Are you prepared to seek your vengeance?

Damona was breathing hard, as though she had been running desperately again through the night to save her husband and children. There was a terrible pain in her belly. Her womb was crying out, protesting the hatred that filled it, yearning for the burdens it had once carried in joy. "I am ready," she said.

The Goddess Sekhmet spoke. *First you must renounce She who is My Sister. Do you do this of your own will, in freedom and of your own choosing?*

For an instant Damona wavered again. But this time it was an instant only. "I do," she said harshly. "I renounce the Goddess. And Her Guardian with Her."

Very well, Priestess, Sekhmet said. *Be still then, and look upon my power.*

Before Damona's eyes a shimmering reflection was forming itself out of the air. She saw herself, or rather, the new self that the Goddess had created. Damona's hair had always been her pride, and the magic had restored its beauty. Sleek and thick, it hung down her back as it always had, with one stark difference.

It had turned completely white.

Other Eos titles by
Sarah Isidore

The Daughters of Bast:
The Hidden Land

THE DAUGHTERS OF BAST

⟨ Shrine of Light ⟩

SARAH ISIDORE

An Imprint of HarperCollinsPublishers

This is a work of fiction. Names, characters, places, and incidents are the products of the author's imagination or are used fictitiously and are not to be construed as real. Any resemblance to actual events, locales, organizations, or persons, living or dead, is entirely coincidental.

EOS
An Imprint of HarperCollins*Publishers*
10 East 53rd Street
New York, New York 10022-5299

Copyright © 2000 by Sarah Isidore
Library of Congress Catalog Card Number: 00-130990
ISBN: 0-380-80319-4
www.eosbooks.com

First Eos paperback printing: July 2000

Eos Trademark Reg. U.S. Pat. Off. and in Other Countries, Marca Registrada, Hecho en U.S.A.
HarperCollins® is a trademark of HarperCollins Publishers Inc.

Printed in the U.S.A.

WCD   10   9   8   7   6   5   4   3   2   1

In memory of Kona, my daily writing companion
and my most non-judgmental critic.
I miss you.

Before St. Patrick came to Ireland, tales were told of a slender black cat who reclined on a silver chair in a cave at Clough in Connaught. The cat delivered oracular pronouncements and abused anyone who tried to deceive him.

I

YOUR TIME IS FINALLY THROUGH, Sister.

Satisfaction rumbled like far-off thunder in the voice of the Goddess. She stood in the pink-tinted chamber, a mighty figure hardened in the forge of old blood, her yellow eyes blazing as she glared in triumph at the one to whom She had spoken.

The days of Your shrine will fade and crack as surely as the Red Land in the Dry Season, and so, too, will pass the power of Your Priestesses, those troublesome descendants of that even more troublesome girl you insisted on taking under Your protection.

And what of Your time, O Sekhmet?

The answering voice was filled with light, and with the rhythms of ancient music. The second Goddess sat upon Her golden throne, bathed in the glimmer of Her divinity. The green eyes in Her enormous cat face burned as deep as Her power.

If My worship is to give way before this new god, She said in that gentle ringing voice, *Yours is doomed to no less.*

My worship? Spears of crimson darted about the other Goddess's massive form. She snarled, and the fangs in Her lioness's mouth gleamed. *The days of My worship are long since turned to dust; You know it well. You told me once that I lacked foresight, O Bast, and You spoke true. I lacked the wisdom to inspire a line of women dedicated to Me. While I was drinking My fill of blood, You were seeing far. But I, too, am a Goddess. My eyes can see as far as Yours, now that I have the wit to use them.*

I

Your vision is clouded by Your hunger, Sister, Bast replied. *It always has been. You see the past and the future in shades of red. Truth must be seen clearly, if it is to be seen at all.*

Sekhmet flung up Her arms, and that bloody light showered and crackled all about Her. *It is the present I am concerned with. The days of the Caesars have vanished into the sun, burning away as brightly as the time when Our once-mighty Pharaohs ruled the Black Land. A new power walks the earth now, and from it will spurt more blood than even I can drink.*

The green eyes of the Cat-Goddess burned into the yellow ones of the Lion-Goddess. *There is no place in the world of this new power for either of Us. We Old Ones made room in Our hearts for other gods and goddesses whom mortals wished to worship. But this god does not possess such generosity. He will tolerate no others save Himself among His followers.*

There will be room for Me. The ivory fangs in Sekhmet's giant mouth bared themselves, and they were tinged with scarlet. *I will see to it.*

You will see to nothing. Bast leaned forward on Her throne. *Your eyes tell You no more now than they ever did. And You are wrong about My shrine. It will continue, in a smaller way, perhaps, and yet it will continue, as will its Priestesses: the daughters of Veleda.*

Sekhmet's hiss spun through the echoing chamber. *That creature was as irritating a mortal as I have ever encountered. Her descendants, though, are not cut from the same bolt of cloth. They have, none of them, ever possessed the unique qualities that made her so difficult.*

The times they lived in have all been different, Bast said serenely. *Especially now. But they are Veleda's daughters nevertheless. In them will My memory survive.*

Sekhmet fell silent, watching Her Sister with narrowed glittering eyes. *I will wager,* She said at last, *that I can turn this latest Priestess from that shrine of Yours, O Bast.*

The Cat-Goddess's laughter rippled and purred through

the glimmering chamber. *Either the drinking of blood or the thirst for it has addled Your wits, Sister. Even in this unsettled world, such a thing cannot be done. The daughters of My shrine are loyal, as loyal as their foremother once was. You overestimate Your influence, O Sekhmet.*

And You underestimate Yours, O Bast. It is precisely because of this unsettled world that I can succeed. I offer You a challenge, Sister. Not only will I turn this latest Priestess from You, but I will bring her to Me. To Me! As My Priestess, no longer Yours.

The words excited the Lion-Goddess even as She said them. She swirled about the chamber, pacing closer to Bast. The other goddess watched Her, Her stillness graceful and contained, accentuating the anger that roiled through Her Sister like flames simmering beneath a kettle.

I will take the memory of You for Myself, Sister. Sekhmet flung out the threat, a warning as well as a promise. *I will start My Own line of Priestesses, beginning with the one I turn away from You. She and those after her will be dedicated to My service. You will be forgotten, O Bast, and blood will flow in My name, as it did in the days of My glory.*

Bast's long green eyes were unfathomable. *There is only one way to prove You wrong, O Sekhmet,* She said. Her voice was so quiet that only another goddess could have heard it.

Indeed. Now Sekhmet had truly wrapped herself in triumph. *On that, at least, We agree. But I will give You cause to regret accepting My challenge, Sister.*

Perhaps. The Cat-Goddess's voice was gentle as a kitten's purr. *And perhaps not. Even goddesses can see only so far.*

"We will have visitors soon."

The cat's voice was light and clear, each word enunciated with careful precision. He sat quietly in the stone chamber, relaxed and yet utterly alert, as only a cat can be. His eyes were a deep fiery orange, and in the light of the flaring torches they glowed bright as the golden couch beneath him.

The woman he had spoken to turned from setting another

torch in its wall niche. "Of course," she said easily. "Else you would not be down here, when you could be in the woods or by our hearth finding yourself a comfortable place to take a nap."

The cat yawned, revealing long fangs white as ivory. "It's raining. Even without visitors, I would not be out wandering about."

"So it is." The woman smiled. There was a strong resemblance between her and the cat, despite the fact that one was human and the other was not. The woman's hair was as sleek and thick and black as the cat's shining pelt. Her eyes appeared in certain lights as orange as those of her feline companion. She had that same catlike comfort in her body, moving with easy grace as she lit another torch and placed it in its niche. "Who is coming," she asked, cocking her head. "Can you see?"

The cat flicked his tail at her question. "Not today; it has not been shown to me." He flicked his tail again. "After all, Damona, my furless one, is it not enough that I tell them their future? Must I give you a description of each man or woman before he or she even arrives?"

"Ah, sacred one." Damona came over and stroked a hand along the cat's back. "You are testy today. Shall I tell whoever is coming that you do not wish to use your powers this day?"

The cat stretched under the woman's hand, slitting his eyes in pleasure. "No," he growled, his clear voice distorted by the purr rumbling in his throat. "There is no need for that."

"Then I will go and meet our visitors." Damona stroked the cat a moment longer and turned to leave the stone chamber.

"You won't need a mantle," the cat called after her. "The rain is stopping. Although," he muttered as he set to grooming himself, "it's still not fit weather for a cat."

Damona walked back along the passageway that had been

cut into the living rock so long ago it was said that the Goddess Herself had done it.

The Goddess.

To think of Her was to feel devotion. A flood of warmth kindled itself within Damona's breast; her steps slowed. She saw the Lady of Silver Magic as she had always seen Her, from the time the enormous glowing figure with the body of a woman and the head of a cat had first appeared to her when she was small. She saw the beautiful temple of pink stone and its courtyard filled with cats. Her soul traveled along the inner passageways to the sanctuary itself. And there sat the Goddess on Her golden throne, Her green eyes filled with wisdom and the sights of ages past.

Bast, She was called in that tongue, but She possessed many other names as well. Goddess of the Shrine, Mistress of Wisdom, the outland Goddess, and Lady of Joy, were only a few of them.

Her ancient glory shaped the days of Damona's life, just as it had shaped the lives of all those who had come before her. It was a welcome and willing bondage, a servitude that had ever been filled with joy and love, with the wise glowing eyes of her goddess and the sound of distant voices chanting in an unknown tongue. Always had it been so. Damona had never questioned it. There was no reason to. It was her destiny, what she had been born to.

The passage was black as a chieftain's tomb, lighted only by the small lanthorn Damona carried. Yet she found her way with ease. Beyond counting were the number of times she had walked this path, since she was a chubby weanling still holding to her mother's skirts for balance. The corridor was as narrow as it was dark, the ceiling so low she had to stoop as she walked. It had been shaped that way for a purpose: so that all who passed through it would lose their pride before they came to the inner shrine.

A finger of light reached toward the lanthorn, widening gradually into the mouth of the passageway. Damona straightened, snuffing out the lanthorn and setting it aside as she came out into the open air. As the cat had said, the rain had indeed stopped, though the world still smelled of it. Damona breathed in the odor of wet leaves and grass. Iron-gray clouds tossed themselves across the sky, chased by the breezes of the departing storm, and in the brightness of the clearing day she saw the party of riders break from the trees and canter up the slope that led to the shrine. Her lips tightened as she saw the figure in the lead. Muirchertac, the king of her tuath, was coming again.

The telling of truth was seldom easy. Damona had learned this lesson very early, and she had never forgotten it. "People come to us because they seek wisdom," her mother had often said before she left this world for the next. "It is the gift the Goddess of the Shrine has charged us to give them." But Damona had learned something else: the honesty that accompanied such wisdom was not always as welcome.

She thought of that now as the men pulled their horses into a trot and rode toward her. Muirchertac's hair was stiff with lime, washed so heavily in the stuff that it had become three colors: dark at the roots, brown near the middle, and fair at the ends. He was a handsome figure, for all that he sat so poorly in the saddle. The stallion that carried him was as handsome as his rider, a fine animal but, clearly, an unhappy one. He trotted stiffly, his mouth half-open under the pressure from the bit, his ears flattened in protest. The *Tuisech* was a big man, and he was heavy in the saddle, bouncing to his mount's gait without balance while his hands tugged and sawed at the horse's mouth.

Damona's own mouth twitched in sympathy. She stepped forward, as much to welcome her visitor as to relieve the stallion of his burden. Stretching out her hands, she shaped the secret signs of welcome and protection. "Blessings be upon you, my lord Muirchertac," she said in her low, calm voice. "In the name of the Goddess, I bid you welcome to Her shrine."

The stallion jerked to a halt, tossing his head angrily at the king's hard tug on the reins. The man looked down at the woman standing before him. His features were even and well formed. The multicolored hair stood tall and unmoving above his red-patterned tunic or leine. A green mantle known as a brat was wrapped over the loose-belted garment, its folds fastened with red-enameled fibulae. He gave her a smile flashing and white, but lacking in warmth. Droplets of rain still glittered in his hair and beard, setting his neck torque of rare gold, the mark of leadership, aflame in the wet sunlight. Behind him his nobles, almost as richly dressed as their lord, drew in their mounts, the animals stamping and snorting as they came to a halt.

"Greetings, *Banfhili*." Briefly Muirchertac inclined his head, using Damona's proper title: the ancient words that meant "woman-seer."

"May this day be a favorable one. For all of us." His voice was deep and resonant, but a fervid glint at the back of his bright blue eyes belied the dignity of his tone.

Tuisech Muirchertac was a man out of harmony, with himself and his world. The stallion knew it, and so did Damona and anyone else knowledgeable in the mysteries of Druidcraft. He came to the shrine often in a search for wisdom, but he rarely departed with any. His visits were tension-filled affairs, marked by the unease that ever dogged his royal soul. Damona sighed inwardly, readying herself for the difficult time that almost certainly lay ahead.

"Come down off your horses," she invited. "My husband will see to them for you."

The king motioned to his men. "My escort will stay with the beasts," he said as he swung down. "I trust that refreshments will be brought to them, as well as to the horses."

"As always, my lord," Damona said smoothly. They held the same conversation each time he came; it had become as much of a ritual as the actual ritual itself. She stepped aside, waiting, as custom dictated, for the *Tuisech* to precede her.

Muirchertac favored her with another brusque nod, walked past her, and strode off through the trees. He would bathe in the sacred spring hidden within a grove of ancient hawthorn trees, purifying himself to receive whatever knowledge the guardian of the shrine chose to reveal to him.

Damona glanced at the nobles. They had dismounted and were watching their king as he disappeared amongst the trees. "How fares your lord this day?" she asked.

The man holding the reins of the king's stallion shrugged. "He is as he is, *Banfhili*. Though today, he seems even more changeable than usual. And his mood is not pleasant. The queen did not want him to come here. They had words over it, very loud it was. Take care, lady, handle him gently."

Damona's hazel gaze was enigmatic. "It is not I who will handle him but the Goddess and Her Guardian."

She left the chieftains and strode toward the earthen embankments that marked the enclosure of her family's rath. It was the month of Seed-Fall. The festival of Samhain was fast approaching and Cuchain was up to his elbows in work. Her husband was a *Boaire*, a cattle-lord who possessed both land and beasts. On this day he was supposed to be supervising the yearly culling of the cattle herds. The animals had been brought in from their summer pasture and now decisions had to be made as to which would be slaughtered for winter food.

But Cuchain had already seen the riders, and had left the herds to wait for her on the path. Damona smiled to see him. Five years and three children had they been wed and waking up beside him had lost not one whit of its sweetness. Just to see him standing there, tall and fair, his reddish brown hair damp and curling with rain and sweat, brought a familiar warmth to her belly. As a Druid she belonged to the noble class, and so had married beneath her. But that had not mattered then, and it did not matter now.

Bast had blessed their union. The Goddess had surrounded each moment with light and joy, for She was not a Goddess Who demanded celibacy from those devoted to Her service. She took pleasure in the making of life. And oh, it had been a pleasure indeed, and still was. The seasons had been kind to this man of hers; he was still as fine and comely as a young stag.

"So he's come again." Cuchain's wide brow was furrowed, his deep voice rumbling with distaste. "His presence will shed a darkness over the rest of the day."

"I know, dear one." Damona sighed. "But he'll soon be gone."

Cuchain shook his head. "He is quite mad," he said seriously. "A fine thing it is, for our tuath to be ruled by a *Tuisech* in the grip of madness."

Damona laid a soothing hand on his arm. "The Shining Ones gave him his position and They must have had their reasons for doing so. Anyway, his councilors and the queen have wisdom enough. Between them, they keep him from doing anything too foolish."

"For the time being." Cuchain's face was grim. "But if the Shining Ones gave him his position, They must also have given him his madness. No mortal can control the Shining Ones, which means that no one can control Muirchertac."

"The Goddess of the Shrine can control him," Damona said serenely. "And She will, though it be unpleasant for the rest of us."

Cuchain's big hand covered hers where it still lay on his arm. "I fear for you, wife," he said in a low voice. "If the Guardian says aught to displease him—"

"Do not." Damona's tone was quiet and inflexible. "The Guardian will speak as the Goddess bids him, and it is my task to see that wisdom and deliver it to the one who has come seeking it." She touched the luminescent Druid's egg hanging on a thong about her neck. "You know this is my work, dear one, as it has been for all the daughters of my *fine* since our line began."

Cuchain tightened his grip on her hand. "I know it well," he said heavily. "But only on the days that *he* rides here, do I wish that you were a woman, as other women, without this sacred burden." He withdrew his hand. "Well, I shall go and see to their horses. I'll have Deirdre and Eichne bring mead and cheese and bread for the nobles."

"Tell them to bring some of the small apples for them as well. They'll expect it." Damona kissed him lightly. "Try not to worry. It will soon be over."

She went toward the spring to wait for the king. After a short time he came back through the trees. He had cleansed himself from head to foot and wrapped himself in one of the loose robes kept there for that purpose. His wet hair was slicked down close to his skull, dark with water and lime, but his eyes were no calmer than when he had left.

"My wife was opposed to my seeking this divination," he said without preamble. His tone was angry and conversational at once. "She has deserted the Shining Ones for this new god of the Christians. She calls herself one of them now, a Christian. She insists that this shrine is an abomination." He snorted. "These sacred rites an abomination? Ha! Foolish woman."

Carefully Damona kept her face smooth of expression. She had already heard this. Although the new religion of the one god had arrived on the shores of Eire with the fervor of Patrick, its determined bearer, it had only recently begun to make inroads this far into the island's interior. Once begun it was spreading rapidly, although here in Muirchertac's tuath, as well as those neighboring it, the old ways largely prevailed as they always had.

"Are you certain she said this, my lord?" she asked carefully. "The queen has always seemed to be a most sensible woman."

"Not any longer," Muirchertac snapped. "This new religion has turned her into an imbecile. Last week she let them sprinkle her with water, just as our own Druids do, only she behaved as if this were something miraculous—baptized, she calls it, and now she'll speak of nothing else. In truth, I can hardly bear to be around her. I was hoping, *Banfhili* . . . "

He fell silent, and Damona prompted him gently. "Hoping, my lord?"

"By the dark face of Macha's bloody incarnation." Muirchertac let out the oath with relish. "I was hoping you would instruct the Guardian to tell me what to do about her."

"Ah." A deep sense of foreboding washed over Damona. "Lord," she said in a firm voice, "you will learn what you are meant to learn. I can promise you nothing more than that."

The king scowled. "I am not some farmer coming to see if his hives will bear sufficient honey or his cows enough calves. I did not come to your shrine only to seek guidance about my foolish wife, but to learn of other, far more important matters. The matters of a *Tuisech*. I *will* have my questions answered. All of them!"

They had almost reached the stone passage that led to the chamber of the Goddess. Damona stepped abruptly in front of Muirchertac, forcing him to halt. They were nearly the same height, and she stared directly into his eyes. "In this place," she said, "no question is more important than another, just as no man is more important than another. The Goddess looks at all of us with the same gaze, and She speaks as She sees fit. As for calves and honey: they are as much your concern, my lord, as those of your farmers. Without them, where would the wealth of this tuath, *your* tuath, be?"

There was considerable risk in chastising Muirchertac so openly. The instability that sat on him was as heavy as the air before a storm. Yet she must speak. She was Priestess of this shrine; and not even from the king could such arrogance be tolerated.

Muirchertac's eyes were bloodshot from traces of lime that had dripped down his face during his bathing, and they seemed to flame even redder at Damona's words. He stared at her, spittle gathering in the corners of his mouth, but she went on before he could speak or otherwise react. "It is time to enter the inner sanctuary, yet your words are not those of one who has been cleansed in mind and body. I cannot allow this divination to continue if you remain so wholly within yourself."

The sternness of her voice and demeanor penetrated the haze of rage that had begun to overtake the *Tuisech*. He blinked several times, swallowed, and hitched the folds of the robe up over his shoulder. "Yes, yes," he muttered, drawing one hand roughly over his face. "I have been within myself." He took his hand away. "*Banfhili*—lady, I crave your pardon. You are a Priestess. You rule in this place, not I. It was ill done of me to come to you in anger."

Damona studied him. These abrupt mood swings between rage and contrition were all too familiar. She had seen them in many of Muirchertac's previous visits. But his remorse was sincere; she knew that, too, although it might only be for the moment. She made a silent prayer to the Goddess to give her forbearance, and said aloud, "It is not my pardon you should ask for, but that of She to Whom this shrine is dedicated. Are you ready to hear Her words and honor Her?"

"Lady," Muirchertac replied at once. "I am."

She stepped aside to the mouth of the passageway, bending to pick up the lanthorn and rekindle it. "Then enter."

They went silently along the dark corridor. The *Tuisech* followed close in Damona's shadow, seeking the dim glow of her small lanthorn. He was quiet now, and very circumspect. But that was to be expected. The walk through this ancient tunnel that led deep into the living rock was daunting, even for a king. They were approaching the womb of the Goddess, and Her power was already making itself felt, reaching out to enfold them and draw them in. Muirchertac had no more power here than any other mortal. This was Her place, and he came to it only as a supplicant.

The inner chamber was still lit by the torches Damona had placed in the wall niches; after the gloom of the passage it seemed bright as day. The long golden couch gleamed in the light. The large black cat sat upright on the embroidered cushions, waiting for them. The white mark on his chest glimmered, and he watched with eyes as glowing and orange as the torches around him, as the two humans entered.

The presence of the Goddess dropped itself about Damona like a mantle of light. The enormous cat face seemed to hover above the watching cat; even as she looked his sleek ebony fur took on the familiar glint of power. She glided up to the couch to stand beside its occupant, and Muirchertac knelt silently before the equally silent animal.

Those who came seeking wisdom had to wait for a sign from the Guardian of the Goddess before they could speak. It was some moments before that sign came. The cat stood up, rubbed himself against the woman's arm, and sat down again.

"You are in the sanctuary of the Ancient Queen, the Lady of Silver Magic." Damona's voice filled the chamber, each word ringing low and musical. "What have you come to learn from Her?"

"Sacred One." Recognizing that it was the cat addressing him, and not the woman, Muirchertac's gaze rested on the former. "It is no longer the season for war, but I wish to gather my army and make one last raid into the tuath of the *Dal gCais* before the coming of Samhain and the cold weather. Will the omens be favorable for undertaking this *taine*?"

The cat looked at Damona. Studying his eyes, she nodded her understanding. "The warmaking season is over," she said to the king. "Why are you so eager to fight again?"

"Guardian," Muirchertac said shortly, "I am a king. Kings are always eager to fight. It is the task laid upon us by the gods." His voice was respectful, but it contained an impatient note that verged on anger. In spite of the intimidating atmosphere of the inner chamber, the *Tuisech*'s volatile nature was already asserting itself. He was not accustomed to being questioned, even by a representative of the Goddess. Although he had come here so many times, such questioning was still not something he took well.

The cat's serene detachment did not change. "The task laid upon a king by the gods is to rule," he said through Damona. "Wars should be fought only when necessary."

"This is necessary." Muirchertac's bearded jaw jutted forward. "Some of their warriors raided cattle from the borderland between our tuatha. The act must be punished. I must have those cattle back, or others to replace them. Winter is coming, and the people will have need of them."

The cat's orange eyes went to Damona's golden ones again. "There is another reason for this *taine*." The *Bhanfhili* spoke sternly. "You are in a holy place. Speak the truth. All of it."

Muirchertac averted his gaze. "Very well. There is indeed more. I am a *Tuisech*. At present I lead only this tuath, but I am a great man. The gods mean for me to be more." Emboldened by his own words he stood taller, thrusting out his chest. "I intend," he said in a grand voice, "to be a *Ruiri*, a great king who rules over more than just these lands. My plan is to conquer the tuath of the *Dal gCais*. By Samhain the folk of that country will be calling me their overlord."

"No, *Tuisech*, they will not."

Damona needed no communication with the Guardian to know the correctness of her words. Her own power told it to her as infallibly as the magic of the cat. More words came bubbling out, rushing from the Guardian's mind to hers, and out through her lips, flowing so swiftly that her thoughts and those of the cat were one and the same.

"No *Ruiri* will you be. Even your days as *Tuisech* are numbered. If you undertake this war, the Goddess and Her Sacred Brethren will frown on you. The Shining Ones will turn Their faces from you. The boundaries between the Otherworld and the world of mortals will fade and you will wander away from the land of the living, lost forever in the space between the worlds. Your soul will cry out, but none will hear. For you have set yourself against the faces of the gods. A poor *Tuisech* have you been. An even poorer *Ruiri* would you be."

"Paps of Danu!" Spittle gathered once more in the corners of Muirchertac's mouth. "How dare you!" he shouted, and the spittle turned to foam. "Your words are meaningless.

Your goddess is not even of Eire. She is a foreign goddess, an abomination!"

The cat came to his feet with a single lithe movement. "I have given you the gift of truth," he snarled, and now he spoke in his own voice, rather than that of Damona. "My knowledge comes from the Goddess Herself. If you do not desire such gifts and the price they bring, you should not have come here."

The animal's light voice rang against the stone walls. It stopped Muirchertac's outburst as abruptly as a deluge of cold water. In all his visits to the shrine, the cat had never spoken to him directly, only through Damona, his Priestess. Indeed, the king was not aware of anyone the cat had ever addressed. It was rumored that he could not speak in the manner of a human, that the Goddess sent him his amazing powers of divination and Damona interpreted the prophecies through the use of magic.

Now the *Tuisech* heard for himself how wrong those rumors were. He gaped at the animal, his fury momentarily forgotten. But it was the cat who was angry. His long tail was fluffed to twice its normal size, the whole of its length lashing against his flanks. He glared at Muirchertac, his eyes narrowed to glittering slits.

"Leave this holy place." The cat's voice was a snarling hiss, through which the words bubbled, clear and unmistakable. "You deface it with your presence. Henceforth, you are banished from the sanctuary of the Goddess. Do not come here again."

Still stunned by what he was witnessing, Muirchertac did not move. The cat spat, this time in the manner of a mortal cat, and lashed a front paw through the air. "I said leave!"

He yowled the command with such power that the king clapped his hands over his ears and fled.

Seated on Her throne, Bast raised Her hand. The panel of light emanating from her fingers widened, showing Her the mortal king as he blundered away in terror from Her shrine.

You hoped that Mau would not send him off like a blubbering fool, did You not? Her question was addressed to Sekhmet, Who stood watching the panel of light with narrowed eyes. *You were hoping for the blood the countenancing of a cattle raid would have brought You.*

The Lion-Goddess bared her teeth. *It is not over yet,* She growled. *And whatever happens, Sister, remember You this: her deeds must follow from her own choosing. If she is truly Yours, then she will need no influence to make her choice.*

Damona stood next to the cat, listening to Muirchertac charge down the narrow passageway, made clumsy by his fear and anger. "This has ended even more badly than I had feared," she murmured.

"It could end no other way." The cat's fur slowly smoothed itself. His voice was regaining its customary lightness. Yet there was no lessening of the power that still glowed about him. "The truth is the truth. His plan was ill conceived and not favored by our Goddess. If he goes to war against that tuath, he will die, just as I said. And so will many others."

Damona shook her head. "Perhaps that would be best. Not for others to die, but for Muirchertac to. The Otherworld may be able to deal with him better than we in this world can."

"It is not his time, not yet."

The cat grew very silent, staring at Damona with great eyes that seemed to grow until they filled the quiet chamber. There was no sound between them, only the soft hiss of the torches and the sound of Muirchertac's thudding footsteps as they receded into the distance. Damona felt the presence of Bast, but for the first time in her memory, her sense of the Goddess was strangely muted, as if a barrier had suddenly risen between them.

The cat's whiskers quivered. Damona reached out to touch the animal's head. "What do you see, sacred one?" Her voice was hushed. "What are you picturing of my fate?"

The cat pushed his head gently against her hand. "I see that it is time for you to leave, furless one. Go out to your rath and see your family."

"Yes," Damona agreed with a sigh. "I had better go and see what has become of our royal visitor. I'll try to calm him down, though it won't be easy. This is the worst I've seen him."

As she picked up the lanthorn and started for the passage, the cat suddenly spoke. "Damona."

She turned back at once. She had heard that note in the Guardian's voice before, and her flesh went cold at the sound.

The cat's eyes were very wide. "Take your mate and your little ones. Take them out into the forest and keep them there."

Damona stared at him. She nodded once, then strode swift and silent from the sanctuary. Out of the passage and in the daylight she immediately began looking for the king. But there was no sign of him. She headed for the place where his nobles were to have had their refreshment while they waited for Muirchertac and saw Cuchain waiting there instead. The instant her husband caught sight of her he hurried forward.

"He's gone," he told Damona tersely. "He came storming over to the chieftains shouting at them in such a frenzy that no one could understand a word. Then he tore loose the reins of his horse and lashed the poor creature out of here at a mad gallop. The chieftains had no choice but to follow him." He pointed up the hill. "They're already out of sight. What happened in the sanctuary, dear heart? What did the Guardian see that enraged him so?"

Damona did not reply. Her hazel eyes searched the wooded hills. Her outer gaze could not see the *Tuisech* and his train, but her inner gaze saw the party of men thundering down the forest tracks, colored by the hues of their king's rage.

"Cuchain," she said. "We must gather everyone together— get the children, and take ourselves into the woods."

Cuchain stared at her as if she had run as mad as Muirchertac. "Have you lost your wits, woman? It's enough time I have wasted idling about entertaining those nobles. I cannot leave the herds now; you know that! Winter is hurrying down upon us and with all the work that needs to be done—"

"Husband," Damona said in the quiet tone that always drew his attention, the tone she only used when she spoke of matters of Druidcraft. "We must leave our rath. At least for a while."

Cuchain's blue eyes did not leave hers, and his expression slowly changed. Questions whirled over his features, but he asked none of them. He knew his wife too well. "We had best gather everyone up and hurry then," he said.

2

THE FAMILY'S RING FORT WAS always a busy place and this day was no exception. The farmyard within its rampart rang with the laughter and talk of several servants as they worked at churning butter and making cheese. Milch cows munched on scattered piles of hay. Pigs wandered about, fattening themselves on whey and table scraps. Dogs ran toward Damona and Cuchain, their tails wagging. After them came Eichne, followed closely by her sister Deirdre.

Dark-haired like their mother and with the blue eyes of their father, the two children were as alike as drops of rain. Twins carried great power, and they were exceedingly rare; to have both survive to their sixth year was even rarer. Certainly there had never been twin daughters born to the ancient line of Priestesses before. Only one of them could be chosen to succeed Damona, and thus far the choice had not been made clear.

Soon, though, Damona would have to ask the Goddess for guidance, for in another year the girls would be of an age to be sent to other families, who would complete the process of rearing them. Fosterage was the custom for nobility and those of the *Boaire* class. However, as heir to her mother's position, Damona had not been fostered. Whichever of the twins succeeded her would also stay at the shrine, to be taught by Damona, as her own mother had taught her.

It was heart-searing to think of that separation, and for now Damona yearned to keep her daughters close to her every moment of every day. Eichne and Deirdre were small hearth-fires in their mother's breast. She was in no hurry to see the day when one of them would be parted from her, to grow up in another woman's household until she was of an age to be married.

"Mother," Eichne cried excitedly, tugging at Damona's sleeve, "I brought food and drink for the nobles, and they smiled at me and praised me. Did they not, Father?"

Cuchain grinned down at her. "They did indeed, daughter."

"And I, too," Deirdre chimed in. "I carried the mead and the tray of apples. They praised me, as well."

"Of course they did," Eichne told her. "They could not tell us apart."

Damona put her arms around both girls. "No one can, except for your mother, and usually, your father. Now come along. We must go into the house and make ready to leave. Deirdre, go you and find Cliodna and your little brother. Tell her to bundle Libran well and bring him to the house."

Both girls bounced on their toes in unified anticipation and curiosity. "But why? Where are we going? Doesn't Father have to be out with cattle? And what about your duties at the shrine?" The questions flew out in a rush, running together as much as the twins' voices.

Cuchain gave Deirdre a gentle push. "Go on, child. We have to hurry."

As Deirdre ran off, Eichne bounced along beside her parents, chattering and asking questions, seemingly unconcerned at the noncommittal answers they gave her.

The round wattle-and-daub house was redolent with the odors of roasting pork and simmering barley porridge. The good food smells masked the other, less appealing scents that were always present despite the fact that Damona herself had just strewn fresh rushes on the floor that morning and covered them with rugs made of calfskin. As the wife of a *Boaire,* this was just one of her many duties, but as *Banfhili* of a sacred shrine, her responsibilities as a Druid preceded those of her home. Thus she had more servants than was usual to help her with the many tasks of running the household.

A young boy sat by the stone-lined hearth that stood at the center of the house, turning the roast on its spit and catching the drippings in a wooden bowl. His mother, busy slicing onions and parsnips into a bronze cauldron filled with water and heated with red-hot stones from the fire, watched him with sharp eyes as she periodically rose to stir the porridge.

Both the woman and her son looked up in surprise as the family entered at this unusual time of day. Before either one could speak, Cuchain gestured tersely at the boy. "Run out to the herdsmen and tell them that I said to bring the cattle and the other beasts inside for the night. I will attend to the culling"—he glanced at his wife for confirmation—"tomorrow."

Damona lit a rush candle, for even at this time of day the house was dark. The smell of the beef tallow the rush had been dipped in added its pungency to the other odors as it fluttered into life. "Or the next day perhaps," she said evenly.

Her husband nodded. "And," he added, "tell the herdsmen that after they have seen to the cattle to go to their own homes."

The boy gladly up leaped from his boring post beside the fire. "May I go with him?" Eichne cried. At her father's confirming nod, she flung herself after the boy.

"Cummen," Damona said to the woman, as the children dashed out. "Help me to start packing food. All the bread fresh-baked today, and whatever cheese is ready. Take the pork off the spit; we'll slice off whatever meat is done."

Cummen stared at her mistress with worried eyes as she set about these tasks. "What has happened, lady?" she asked. "Do the *Tuisech* and his train remain here still?" Like all the people in the tuath, the servingwoman was well aware of Muirchertach's unpredictable moods, but because she served in the rath of the *Bhanfhili,* she had had more oppor-

tunity than most to see the king's sudden rages, and thus
more opportunity to learn to fear their consequences.

"They are gone," Damona told her. "And now we must be
as well."

The servant's lips grew thin and tight. Questions spun in
her eyes, but the expression on Damona's face convinced her
to say nothing more. Her mistress was a Druid. Cummen
knew full well that when Druids did not wish to speak of a
thing, nothing in this world could make them. Her mouth set
in an even grimmer line as she quickly went about wrapping
bread and cheese in cloths. Cuchain buckled on weapons,
and Damona carved slices of pork off the steaming roast and
bustled through the house's single large room, gathering up
essentials from the sleeping cubicles that lined the walls.
While they were at these tasks Cliodna, the children's nurse,
came in with Libran and Deirdre in tow. The small boy
promptly toddled to his mother, and Damona cuddled him
with one arm while she rolled up bedding with her free
hand.

By the time Eichne and the cook boy came dashing back,
panting out that Cuchain's message had been delivered, the
family was ready to leave.

Damona laid a hand on Cummen's shoulder. "Thank you
for your help," she said kindly. "Now take your boy and seek
your own house."

The woman gave an emphatic shake of her head. "I will
not," she said stoutly. "With my husband gone to the Otherworld these past two years and our *fine* living off in the
south, my son and I have no one. You have been good to us,
lady. We will go with you, wherever that may be."

Damona hesitated, but Cuchain said, "Come with us,
then, Cummen. Your loyalty becomes you."

"I, too, will go," said Cliodna, the young woman who
served as little Libran's nurse. "The boy will have need of
me." She grinned wryly. "And anyway, my man will be too
busy bedding down the cattle and the other beasts at such an
unaccustomed time of day to worry about bedding me!"

Her comment relieved the tension that had gathered subtly in the room, and the adults all laughed. But when the laughter had faded, Cliodna looked at Damona with concern in her eyes. "Will we return before my man does notice I am gone, lady?"

"I pray so," Damona said gently. "But the answer to that is in the hands of the gods."

As Erin, Goddess of the sun, lowered Herself toward the green rolling hills and a veil of purple clouds, Damona, Cuchain, their children, and the servants, headed deep into the woods.

A fire crackled cheerfully in the central hearth of Muirchertac's great hall. The *Tuisech* paced back and forth, shaking with fury. His fine clothes steamed in the heat from the fire, and his lime-stained hair draggled about his shoulders in stiff strands. The rage that burned within him had not abated during the ride back. He had exhausted his horse and those of his train, but his anger it had only grown.

"I, not a *Ruiri*," he muttered over and over. "I, not a *Ruiri*!"

Each time he said the words his fury fed on them, and his pacing quickened until he was actually running to and fro in front of the fire. Several servants peeped cautiously at this peculiar sight from the safety of the doorway. They stepped aside in hasty respect as the queen appeared. She stood among them for a moment, watching her husband, then strode into the hall, the folds of her gold-belted laine swishing about her ankles.

"My lord." Lady Rionach's voice was calm, providing a counterpoint to the king's mumbled ravings. "What has happened to upset you so?"

It was several moments before Muirchertac seemed to hear her. Blinking, he came to a halt and stared at his wife. "You were right," he finally said to her. "You told me that place was an abomination, and you were right. I should not have gone there. I should not have!"

The queen knew what he was referring to, but she took little satisfaction from it. To hear that Muirchertac's visit to a shrine of the old gods had gone badly did not bode well. These moods of her husband could be dangerous to anyone who crossed his path. She had no wish for herself or anyone else to suffer from them.

"Calm yourself, my husband," she said in the soothing tone she always used when the *Tuisech* was enraged as he was now. "Would you like some ale? I will bring it to you myself."

The king spun on her. "The creature told me I will never be a *Ruiri,* that even my days as a *Tuisech* were numbered. And then—as if that were not enough—he banished me from the Shrine!"

"The cat said this to you?" Rionach was quite familiar with the Guardian of the Shrine; she had visited there herself. But that had been before her acceptance of Christianity and the One True God.

"Do not trouble yourself about what you heard there," she went on in the same soothing voice. "I have told you that these places of the old gods no longer have any power. There is only one true power in the world now: that of Jesus Christ." She touched the ornate cross that hung between her breasts. "This cat belongs to an old and evil magic brought about by Druids who are opposed to the holy light brought to Eire by Patrick, the messenger of Jesus. It is more than likely that the cat itself did not even speak to you. The woman-seer probably laid a spell upon you."

Muirchertac looked at her. His earlier terror at hearing the cat's terrible voice had faded. Indeed, he had almost convinced himself that the incident had never happened, that the creature had not spoken at all. And if it was not the cat's voice that he had heard, then his wife was correct. There was only one other who could be responsible: the *Banfhili* herself.

"Ah!" His blue eyes lit up. "Truly, my wife, this new faith

has given you wisdom. I know what I should do now." He slammed a big fist into his palm.

The queen regarded him with sudden wariness. "And what is that, my lord?"

"Is it not obvious?" Muirchertac was practically dancing. "You and your Christians have given me the answer. The place is an abomination, and what does one do with abominations? One destroys them, and slays all who countenance them!"

"No, my lord." A wave of alarm coursed through Lady Rionach. Followers of the old religion those at the shrine might be, but she had no wish to see them harmed. Shrines to the old gods were all throughout this tuath and indeed, the entire island of Eire. If one began killing them, where would it end? "Yes, the shrine is an abomination," she said hastily. "But the way of Christianity is not to kill innocents—"

"Innocents!" the king roared. "There are no innocents at that evil place. They are all against me. Have I not just this moment told you how I was treated?"

Rionach strove to keep the growing anxiety from her tone. "Yes, yes, husband, but the folk there are not evil, only misguided. They must not be killed. They must be brought to salvation, as must you, my lord."

But Muirchertac was no longer listening. He charged away from the hearth, shouting for the servants. "Attend me," he roared. "Send messengers out to gather my chieftains. I have a task for us, and it must be done quickly."

The children huddled sleepily around the fire, nestled up against their parents. Their bellies were full, they were wrapped in furs against the evening chill and they were content as only tired, well-fed children can be. Near them Cuchain talked quietly with Cummen and Cliodna. But Damona sat in silence, staring into the flames as darkness stretched out to swallow up the last threads of daylight. Deirdre was curled on one side of her and little Libran on the other, yet she took small comfort from their familiar warmth.

The Guardian's words were still with her. They pressed against her as closely as the sweet bodies of her children. She had followed his warning; they had gone deep into the forest, just as he had told her to, and yet it was not enough. Premonition ground in her bones. The sensation of safety, so often elusive, was even more difficult to grasp hold of on this quiet night in the last fleeting days of summer. There was darkness beyond darkness in these woods. It hovered above her, looming over the heads of her loved ones, vast beyond knowing, inexorable and waiting. She sat before the fire, her arms tight about her daughter and son, as still as a doe scenting a pack of hunting wolves.

Abruptly Cuchain straightened up, dislodging Eichne from her comfortable position. The child muttered fretfully as her father stared into the gloom beyond the firelight. "Listen," he said tensely. "Do you hear it?"

The two servingwomen shook their heads. But Damona drew Deirdre and Libran closer, so tightly that the children squeaked in protest. "Pay no heed, husband." Her voice was quiet and fierce. "No matter what sounds your ears may bring you, pay no heed."

"Then you hear it, too"—Cuchain caught himself, listening again, straining to hear. "Horsemen," he said in a low growl. "Many of them."

The eyes of the servingwomen widened. "Who would be traveling in such numbers at nightfall?" Cliodna whispered the question as if she were afraid that the distant riders would hear her.

Cuchain answered her grimly. "Men who are coming for no good purpose."

He looked at Damona, and she looked back. So this was who the Guardian had warned her of. The reason for his insistence that they all come away into the woods lay before her, as clear as the sacred spring. She shuddered at the seeing of it. Men and death, galloping together, bound up in the thirst for blood.

"They are bound for the rath, aren't they?" Cuchain's voice grew harsh when Damona did not answer. *"Aren't they?"*

"It does not matter."

Damona bit out the words, turning from her private visions to stare hard at her husband. A shadow had suddenly dropped over his familiar features. The others could not see it, but her Druid sight showed it to her clearly. The darkness that had been hovering in the night shadows now joined them around the fire. She could feel it swirling, concentrating itself on Cuchain. She half rose, still gripping her children.

"We must stay here, husband." She heard the tremble in her voice and fought to muffle it with a layer of quiet urgency. "The Guardian warned me this might happen. But here we will be safe."

The sound of hooves was growing louder. The thunder of it rolled forth on the still air, turning the peace of the approaching night into something hostile and fraught with menace. Libran whimpered in displeasure at being awoken. The twins stared up with wondering eyes at the sudden noise.

Damona reached out and gripped Cuchain's muscled forearm with hard fingers. "I see that something is upon you, husband," she hissed. "You must push it from you; love of my heart, you must. Pay no heed to the riders. You dare not."

Cuchain sat back. Beneath her fingers Damona could feel him tremble. "The *Tuisech's* madness has overwhelmed him," he said in a harsh whisper. "He means to kill us, doesn't he?"

Deirdre shifted uneasily, and Damona gave the child a reassuring squeeze. She forced her gaze from his face to those of her other children and two women. "Muirchertac and his men will look for us, but they will not find us."

The trembling in Cuchain's arm had stopped. The powerful muscles were stiff as iron beneath Damona's hand. "And the rath? What will become of the rath?"

"If we are fortunate, nothing. But if the king's rage overcomes him, then remember you this, my husband: houses of wattle and daub can be rebuilt and goods replaced. Only lives, once taken, cannot be brought back, not in this world."

He looked away from her. The horses had passed on, but to the ears of those listening the direction they were heading was all too clear. Distant shouts drifted through the trees, borne toward them on the still air.

All at once Cuchain drew in a sharp breath, a sound composed of fury and anguish. The shadow on his face grew darker. "Flames," he snarled. "By my head, I smell the flames."

"Perhaps, lord," Cliodna said in a quivering voice, "it is naught but the smoke from our own fire."

"No." Cuchain's eyes widened. In the blackness of the shadow his features were all but obscured. Only his eyes were visible, blazing blue and distant, as if he could see what was happening beyond the safety of these woods. "They are setting fire to the rath."

He lunged forward, heedless of Damona's grip on his arm. Her other hand shot out to seize him. "Let them."

His gaze turned on her, tortured and disbelieving. "Let them?"

"Yes!" Damona held him desperately, struggling for the words to persuade him.

Certainty washed through every pore of her, as inexorable as the premonitions. In her inner gaze she saw the Guardian, and reaching far above him was Bast. The sight of the Goddess dwarfed his cat form. Her shining figure vast and glorious as always. But Her eyes were different. There was a look of warning in them, a look so powerful it was almost pleading.

At last Damona found herself able to give speech to what was in those mighty eyes, and she cried out each word. "We must bide here until they are gone. Heed me, Cuchain. If we are to live through this night, we have to stay here!"

For a long shaking moment Cuchain held still, his tortured gaze staring into Damona's. She could see the struggle waged within him. The darkness on his face fought with the glow in the eyes of Bast. Then he spoke. "Do not ask this of me." His voice was as tortured as his eyes. His hands, callused and rough with work, covered hers. "What kind of a man would I be to stand by while our home is being burned?"

"Cuchain, dearest of my life, no." But Damona could see that the darkness had won. It was pushing him away from her and from safety, striking at the place where he and all males were the most vulnerable: his sense of honor.

"I must go!" The big familiar hands pulled hers away. Cuchain jerked to his feet, freeing himself from her desperate grip.

"Cuchain!"

But he was already gone, running off through the darkness, racing toward the lurid glow that had begun to glimmer through the trees.

"Lady," Cummen cried out. "What shall we do?"

"Stay here with the children." Damona whirled on the servingwomen, fixing them with her eyes. "Do as I bid you. No matter what happens, stay with the children."

She ran after Cuchain, turning only once to glance behind her. Framed in the fire glow, Eichne and Deirdre stood beside Cliodna, silent and afraid, watching her with big eyes. Next to them the cook boy stood with his mother, his chin jutted out, looking as if he wished to follow Cuchain, rather than staying behind with the women. Only Libran had fallen back into sleep again, nestled safely in the arms of his nurse.

Sekhmet's fangs glittered white.
It has begun, She exulted. Now We will see what Your Priestess does.

With fluid grace Bast rose from Her throne.
She said nothing.

The woods themselves seemed to unite against the idea of
Damona following her husband. The faster she ran, the more
they impeded her progress. Bushes slashed at her legs, tan-
gling the folds of her laine around her ankles. Tree limbs
grabbed for her hair, as if they, too, were desperately trying
to hold her back. The voice of the forest spoke to her Druid
ears, pleading with her to turn around. She did not listen.
She could not. For her ears were also bringing her other
voices, voices raised in the harsh roar of violence.

The sounds of battle froze her blood, and Damona desperately increased her pace. Suddenly a familiar shape leaped
out of the trees, landing squarely in front of her. The
Guardian's orange eyes blazed at her.

"What are you doing?" he demanded in a harsh growl.
"Did I not warn you to stay away?"

Damona started to slip around him, but the cat was in
front of her again. Dancing with impatience, she cried out,
"Cuchain would not heed me. I must go to him."

"Furless one, you cannot. It is already too late for him.
There is a power at work here that you do not understand. If
you do as your heart bids you, you will set other deeds in
motion—"

"Get out of my way!" Damona shouted hoarsely. "He is
my husband!"

This time the cat did not attempt to stop her.

Muirchertac had had an extremely difficult time persuad-
ing his chieftains and their followers to ride with him on this
mission of destruction. Even had the Shrine of the Guardian
not been so well known throughout the tuath, to propose
such a deed was an unheard-of and dreadful thing. Only the
Romans demolished holy places, as they had done long ago
in the conquering of Gaul and Albion. For the people to

destroy one of their own sacred sites would surely bring the direst of ill fortunes down upon the destroyers.

However, there were those among the chieftains and their trains who had chosen to become Christians, who did not share the queen's desire for peaceful conversion of others. These men accompanied the *Tuisech* willingly, eager to prove their loyalty to him, as well as to the priests of the new religion. Despite that, most of the nobles were still faithful to the ancient ways they and their forefathers had always followed. They had no wish to be a part of this blasphemy against one of the Shining Ones, and they said so.

Their refusal had sent Muirchertac into a rage. Shaking his fist, he roared out oaths and imprecations and threats of what he would do to these men who dared refuse him. His madness was the greatest threat of all, and therefore, the most effective persuader. Every man knew the violence he was capable of committing when his fits were upon him. No one wanted that rage turned upon himself, his lands, or his kin. So they forced back the protests hovering on their lips and set out to ride with their king, grim-faced and profoundly uneasy at what they were doing, but too bound by fear to act as their hearts bade them.

Now they galloped down upon on the rath. Muirchertac's fury had not abated during the wild pace he set for himself and his followers. Indeed, the fit that had swirled down upon his mind had only fed on itself as he raced through the gathering night. The darkness advanced to meet him, and it seemed that the shadows merged with the blackness in his soul until whatever vestige of rationality left in his mind had been swallowed up. Only grim purpose drove him now, a purpose shaded with blood and death.

The boundaries of the large ring fort were composed of an earthen embankment and a ditch. But these earthworks, impressive though they were, were meant to provide protection against wolves or thieves, who might be tempted by the cattle, pigs, and sheep, penned up inside the rath at night.

They had not been built to withstand a charge of armed horsemen.

Screaming out a garbled war cry, Muirchertac lashed his foaming stallion forward, sending him plunging over the low embankment, through it and up the ditch. The retinue of nobles and warriors sent their mounts clambering after him. Dogs erupted into a frenzy of barking as the riders burst into the enclosure.

Several herdsmen came stumbling out from their sleeping places. Despite the orders of their lord to leave the rath, they had not gone. The task of bringing in the cattle and getting the herds settled for the night had taken longer than they had anticipated. Finding roast pork and bread and cheese in the house, a few of the men had decided to eat their evening meal and spend the night in the rath, rather than going out to face the unseen dangers of the woods after dark.

It was a decision that would cost them dearly.

Riding down on the nearest of the herdsmen, Muirchertac yanked out his sword with a great ringing clash of iron. "Evil one," he bellowed down at the astonished man, and struck off his head. Blood gouted up from the neck stump so violently it splattered both the king and his horse. The severed head hit the ground, bouncing and rolling, the astonished expression on its face still fixed in place.

Muirchertac wheeled his plunging stallion. "Burn this accursed place," he screamed at his men. "Turn it to ashes for the new religion!"

The remaining herdsmen, as confused and astonished as their comrade who had just been killed before their eyes, ran for their lives.

Many in the king's retinue hesitated, reining in their nervous horses in horror at what they had just seen. But Muirchertac's words galvanized the Christians among them. These men leaped off their horses, ran into the deserted house, and came back out with lighted torches. Remounting their horses, they set out to do as their *Tuisech* bade them.

Muirchertach snatched a burning brand from one of the men. Driving his heels into the flanks of his horse he drove forward to where the hay was stored and jammed the flaming end into the thick sweet-smelling piles. The hay caught fire instantly, bathing the enclosure in a yellow light that revealed the riders setting fire to the other buildings.

It was that glow which Cuchain, and then Damona after him, had first seen as they sprinted frantically through the forest. It grew brighter and brighter as Cuchain hurled himself through the trees toward his home. His desperate feet took him through the last of the woods and on into the flat, tilled fields of his rath. The fields had already been harvested of their bounty. They lay flat and rich and empty, waiting for their winter rest. Cuchain sprinted through them, stumbling over the deep tracks left by running horses.

He heard sounds, chief among them the terrified bellowing of cattle. Finally, the low embankment of the ring fort loomed up before him. He flung himself over it, ran through the ditch and burst into the enclosure. The scene that met his eyes was beyond all reason. Cattle, sheep, and pigs were dashing everywhere, their forms illuminated by the lurid blaze of burning sheds. Mounted riders were charging through his home, the eyes of their horses rolling white in the fire glare as they plunged past the stampeding cattle.

Cuchain stumbled over something. He glanced down and saw the body of a dog. Beyond it lay another shape twisted and still amid the flames and the heavy smells of blood and death. It was the body of one of his herdsmen.

Cuchain stared at it incredulously, his thoughts hazy and whirling. Through the clamor a familiar voice suddenly smote his ears. He looked up in a wildness of horror and fury. His gaze picked out one of the horsemen. A blast of rage seared through him, white-hot, and as red as the flames consuming his rath.

"How dare you!" he roared out. "You, the *Tuisech* of my own tuath, riding here against your own people!"

One of the chieftains saw Cuchain, recognized the *Boaire,*

and forced his rearing horse over. "Run, man!" he shouted down at him. "This time he is completely out of his head. He'll kill you for certain."

"In the name of all the gods, why is he doing this?" Cuchain shouted back.

The noble made a helpless gesture. "He says it is for the new religion, but he is mad. Now do as I tell you: run. Run, before he sees you."

But Cuchain could not run. He looked about him, at his animals being chased and cut down by Muirchertac and his followers as the storehouses of food that would have kept his family and his herds fed through the winter blazed against the sky. He looked at his house, the house he had built with his own hands and inside which he and Damona had created their three children. Someone had set fire to it, perhaps Muirchertac himself, and the thick walls of wattle and daub sent long tongues of flame up into the night. Cuchain looked at all of these things. And the mysterious power that had sent him back from the safety of the forest told him he could not leave.

The blade of his sword sang against the clamor as he yanked it forth from its scabbard. His battle cry was a howl composed of rage and grief and pain as he charged forward.

3

"LADY." THE GUARDIAN'S TAIL lashed furiously against his sides. "You must stop this. Will you allow her whole family to die?"

A sigh rippled through Bast, as vast as the wind soughing through a great forest. *O Mau,* she said. *I accepted a challenge. I cannot interfere.*

"Challenge? Pah! May there be a pox on such challenges. Sekhmet drew You into this only because She wants blood."

No, little one, there is more to it than that. Far more.

The cat let out a hiss of frustration. "When it comes to You and Your Sister, there is always more. But the feud between You should not involve the lives of mortals. This is not like You, Lady. Damona is Your dedicated and loving Priestess. Mistress, how can you reward her with such cruelty?"

O My loyal child. The grief in the Goddess's voice was as infinite as the sea. *Much is at stake. This time Sekhmet desires more than just blood. She turns Her gaze to the future and She wants what I have and have had: a tradition of Priestesses dedicated to Her. If She can succeed in drawing Damona away from Me, the line that began with Veleda will end.*

The Guardian's orange eyes blazed. "If You allow the actions of this night to continue," he said angrily, "her line may end either way."

A long silence hovered between the cat and his Goddess.

Veleda made a choice, Bast said at last. *And she made it of her own free will. Damona must do the same.*

* * *

35

Damona came up short, staggering in horror as she saw the bright flames joyously devouring her rath. She coughed and rubbed at her eyes. The air reeked with smoke, bearing the odors of burning hay and barley and charred flesh to her on clouds of death. Unlike Cuchain, she did not need to stumble over bodies to know what was happening inside the ring fort. Her Druid-sight was merciless, and it showed sights to her inner eye that made her weep.

"I thought they would seek to harm only us, not the servants," she cried aloud, her anguished words meant for Bast, the Goddess's Guardian, and whatever other Shining Ones might be listening.

None of them answered her. But for a fleeting instant the Goddess arose before her eyes. The glowing gaze stared into hers. It seemed as if She would speak. And then she was gone.

In new terror Damona ran on. Cuchain was surely in the thick of that tumult of screaming and fire and smoke, fighting a doomed battle against those who would destroy his home. The familiar length of the broad ditch loomed up before her; she leaped through it, and raced up the embankment.

A horseman came clattering toward her. His eyes were wild in the light cast by the fires. His sword was unsheathed and its long blade shone red and glistening in the lurid glow. He rode directly at Damona, screaming the same refrain over and over. "Destroy the stronghold of the pagan Goddess!" His crazed words battered at Damona's ears. "Burn it for the new religion!"

Damona flung up her arms just as the lathered horse reached her. *"Be gone!"* She shouted out the command in a voice of power, strengthened by the fury boiling within her.

The horse reared wildly, hurled himself away from her, and stampeded in a frenzy of bucking in the other direction. His rider's sword went flying as the chieftain tried vainly to control him. But the animal ignored the tugs on the reins and continued his flight. Behind him Damona snatched up the bloody sword from the trampled dirt and ran on.

In the center of the ring fort there was chaos. Clouds of smoke drifted across the enclosure, one moment making it almost impossible to see, the next moment abruptly lifting so that the sights of this night were revealed with a painfully vivid clarity. The carcasses of the rath's animals lay everywhere, their blood pooling in the dirt. Mingled with them were the bodies of herdsmen who had not been able to escape in time.

Damona was beside herself with fury and terror. Her eyes searched desperately for Cuchain. Where was he? Had he already fallen prey to the wrath of these madmen and their even madder king? She spread her arms again, barely noticing the weight of the sword she still grasped. *"Beloved!"* she shrieked, and the voice of power seemed to tear her lungs raw with the effort. *"Come to me!"*

Another horseman charged at her. She swung the sword savagely, the weaponscraft she had learned as a girl rising up to give strength and skill and speed to her arm. The blade slashed into the man's thigh, but it was her words and not the wound that caused his eyes to widen in horror. *"The curse of the Goddess be upon you for desecrating this place."* The power crackled out of her in a sibilant hiss, freezing the chieftain upon his horse. *"Your wound will blacken, along with your soul. And screaming in agony will you die."*

The chieftain threw away his sword. In recognizing her, his wits had come back to him with a rush, though not in enough time to save him. "Forgive me, lady," he babbled frantically, trying to make himself heard above the din. "Not of my own will did I come here to do harm to you and yours. Remove your curse and forgive me. I beg you!"

But Damona had already turned away, losing herself in the smoke as she went on searching for Cuchain. His spirit, sweet and strong and unique to himself, touched her before she actually saw him. Streaked with blood, stained with dirt and smoke, he was answering her summons, fighting his way toward her across the enclosure. Damona's heart wrenched. To see him yet alive was a joy, but the look on his

face stabbed her as sharply as any sword wielded by these
invaders. His expression was dazed and dark, although
surely it was but a reflection of the agonized and enraged
expression her own face must bear.

A scattering of cattle plunged past her, obscuring her
vision. She had to leap back and around to avoid them. Several chieftains were chasing after them. However, these men
were halfhearted in their efforts. All Damona had to do was
raise her arms in the familiar gesture of power, and they
wheeled their horses and scattered as wildly as the cattle.

As the last of the cattle and horsemen swirled away,
Cuchain was revealed to Damona's gaze once more. In the
few instants it had taken for the animals and riders to stam-
pede past, three mounted nobles had seen Cuchain and were
galloping up to encircle him. Unlike those who had just fled,
these men were utterly caught up in Muirchertac's fanatic
purpose. Howling in triumph, they closed in about the
Boaire. He met them bravely, and the clash of swords rose in
a fierce discordant melody.

Damona's throat closed up. She started to scream
Cuchain's name, to send out a storm of shrieking curses so
that the three chieftains would flee in terror. But whatever
dark power had taken over Cuchain's reason and sent him
here to his death now descended on her as well. Her voice
failed her. She found herself choking as if hands had suddenly closed about her neck. She fought the sensation with
all her strength. She could not speak, but she could move,
and she forced her legs to hurl her forward. Yet, even as they
did, the end came.

A man on foot, fighting against three armed and mounted
warriors, cannot hope to live. Cuchain did not cry out; he
made no sound at all as a sword slashed into his shoulder,
severing the arm that held his own weapon. A second blade
followed almost immediately, slicing into his neck. Still, he
did not cry out.

Damona cried out for him. As suddenly as it had come the
sensation of choking that had constricted her throat freed

her. Her voice rose in a keening wail, flying up to join Cuchain's soul as it left his earthly body. His spirit touched her, enfolding her in a swift embrace that was as solid and real as his bravery and his love. Then he was gone, carried away to the Otherworld on the echoes of her grief.

Damona surged forward. She was conscious of only one thought: to avenge the death of her love. Some dark power was present this night: perhaps Muirchertac's madness had grown so powerful it had gained a life of its own. It had lured Cuchain to his death and had held her helpless while he died. As a priestess, she knew of such dark things; all those trained in the mysteries did. Light and dark were companion forces balancing out the world, each unable to exist without the other. Damona raged with the desire to call upon those forces now—light or dark, it made no difference—she had just seen her husband murdered before her eyes. She was bound to do something.

"Mother, Mother, where are you?"

The cry slashed her ears as sharply as the swords that had taken Cuchain's life. It was Eichne's voice, although she had not heard the words with her ears but with her soul. In the name of the gods, her children had left their place of safety and returned! Damona froze again in her tracks, gripped by a terror so great she was momentarily helpless in the face of it. Then her strength returned in a rush, aided by the power that belongs to all mothers when their children are threatened. She wheeled around and ran in the direction her inner sight told her to take. Cuchain was dead; she could not bring him back to her. She could only avenge his death. But her children were still in the world of the living. Them she could save.

She ran, threading her way between dead cattle and pathetic huddles of bleating sheep. Showers of embers fell sizzling on her skin and hair. She stamped them out with unfeeling hands as she dodged falling chunks of burning wood. Even the horsemen were fleeing, realizing that their work was done. The fires were raging out of control. The

clouds of smoke were as thick and black as this night of
death, and they obscured her from the sight of Muirchertac
and his raiders.

The broad ditch that encircled the rath was containing the
fires, and as she leaped down into it, Damona caught sight of
her children. They were running across the fields, straight
toward the rath. Cummen and Cliodna and her son were with
them. Cummen was holding Eichne and Deirdre by the
hand. Cliodna ran awkwardly behind, clutching little Libran
in her arms. The voices of her twin daughters echoed again
in Damona's head as she saw them.

Had the evil that had brought Cuchain to his burning
home brought her children as well? Perhaps she herself had
brought them. When she had been seeking out Cuchain in
the midst of all this destruction she had not called her husband by his name, but by her love. In trying to summon him,
could she have also summoned the rest of her beloved ones:
her precious children? Regardless of the reason, they were
now running straight toward her, and to their deaths.

"Nooo!" It was not the voice of an avenging Priestess that
shredded her throat this time, but the shriek of a mother for
her little ones.

Something hard came down across the back of her neck,
knocking her to her knees. Her vision blurred and reeled, but
waveringly she still saw Cummen running, holding on to the
hands of Eichne and Deirdre, only now she was running
away from Damona, not toward her. Damona knew she had
to rise; the impulse to struggle to her feet was overwhelming. But even as she did, the object hit her again.

The world broke apart in an explosion of sparks. She was
tumbling into darkness, and she strained to catch sight of her
children. She saw her twin daughters. Their tender little legs
were pumping frantically as they clung to the hands of the
servingwoman and tried to keep up with her. Their forms
were brightly illuminated by the fires blazing over the rath.

But the flames revealed another picture in her fading
vision: the horsemen that had swept past Damona and were

now thundering down upon them. Muirchertac was in the lead. His bellowing voice was unmistakable, crashing against Damona's ringing ears like the hammer of an iron-smith. He caught up with Cliodna and Libran, and delivered a terrible blow with his great sword that felled both nurse and child. Dimly Damona heard the voices of his men shout-ing out for him not to do this, but the *Tuisech* ignored them as he rode down Cummen and the twins.

Their screams were thin little wails in the smoke-choked air as he cut them all down.

Damona took that sound with her into the blackness.

Damona awoke to a vast unmoving stillness. At first all she was conscious of was the pain that clawed through her her head and along the back of her neck. Slowly, she became aware of other sensations. She was lying in the ditch that now protected only scorched ruins. She was covered with ashes and dirt. Her bruised body shivered violently from the dampness of the morning mists.

Trembling with the effort, she raised a hand to the back of her head. Her hair was as dirty and matted as the mane of an unbroken colt in winter, and feeling through the tangles she encountered a large mass of warm sticky blood. Her head throbbed sharply, sending new waves of pain spinning through her as she touched it.

She closed her eyes as her muddy thoughts gradually cleared. Memory returned with a rush, and she doubled over, clutching the womb that had protected her children while they were growing and then expelled them into a world where she could no longer protect them. She moaned, rock-ing back and forth in her grief. So Muirchertac and his men had thought they killed her and had left her for dead. Oh, how she wished they had. The physical agony of her wound was as nothing compared to the anguish in her soul.

She huddled in upon herself and wept. The odors of death surrounded her. All about the destroyed rath, the birds and insects that scavenged upon death were already descending, eager to inspect what the night had left them. Even the fires had died, though their smoke was still heavy and rank on the dawn air. Flies buzzed as they swept down over the carcasses of sheep and cattle.

"Lady, where are You?" she cried. "And where were You last night? I am Your Daughter. Why did you not protect us?"

Trembling, she waited, yearning for the familiar presence that had been so terribly silent. But the Goddess gave her no sign; not even the Guardian's lithe form slipped up to join her. Had he, too, been slain?

The dampness of the wet grass seeped into her torn bloodstained laine. Unheeding, she wrapped her arms tight across her breasts, pressing hard as if physical strength could push her agony into the soft flesh and beyond. The blood drenching her hair slowly crusted, drying into thick sticky strands about her shoulders and chest. Bound by her suffering, she took no notice of her state, only knelt and continued to weep with an unceasing tearing rage. Her keening breathed pain into the very air.

At last she raised her twisted face to the overcast morning sky. "The blood-price must be paid!" The words ravaged her throat, writhing up into the pale gray clouds. "Help me to take my payment. Help me gain my blood-price!"

She shrieked out her plea again and again. The cry tore apart the morning, but the morning listened, uncaring and silent.

Then, a clear dark voice answered her.

"I will help you," the voice said, and there was a smile as thick and shining as blood in its dark rhythm.

Slowly Damona unwound her arms. This was not the voice of Bast; nor did it belong to any Shining One familiar to the land of Eire. "Who be You?" Her own voice was ragged, grated as raw as her soul. "Though perhaps I should not care. For at least You have answered me."

I have indeed.

Damona's eyes, bloodshot by smoke and tears, blazed. She thrust a fist in the direction of the voice. "Then where were You when I had need of You? And where was Bast, the Lady of Silver Magic? All my life have I served Her, and yet my home lies in ashes and my family sprawls murdered before my eyes! Is this how She repays my devotion?"

The Goddess's voice was calm. *I am not that Goddess. But I am Sister to the one you speak of.*

Damona slumped. "Then the Lady Bast is truly gone," she said dully. "And so is Her Guardian. The power of this shrine is destroyed. A new power came here last night—the power of Muirchertac's madness I think it was. The daughters who would have come after me to continue the sacred tasks are dead. I can be of no use to You, unknown Goddess, not You or any other Shining One. Why have You come?"

Why, child, the Goddess said. *I came because you called Me. And, unlike My Sister, Who may or may not grieve for you, but nevertheless, has done nothing for you, I can help you.*

Damona's awareness sharpened. "How?"

Power rippled through the Goddess's reply. *It was not only your king's madness that wrought these deeds, but the madness of the new faith, the followers of which will countenance no faith but their own. Punishment is warranted against them all.*

You are consumed with rage, are you not? The darkness in the mighty voice grew thicker, each word digging itself into Damona's heart. *It eats into your soul like flames consuming dry wood. Retribution is what you desire now, and that you desire above all things. Well, you have called out to the proper Goddess. If there are two things I know of, they are rage and retribution. They are My gifts and the source of My strength. I will enable you to achieve both. That is what you want, is it not?*

Damona stared out over the charred ruins of her life. Long and long she looked at the smoking ashes, at the bodies both human and animal, tumbled here and there. The grove of sacred hawthorn trees had been burned, the spring defiled with the carcasses of animals. The entrance to the inner sanctuary had been blocked up with boulders. The bodies of her children lay somewhere in the fields, but the remains of her husband would never be recovered. He had fallen within the enclosure and so had been consumed by the fires. She could not give him a warrior's burial as he deserved. Muirchertac had robbed her of even that.

The yearning for blood-price gaped in Damona like the fatal wounds in the bodies of her family. Yet did she truly want what this goddess was offering? Blood and death seeped through Her words. Her promise rang with a coldness as deep as a moonless night in winter. There was danger in Her presence; Damona could sense it as surely as she had once felt the quickening of her children in her belly. But that had been a joyous thing. This sensation stank of evil.

Damona was Druid-trained. She could see the opening of a path before her, and it was as dark as the voice of this unfamiliar goddess. To walk down that path was to enter a realm she had never thought to enter, a realm far distant from the ways of Bast: the ways she had followed all her life.

She wavered. In spite of the grief and terror and rage, she wavered. Suddenly, for an aching heartbeat she felt the presence of Bast. But the Cat-Goddess said nothing. She did not speak to her as this new goddess had. She offered nothing, no consolation, no guidance, not even chastisement for the destruction of Her shrine. She only waited.

And in that silence of waiting, Damona slowly turned away. She filled her inner sight with the scenes of last night and her outer gaze with the devastation that lay before her now.

"It is what I want," she said, when she was through looking. "Tell me what I must do, and I will do it. But first, I have to bury my children."

There are few tasks more difficult than the burying of one's children. Damona made herself hard inside. She squeezed her heart into a tight unyielding knot that would feel nothing. Her face was carved in stone, her eyes dry and

burning, as she gathered up the small bodies of Eichne,
Deirdre, and Libran. The wounds that had taken their lives
were terrible. It was a small blessing to realize that in suffering such dreadful blows, they must have died almost
instantly.

The suffering of their mother was nowhere near as short-
lived. Damona swallowed again and again, her gaze turned
inward, while she arranged the pitiful little corpses and
brought water to cleanse and purify them. Until now, she
had thought herself blessed by the Great Mother, and in particular, by the Goddess whose shrine she kept. She had
borne three healthy babes, and they had all lived past
infancy. This was wondrous indeed, for it was rare for one's
children all to survive past the age of three or four. Fevers,
not enough food during hard winters, and a host of other
dangers carried them off with painful regularity. Damona
knew of many women who had borne twelve or more babes
during their birthing years and had seen only two or three of
those children reach adulthood.

However, the blessing had turned to a curse. Her little
ones had survived fevers and hard winters only to die at the
hands of their own king, the very man who was charged to
protect them as members of his tuath. Oh, hard and hard was
this day. And it would become only harder still.

An agonizing time later, it was done. It would have been a
mercy if Damona's eyes and thoughts had dimmed along
with the brightness of her children's lives, but it had not.
Indeed, her mind was clearer than ever, as if the gods meant
for her to carry every detail of this morning with her to her
own grave. She had gone far from the desecration, choosing
a small opening set deep into a slope wooded with young
birch trees for the burial of her children. There were no
grave goods to put in with them, no jewels, fine tunics, toys,
or other sweet things to remind them of their brief time in
the lands of the living. Everything they had ever been given
had been destroyed in the fires.

Eichne, Deirdre, and Libran were in the Otherworld now

with their father. Damona told herself this as she blocked up the opening to the cave. For all eternity they would live in the Blessed Realms, biding there in happiness and safety.

Thus had it always been taught, and Damona knew in her heart that this was true. Yet she could find no happiness in it. These deaths were wrong; they went against all that was harmonious in the world. She could feel hatred rooting in her womb, replacing the lives she had once nurtured, expanding until she was the hatred itself. Her world and all she had loved in it was gone. There was nothing left for her but to punish the man responsible for bringing this about.

"Come to me again, foreign Goddess," she cried. "Come and tell me what I must do." She waited, her cry quivering on the quiet morning, drifting in the air that still reeked with the smoke of the fires.

I am here, the familiar voice said. *Are you prepared to seek your vengeance?"*

Damona was breathing hard, as though she had been running again, running desperately through the night to save her husband and children. There was a terrible pain in her belly. Her womb was crying out, protesting the hatred that filled it, yearning for the burdens it had once carried in joy. "I am ready," she said.

The Goddess spoke. *First, you must renounce She Who is My Sister. Do you do this of your own will, in freedom and of your own choosing?*

An image formed sudden and unbidden in Damona's mind. The Goddess of the Shrine stood there, shining before her inner eye. She was radiant, her woman's body glowing with light. Her great cat face gazed on Damona with its unknowable wisdom. Grief shone starkly in the enormous green eyes; tears glimmered in their depths. The Guardian stood at her side, staring gravely at Damona. His orange eyes were wide and unblinking.

For an instant Damona wavered again. But it was an instant only. She pushed the images away from her, sent them swirling into the darkness possessing her soul. "I do," she said harshly. "I renounce the Goddess. And Her Guardian with Her."

A triumphant sound rippled along Damona's nerve endings, like a massive chuckling purr from some great beast. *Very well, Priestess,* the Goddess said. *Be still then, and look upon My power.*

The morning went suddenly still. Birds that had been chattering and chirping their greetings to the new day ceased their music. Flies buzzing in black clouds over stiffened bodies went silent. The breezes rustling through the trees abruptly vanished. Even the smoke, with its heavy odors of death and destruction, seemed to dissipate.

Into this new deep silence came the magic. It started slowly, feeling its way, searching for its purpose. Then it found her.

Damona swayed under the force of the impact. In discovering her, the magic discovered itself. It breathed all about Damona, enfolding her, wrapping itself around her with a presence as physical as that of any mortal. Inexorably the power increased, seeping into Damona until not a pore of her body or mind was left untouched. The spell was dark, as red as new blood, and she swam in the midst of it, unthinking, and strangely content.

Yes, she thought dreamily, this was what she wanted. Let the foreign Goddess work Her ways. Bast, the Goddess she had dedicated her days to, had not seen fit to protect it or her. Let this dark magic be done. She was willing. Somewhere deep inside of herself, she laughed.

It was not a happy sound.

She felt herself flying apart. All the pieces of her soul and body were swirling into the red darkness. Her life was disappearing into that darkness, but then what did that matter? Her life had already been taken from her. Now, she would be given a new life, and in it she would take her revenge.

The voice of the Goddess throbbed in the darkness. *You are yourself no longer. And yet, you are more yourself than you have ever been. Glory in your hatred. Take pleasure in your rage. These things will make you strong against your enemies. My power is old beyond knowledge, and the secret of it lies in blood. Now, your power, too, will lie in blood. Worship Me, and you will be invulnerable. Worship Me, and those who wronged you will scream out for mercy, a mercy you will not give them. Cry out in your anger. And know that I am what you seek.*

I do. Damona spoke the words silently. *I cry out, Lady. I ask for your blessing of blood.*

She meant it. With every shred of her torn and battered soul, she meant it. A terrible pain went through her head, that sacred repository where everyone's soul resided. The bits and pieces of her that had flown apart were reassembling, and their coming together seemed likely to tear her asunder all over again.

It is done, the Goddess said. *Look upon yourself.*

The magic went into violent motion, moving with a whistling speed like the wind singing down through a smoke hole. The bloodred darkness lifted and departed, allowing the sounds of the new day to return in its wake. But before Damona's eyes a shimmering reflection formed out of the air. She saw herself, or rather, the new self that the Goddess had created. As though she were gazing into a clear scrying bowl, she stared at the sight being revealed to her.

A woman looked back, serene and alluring and murderous with purpose. She was Damona, and at the same time, she was utterly unrecognizable. Gone were the bruises, the dirt, and the blood. The torn clothing, the tangled hair, even the wound at the back of her head had disappeared.

Damona's hair had always been her pride, and the magic had restored its beauty. Sleek and thick it hung down her back as it always had, with one stark difference. It had turned completely white. Silvery as new-fallen snow, this new hair glowed in the pale sunlight, its pristine color broken only by the great swaths of red that bloomed back from each temple.

The hair I have given you bears My mark. Satisfaction

throbbed in the depths of the Goddess's voice. *Red is the color of blood, and, therefore, it is sacred to Me. You will carry the red as a reminder of the pact between us. As for the white, you will carry that to remind you of your grief, and your hatred.*

Damona continued to stare at herself. She was the same height, but her breasts were fuller and higher. Her body had become more slender, bearing no signs of childbirth. A laine of the softest wool, shimmering red as the streaks of hair at her temples, draped her body, fastened at her slender waist by a belt of heavily worked gold. A brat of deep blue lay across her shoulders, held in place by a wide silver brooch. Bracelets gleamed on her arms, and jewels glittered at her ears and neck, setting off the face that had been transformed by magic.

It was a magnificent face, dominated by eyes as deep and brilliant as the mantle about her shoulders. Damona had been a pretty woman, but the stranger who stood in her place was beyond beauty. She was incomparable. Yet behind those glorious eyes there burned a grim and terrible devotion to purpose. A mortal would not be able to see that latter quality in her. He would be too dazzled by the outward appearance to see what lay beneath it, and that, of course, was the point.

I have gifted you with great beauty, the Goddess said. *And I have gifted you with something more important than beauty: distinctiveness. Your coloring is like no other. It will draw attention to you, and your power will hold that attention, so that you may work your revenge as you will on the one you hate. Are you pleased?*

"Oh, aye." Damona smiled, and saw this reflection of her new self smile back. "I am pleased, Lady. Most pleased."

Then serve Me well. For in serving My purpose, you serve your own. Your festival of Samhain draws nigh. It will be the proper time for you to appear in this guise I have put upon you.

Damona said nothing. Samhain, the time of the sacred fires, was indeed upon them. Every year the cattle were brought back from the high pastures to be culled for the coming winter. Samhain was one of the most important festivals to come during the wheel of the year. It was a time of rebirth and renewal. It was at Samhain that she and Cuchain had been wed, for it was then that courtships and weddings were celebrated. Ah, how clearly Damona remembered those times: the lowing cattle, the blazing fires, the bidding farewell to summer and the acknowledgment of winter and yet another turning of the year's wheel.

Damona's soul cried out, but fiercely she silenced it. Samhain was a time of danger as well as joy. It was then that the barriers between the worlds lowered, allowing spirits, and even mortals, to pass back and forth. A thought blazed across her mind. Perhaps . . .

Do not think of it. The Goddess's voice clanged about her. *Even if you crossed to your kin or they to you, it would not last. You know this. The lowering of the barriers is only temporary. What I offer you is permanent.*

"Permanent?" Damona ran a hand along her hair and over her body, feeling the strangeness of it. Magic, in all its forms, pulsed in this place of grief and pain, and nowhere was it stronger than here inside herself.

Permanent, indeed. For what is more lasting than successful retribution? Now go. Find this out for yourself. Seek out your revenge.

The reflection of the stranger who was now Damona began to break apart, dissipating into the air. When the last trace of it was gone, Damona turned to go. She did not look at the burial place of her children. She did not look at the smoldering ruins of her rath, the blackened mounds where the ashes of Cuchain lay. But she did pause and turn back.

"Lady," she said. "What shall I call You?"

Her question was greeted with silence. Suddenly a red-tinged blackness whirled out of nowhere. It grew and grew, rapidly taking over the brightness of the day. Damona stood in her new shape, watching in utter stillness as yet another figure began forming in its depths. This was no reflection of a mortal woman overlaid with magic. This was a goddess. She was gigantic, in the soaring overpowering way that only a Shining One could be. A linen garment of bright scarlet clung to her body, so tight-fitting and sheer that all the power and beauty of her female form were clearly revealed. A strong neck stretched from her sleek, muscled shoulders, and atop this neck was the head of an enormous catlike beast.

Damona had often seen the Goddess Bast. She, too, was part-animal, part-woman. But the cat's face that Bast wore had always been gentle and benevolent, radiating strength and power and love and wisdom and joy, all mingled together in a blend beyond the capability of mortal speech to describe.

This new Goddess radiated strength and power as well, but without any of the other qualities of Her Sister. Ferocity burned within and without Her. She was, as She Herself had said, an avenging force, a goddess of retribution and vengeance. She did not belong to the land of Eire. She was as utterly foreign as Her Sister Who had come to Eire so long ago and stayed on with Her Guardian to offer wisdom.

Yes, She was foreign and savage. She was precisely what Damona needed.

The Goddess looked at her with burning yellow eyes. Her lips parted, revealing a massive red tongue and glistening ivory fangs as long and deadly sharp as a warrior's spear. Damona fought the impulse to cover her eyes and shrink back from that fearsome sight. The massive rumbling sound she had heard before beat at her ears. It was a purr, she suddenly realized. The Goddess was pleased. It was a deeper, fiercer sound than the purr Damona had sometimes heard the Lady Bast make, but it was a purr nonetheless.

You are strong, the Goddess said approvingly. *Strong in the way that she who came before you was strong. But she, and those of her line who came after her, always rejected My gifts. They chose to serve My mealy-mouthed Sister, not Me.*

The hard knot that was Damona's heart constricted. The

magic had not changed her heart, only made it smaller and harder. "Perhaps," she said from new and bitter wisdom, "they did not see their families murdered by their own king."

The Goddess's voice was a deep and oddly musical growl that tolled through every fiber of Damona's new body. *When the blood of your enemies stains your hands, and you wear their souls like ornaments around your neck, then will you know joy again. Happiness will cause that heart of yours, which is now small and shriveled with pain, to grow large again. Happiness that only My gifts have given to you.*

Before Damona's gaze, the immense figure began to fade. "Wait," she called. "You still have not told me Your name."

I am Sekhmet, the Goddess said in Her deep ringing voice. *And now that you have seen Me, you will not forget.*

As Damona turned again and began to walk, Sekhmet flamed back into the Realms of Magic.

You see? She roared. *You gave her a choice, and she has made it. I wager now, Sister, that You regret Your foolish generosity.*

At the Cat-Goddess's feet, the Guardian glared at Sekhmet, but Bast Herself was silent. *Her choice is not carved in stone,* She murmured at last. *Not yet.*

4

TEARS RAN DOWN THE QUEEN'S face. She had been weeping and weeping, and the wellspring of her tears had still not gone dry. Along with her tears she had prayed constantly to the One True God. But neither prayers nor tears had brought her ease.

"Lady Rionach." The oldest of the queen's servingwomen approached her, timid, and yet made determined by her concern. "Will you not rest now? Or perhaps take some nourishment? You have been out here since dawn."

"I cannot." Rionach clutched at her cross, turning a ravaged face to her servant. "Do you not see? I am responsible. The blood of innocents stains me. My soul is tarnished with it. What happened last night is my doing."

"No," the servingwoman said fiercely. Her lined face was hard with anger. "That was not your doing, and you must never think that it was. Forgive the harshness of my words, lady, but your husband is in the grip of madness. It was the madness that drove him to commit the great evil that was done. By the gods, it was not you."

Lovingly the queen's fingers stroked the heavy gold symbol of her faith. "You have not accepted the true Lord," she said sadly. "That is why your eyes are blinded to the truth. But my eyes are all too clear. Over and over have I spoken to my husband of abandoning the old ways and following the Christian teachings of Patrick the Blessed One. I have told him that the shrines he visits in search of truth will never bring him true knowledge, but only evil—"

"You never told him to ride to a holy place, slay everyone there, and burn the priestess's rath to the ground," the servingwoman interrupted angrily. "Their deaths and the blood-price due them are on our *Tuisech*'s head, and his head alone."

The servant clamped her lips tightly together. She did not wish to add that in her mind, the blood-price also rested upon the heads of all those chieftains who had taken part in the horrific deed.

That was not only her opinion, but the opinion of many others as well. From the first moment that news of the raid upon the sacred shrine had spread among the ears of the tuath there had been talk of nothing else. But those who felt as the servingwoman did were not Christians. Some who belonged to the new faith had actually agreed with the attack, pointing out that it was not madness but Christian dedication that had driven the chieftains who rode with Muirchertac.

The servingwoman thought that such talk was blasphemy, a sign of horrendous ill fortune with Samhain about to begin. Even worse was the queen's refusal to speak with the tuath's Druids who had come to see her in the wake of the tragedy. To reject the guidance and wisdom of the tuath's religious leaders only compounded the evil consequences that must surely follow the events of last night. But the servingwoman, seeing the agony in her mistress's face, said none of this aloud.

Lady Rionach looked past the other woman's shoulder. Her light green eyes were haunted. "We will all pay for the evil of last night," she said quietly. "May God have mercy on our souls. For in one way or another, we will all pay."

There was always a great deal of hunting to be done before Samhain. Meat in plenty had to be provided for the people, so much so that everyone lolled about with aching bellies. A well-fed tuath was a strong tuath, and it was an omen of good fortune to see haunch after haunch of venison and boar spitted and roasting over the coals. The culling of the herds and flocks was over. Those animals not likely to make it through the winter had already been slaughtered, and though some of their meat would be used at the feast, most had been stored away against the cold cruelty of the snow season. To eat too much of that flesh now could mean starvation later, so the emphasis was on eating rich game meat at Samhain, especially since such animals would be scarce during the long winter months.

On the day of Samhain Muirchertac led a party of chieftains out on the last hunt to be made before the festival began at sunset. Many of his nobles had been avoiding him, and they sent a host of various excuses as to why they could not join their lord on this day. Those who did join him were Christians, most of them the same men who had willingly participated in the massacre. It was a smaller group than usual that rode out into the woods, but Muirchertac did not seem to notice this, any more than he had noticed the reaction of his tuath to his attack on a sacred shrine.

The *Tuisech* had already passed into a blithe unawareness of that night and what he had done. It was not that he had forgotten those events, just that they no longer mattered to him. He felt not the slightest tinge of remorse or regret for the destruction he had caused. His madness shielded him from such troublesome emotions, and the highness of his position protected him—for the time being at least—from the consequences of that madness.

With a clear heart he rode through the dank woods of late autumn. The trees had released their burden of dead leaves, which carpeted the forest floor, crunching and rattling beneath the horses' feet. Through the unclothed branches the sky gleamed a restless, darkening gray, a portent of the stormy weather to come in the months ahead. Trotting alongside the huntsmen, the dogs soon struck up a scent.

Murichertac leaned down from his horse to examine the ground with a practiced eye. "It's the spoor of a stag," he said to his companions. "And a big one. We'll have our-

selves a good chase, and after we've brought him down, perhaps the gods will favor us with taking a boar as well."

And so the hunt commenced. It was a good day for hunting; the scent lay close to the ground, and the dogs were
fresh and eager. The stag was soon flushed from his resting
place in a hawthorn thicket. Just as Muirchertac had predicted, he was a fine beast, his thick winter coat ruddy in the
pallid light, a crown of stately antlers weighing down his
head. The dogs set up a wild outcry at the sight, and the hunt
went forth in earnest. Whooping in joy, the men urged their
horses forward. In the cool air the horses, too, were fresh,
and they leaped ahead as eagerly as the dogs. The quiet
woods shook with the rhythmic thump of hoofbeats, the
shouts of men, and the musical baying of the hounds.

Only the stag was silent. He flew through his wooded
home, familiar with every tree and bush, every clearing and
thicket and stream. As swift and strong as the great god Cerrunos, who himself wore the antlers of a stag upon his divine
head, the animal bounded away from his pursuers on tireless
legs, hidden from them, leaving only his scent behind.

The hunt wore on through the morning, and still, the
hounds could not bring the mighty stag to earth. The horses
were lathered beneath their riders, the men hoarse from
shouting, but the dog pack was relentless. Their tongues
lolled from their mouths as they panted and bayed, but the
scent of the quarry was sweet and heavy in their sensitive
noses, and, as long as they had that smell enticing them on,
they would not stop.

"We'll take him soon," Muirchertac shouted to his chieftains. His teeth flashed through his auburn beard in excitement at the chase. "What a brave beast he is!" And he roared
at the dogs to urge them on.

The stag's trail led through ever-thickening trees and over
a rocky streambed. One of the horses stumbled on the rocks
and came to a jerking halt. His rider leaped off to attend to
him as the others plunged past. Farther on, Muirchertac let
out a string of oaths, as the dogs abruptly stopped and began

to mill around. They had lost the scent. The stag had crossed a swift-flowing brook to throw them off and had apparently succeeded. Sniffing and whining, tails wagging in concentration, the dogs coursed along the banks seeking to rediscover the trail. Muirchertac trotted his horse up and down after them, shouting angry encouragement.

Suddenly one of the nobles called out and pointed. The stag had appeared. His red coat shimmered through the dark bare tree limbs. He was plainly winded, his flanks heaving and trembling, his head lowered with the weight of the mighty antlers. But the sight of his hunters seemed to galvanize him into a new effort. As unexpectedly as he had shown himself he took off again, dashing swiftly into a tangled mass of fallen trees and thick copses of brush and young oak and ash trees.

Muirchertac jabbed his heels into his horse's flanks. "We have him now," he exulted. "Hurry, he'll soon be ours!"

The hounds, relying on their noses and not their eyesight, had regained the scent. Eagerly they set up the music of the chase again. In a flurry of tails and legs and lolling tongues, the entire pack breasted the fallen logs and hurled themselves after the newly discovered quarry. Close on their heels followed the hunters. But though they started out as a group, they soon had to split up. The terrain made it impossible to do otherwise. The deadfall with its huge rotting logs and piles of twisted branches presented an obstacle that would have deterred less-determined pursuers. Several more men fell out of the chase when their mounts stumbled or refused to jump a particularly daunting obstruction. Those that went on found themselves quickly separated by the thickly wooded copses.

As he sent his mount plunging through one of these copses, Muirchertac suddenly realized that he was alone. He thundered on through the brush, the saplings lashing against his face and the sides of the horse. He paid no heed to the stinging blows, focusing all his attention instead on the hunt. But though he listened intently, his keen hunter's ears brought him no news. The stag was gone. Even the baying of the hounds and the pounding pursuit of the following horsemen could no longer be heard.

The tired horse fell into a walk, and the *Tuisech* did not push him on. Anger built in him as swiftly as the chase had before he became separated from it. Perhaps his chieftains were already overtaking the stag and closing in, denying him, their *Tuisech,* the honor of the kill. Such temerity would have to be punished.

"Has your quarry escaped you?"

The voice rippled over Muirchertac's flesh like the sliding of a fur coverlet. The horse abruptly stopped, and the king did not reprimand him. His hand went to his sword as he swiftly reined the animal about. But his hand left the sword haft almost at once.

A woman had stepped out of the thicket through which he had just passed and now she stood on a small patch of grass watching him. Her lips curved ever so slightly as her gaze met his. She was shapely as a young doe, and surely as tender. Her garb was a red tunic and a blue mantle. Her slender waist was belted with gold and her mantle was fastened with silver. She glowed in the dull gray day like rainbow-colored flame.

Muirchertac stared and stared and still, his eyes could not get their fill. He could not take his gaze from her hair. Gleaming like silk, its whiteness was blinding, made even more so by the streaks of red slashing back from each temple. The sight was like moonlight spilling down on fresh blood. Images from the previous night suddenly flashed through Muirchertac's mind. He saw the moon, remembered its cold silver light shining over tumbled bodies and flames and pools of blood.

Why was he thinking of that now? The deed was over and done with, his will worked as the gods meant it to be. The woman's eyes burned at him, as blue and deep as the sea on a day in high summer, and those troubling scenes were promptly replaced by images of a different sort, no less troubling, but in a far more exciting way.

He cleared his throat. "Who are you?" he demanded huskily. "By the antlers of Cerrunos, I nearly swiped your head off. Where did you come from?"

Her wonderful eyes did not leave his face. "I thank you for not harming me, lord," she said in a voice like music. "I heard the noise of the hunt and merely followed it. That is all."

Muirchertac nodded, accepting this. "Why is it that I have not seen you before? Are you kin to someone in my tuath?"

The stranger's lips twisted ever so slightly. "In a manner of speaking, my lord," she said.

"Ah." Muirchertac's gaze traveled boldly over her. "Well, it is plain to be seen that you are no servant. What noble *fine* do you belong to?"

She regarded him in silence. "I have no *fine*," she said at last, and her lovely voice was so soft that the *Tuisech* had to lean forward over his horse's withers to hear. "I belong to myself, my lord, and to those I serve."

He misunderstood, as of course, he was meant to. "Then you are a servant." His gaze grew bolder, and yet more hungry. "I'll be bound, I would not have expected it by the manner in which you are clothed. Your master must value you highly."

"I have no master."

"Do you not?" Muirchertac grinned. "Your mistress, then."

The woman continued to watch him. "She whom I serve has freed me to do as I wish. For now."

"Indeed."

Muirchertac was truly delighted. The stag and the excitement of the hunt were utterly forgotten. Here was a different form of hunting, one that was even more satisfying. The gods had clearly sent this delectable woman to him as a sign of their favor before Samhain. A bit of love play would not go amiss before he rode back to his hall to ready himself for the lighting of the sacred bonfires and the rest of the night's rituals. In any case, his men had surely caught up with the stag by now and dispatched it. Muirchertac discovered that he was no longer angered at missing the kill.

He swung a leg over the back of his horse and slid lithely to the ground. "Then you are free to serve me, my beautiful one." He made his voice low and seductive, using the tone that he knew both his queen and the serving girls liked. "I vow that I will use you wisely and well, and that we will both find pleasure in it."

But as he came toward the woman she put up a hand. Muirchertac halted in his tracks. He was unable to say why he had stopped; the woman had neither touched him nor uttered any words of magic. Yet, though his body urged him to leap forward and bear her to the grass, he did not stir. Something far stronger than sexual desire forbade him.

"I do not doubt," the stranger said calmly, "that we could find pleasure in each other, my lord. But not at this moment, and not in this place."

Unmoving, Muirchertac stared at her. He did not wish to stand here like a tree stump. Gods, how he wanted to grab hold of the woman, pull off those garments, and expose the flesh underneath. But he could not. There was a dark and mysterious power here, and whether it was her doing or that of some Shining One he neither knew nor cared. A sane man would have questioned it, but Muirchertac, though he acceded to the power holding him in place, was sublimely indifferent to the power's possible dangers. He only knew that he desired this woman, and her refusal only increased that desire.

His brow darkened. "I want you, woman," he growled. "And I am a *Tuisech*. A great *Tuisech*."

"You will see me again," she said, and gave him a wide smile.

Muirchertac drew in his breath at the dazzling sight of that smile. "Maiden, Mother, and Crone," he whispered.

"Your face is brighter than the countenance of the Sun-God-dess Herself." His voice grew louder. "Indeed, I will see you again, woman. I order it."

The moment the words left his lips, his eyes widened in consternation. The spot where the woman had been standing was empty.

Her voice drifted about him, as sweet and teasing as her smile. "You cannot order me, my lord. Even a *Tuisech* as great as you may not command me in such matters as this."

Muirchertac's blue gaze grew wild. He searched the copse for her, stared up into the thick branches that arched over-head. But he found no sign of her. His eyes grew wilder, flaming with the anger that always bubbled so close to the surface of his unstable character. "Where are you?" he called. When he received no answer he raised his voice, shouting until it cracked. "Show yourself! By what magic have you hidden yourself from me?"

Soundlessly she stepped out from a massive oak tree. "Woman's magic," she said, and each syllable that floated up from her throat was like music. "Nothing more, my lord. For you are a great *Tuisech,* and I, after all, am a mere woman."

Muirchertac stared at her. Somehow the act of disappear-ing and reappearing seemed to have only increased her beauty. "Ha," he grunted, thinking of the queen and all the other women he had known. "There is no such thing as a mere woman. But"—he swallowed his anger and his impa-tience—"very well, then, I will not order you. Lady, will you return with me to my hall?"

The thought of what the queen might say to this question did not occur to him. He was too caught up in the strange woman's splendor to think of such things, and it would not have mattered to him if he had. The queen and her Christians had the peculiar idea that a man should cleave only to his wife. But anyone with a grain of sense knew that such an outlandish notion was pure nonsense. All men, and lords in particular, were judged by their vitality with women. For a *Tuisech* it was even more important; for such was the strength of the tuath ensured, symbolically as well as physically.

Muirchertac grinned, thinking of the pleasure he would have in demonstrating his virility with this mysterious, enchantingly lovely woman who was surely more beautiful than any goddess ever seen by man. But his grin faded at her reply.

"No, my lord," she said. "I will not."

The king's face darkened. "You gainsay me?" One of his swift rages began to sweep over him, blackening his handsome features still more. "I have asked you in courtesy, not commanded—"

"I did not say I would never come," she broke in gently. "Only that I would not return with you now."

She stepped forward, and her blue eyes fixed on his. Muirchertac tumbled into those shimmering depths and felt himself immersed by her beauty and his desire. Confusion replaced his fury. He faltered, not wanting to leave those eyes. "When?" he heard himself ask. "When will you come?"

She smiled again, gliding toward him, so close that for the briefest instant her full breasts brushed against his arm. Muirchertac grabbed for her. His hands clutched empty air, and her beautiful, mocking voice surrounded him. "When it pleases me."

This time, though the *Tuisech* searched and searched, she did not return.

5

THE SHADOWS OF THE SHORT FALL day lengthened and all throughout the land the magic and power that attended the three days of Samhain was beginning to stir. In the oak groves atop the highest hills in the tuath the Druids were gathering. The sacred tindle fires were laid, waiting to blaze into life and send their bright beacons up into the dark sky. The offerings of crops had been brought to the hilltops, along with the black sheep that would be sacrificed in memory of those who had died during the past year. Every morsel of grain and fruit that could be harvested had been taken in, for it was ill luck to leave any food on vine or tree or ground after Samhain, lest it become tainted.

In their houses the people extinguished their hearth-fires and in the growing shadows, lighted lanterns carved in sacred shapes out of hollowed-out turnips. Not until the next morning would they be able to kindle their cooking fires again, and then only with embers from the holy tindle fires lit this night by the Druids. It was a time of endings and beginnings. The Sun-Goddess was departing, taking with her the season of light and warmth and life. Now it was Cailleach's turn. The ancient goddess in the guise of an old woman would strike the ground with her hammer, and the earth would grow hard and cold and dark, ushering in the season of winter.

The next three days were imbued with excitement and dread. The feasting and revels would take place only in daylight, for at night it was dangerous to be abroad. The mounds of the Sidhe opened then, allowing the ancient magical race that had once ruled Eire to come forth and abduct any person foolish enough to be wandering about.

But the Sidhe were not the only spirits to swirl through the land during the dark hours of Samhain. Guided by the great bonfires, the dead, too, left the Otherworld to walk among their relatives once more. They were welcomed home with offerings of barley and milk, for the dead were not feared as the Sidhe were. In death a person was only as threatening as he or she had been in life. The spirits of the dead could be wild and powerful, but there was no evil in them, and this was their time.

However, on the eve of this year's Samhain, ill omens were already glowering down from the darkening sky. The *Tuisech* had been late in accompanying the Druids to light the bonfires, in itself a portent of the greatest bad fortune. It was whispered that he had gone out hunting, become separated from his men, and not returned. The chieftains had gone out searching for him, and they had finally discovered him running through the woods calling out for some woman he had supposedly seen.

Muirchertac had to be virtually dragged out of the woods and back to his hall. And now, though he had at last arrived on the high hill upon which the first of the tindle fires was always lit, he was plainly preoccupied and distant.

The Druids studied him with barely concealed rage. This latest disrespect simply placed the seal on the horrendous deeds the *Tuisech* had already committed. They were infuriated. Had this been another time, they would have immediately acted to strip his kingship from him. But Christianity was sweeping through Eire, weakening the ancient power of the Druids in its wake. Those tuaths where the age-old influences still held sway were becoming increasingly important. Muirchertac's own queen had become a Christian; it was essential that Muirchertac, no matter how mad his behavior might be, not follow her example.

And so, although there were some among the grim-faced

men and women gathered in the oak grove who did not agree with the decision, the Druids did not chastise their *Tuisech*. In any event, Muirchertac seemed neither to notice nor care. He had said little to them. But then, it was not necessary for him to speak. These were Druids. They could see and feel forces gathering, forces vastly different from the powers that usually attended the coming of Samhain.

"The fires and offerings will have to be great indeed this Samhain," one man whispered to another, as they both watched the king move restlessly in the dying light. "For there is evil in the air this night."

The woman he had spoken to shook her head. "After what this *Tuisech* has done, we can light fires that reach beyond the sky itself, and it will not be enough."

The bloody massacre of the other night had left a stain that occupied both the Druids' and the people's minds. Everyone knew of what had happened at the shrine of the outland Goddess. And, heaping one grim portent atop another, the queen had refused to attend the Samhain festivities, claiming that as a Christian, she must no longer take part in pagan celebrations. Fortunately, most of those who had joined the new religion did not choose to follow her example. Samhain was one of the most important times in the wheel of the year, and it would take a brave Christian indeed to risk offending the powerful forces set loose to roam during these three days by refusing to honor the festival.

The folk of the tuath, who sat in their cold houses lit only by the candles flickering inside the sacred lanterns, whispered of these dark and terrible things. Only the very young did not know of Muirchertac's madness. Disturbing as the king's instability was, it had largely been kept in check by the queen, enough to prevent any great harm from being done. Last night had changed all that forever. With the falling of darkness the doors between the worlds would open, and the ones whose blood had been shed in a sacred place would come forth. There would be consequences for what the *Tuisech* had done. But the people who muttered of this in their homes knew that when there were consequences to be paid, great lords rarely paid as high a price as the common folk did.

Throughout the land, children crouched beside the walls of their houses, peeking through slits in the wattle and daub. As always, they were the ones who saw the first of the fires flare into life, and eagerly they cried out to their families, "It has begun!"

Atop the mountain where the distracted *Tuisech* stood among the Druids, the High Druid raised his arms. "The season of the sun is passing," he cried. "And the season of darkness is beginning. Now will the earth fall into her winter's sleep. Cold and quiet will she lie, waiting for the light and warmth of Imbolc, the spring season, to awaken her. Let these holy fires strengthen the Lady of the Sun for Her battles with Cailleach and the darkness. Let our prayers and offerings make her victorious."

He took a lighted brand from the first fire and used it to kindle the second. "Shining Ones, let the doors between the doors open. We bid welcome to you, spirits of the dead who come to us from the Otherworld. See these sacred fires and use them to guide you to the homes of your loved ones. For they await you with offerings of peace and remembering. Accept them and go in peace."

All these were the traditional words, spoken in solemn cadence, as they were every year. But the listening Druids heard other words as well. Other voices twined on the wreathing curls of smoke, and there was an ominous sound to them. These were not just the whispers of the dead swooping over the beacons provided by the tindle fires. Something different was in the land. Perhaps the fires had released it, or perhaps it had been there already. There was a heaviness in the air; every Druid could feel it.

The crop offerings were brought forth, followed by the bleating sheep. The praying and dancing around the fires that would go on all night began, and there was a fervid quality to it that had never been present before. But even as the men and women danced, in the soul of each one a fear was kindled that burned as bright as the flames.

All their efforts might not be enough to safeguard against what was coming. What had been brought by the actions of their king.

Deep in a grove of yew trees Damona looked up through the branches, watching as the distant fires bloomed on every hilltop. Yew trees were sacred, and Damona had chosen to wait among them for the oncoming night. She stared unceasingly at the orange flickers, and memories wreathed about her like smoke from the bonfires.

Once she had thought them beautiful, these great tindle fires of Samhain. She had gone along with the other members of the Druid class to the high places, while her family stayed in their darkened house below, waiting for her to bring an ember from the sacred fires at daybreak. She had prayed and danced, and brought forth a black sheep from their own flocks as an offering and a remembrance.

Now her house was no more. The rath and the flocks it had sheltered were no more. Her family waited for her in the Otherworld, and she had not even a black sheep to sacrifice in their memory. Damona stared at the fires with wide tearless eyes and dug the nails of her newly formed fingers in the flesh of her new palms until they bled.

Fire. Never again would she look at it as a thing of holiness and beauty.

Samhain was known as a time of Letting Go. For an aching moment Damona heard the voice of Cuchain winding about her as tight as his arms. She refused to do as he bade her.

No, she told him. *I will let go of you, my dearest, but not of my vengeance.*

On the third and final day of Samhain the woman who had haunted all of Muirchertac's thoughts, sleeping and waking, since he had first seen her, came to him again.

In spite of its inauspicious beginning, Samhain had gone

on as it did every year. The sacred fires had burned as they
should, the offerings had been made and the hearth-fires in
all the houses rekindled. Huge feasts had been prepared
from the new fires, feasts they were still eating. People had
garbed themselves in the skins of slaughtered animals for
good luck and were parading about in a cacophony of
singing and shouts.

The people's mood was considerably lighter than it had
been on Samhain eve. The rituals of the festival had proceeded as they should, with no more ill happenings to mar
the holiness of these three days. Only Muirchertac and his
behavior marred the tuath's sense of relief, and most people
shoved those evil memories away, lest the remembrance
bring bad fortune in the coming year. For the Druids it was
not so easy. They walked among the celebrants, grim-faced
and unsmiling, watching the skies and trees with grave eyes
as they searched for signs.

Muirchertac, too, was searching, though not for signs.
Throughout these three days he had wandered amongst the
celebration, staring into faces, pushing his way through the
crowds when he caught a glimpse of long pale hair or a red
tunic. Each time he had been disappointed. The face he
peered into belonged to either an old woman or a startled
young one. With a muttered oath Muirchertac would fling
himself away and resume his search. Both chieftains and
Druids tried to dissuade him from this worrisome behavior,
but Muirchertac disdained them all.

Now Muirchertac stood at the edge of the woods that bordered his hall, glowering into the trees. A group of farmers
paraded past clad in fresh cowhides, but he took no notice of
them, not even when they paused in respect to offer him
their greetings. He had already seen that the woman he
sought was not among them. There was no further need for
courtesy. Anger and frustration welled up in him as the
farmers exchanged troubled looks and went on their way. He
slammed a fist into the rough bark of an elm tree.

"By Cailleach's hammer," he exploded. "Where *is* she?"

"Why here, my lord," a maddeningly familiar voice suddenly answered. "Where I have always been. Waiting for you."

The voice was as musical as Muirchertac remembered. Each word vibrated inside him as though he was listening to the deep notes of the sweetest bard's harp in all of Eire. He whirled around, his bloodshot eyes blazing. "Waiting for me you say!"

He could barely contain his fury. When he finally found this creature he would sate his desire upon her and then beat her soundly for playing with him in so frustrating a manner. "You have been using magic to hide from me," he snarled. "Show yourself, woman. I command it!"

At once the gentle voice lost its melody. Cold as the coming winter, the woman spoke to him. "You, my lord, may command me in nothing; I have told you that. Mayhap it would be best if I left you now."

"No!" Muirchertac leaped forward, his keen hunter's gaze wildly sweeping the forest. He found no sign of the woman. All impulse to do her violence left him in the frantic realization that she could indeed take herself from his presence as mysteriously as she had come back. "Stay, woman, stay," he said hurriedly. "I will do you no harm."

There was a silence, broken only by the *Tuisech*'s harsh uneven breathing.

"Do you ask this of me?" she inquired at last.

Muirchertac jerked his head in assent. "I do," he said at once. "Show yourself to me, lady. Please."

"Very well." And suddenly she was standing before him.

Muirchertac had barely slept in three nights, and he filled his exhausted eyes with the sight of her. She was every bit as beautiful as he remembered. He could not take his gaze from her. She drew him toward her, held him entranced as if he were bound with links of iron. Truly, there was magic here, and woman's magic or no, he did not care. She created a hunger in him that no food could satisfy. Her beauty dug at his soul with cruel fingers, burrowing an emptiness into his soul that he knew would never be filled until he possessed her.

"Come with me," he said hoarsely. "Come back to my hall. Look you"—he gestured with his arm—"it is just there."

A slow smile curved the woman's lips. Muirchertac watched it in a trance of longing. "My lord," she said. "What will you give me if I do?"

The *Tuisech* lunged forward in an effort to seize her. But suddenly his feet would not obey him. They held him to the cold ground like wet flesh to frozen iron. The woman smiled at him, beyond his reach and as impossible to grab hold of as a spring breeze.

"Anything," he cried, gritting his teeth. "Release me from your magic that keeps me from you. Come to me, and anything you desire will be yours. I vow it upon my blood." He placed a hand on his golden torque to signify the truth of the oath.

"Upon your blood?" The woman stood still, regarding him with an expression that Muirchertac might have found menacing, if he had not been so besotted. "That is a serious oath indeed."

"Nevertheless, I make it in truth. Come with me, lady, and you may ask what you will."

The woman walked toward him, or rather, she flowed, so light and graceful were her movements. The folds of her red tunic moved about her with a life of their own as she stopped just out of the king's reach. "There are two things I would ask of you," she said sweetly. "If you truly want me with you."

Eagerness both urged Muirchertac forward and held him back. "What are they? Tell me."

"First"—the woman's voice hardened—"you must banish all those who follow the new religion from your hall. All signs and symbols and followers must be sent away. If ever you speak of anything Christian or allow a priest of that religion into your hall, I will leave you, and I will not return."

Muirchertac nodded. It was a simple enough thing. He felt no bonds of loyalty to Christianity. The new faith that had served the purpose of his anger toward the shrine of the outland Goddess on that bloody night was already a distant memory: it meant nothing more than that. "Agreed," he said cheerfully. "What is the second thing?"

The woman's face was as serene and unyielding as a Roman statue. "You must banish your queen and her kin, even your children by her, from your house."

Muirchertac's eyes widened, and some of his entranced eagerness faded. This request presented more difficulty. It was one thing to take another woman to lie with and enjoy, even to install her in his house as a secondary wife; it was quite another to send away one's wife, particularly if she was a queen and of noble blood herself.

"Lady," he faltered. "She is the queen. Surely . . . "

The woman took a single step closer. "Do you want me?" she asked softly.

Her presence seemed to surround Muirchertac. Heat wafted toward him as though she were made of fire. He looked into her face, gazed at her eyes, and felt himself growing dizzy with longing. His thoughts, never very clear in the best of circumstances, ran as muddied as a spring stream. "Yes," he said. "More than anything do I want you. More than food or drink or breath itself."

"More than banishing the queen and the children of her body?"

Muirchertac shivered at that melodic, relentless voice. For a moment he saw himself teetering on the brink of a terrible chasm. Something deep inside urged him to turn away from this beautiful creature, to run as far and as fast as his strong legs could take him. Her magic would not be able to hold his feet in place if he turned and fled. But stronger than that small voice of warning was his aching lust, his utter fascination with this stranger. Beside it the voices of warning and his bonds to Rionach were a pale and small barrier indeed.

"Yes," he growled. "More than that. I will do it. I will send the queen away. But"—he hesitated—"my daughter and son, they are of my body, too, lady. Must you see them gone as well?"

"I must." Darkness came over the woman's lovely face, but Muirchertac was still too absorbed in his fascination with her, and now, his unhappiness at the thought of banishing his children—one of whom was his heir—to see it. "The children must go with their mother. It is the proper way of things. And in any case, they have been tainted by her love of the new religion."

Suddenly she stretched out a hand and laid it on his chest. It was brief, only the lightest of touches, and then she drew her hand back. "Do it," she whispered. "And then you will have me with you."

Muirchertac staggered. With all his will he wanted to leap at her again, but her powerful magic still held his feet rooted in the ground. His whole body burned from the memory of that touch, and his resistance to her demands melted away in the flames. "Very well, very well." He scarcely realized that he was speaking. "The children, too."

The blue eyes with their long pale fringed eyelashes watched him. "Remember, my lord," the woman said. "You have given me your oath."

"Of course. " Muirchertac snapped out the words in an agony of impatience. "I honor my oaths always. What sort of a *Tuisech* would I be if I did not? Now remove whatever spell you have put upon me so that I may lift my feet and bear you into the woods. We will find some quiet place where the grass is still soft—"

"No." The woman spoke with quiet firmness. "I will not be tumbled into the bushes like some newly taken slave from Albion. I will come through the door of your hall at your side and be treated with respect by those within. But first, you must go back and do as you promised. When that is done, I will come to you." She waved a hand. "Take your leave, my lord."

Muirchertac found that his feet would obey him once more.

"Hurry," the woman said. She smiled at him, the splendor of it making Muirchertac gasp. "The sooner it is done, the sooner you will have me."

Reluctant and eager at once, the *Tuisech* lifted first one foot, then the other, and turned to leave. As he began to walk toward his hall, a sudden thought struck him like an arrow. He paused and looked back at her, and a wide grin broke over his face. "I see it now," he exclaimed. "The Christian god has sent you to me as a gift for my destruction of the place of evil, hasn't he? You are my reward!"

The woman stared at him with those brilliant blue eyes. She seemed to shimmer before the *Tuisech*'s gaze, almost as if another shape were striving to break free from inside her. Muirchertac blinked his eyes and her form steadied itself. It was his weariness, he told himself. She was the same as she had been. "You are my reward for what I did," he repeated.

The woman continued to look at him, and her voice was very low. "Oh, yes," she said. "I am indeed."

6

MUIRCHERTAC HAD NEVER SEEN
Rionach angry, not truly angry in
the way that she was now. Theirs
had been an arranged marriage, as
customary as the lack of love that
often attended such unions. But
Lady Rionach had treated her husband well. During their three years
together she had given him a strong and healthy son to continue his line, and after that, a fine daughter. She had ever
behaved properly in her position of queen. Indeed, she had
guided Muirchertac in the ruling of the tuath with a subtlety
and skill that hid itself under the guise of dutiful respect. So
well had she done this that the *Tuisech* had no idea of how
greatly he had come to depend upon her guidance.

But Rionach walked a narrow ledge between rationality
and the king's ever-changing and unpredictable moods. He
had never seen her angry because she had never dared to be.
But in the space of a moment that had all changed.

"You would do this to me?" The queen's light green eyes
were even paler with fury. "To me!" She flung herself
toward Muirchertac, thrusting her face up at his. "I am your
wife, your queen, in the eyes of the law and of God. You will
not put me from you. I have given you no cause!"

Muirchertac stared at her, astonished by her rage. "I will."

He was surprisingly calm. But in his mind the image of
the stranger woman remained, clouding every other thought.
Her oddly marked hair shone snowy white against her blue
brat and red laine, as vivid as though she was standing
alongside him. She was waiting to join him. The urge to ful-

74

fill the tasks that had been laid upon him was so strong he could think of nothing else. The sooner those things were done, the sooner he would have his heart's desire. Why did Rionach not understand that?

"You must depart from my hall," he explained reasonably. "I am lord here, and it is what I want."

"What you want?" Rionach nearly struck him, so great was her anger. "No, husband, that is not the end of it. There is what I want, as well. You may not divorce me. I am not barren, and I have not been unfaithful to you. You have no cause."

"Divorce!" Muirchertac was nonplussed. "I have said nothing about divorce. I simply want you to go." He went on impatiently, repeating what the stranger woman had said to him without being aware of it. "All things Christian must disappear from my hall. I am banishing all those who follow the new religion. Every sign, symbol, and follower must be sent away. No one will speak of anything Christian, nor allow a priest of that religion into my house."

"But why?" Rionach turned a shocked face to him. The words, along with Muirchertac's peculiar demeanor, finally penetrated her fury. Her anger abruptly disappeared. In its place she felt disbelief, and a steadily growing fear. "Husband," she began. "What has happened to you—"

Muirchertac waved a hand to cut her off. A smile broke over his attractive features, sly and secret and eager. "There is no need to concern yourself, woman. My reasons are my own. I am *Tuisech*, and this is my hall. I will do as I please. You will go from this place as I command. When I desire you to return, I will send word."

For several long moments Rionach stood regarding him in silence. At last she straightened her shoulders, standing straight and tall like the queen she was. "I will wait for that word," she said with frigid dignity. "And I will not take my own right to divorce you, as your command this day enables me to do."

She swung sharply around on her heel and strode to the

door. But Muirchertac's voice stopped her. "The children, too, must go."

Rionach went very still. Slowly she turned and stared at him. "So you repudiate the children of your blood?" Her voice was low and just above a tremble. "You would send away your own son, who will inherit after you?"

Muirchertac hesitated. A frown started between his brows. For an instant he seemed to be thinking, truly thinking about what he was doing. Then the moment passed. He grinned. "I will make new sons as comely as gods."

And so it was done.

Muirchertac banished his wife and children and all those who had become Christians from his hall.

Damona watched the queen's procession ride out from the hall and turn their horses to the beaten track that led south. The animals moved slowly, as if they were as confused and reluctant as their riders. The queen rode at the head of the train attended by armed men she had demanded her husband send along to see that she departed his hall in safety. Her children followed behind her with their nurses, all of them riding in an open cart flanked by more guards.

Within her shell of magic, Damona shivered at the sight of those children. Pain stabbed through her, but she shivered at the fiery anger of Sekhmet as well. The lion-headed goddess had not been pleased at the sending away of the children. Damona had done this of her own will, and the Goddess's displeasure swirled around her.

But she could not have done otherwise. Hatred coursed through her like a great river, and yet there were eddies in that thunderous flow. For what she meant to do the children should not be present, lest they take harm from the revenge she would wreak upon their father.

Queen Rionach, who had surely led Muirchertac down the path of murder and sacrilege, Damona hated. She could have happily let her stay in the hall and suffer at her husband's enchantment, but her children were innocent.

Damona was a mother herself, or she had been. Deprived of her children, she could not deprive these little ones of their mother, accursed Christian though she might be.

The weather was turning steadily colder. There had been a frost in the night, and it had whitened the ground. The hooves of the horses clip-clopped against the frozen earth as they wound their way down the track. As the last of the banished ones departed, Damona felt the surge of mercy that had caused her to spare the children and thus, their mother, departing with them. Her empty womb again grew hard as stone, her heart clenched once more to its purpose.

When the last of the riders had vanished over the hills, she left her hiding place in the trees and walked briskly along the same path the queen and her retinue had taken. But her way led toward the king's hall, not away from it. She passed through the earthen walls that protected Muirchertac's house and stopped before the great open doorway. Two warriors came out to look at her. They were distracted and upset by what had just happened, or they would have taken more than just a passing notice at her beauty. However, with matters the way they were, both men merely glanced at her.

"What is your purpose here?" one of them inquired curtly. He took a second look at her, narrowed his eyes at the gold jewelry and fine clothes she wore, and added a belated, though grudging, "Lady."

Damona smiled. "Tell your lord that I have come. He is expecting me." She saw the man's uneasiness at this announcement, and narrowed her own eyes. "He will not thank you," she said, "for any delay in telling him that I am here."

The warrior frowned. "The *Tuisech* is . . . not himself." He and the other man exchanged glances. "You do not want to see him, lady, not today."

"Do not presume," Damona said calmly, "to tell me what I do or do not want. Go to your lord and speak to him as I have instructed you."

Both warriors stiffened angrily at her tone, but her glowing blue eyes met theirs, and they stared at her in sudden wonder, clearly seeing her for the first time. "I will find him," the first man said. "How shall I introduce you?"

Damona gave a regal nod. "My name is Niam." The name popped from her lips unbidden. But it was fitting. Niam meant "brilliance," and with this luster of magic upon her there was no woman in Eire more brilliant. Long ago, Niam had been a princess of the legendary Tir-na-nOg, the race who lived in the Land of Youth. The original Niam had taken a mortal chieftain to the Otherworld, just as Damona intended to send Muirchertac.

"From this time forth," she added, "you will remember it."

The warrior disappeared within the recesses of the hall, leaving his companion to shift his feet and wage an unsuccessful battle to take his eyes from Damona. Only a few moments passed before the king himself came hurrying to the door, striding so quickly that he was nearly running. Before the astonished eyes of the two warriors he rushed up to the woman, and jerked himself to a halt as if he feared touching her.

The woman gifted him with a glittering smile. "Am I welcome within your hall, my lord?"

"Lady," Muirchertac roared so loudly that all the servants within hearing distance halted whatever they were doing and stared. "You are."

She held out her hand. "Then take me inside."

Muirchertac's eyes blazed. His intention was obvious. He plainly wanted to sweep her up and carry her off to his bedchamber. But something in the woman's manner just as obviously prevented him. As the warriors and everyone else who was nearby looked on, he held out his hand instead. "My queen," he said breathlessly. "My new queen."

There were many sources Rionach could have gone to in order to seek justice for what her husband had done to her. The Druids would have interceded at once, and there was of course her own *fine,* the members of which would be outraged at this dishonor. There were also the Brehons, the arbiters of the ancient and highly complex laws that had always governed the land of Eire. No one—man or woman, king or slave—was exempt from the judgment of a Brehon, and even in his madness, Muirchertac would have been hard-pressed to explain his actions in light of the laws governing marital obligation.

But the Brehons were closely linked with the Druids; many, in fact, were Druids, and Patrick taught that the Druids were enemies of Christianity. Then there was Rionach's *fine*, which still held firmly to the old religion, not the new. There was not one family member save Rionach herself who had embraced the One True God. This meant that there was only one place the ousted queen could go to for help. The arbiters of her own recently adopted faith: the new officials of Christianity.

With her retinue following along behind her, the queen rode straight to Bishop Cairnech, the highest-ranking churchman in the vicinity.

Bishops were still a new phenomenon in this part of the country, though their influence was spreading. Unlike Gaul and Britain, from where the new religion had come, Eire was a land of farms and isolated raths. There were no towns and cities, or even large villages, where Christianity could concentrate a power base, and thus different measures were required, not only to ensure the flow of converts, but to keep them within the fold once they had been converted. The solution had been for the church to give bishops—its most powerful churchmen—a status equivalent to that of the king of any tuath, equivalent to the status of Muirchertac himself. The one problem was that only other Christians recognized that authority.

Rionach was granted an immediate audience with Bishop Cairnech. A young priest led her to the chamber where the bishop greeted his most honored guests. A fire blazed cheerily in the hearth and a servingman appeared promptly with heated wine, which Rionach had no appetite to drink, despite the long cold ride. She was staring dully at her goblet when Cairnech strode in.

The bishop was a dark man, his features swarthy and his hair a dense black sprinkled with gray. It was said that he was related to the earlier inhabitants of Eire whom the tall fair Celts had defeated when they migrated to these shores. The bishop had once been known as a bold warrior. These days he was a heavyset man whose muscles had begun to go to fat now that he had given up warrior ways to take on the mantle of Christianity.

Brown eyes that had once blazed with the delight of battle now blazed with religious fervor as he came forward to greet Rionach. She was an important addition to the fold, a convert of noble blood, who had brought many others along with her, and he welcomed her warmly. But his warmth turned to shock and anger as the queen poured out the tale of what Muirchertac had done to her.

"This is unconscionable," he said when she had finished. "This time the *Tuisech* has gone too far. He has committed a great sin against the laws of God."

"Not in his eyes," Rionach said. "A man can always take another wife." Her mouth twisted bitterly. "A man can, although a woman may not."

"Only by pagan law," snapped the bishop. He crossed himself. "Church law forbids such alliances. They are forged in evil. The Gospel teaches us that marriage is a sacrament, not to be tainted by a man taking other women into his bed. You know that well, my daughter!"

"Still," Rionach replied, "many men do so all the same, even those who have accepted the true Savior. In matters like this the Brehons have more power in Eire than the Gospel. The law is clear. My husband is not only allowed to take this creature into his house, but if he makes sons upon her, they will share in the inheritance rights equally with my own son." Her gentle features grew set and hard. "What he cannot do is banish me from my home. I have been a good wife to him—"

"Of course you have, daughter." His dark features tense and angry, Bishop Cairnech began to pace as he said this. "That is hardly the point. What matters is that you must be restored to your former position at once."

Rionach let out a shaky breath, allowing a brief tear to open in the rigid mantle of composure she had wrapped about herself. "Yes," she said heavily. "That is why I have come. I did not know where else to go. And yet, holy Bishop, my husband is not a Christian. There may be aught you can do to help me."

"We shall see about that," Bishop Cairnech declared with a heat that recalled the warrior he had once been. He called out for his steward and when the man appeared, he issued terse instructions.

"I have an errand for you. Take one of my best horses and go you to the *Tuisech*. Listen carefully, so that you may repeat my words exactly as I tell you. Say this: 'You, my lord, have erred grievously in what you have done. Your wife is dutiful and above reproach, yet you have put her from you. This is an offense in the eyes of God and man. However, there is still time for you to redeem yourself. Renounce your actions. Welcome your lawful queen back to your hall. Do this at once, and the One True God will reward you.' "

When the steward nodded his understanding of the message and departed, Bishop Cairnech turned to Rionach. "There, my dear," he said with a reassuring smile. "My man will deliver the message, and this will all be put right. You'll soon see."

"Perhaps." Rionach's tone was as doubtful as her face. Her eyes had followed the steward as he left, and they still lingered on the open doorway. "I will pray that it be so, Holy One, but I fear that things may not be put right so easily as you think. My husband is very . . . well, you know what he is like."

"The whole tuath knows." The bishop poured himself some wine. He glared down into the ruby depths, and slowly his dark features smoothed themselves out. "But," he went on serenely, "God will chase the madness from the heart of your lord and restore him to his senses." He crossed himself. "In the meantime, my lady, you, your children, and your retinue, are welcome in my hall. I invite you to stay here under the protection of the Church."

Rionach inclined her head. "I thank you for that, Holy One." She spoke with practiced courtesy, but her gratitude was genuine. She did not add that she feared her stay in Bishop Cairnech's hall might turn out to be a very long one.

Muirchertac felt as if he were drowning in a lake of pleasure and pain.

Never had he known such ecstasy lying with a woman as he had experienced with this wondrous stranger who had sought him out of her own mysterious choosing. And never had he known such horror in the dreams that came to him when, exhausted after their lovemaking, he tumbled into sleep. A sane man would have drawn a connection between the woman and the dreams. But Muirchertac was as besotted by Lady Niam as he was by his madness. The two were already becoming so tangled that those about him were no longer able to tell the difference.

Muirchertac gave Niam free rein to do as she liked in his hall. He was in little shape to do anything else. When he was not coupling with his new woman he was either wandering about thinking of her, and yearning for the next time, or tossing in the grip of nightmares. Any pretense at ruling the tuath was completely forgotten. In any case, Rionach had handled most of those details and, without her, Muirchertac had lost all sense of anyone but Niam, and only Niam. And, of course, the dreams.

Lady Niam, however, was in full possession of her senses, and she had no qualms about exercising her power. The servants were at turns bewildered and terrified of both her, and the changes that had been wrought in her name. By the end of the second day the terror was uppermost. When Bishop

Cairnech's steward rode up to Muirchertac's hall he found himself refused entrance.

A haggard pale-faced warrior ordered him brusquely to leave. "You are not welcome," he told the steward. "Neither you nor the message you bear."

The steward glared down from his horse. "I just told you I am here on official business of Bishop Cairnech himself—"

"That means nothing," the warrior interrupted. "Not anymore. Turn your horse around and go back to your master."

The steward's anger grew. "How dare you say it means nothing. I represent the bishop! I have been charged to deliver my lord's words directly to the *Tuisech*. I must see him, and at once!"

"What you must do," the warrior said firmly, "is ride away from here at once." He paused, eyeing the steward as he sat upon his tired horse. "Are you a Christian?"

"Of course I am!"

"Then if you have a grain of sense, you will heed me. Christians are no longer welcome inside this hall. Believe me, man, I am doing you a favor by telling you this. You do not want to enter here."

"By what authority are Christians no longer welcome?" demanded the steward. "Has the *Tuisech* decreed this?"

The warrior's face was suddenly paler. "In a way, perhaps. But if you want my opinion, his madness has decreed it. Lady Rionach was able to keep him in check, until he committed the sacrilege at the shrine of the outland Goddess and sent her away. Nothing has gone right since."

"But that is why I've come," the steward protested. "The queen has sought refuge with my master. She and her train are lodged at his house. The message I carry is about her."

The warrior shook his head. "It doesn't matter. She who has replaced Lady Rionach"—the steward was shocked to see him make the sign to protect against evil—"is no Christian. She will not countenance anyone belonging to that faith in this hall, much less around the king." He gestured roughly

with his spear. "Go now. Go before she sees me talking to
you. It will not serve well for either of us if she finds you
still here."

His response left the steward far from satisfied. How
could he return to the bishop with this important message
undelivered? What would he tell him? He started to argue, to
protest, but the warrior barred his way, refusing to say anything more. Soon, another equally intransigent warrior
joined him, and the steward was forced to turn his horse's
head back in the direction of the bishop and ride away.

By the time three days had passed, the servants came to
know when Muirchertac was being ridden by one of his
nightmares. His shrieks and moans would echo throughout
the hall, making it impossible to concentrate on anything
else. Shivering, the men and women of the hall listened to
their lord and made signs against evil and wished desperately that they were anywhere else but where they were. But
as concerned as the servants were, the chieftains of the tuath
were even more worried. And they had more power to act
upon that worry.

Word of the queen's banishment traveled quickly
throughout the tuath. As soon as the Christian chieftains—
those men who had ridden eagerly with Muirchertac to burn
the shrine—learned of it, they gathered to confront their lord
over his shocking actions. To their astonishment and anger,
he would not see them. He would not even allow them inside
his hall. Outraged, the chieftains milled around in the outer
enclosure, shouting and gesturing. The situation had grown
very tense indeed, when a woman none of them had ever
seen before stepped out of the great doors to address them.

She drew the eye of every man there, enthralling and disturbing them at once. The sight of her hair, frost white with
red streaks arrowing back from each temple, was so unusual
it was almost frightening. Her beauty burned in her like a
flame, though her eyes were as cold as a frozen lake in the
dark of night. When she spoke, her voice was just as cold.

"Your presence is creating a disturbance," she said. "The *Tuisech* commands you to ride from his hall at once."

"Commands us?" shouted one of the nobles. "We are his chieftains. Who are you, a woman, to tell us what he commands?"

The woman's gaze fixed on his, and the man found his eyes spinning away from hers as if he had been struck. A tiny smile drifted across her face, and vanished just as quickly. "I speak for the *Tuisech* in this matter," she said in that clear frozen tone, ignoring the fact that he could no longer look upon her. "I, and no other."

"Who are you?" another of the chieftains called out. "Your face is not familiar to me, lady."

"Is it not?" Something came into the woman's voice, then. It laid cold fingers against the flesh of every man present and sent chills racing along their spines. An uneasy silence fell, and into it the woman dropped more icy words. "That is not important. What matters is that I am bidding you leave in Muirchertac's name."

New anger erupted among her listeners. "Only the *Tuisech* may bid us do that," a voice roared. "Or his queen. And the Lady Rionach, who has been blessed by the One True God, is not here. By what evil has she been sent away?"

The woman drew herself up. Several of the servants peering out from inside the hall gasped and made the sign against evil. A number of the chieftains crossed themselves. Flames seemed ignite within the folds of the woman's red tunic. To the eyes of the watching men fire was suddenly glowing all about her. And behind the woman and above her yet another figure was taking shape, hazy and shifting but clearly visible. It was a monstrous form, a creature with the body of a woman and the head of a beast, a vision straight from the realms of nightmare. The nobles' horses danced and snorted at the sight, and the unearthly vision opened its giant jaws and snarled.

Dwarfed by that terrible figure the woman's voice still rang out, clear and cold. "Your Christian queen is gone by my doing," she said. "And I am the lady here now. If you are wise, you will not question it. Now be gone!"

The chieftains wheeled their panicked horses and went.

It was clear to all within the tuath that stronger measures were needed. Although Rionach was a Christian, and the majority of folk in the tuath were not, she was a popular queen. Without her steadying presence matters fell rapidly into chaos. Muirchertac would no more see his non-Christian nobles than he would the Christian ones, and thus there was no one to lend the unstable king balance.

On the third day of Niam's arrival at the hall, a group of nobles sought out the High Druid and asked him to go to Muirchertac.

"I have seen him unsettled before," one of the nobles said. "We all have. But this is different. He is under an enchantment from the stranger he has taken into his hall."

The High Druid frowned. "So say the unbelievers, the same men who encouraged Muirchertac in his desecrating of a sacred place. This woman is not a Christian as Lady Rionach was, and that upsets them."

"Neither does she seem to be one of us," the noble pointed out. "But if she is faithful to the sacred ways, then she will listen to you, High Druid. Influence her, and you will be able to influence the *Tuisech*. Things can be set right again."

The High Druid's greenish blue eyes had faded somewhat with age, but they were still piercing. He turned them on the younger man, staring until the latter looked down. "Things will never," the old man said flatly, "be set right in this tuath, not so long as this new religion spreads among us like a miasma. Lady Rionach had the ear of her lord. She counseled him to take his unbeliever chieftains and destroy a holy shrine. And when Muirchertac's eye strayed and he put her from him, she did not avail herself of a Brehon who would have brought the weight of law to bear on her husband. Instead, she went weeping and wailing to yet another Christian. Perhaps it would be better if she stayed gone."

"We do not know for certain that the queen had a hand in what happened at the shrine," another chieftain said. "I have heard rumors that she was against the deed, and that she wept so much after it was done it was as if her own *fine* had been slain."

"Holy One." The oldest of the chieftains stepped forward. "You must do something. You cannot allow this to continue. Christian or true religion, it does not matter. The tuath is falling apart. The servants in Muirchertac's hall are terrified of this new woman. I do not believe her influence is a good one. My own slaves have brought me word from those in the king's house. They tell me that he has grown even madder since she has come than he was before. The Christian nobles say—"

"I know what they say." The High Druid scowled. "She frightened them by calling upon the outland Goddess of the shrine they desecrated," he went on with contempt. "They deserved to be frightened. Indeed, both the woman and that goddess were kind to them. They deserved far worse."

The old chieftain threw up his hands in a gesture of frustration. "And what if they did? Holiness, you are wise beyond all of us. Look beyond your anger and see what is true. In the state he is in, our *Tuisech* is a threat to Christians and us alike. This woman must be brought under our control, or sent away, so that we may regain our influence over him. But things cannot continue as they are. A blemished *Tuisech* is a threat to us all. It will not take long for our neighbors to see what is going on and take advantage of it. They're probably aware of it already. The only reason they haven't attacked us is because of the weather. Thank the gods for winter and the Time of Cold."

The High Druid gazed thoughtfully at the grizzled old chieftain. "Yes," he said after a moment. "Truth has come from your lips, and above all else, I am bound by truth." He sighed. "I will go to the hall of Muirchertac."

7

THIS ONE HAS THE ABILITY TO KNOW your secret. Sekhmet's voice hissed inside the head of Damona, the woman who now called herself the Lady Niam. *He will quickly see behind the illusion. You must not allow that to happen. Use your power.*

Damona gazed at the High Druid as he walked toward her. He had come to the doors of the hall, and the warriors that stood guard there had instantly granted him entrance. The warriors were of the old faith; not even with their fear of the mysterious woman who had come to reign in the king's hall would they dare deny the High Druid himself. Indeed, they were pathetically grateful to see him, whispering their desperate hopes that he would be able to set things to right.

So the High Druid entered the king's house and allowed his inner sight to lead him to the reason for his visit. Magic was present for certain in this great hall, and mingled with it was the reek of madness. The rafters vibrated with unseen voices, the smoke from the hearth-fire wreathed up to the ceiling heavy with shapes of ill omen. Servants peeked at him from corners and doorways, their faces pinched and drawn.

The High Druid nodded to those who would meet his gaze, offering them silent reassurance as he walked on. At length he found the woman. She was standing in a small chamber that overlooked the courtyard and was clearly waiting for him.

Damona's gaze did not flinch from that of her important

visitor as he approached. The High Druid moved with a slow and careful dignity, wrapped in a majesty that Muirchertac, for all his royal blood, would forever lack. His farseeing eyes were as clear and steady as a lake at sunset, and they stared searchingly into her face. His hair flowed over his shoulders, as snowy as her own frosty mane, blending into the pristine folds of the formal robe he had donned for this occasion.

As he came closer Damona strained to pay heed to Sekhmet's warning. But a tinge of reluctance dogged her. She knew the High Druid; in her old life she had talked with him many times. He was a good and wise man; not to give him the reverence he deserved was as foreign to her as the lion-headed goddess herself.

"The gods give you good, Holy One," she said.

The Druid stopped in front of her. "And you, my child." He stood there, regarding her with those steady eyes.

Damona smiled, regarding him as directly as he studied her. "Is there a ritual to preside over that you have dressed yourself so this day?" she asked politely.

"There is not." The Druid's face grew sterner. "But with all that has befallen our tuath, the trappings of ritual seemed called for."

"And I am one of those things." Damona did not quite sigh. "You seek to protect yourself from me. There is no need, Holy One. Not for you."

The High Druid did not respond to this. "Your face does not belong to one of the folk of this tuath," he said thoughtfully, and without preamble. "How is it that the *Tuisech* has welcomed you into his hall and sent his own lawful wife away in your stead?"

"The *Tuisech*," Damona said, as if it explained everything, "is quite mad."

"Indeed." The blue-green eyes narrowed. "But what have you done to increase that madness?"

Fool! Sekhmet's voice snarled inside Damona's head. *Do*

not bandy words about with this priest. Destroy him. I will help you do it.

Damona felt the strength of the Goddess begin to swirl about her. It touched her with a searing heat, licking along her limbs like the flames that had consumed her prior life. "Go from here," she said in a sudden harsh tone that was no longer her own. "I will answer none of your questions."

The High Druid did not move. His sea-colored eyes grew more piercing, and Damona could feel him calling upon his own power. "No, you will not," he said in a ringing voice. "But She who is with you will answer what I ask. I call upon Her now. Outland Goddess of the Shrine, acknowledge me, and we will speak of the wrong that was done You by unholy men."

The heat that bathed Damona grew more savage. She raised her arms, and her blue eyes blazed suddenly yellow. A person not initiated into the mysteries would have fallen back in terror, but neither the High Druid's calm demeanor nor his strength wavered. "A glamour has been laid upon you, my child," he said gently. "Your soul resides in a body given to it by the magic of your goddess. But She and you are both set upon a course that is ill-fated."

Damona bared her white teeth, which gleamed in what should have been a smile, but was not. "Ill fate," she repeated, and laughed. "My lord Druid, you know nothing of my course, or what has set me on it. I, on the other hand, know far too much."

"Courses can be changed." The High Druid's voice was still gentle. "For the living. But the fates of the dead cannot be altered. A great desecration was committed against the shrine of the outland Goddess. Madness rode that night: the madness of the *Tuisech* and the madness of this new faith that will not tolerate what has come before. Honor must certainly be restored and blood-prices paid, but the dead are in the Otherworld now, and not even the magic of your outland Goddess will bring them back . . . "

His voice abruptly trailed off. His eyes sharpened, fixing intently on the woman who stood before him. "You," he breathed. "In the name of Mother Danu, you have returned—no"—he closed his eyes, then opened them, still staring at her. "You were never gone. They did not kill you. Praises to the Shining Ones, your goddess protected you. And She protects you now, Priestess of the shrine, is that not so? It was She who sent away the chieftains who came to this hall. And well that She should, for they were the ones who rode against Her holy place. So She has laid this illusion upon you—"

A burst of flame shot out. Damona felt it searing through her, issuing from the hand she had just raised without her volition. Sekhmet had commanded the movement. The flame was formed of illusion as much as the shape that lay upon Damona, but it still appeared real enough for all that. To Damona it mattered little that the Druid thought the Goddess of the Shrine was responsible for all that had happened since the destruction. What difference could it make? Neither one was a deity the High Druid worshipped. But to Sekhmet it mattered a great deal.

I determine what is fate, the lion-headed goddess roared in a voice that set the very rafters aquiver. *You are a puling mortal who worships gods other than Me. It is not for you to know My secrets.*

The High Druid was strong, but he was a mortal, and what he faced was the anger of a goddess. He stumbled backward as the tongue of flame struck him, and fell to his knees. Eyes blazing, he leaped to his feet with an agility that belied his age, only to be lifted into the air by another leaping flame. The strength of it flung him against the wall with bruising force. His body impacted against the unyielding stone with a painful crack, and he slid to the floor. His silvery head left a smear of red on the stones behind him.

Damona broke into a sudden trembling as she saw that he was unconscious. Her shaking did not come from fear.

Within her a battle raged. Sekhmet was not only beside her, but also inside her. She could almost feel the mighty jaws of the lion-headed goddess snarling at the sight of the blood slowly trickling from one corner of the Druid's mouth.

The Goddess roared at her again in the voice of a lion. "Kill him," She screamed. "Use the flame I have kindled within you. Do it!"

She could have done it Herself, of course. She required no mortal to commit such acts for Her. But Sekhmet had another purpose, and Damona, who knew about the bindings of power, recognized it at once. There was a heavy importance to her slaying the High Druid herself. His blood would be a powerful weapon, an act that would bind her to Sekhmet even more. And it was so easy. All she need do was lift her hand, and the flame would hurl itself forth again. It was a dizzying sensation, painful and pleasurable, like drinking too much wine or lying with a man for the first time.

But something else was stirring inside Damona, and it was refusing to be pushed aside, even by the power of a goddess. The reverence she held for the High Druid gripped her relentlessly. A Christian's fate would have been sealed, but this was the most holy priest of the Ancient and True Ways. Consumed with the hunger for revenge she might be, yet she was not so utterly caught up in her plans that she could ignore all she had once held sacred. To realize this was a new discovery. It loosened something inside her that had been wound painfully tight.

"I will not," she said, speaking to herself, as well as to Sekhmet. "He cannot harm me. And I will not harm him. My quarrel is not with the Druids."

Your quarrel is with all priests. What did these Druids of yours do while your home was being burned and your family slaughtered? They were sitting on their safe and well-fed behinds afraid to interfere for fear of losing their power, a power they are already losing in any case. Slay him now, so that I will know you are dedicated to My service.

"No," Damona said again. "I will not."

Even as the Goddess roared about her, blazing in Her fury, Damona raised her own voice, calling out for servants.

Three came running, swift and reluctant at once. By now everyone in the hall had seen at least some evidence of the power that Damona wielded. They had glimpsed the form of the mighty outland Goddess who accompanied the stranger woman. They had listened to the tortured dreams of their *Tuisech*. They did not know Damona's true identity, but they knew her power. The three servants who answered her summons were terrified of disobeying her, though they were equally terrified at what the results of their obedience might be.

Damona took no notice of the expressions that seemed to collapse their pasty faces as they saw the High Druid lying on the floor. "Take him to the herb room," she ordered. "I will make up a poultice for his head, and then you must carry him back to his house."

As the frightened servants lifted the High Druid and bore him away Sekhmet's voice rang dark and angry in Damona's head. *Your disobedience has not pleased Me. I have given you great power, but you have not seen fit to use it. Your heart is soft and your will is weak. Such qualities were not why I came to you. Remember, woman, you called out to Me. It was My help you sought. Have you forgotten your quest so quickly?*

Damona stood very straight, wrapped in her guise of magic. She watched the senseless body of the High Druid being carried down the corridor. The small procession had turned a corner and two of the servants peeked nervously back over their shoulders just before they were out of sight.

"Great Lady," she said quietly. "I have forgotten nothing. My will is as strong as ever, and as for my heart: I no longer have one. I thank You for Your power. And have I not been using it with good skill? Is the murderer not completely under my thrall? I am mistress in his own house, his wife and children are banished, and servants and warriors alike dread my displeasure.

"But if I had killed the High Druid, all the folk of this hall would have fled. Druids from our tuath and all others would have come against me, along with every noble, *Boaire,* and freeman faithful to the old ways. An enormous problem would have been created, and for what purpose? It would only interfere with what I came here to do. Everyone wants Muirchertac dead. His madness is a blemish, and a blemished king blights the very land he rules over. Now I have made his madness worse. By the time I take my revenge the people will be so grateful they will hold feasts in my honor."

She felt the Goddess's presence swirling about her, but the fiery anger was lessening. Sekhmet was a being of fire and blood and raging impulse, but She was a goddess nevertheless, and She saw far. She saw the logic in Damona's words, and the flames of Her displeasure cooled still more.

You speak with wisdom. The words were a grudging hiss in Damona's ears. *For a mortal, that is,* the Goddess added in a rumbling growl. *Very well, I will not smite you as I was tempted to do. Continue with your plan. But be swift in your revenge. I am growing impatient for the taste of blood.*

Damona glanced down the empty corridor. The servants would have reached the herb room by now and would be waiting for her along with the injured High Druid. She would bind the wound in his head and see to it that the servants took him safely out of this doomed place. Then she would be free to return to her own madness. In a way, she thought to herself, it will be a relief.

"Be assured, Great Lady," she said. "I, too, am impatient."

Muirchertac lay in his bed, staring raptly at the hangings that enclosed his sleeping cubicle.

These days it was rare for him to be so quiet. All around him there was rustling silence, as the house folk snored and breathed deep in this equally rare patch of undisturbed rest. Even in the hall of a great lord all the house folk slept in the vast central room where the hearth-fire would warm them through the damp nights of Eire. The *Tuisech* slept with them, although his position merited the privacy of a box along the wall curtained in the richest and thickest bed tapestries available and large enough to hold a comfortable bed.

However, even the heaviest of material could not conceal what went on behind its heavy colorful folds. The moaning and shrieking would start after sunset and continue unabated, until first light. At first the sounds had reeked of pleasure and lust, but no longer. Other emotions had gradually overtaken the cries of that first day, and now the king's voice rang only with terror.

Sitting up on the other side of the bed, Damona watched him with merciless blue eyes. The strength of her spell had progressed so far that the need for physical intimacy was no longer required. Muirchertac believed that he was still coupling with the magnificent woman he had sent away his wife and family to possess. He felt her body in his mind, saw himself thrusting into her softness, sweated and grunted with the absolute pleasure of the sexual act. And while he moaned and moved his body back and forth Damona would lie on her side, head propped on one elbow, staring at him with a hatred that was depthless in its determination.

On this night, as on the others preceding it, Muirchertac had engaged in his imaginary lovemaking on into the morning, finally collapsing into this state of rapt and staring exhaustion. It was a familiar sight. Soon his eyes would close, the nightmares would come, and the screaming would begin again.

He was still a handsome man, this king of her tuath, Damona reflected, as a tentative dawn approached, sending gray fingers of light creeping under the edges of the bed hangings. Surprising, really, considering what she was putting him through. Yet his body had remained strong and comely. His broad chest rose and fell, gleaming with its mat of rich auburn hair. A smile had settled over his unkempt yet even features, and his blue eyes glowed with the pleasure of the sensations she had placed there. Physically, he was perfect. Only his mind was marked, torn apart by madness and the dark magic she had worked upon him.

And she was far from through.

Damona leaned forward. Her voice was so soft it was not even a whisper; the bed hangings made more sound as they rustled with errant breezes from the hearth, where the fire had burned to coals. "From this moment forth," she murmured, "sleep will come ill to you, even more so than it has before. The dreams will grow worse, and now you will have to rise from your bed and go in search of them. If you find them, perhaps this torment will cease. If you do not, I will have to leave you. No more will you know my body. No more will you possess my beauty. I will be gone, and you will be alone."

Muirchertac turned his head to look at her. His eyes were glazed. "But I have done all that you asked," he said hoarsely. "What more can I do?"

Damona smiled down at him. "That," she said with a terrible tenderness, "you will soon discover. Now close your eyes, my lord. Mayhap the gods will be kind and you will sleep after all."

Obediently the glassy blue eyes closed. "Do not leave me, Niam, my beautiful one," he murmured. "There is a great pain in my soul. Stay by my side and grant me ease from this torment that possesses me."

"Ah, but I must." Damona's soft voice hid the smile of satisfaction that curved her mouth as she studied him. "The business of your hall must be tended to, and who else is there to do it but me?"

She threw off the rumpled bedcoverings and arose. Muirchertac lay quietly as she dressed. His eyes were still closed, but now his handsome worn features were twisted with suffering. "Please," he whispered. "Stay, Lady Niam. I beg you."

Damona's smile widened as she left the sleeping box. His pleading voice drifted out at her from behind the bed hangings. The servants who were rising from their own beds shivered and made the sign against evil, taking care that the new mistress of the hall did not see them doing this.

That day Muirchertac did not get up from his bed. He refused to taste the food and drink his worried steward brought to him. But when darkness came, he got up and began to roam. All throughout the night the house folk lay in fearful silence, listening to their lord walking about, muttering and cursing and calling out for Lady Niam. No one got any sleep that night: no one but Lady Niam herself. She alone rose the next morning as blooming and fresh as those about her were haggard and wan.

The pattern went on for the next night and the next, until the servants were ready to drop from exhaustion and fear. Finally, on the third night, as Muirchertac was wandering restlessly about, words suddenly touched him, fluttering about his ears as lightly as feathers. His footsteps slowed and paused.

"What," he asked loudly. "Is that you, my love?"

He had come to the lower part of the hall, the place where food was prepared and stored, and great vats of wine and mead were brewed. The large dark room was empty, the servants having long since sought their beds; no one was about to hear or be disturbed by him.

The voice spoke again. "Come," it whispered, urging him on. "Hurry. There is danger."

The *Tuisech* walked restlessly forward, stumbling heedlessly against wooden benches and tables and barrels of grain and salted fish. He paid no attention to the obstacles. His eyes searched the darkness eagerly. He held his arms outstretched waiting to embrace the woman he sought. "Danger?" he said, and laughed. "There is no danger. You play with me, lady. Step out of the shadows and come to me."

The familiar voice hissed, stabbing at his ears. "There is danger indeed. Look before you."

Muirchertac stared dazedly about him. His eyes widened in horror. An orange glow was illuminating the storage room. Flames were igniting in the dark corners, curling up around the benches and thick tables and barrels of stored goods.

There was no greater threat to a wooden house than fire. Muirchertac exclaimed in terror and lunged forward. But smoke had leaped up, along with the flames, and he could no longer see his way. He crashed blindly ahead, calling out for Niam, bruising himself against the barrels and vats.

"This way," the voice lured him. "Come this way, my lord. Before you is a place of safety, but you must hurry."

Desperately Muirchertac followed the sound of the familiar voice. "Where are you, Niam?" His frenzied shout echoed off the walls. "We must get away from this room and out of the hall before the roof falls in! Where are you? Answer me!"

"Here," the sweet voice replied. "Step up closer, and you will see me."

The *Tuisech*'s foot stubbed itself against something hard. The flames were surging ever more fiercely, and their heat was toasting his flesh. He coughed harshly as smoke seared his lungs; his watering eyes could not make out any shapes in the sudden terror that was washing over him. "Where are you?" he wailed. "I cannot see you."

"I am in here. Hurry, my lord, come into this cauldron with me. You will soon be safe."

Finally, he saw her. The hard surface he had bumped into was a great vat of wine, and Niam was standing in the middle of it. She was nude, her white hair flowing about her shoulders, the ends stained red where they floated in the dark liquid. Her breasts lifted round and rosy sweet, the flesh gleaming bronze in the glare of the flames, as she stretched her arms out toward him.

Muirchertac gasped in relief and desire. "Yes, yes, that is the way." Swiftly he stepped up onto the edge of the cauldron. As he did so a wave of dizziness caught at him without warning. Arms flailing, he swayed in an instinctive though futile attempt to regain his balance.

"Niam," he cried out as he fell. "Ni—"

He tumbled into the vat of wine with a huge splash.

The cold wet impact momentarily cleared the *Tuisech*'s head. There was no fire, he realized now; it had been naught but a dream, or perhaps the conjuring of magic. Niam, that elusive creature, was not only safe, but she had already slipped out of the vat and was no doubt standing behind a barrel laughing at him. Cursing, he started to pull himself up over the lip of the great cauldron.

The wine surged up around him as though it was alive, as though it had suddenly developed a will and a consciousness of its own. And that will was devoted to seeing that Muirchertac did not climb back out of the vat. The *Tuisech* struggled. His feet fought for purchase on the cauldron's curved bottom, and his hands grasped the rough iron edges in an effort to pull himself up. He was a strong man, even in his wasted state. It should have been easy.

It was not.

The more he tried to haul himself out of the vat of wine, the more stubbornly the rippling liquid pulled Muirchertac down. The wine seemed to have sprouted a hundred writhing fingers. They clutched at the king's beard and hair in a remorseless and loving embrace, wrapping themselves about him, coaxing his head below a surface splashing red as blood with his struggles.

Bemused, he gulped down great mouthfuls of the stuff, coughing and choking. His movements were becoming as slow and confused as his thoughts. Why could he not get out of this thing, he wondered sluggishly. It was only a vat full of wine. Standing up and stepping out of it should be a simple matter, and yet it was not. Somehow this simple cauldron was taking on the dimensions of the sea itself, its ruby depths growing so deep it seemed as if his very feet could no longer touch the bottom.

With a desperate effort he lunged upward, snatching at the elusive rim of the cauldron. This time his head just managed to clear the edge. For an instant he thought he was free. Then his muscles lost their strength, and the wine reached up for him. But before the insistent liquid fingers jerked him back down, he saw something that made him cry out with joy.

The Lady Niam was standing beside the vat, fully clothed and unaccountably dry, staring silently down at him.

Muirchertac's bulging eyes fixed on her. "Thank the gods," he gasped, spitting out a mouthful of wine. "Help me, Niam, my beloved one. Help me."

The woman's expression did not change. "As you helped my husband, lord?" she asked in a strange unemotional voice. "And my helpless little children?"

The chilled words struck at something in Muirchertac's soul. A note sounded deep within him. The scales fell from his eyes. For a stark instant his lover's face shimmered before his wine-splashed gaze. Other eyes stared into his, other features formed before him, and a wild question bubbled out from his throat. "Who are you?"

Lady Niam bared her teeth. "Why, my lord," she said. "Do you not know me? In these, the last moments of your life, I would that you know who is responsible for your death."

She raised her arms and, apparently addressing someone other than Muirchertac, said, "Let him see me as I truly am."

A mist swirled up around her and when it cleared the struggling *Tuisech* gaped at who stood there. "You," he gurgled through the wine sloshing into his throat. Surely his eyes were playing tricks on him. He had swallowed so much wine that he must be very drunk. Yet something told him this was no trick. There was darkness here, and it was all too real.

The beautiful Lady Niam was gone. Instead the *Banfhili* of the shrine he had destroyed stood before him. Her hair was tangled and matted with blood, her tunic torn and blackened with smoke. Her eyes blazed at him like the gaze of an animal about to leap on its prey.

"You—you are dead," he stammered. "What magic is this? Where is the Lady Niam?"

Damona laughed. It was a dreadful sound.

"Your wits were never the sharpest of spears," she said. "Even before I laid this enchantment upon you. And now, they have grown even duller. Do you still not understand?"

Muirchertac did understand. At long last he did. "You cannot do this!" Wine surged into his mouth, sweet and cloying, and frantically, he spat it out. "I am the *Tuisech*. Your *Tuisech*!"

Damona's laugh had madness in it. "Die, slayer of children," she cried in a guttural voice. "Die with my curse upon you. May you never find peace, not in the realms of the dead, or in any other world."

A sucking sound swirled up from the depths of the cauldron; all at once a whirlpool was leaping up, hurling the wine around and around the round iron sides. Muirchertac's scream was lost in a horrible bubbling and sputtering as he struggled to right himself. But the suction was relentless. The *Tuisech* was swept below a surface as vast and unfathomable as a lake of the Goddess, as gleaming as freshly spilled blood. One arm thrust frantically out of the dancing wine. His mouth surged above the surface one last time.

"Rionach," he gasped. "Rionach!"

And he was gone.

8

DAMONA STOOD BEFORE THE CAUL-dron. Her eyes were lowered, fastened on the quiet pool of deep red liquid before her.

The vat of wine had become a vat of wine again. Its depths could be plumbed now, and as she watched the cauldron slowly gave up its secret. Muirchertac's large body drifted upward, breaking gently through the rippling surface. Face downward, his outspread limbs bumping against the sides, the drowned *Tuisech* floated in the placid embrace of the wine, his auburn hair trailing out behind him.

It is done. The voice of Sekhmet billowed through the quiet storeroom, breaking the sudden silence that had descended. Her image swept up against the darkness, towering up to the ceiling and beyond. She was vivid in the gloom, sharply delineated against the barrels and vats, as if the death of Muirchertac had invigorated her. *You have done well, Priestess.* The Goddess pulled Her lioness lips back into a snarling grin, exposing bloodstained fangs. *I am well pleased. This one's blood has helped to quench My thirst, though I am far from satisfied. Yet, it is a good beginning.*

Damona gazed down at the body of the man her magic had killed. So this was what revenge tasted like. It was not what she had anticipated, what she had longed for. The mists she had wrapped about Muirchertac had enfolded her as well, and now she felt them slowly lifting, leaving her as if her time in the *Tuisech*'s hall had been no more than a dream. The hatred that had submerged her all these days, drowning her as utterly as the wine in this cauldron had immersed Muirchertac, was suddenly gone. She stared into the cauldron, and the chains of grief and pain her revenge was supposed to have broken seemed heavier than ever.

"I expected to feel joy," she said, speaking more to herself than to Sekhmet. "I thought his death would cleanse me. Instead, I feel—sadness."

Sekkmet made a growling noise deep in Her massive throat. *It is but the weakness of your former life that speaks to you. Do you stand here and tell Me this creature did not deserve to die for what he did?*

"No." Damona gave an emphatic shake of her head. "I am not sorry for his death. But my husband and children are still in the Otherworld, and there they will remain."

She fell silent. Slowly, like the wine that rippled about Muirchertac's corpse, a shudder went through her, cascading through every muscle. Images of herself as she was now cascaded through her mind; she saw the terror in the eyes of the house folk whenever they looked at her; she saw herself standing by while Sekhmet sent flames leaping out at the High Druid. She stared at what lay behind the façade of beauty the lion-headed goddess had laid upon her. For the first time, she looked with true vision not clouded by hate, and what she saw was ugliness.

She lifted her eyes from the cauldron and its royal occupant. "By all the Ancient Harmonies," she whispered. "What have I done?"

The Goddess's growl became a snarl. *You have done as I instructed. I gave you great powers, and you used them to slay your enemy. That is as it should be. But the king was only one enemy. The tasks I have set you are not yet finished.*

"They are." Damona was trembling in every limb. "Lady, you have seen to it that I received the blood-price for my *fine*, and I am grateful. I will offer up prayers to you. I will make sacrifices in Your name. But this must end. I will take no more lives, Lady. Call back the magic shape you have put upon me and let me resume my own true form so that others will know me again. I must—"

A roar echoed through the quiet storeroom. Sekhmet's red-tinged figure grew bright and blazing. She towered up before Damona, terrifying in Her rage. *A mortal dares give Me orders? I am the Goddess of Death and Destruction! You, who have seen My might should know better. It is not for you to say when you are through; that is My right. You have given yourself into My service, and only I will say when you are freed of that duty.*

Damona stared into the enormous eyes flaming red and yellow with anger. She had indeed given herself into the Goddess's service. And she had done it willingly.

Yes, willingly, Sekhmet hissed, seeing the thought in Damona's mind. *Now go from here. I will not take this guise of magic from you; not yet. Long and long have I waited for an opportunity such as the one you have brought Me. There is blood on the wind in this land, and I intend to drink my fill. With you as My instrument, the followers of the old faith and the followers of the new will slay each other. It will be a feast greater than I have tasted in many a century.*

"So that is why You came to me." The sense of having awakened from a deep sleep grew ever more powerful. Damona looked from the body in the cauldron to the shimmering face of the Goddess. Her eyes were wide, the hazel gaze of her true face shifting through the brilliant blue stare of the magic. "This was Your plan all along. To set my people at each other's throats."

Sekhmet let out her thundering purr. *Of course it was. Would I offer my aid to a mortal who has always worshipped My Sister's goodness, rather than My strength? And we have both benefited, have we not? I, in My thirst, and you, in your revenge. Your enemy is destroyed, but he was only one among many. There are others who rode with him on that night. Are you grown so weak that this no longer matters?*

*Blood calls out for blood, woman, and you have thanked Me
too soon. The price is not yet paid.*

As swiftly as it had appeared the enormous shape began
to fade. *Remember.* The Goddess's great voice coiled all
about Damona. *You called out for Me, and I came. You are
bound to Me now, Priestess. Do not forget that.*

The resulting silence pounded in Damona's ears. She was
alone again, profoundly so, for now she had not even the
warmth of her hatred to comfort her. She looked within herself, seeking to rediscover that hatred, to rekindle the flames
that had driven her. For Sekhmet was correct: Muirchertac
was not the only man who had committed sacrilege and
murder. Other men still walked free who must be called to
account for their deeds of that night. Perhaps in the Goddess's plan for blood there lay justice as well. Should not
the followers of this new religion that had invaded Eire be
punished?

Long moments passed, and Damona stood before the
cauldron and what it contained. A precipice had opened
between what she had been and what she was and she hovered between the two, balancing on an edge as thin as a
knife blade. The madness and hatred that had possessed her
was a cavern, black and swirling and without end. It beckoned to her, strangely inviting in its darkness.

To tumble back into that blackness was compelling. After
all, this awakening of hers was not welcome. What was left
of her old life but ashes? She had already bound herself to
Sekhmet. It would be far easier to continue on her present
path, to steep herself in the blood the Goddess sought, than to
embark on a struggle with this powerful deity and the darkness in her own soul. Let them all slay each other. What did it
matter to her? All those she cared about were gone anyway.

At last she shook herself and wrapped her arms across her
chest. "No," she said to the body in the vat, "you did what
you did because of your madness, not out of any loyalty to
the gods, either the old or the new. And it was my own mad-

ness that has led me to this place. Now I must get myself out."

She spun on her heel and strode from the storeroom.

Word of Muirchertac's death spread throughout the tuath like the fire he thought he had seen when he tumbled into the vat.

Damona had gone directly from the storeroom and roused the servants. "The *Tuisech* is dead," she said without preamble. The collection of sleepy-eyed bleary faces stared at her with one stunned expression as she went on. "He met with a mishap while wandering the hall in the grip of his madness. His body must be taken up and prepared for burial and the news brought to the Druids and nobles."

Silence.

"Lady," the steward finally asked in a quivering voice. "Wh—where is he? And how did this terrible thing happen?"

Damona's crystalline gaze was as blue and empty as the sky. Underneath it her own eyes were burning, but the servants could not see that. All they saw was the beautiful and cold Lady Niam telling them this terrible news without a trace of emotion in her musical voice. "He is in the storeroom," she said. "The one where the mead and wine are kept. He fell into a vat of wine and could not get himself out of it again. He drowned."

The silence deepened. There was no need to voice what the house folk were thinking. Not a man or woman there did not believe that this stranger who had beguiled their king had not led him to his death, perhaps even drowned him with her own hands. But not a one of them dared voice their suspicion aloud.

"Well?" Lady Niam asked impatiently, when a handful of moments had passed and still, no one had moved. "Is there a spell upon all of you? His body lies floating in the vat. Go you and fetch him out."

The sharpness of her tone galvanized the house folk into action. The steward beckoned to the strongest men among the servants and led them off to the storeroom. As they hurried away, Lady Niam singled out another man. "You," she said. "Go to the stables and tell the grooms you have my permission to take a horse. Ride to the High Druid's house as swiftly as the beast will carry you. Tell him what has happened this night." Her eyes glittered with an expression that none could read. "I am sure he will want to return with you, so wait for him."

The man ducked his head nervously and ran to do her bidding.

The silence descended again. Lady Niam filled it with her words, spitting them into the quiet like flung stones. "Why do you all stand about staring at me like a gaggle of startled geese? Set about your duties. There is work to be done. Many lords will soon be coming here, and food and drink must be prepared for them." She clapped her hands sharply. "Be off! And bring wood in plenty to rekindle this fire. Can you not see it is nearly out?"

The crowds of servants scattered like the geese they had been described as, leaving Lady Niam to stand alone by the embers of the dying fire. They were too shocked and in too much of a hurry to notice the sudden strangeness that came over the dead king's lover. No one glanced back to see her tensing and glaring up into the rough-beamed rafters. As if she were listening to a voice only she could hear. As indeed she was.

Sekhmet's great voice was purring all about her. *Yes, this is well. Bring the Druid here and his priests with him. Then send word to the Christians. Blood will flow in plenty this day.*

The purr of satisfaction and hunger thrummed past the shell of Lady Niam, reverberating into the belly of Damona herself. She did not answer the Goddess's rumbling voice, but stood silently in the deserted hall, waiting.

Before daybreak had begun to glow above the trees the servant had returned. As Lady Niam had predicted, he was not alone. But not just the High Druid accompanied him. Trotting in a swirl of flowing mantles, wind-tossed hair, glit-

tering torques, and arm-rings, rode all the Druids of the
tuath, along with a host of nobles, every one of whom was
faithful to the old religion.

In the doorway of the hall Damona watched them arrive,
clattering through the dim gray light, trotting along the same
road that the queen had taken such a short time ago in
departing. Outwardly their faces were grim, but masks lay
upon these Druids and chieftains, just as the mask of Lady
Niam lay upon her own face. There was relief peeking out
from behind the grave expressions, and mingling with that
relief was speculation. But anger glinted in their eyes as
well. Chieftain or Druid, suspicion was heavy and dark in all
of these men, and it was directed solely at her.

The High Druid climbed down off his horse. He moved
slowly and cautiously, and two of the other Druids had to
help him.

The old man had largely recovered from the injury
Sekhmet had inflicted upon him, but he was still weak. The
partly healed wound on his head gleamed pink in the dawn-
ing light. Not since that ill-fated day had he been back to
Muirchertac's hall. He had not used his own power or influence to reciprocate for the attack on him; nor had he made
any further attempts to rescue Muirchertac. Damona knew
why. There were wheels upon wheels turning in this tuath.
Muirchertac, whether ruling by himself, or under the magical control of a woman who was herself under the authority
of an outland goddess, was far too much of a liability. Men
wanted to be rid of their *Tuisech*. They were simply uncertain of how to go about it.

"I see relief hiding in your eyes, Holy One," she said quietly. "Just as I see it in the gazes of all those who are with
you."

The chieftains growled amongst themselves and glowered
at her. "Was it your hand that brought him his death,
woman?" one of them shouted at her.

She met the eyes of the man who had spoken. "What difference does it make how he died? He is gone from this

world, and there is not a one of you standing here who is not glad in his heart that he is."

The High Druid released himself from the supporting hands of his fellow priests and stepped forward. "Muirchertac committed a grave desecration, and he has been punished for his deed," he said in a quiet carrying voice. "But do you think to rule this tuath in his stead?"

Sekhmet's presence flamed up around Damona. *You do,* hissed the voice of the goddess. *That is indeed what you want. Tell him so. Take the power that is offered, and bring me more blood.*

Damona spoke above the voice writhing in her ears. "There can be only one heir to the rulership of this tuath. And that is the son Queen Rionach bore to Muirchertac."

The gathering of men gaped at her in stunned silence. From all the vantage points where they had been listening, the house servants gasped. Sekhmet roared in such fury Damona was amazed that no one else, especially the Druids, could hear Her. She forced herself to go on, her voice rising louder and louder above the Goddess's anger. "Clearly, he is too young for the responsibilities now, so his mother must take over his duties until he is able." Her mouth twisted in a line of bitterness. "She was already doing so in any case," she added. "And a far better job of it she did than her husband, the lawful *Tuisech.*"

The nobles had begun to mutter and whisper, taken aback by this astonishing pronouncement by the woman who had beguiled their *Tuisech* and taken over his household. The Druids were staring at her, and the High Druid was staring most of all. His lined features were thoughtful and troubled. He took another step closer. "The magic is loosening its hold upon you, child," he observed suddenly. "Has Muirchertac's death done this? Was that your purpose in coming here, to shed his blood?"

He studied her so intently it seemed inevitable that he must pierce the mask and see who lay underneath. But Lady Niam stepped out of the doorway and into the courtyard.

The reaction from the chieftains was immediate: most moved hastily back, many making signs to protect against evil. Everyone knew of the incident with the High Druid; the fact that he had not again attempted to challenge the power that had injured him only increased their trepidation.

But once out of the hall the stranger turned away, showing them only her straight slender back. "I will go to the Lady Rionach and speak with her," she said with no change in the controlled melodic voice. "No doubt, she will wish to return here at once."

"And you, lady?" The High Druid had to call out his question, for the Lady Niam was already moving away, heading with her uncanny grace toward the stables. "What will you do? In truth, the queen will come nowhere near this hall while you are present."

The woman paused, though she did not turn back to face him. "The queen may have this place back and welcome to her," she said quietly. "I will not be returning."

Will you not? The lion-headed goddess's voice howled on the wind. *Look you at what is coming, and then say that you have lost your taste for vengeance.*

Damona spun around. Though they could not have heard Sekhmet's howl, the others were turning as well. Hoofbeats were thundering on the air, breaking apart the quiet morning. More chieftains were coming, and this time, all of them were Christian. Their faces leaped at Damona, glowing red as if they were bathed in blood: the blood of her husband and children. She knew it was magic. There was no sun to paint the faces of these men with a radiant glow. The Sun-Goddess had hidden herself behind bank after bank of clouds this day. The morning had dawned lowering and dark, with the smell of approaching rain gusting through the trees.

The chieftains drove their lathered horses toward the gathering, and as they drew closer the anger on their faces could be clearly seen. Damona felt an answering rage surge up inside her, rising from her belly to her heart to her head.

You see? The Goddess's words roiled in her ears, gloating. *You are not free of your taste for revenge. And thus, you are not free of Me.*

The horses danced to a halt, tossing their heads and scattering foam from their bits.

"Muirchertac is dead," a burly noble shouted. "Slain by *her* hand, wasn't he?" He thrust a finger at Lady Niam. "She is evil. The spirits of the old religion brought her here, and now she has thrown our tuath into chaos!"

"She is not the only one." The High Druid's words rang out like the tones of a battle trumpet. "You, who have forsaken the Ancient Harmonies, have much weight to bear for the *Tuisech*'s death. You rode with him to burn a sacred shrine and slay those sacred to a powerful goddess. Muirchertac has been punished for that night, but what of the rest of you? Perhaps the Goddess will now turn Her eyes in a different direction."

The burly noble made the sign of the cross. "Jesus Christ will protect us! His is the One True Faith. The old gods are nothing against Him. If Muirchertac had come to Christ as his wife did, then surely the evil of this woman could not have touched him—"

"Think you so?" The High Druid's gaze was frigid. "Evil is evil, and there are more than enough places for it to find a hold, no matter what gods a man worships."

The chieftains who had ridden in with the Druids nodded their agreement, glaring angrily at the newcomers. The Christian nobles returned the glares with equal animosity. It was a situation fraught with tension. Every man here, whether Christian or pagan, knew each other well; they had hunted and feasted together, had gone on cattle raids and fought in battle against the warriors of other tuaths. Marriage bonds tied many of them even more closely together. But now warriors with gray in their beards exchanged narrow-eyed stares with sons-in-law who had given themselves over to new ways.

But magic made a poor target for a man to vent his anger

upon, if he was only a man and no Druid. Not one of the
pagan nobles cared to challenge the power of a woman
whose goddess could defeat the High Druid. These chieftains who had embraced Christianity, though, were another
matter entirely. They were flesh and blood, with only their
swords and their faith to protect them. They were safe targets.

One of the nobles raised a heavy fist and shook it. "It was
you Christians who brought the evil among us!" he roared,
as his horse curvetted nervously beneath him. "Muirchertac
was mad, but he was controllable. Then your new religion
sent him off on the foolhardy attack that led to his destruction. Naught but ill omens have followed. And naught will
continue to follow as long as you Christians are among us!"

The Christian nobles returned a storm of retorts, and gusting voices filled the gloomy morning, as each group tried to
out-bellow the other.

Damona stood watching, all but forgotten in the uproar.
The faces of the Christians swam before her, reeling through
a red haze that made her dizzy. Darkness swept over and
through her. The presence of Sekhmet was very strong. It
seemed the towering form of the Goddess was standing right
beside her. How could the Druids with all their combined
strength not be aware of Her?

Oh, they sense Me well enough, came the familiar hiss.
*But they cannot see Me, and even if they could, they have no
power where I am concerned.* The Goddess made a sinister
chuckling sound. *The High Druid has found that out for
himself already, hasn't he? But look upon them, Priestess.
Look at them all. Barking and snapping at each other like a
pack of mangy curs. Look at your enemies, the ones who
destroyed your kin. Do they show regret for their deeds? No.
They only yelp about the evil you have brought to their mur-
dering king.*

It was true. Damona stared at the gesticulating men who
had destroyed her home. She listened to them yell and felt
her throat grow parched and tight. They should die. They

deserved it as much as Muirchertac had. Sekhmet's thirst for blood seared her flesh. She licked her lips, feeling the Goddess's hunger as if it were her own.

Yes, the Goddess exulted. *That is what I want. Give yourself to the darkness. Set them at each other's throats, and let the blood wash over us both.*

The High Druid thrust himself forward. The fire in the old man's eyes and his sheer presence stilled the voices of the nobles, even those of the Christians. He spoke into the sudden quiet. "We of the old ways once welcomed the new religion to Eire. The gods would have been tolerant of your new god, but neither He, nor His followers would have it so. You vilify the ways of your fathers. You turn your backs on the Shining Ones. Now, even that is not enough. Your new god sends you to destroy sacred shrines. The place you burned belonged to an outland Goddess, but how long will it be until you turn your swords and flames against the ancient groves of our own gods?"

"They are no longer our gods," a Christian noble yelled. "Not anymore. It is time to give way to a newer, more powerful god. We will bring Queen Rionach back from Bishop Cairnech's hall. She will rule the tuath as a Christian, and she will raise Muirchertac's son and heir to do the same."

His fellow chieftains shouted in agreement. But their approval was met with a chorus of anger from the nobles who had allied themselves with the old ways. "No, no, no!" the men roared out. Before the arrival of the Christians these same nobles had been staring in surprised approval at Lady Niam's espousing of that very idea. But now they could not voice their protests loudly and quickly enough. "A Christian will not rule this tuath. We have had enough of Christians!"

The Druids themselves were no less angry than the chieftains shouting on their behalf were. The High Druid, his eyes blazing, gestured for silence, but this time, no one obeyed him. Several of his brethren shouldered forward and flung their arms out until the shouting quieted again. The High Druid's deep voice boomed into the quivering silence.

"Hear me, Chieftains. I speak with all the authority of my office, and in the absence of a *Tuisech*, my word shall be followed. Lady Rionach may act as regent for her son, only if she follows the old ways." He fixed the Christian nobles with his blue eyes. "Has following your Christianity not brought her and this entire tuath enough grief already?"

Thunder muttered in the distance. The rain suddenly swept in, pelting everyone with heavy drops that splattered them like blood. Handfuls of wind rattled through the trees, and from her forgotten place Damona saw one of the Christians draw his sword. Several more followed suit. The sight was like a knife in her breast. She swayed forward, seeing not this gathering of angry nobles, but helpless children being cut down by blades wielded by these very men.

The chieftains who stood with the Druids stared in disbelief at this hostile act, then whipped out their own swords. The darkness gaped before Damona, inviting her into its depths. Sekhmet was howling all about her, exulting in the men's anger, demanding in Her thirst, drawing Damona back into Her clawed grip. And why shouldn't she go back? It would be so easy, not to think, not to remember, simply to hate.

The High Druid and his fellow priests leaped forward. "How dare you," the old man roared. "You would do battle in the presence of Druids? It is for us to say when and where battles should be fought. And this is not the place!"

Shamefaced, the pagan nobles drew back at once, though fury was still boiling over their reddened features. But the Christian chieftains were not so quick to obey. Some of them hesitated and started to lower their swords. However, others did not.

"We follow the word of Christ," the burly noble shouted out. "Not the commands of false priests who are in the thrall of false gods."

"No." Damona whispered the word. She shook herself all over. The action sent an even stronger shiver all through her.

Yet her head was suddenly clear. She felt as though she was ridding herself of magic as well as raindrops.

"No!"

This time Damona screamed the word out. Her cry pierced the clamor of wind and rain and men's voices. They froze in their tracks, swords raised, mouths open, gaping at her with widened eyes. She held them with her own eyes, those brilliant blue eyes that still had the power to beguile, even though the woman inside them was finally fighting free of Sekhmet's influence.

"Do not do this. What man of honor fights against the warriors of his own tuath? All of you are heaping evil upon evil! Nothing good can come of more blood being spilled this day. And if there is one thing I know about, it is blood." Her glittering stare encompassed the Druids, the chieftains loyal to them, and finally swung back to the Christian nobles. "I have no love for any of you," she said in a low harsh tone. "If I were truly wise, I would not care if all of you sliced each other to pieces. But I do care, if only for the sake of this tuath. There is a power here with us, and it cares nothing for the future of our people. This power cares only for blood. Once I thought that was also what I wanted. Now—"

The pelting rain all at once whipped sideways, driving savagely against men and animals alike. The trees bent their heads, groaning as if in fear of the howling wind that slashed through the sky.

Sekhmet's voice rose over the wind. *So you turn from Me still?* She screamed. *You deny Me My thirst, you weak mortal? Then let Me grant you the wish you begged of Me last night. And see how long you remain among the living once these men see you as you truly are!*

A crack of thunder bellowed down from the sky, shaking the ground beneath the horses' feet, causing them to rear and neigh in fear. Their riders struggled to control them, too occupied, at least momentarily, to continue with their hostilities. As the reverberation of the thunderclap rumbled away, one of the chieftains suddenly pointed and let out a hoarse exclamation. More men looked, and they, too, cried out. The Druids were already gazing at what the first noble had noticed. They gathered close beside the High Druid, and only their faces showed no expression.

The Lady Niam was gone.

In her place stood Damona, the *Banfhili* of the shrine.

9

EVERY CHIEFTAIN IN THE COURT-
yard fell back with cries of fear and
astonishment. From their hiding
places the servants drew back in terror. Only the Druids did not react in
fear. They stared intently at
Damona, and the High Druid smiled
a slow sad smile.

"So you have come back," he said.

Damona was garbed as she had been when Muirchertac
last saw her, in the torn bloody tunic of the destruction. Only
her hair was different; the same startling white with crimson
streaks she had borne in her incarnation as Lady Niam. To
the Christian nobles she was a terrifying vision, a glimpse
from nightmares. It was one thing to slay in battle, one man
pitting his strength and skill honorably against that of
another. But women and children had been killed on that
night, and while Muirchertac had been the one whose sword
had cut them down, these men had still done nothing to prevent him. This ragged woman with blazing eyes and
unearthly white hair was a horrifying reminder of that fact.

The burly noble crossed himself frantically. "Away spirit,"
he croaked. "Go back to the realms of the dead. Our lord
Jesus Christ will protect us from your dark powers."

Damona took a step forward, and the noble hauled back on
his horse's reins so that the beast reared up in as much fear as
his rider. "If only it were that easy," she said. "But it is not."
Her burning eyes went from Christian to Christian, transfix-
ing them with the condemnation of her gaze. "Your god must
be a god of blood, to rejoice in the blood of children."

117

"That—that was a mistake," another of the nobles quavered. "It was the *Tuisech*'s doing, not ours, that you and your *fine* were killed."

"Yes," the burly noble cried, having got his horse back under control. "It is God's will that the shrines of false gods be destroyed. Fly back to the darkness, evil one. Before Christ smites you down."

Damona raised her bloody arms, a gesture that caused the chieftains to fall back again. "I am not," she said, measuring out each word, "dead. And if I were it would make no difference. Your god has no power over me."

The Christians fell silent, glancing at each other. The burly noble brandished his sword. "In that case," he snarled, "my sword will have power over you. You have murdered the *Tuisech*. An act of such evil must be punished in kind."

His words set the eyes of his companions to flashing. Emboldened, they pressed their sweating horses forward. Damona did not move. Sekhmet was swirling all about her, the Goddess's giant form shimmering crimson through the wind and rain.

Blood is blood, She hissed. *Yours will do as well as that of any other mortal.*

Damona said nothing. The fear and hatred in the faces of the nobles was as palpable as Sekhmet's thirst. Mingled with those feelings she could sense guilt, but there was not enough of it to sway them from their course. She watched the burly noble spur his horse toward her. The heavy blade of his raised weapon gleamed wet and bright in the rain. She could stop him, of course; even with Sekhmet here she could use her powers to spook the horse and turn the weapon from her. But she did not. She stared at the sword and felt only relief.

A tall figure thrust itself between her and the chieftain on his snorting horse. The High Druid planted himself like one of the oaks of a sacred grove. "You will not," he said in his deep steady voice. "I forbid it. This is no longer a matter of magic, but of law. The *Tuisech* slew this woman's *fine*. And now he himself is dead. If his death was indeed at her hand, then so much the better. The honor-price has been paid."

The noble hesitated, but his eyes were blazing, and he still held his sword poised as if to strike. Behind him his fellow Christians pressed their stamping horses forward. The pagan chieftains pressed their own mounts forward in immediate response.

"How dare you," cried another of the Druids. "No armed strife will there be in the presence of the Brothers of the Oak. All of you—whether you belong to the true faith or not—know this well."

The wind yowled as if it were a living thing, as indeed it was, for throbbing within its high-pitched intensity Damona heard the voice of Sekhmet. The High Druid heard it, too; perhaps he had heard it all along. He gestured to Damona. "Go. Blood will be shed here. I cannot prevent that, and neither can you. But the blood will not be yours. You have lost enough as it is. Hurry now. Do as you must."

Damona faltered for just a moment.

Sekhmet's rage seared through her. *If you do,* the Goddess snarled, *no more of My favor will you see. Defy Me and My anger will be greater than anything you can imagine. Remember your vow. You are bound to serve Me.*

Damona set her jaw. *No longer,* she said in her mind. *My vows to You ceased when You took this shape from me and invited these men to kill me.*

Over the howl of the wind she gathered up the folds of her tunic stiff with dried blood and ran toward the stables. Behind her she heard a new outbreak of yelling and the sudden clash of iron against iron. She tried to shut out the sounds.

She did not succeed.

"My lady."

The servingwoman's voice was diffident. She was disturbing her mistress's prayers, an interruption that would not be taken lightly in view of Muirchertac's recent death.

Slowly Queen Rionach lifted her head. "Why have you disturbed me?" she began, and fell abruptly silent. The maid was staring at her and her face bore an expression so strange that Rionach gathered her skirts and stood up at once.

"What is it, Binne?"

The servant clasped her hands together, twisting and untwisting her fingers. "You have a visitor. Someone who demands to see you at once."

Rionach sighed. It was not unexpected. That she would have visitors was inevitable, something she had resigned herself to, ever since word had reached her that her husband had died. Only a day had passed since she learned of Muirchertac's shameful drowning in a vat of wine. The man who had rushed to Bishop Cairnech's hall with the news was a Christian. He could not wait to tell of the part that the *Banfhili* and the woman called Niam had surely played in that death. The woman who was responsible for driving Rionach and her children from the hearth and home that was rightfully theirs. He had watched the queen eagerly as he spoke, anticipating a glorious demonstration of fury and grief.

Rionach had shown him neither. The bishop had raged up and down in a most satisfying way, demanding retribution for this terrible deed. But the queen herself had outwardly remained calm, almost disturbingly so. What she might have thought was a different matter, but she had shared none of that with the messenger, or even with the bishop, after the man had gone off for his well-earned refreshment and rest.

Rionach ran a hand through her hair and straightened the cross about her neck. "I must see whoever it is, I suppose," she said. "He will only be the first of many others to come. What chieftain is it?"

The servant's face was very pale. "No chieftain. A woman waits to speak with you, lady. She—I . . . "

She broke off, gazing at the queen with huge eyes. "Will you see her in this room?" she asked at last. She spoke in a near whisper, her voice trembling.

"Well, of course," Rionach asked impatiently. "Why not?

What is on you, woman? By my head, you act as if one of the old gods has tried to fly away with you. Which of my friends wishes to see me?" She brightened a bit. "It will be good to see the face of a woman who loves me."

"I—I will fetch her." Binne wheeled around and fled the room. The moment her back was turned and she was certain her mistress could not see it, she made the sign of the cross.

Within a few moments she had returned. Rionach looked up, expecting Binne to enter ahead of the visitor and announce her. But with uncharacteristic haste and surprisingly ill manners, the servant had already rushed away. Astonished, Rionach stared after her.

"What in the name of Heaven"—she stepped forward—"please forgive us. Such a lack of hospitality is completely unlike my servants." She caught herself with a sudden cry, her hand flying involuntarily to her mouth.

The visitor had moved slowly into the room. A spill of light from the window embrasure caught hold of her tall ragged figure, revealing the crusted bloodstains in her torn tunic.

"For love of the true faith." Rionach crossed herself. "I had heard that you were seen, but I did not believe it could be true." The queen's eyes lingered on the strange white hair.

"It was," Damona said quietly. "I am as you see me. Your husband and his men did not succeed in slaying me." Her voice became low and bitter. "Although they succeeded in everything else they sought to accomplish that night."

Rionach flinched. She continued to stare, her gaze incredulous. "And the woman who caused my lord to send his lawful wife and heirs away?"

"We were one and the same."

"Then why have you come?" Anger began to burn through the shock that had gripped the queen. "To gloat over the working of yet more of your evil magic?" She gripped the ornate cross, holding it like a weapon. "I warn you, *Bhanfhili*: be you truly alive or dead after all, this is a house where God rules."

Damona's eyes, hazel again, were deep and dark and steady. "It matters aught to me what god rules this house. And I have not come to gloat. That evil was done is true, lady, but not all of it was my doing. You, who lived with the *Tuisech,* should know that well. Was it your idea that he ride down on my home and family and kill them?"

Rionach lowered her eyes. Her grip on the cross loosened; she held it gently now, and with an aching sadness. "I spoke against it," she said softly, still unable to meet Damona's gaze. "I tried to prevent him from riding out on that dreadful deed. But—when the madness was on him, there was no reasoning with him. When he returned, soaked in blood and shouting with victory, I wept until I thought that blood would flow from my own eyes."

She looked up, fixing a gaze that shimmered with tears on the other woman's dry-eyed stare. "Ask my servants, if you doubt it. I grieved for you, *Banfhili,* for you, your husband, and your poor little children. Oh, how I prayed for your souls, nonbelievers though you were. Ask my servants. They will tell you this is so."

"There is no need." Damona's voice was as soft as the queen's. "Muirchertac brought suffering in plenty to us all. That is why you are not grieving at his death. But now it is time to put things right. And it must be done quickly." She turned away, looking and listening to things Rionach could not grasp. "There has already been fighting between old and new. We must act before matters grow worse."

The queen drew herself up. "My son is heir to the rulership of this tuath," she said implacably. "Do you deny it?"

"I do not."

"Then why—?"

"Lady." Damona's tone was weary. "Because of your husband I lost everything I hold dear. My pain was beyond bearing, and I was willing to do anything to ease it, even if it meant giving myself over to evil. But I am no longer willing. The blood-price has only been partially paid, yet it is already too high. It must not go higher. Return to the hall with your son and take your rightful place. If you do not, our tuath will never recover. I would not have that on my soul."

The two women stood in silence. Finally, Rionach put out a hand, reaching toward but not quite touching Damona's. "Will you come with me?" she asked gently. "I would have it known before all that you and your *fine* were wronged. Never can there be a healing between us all until that is acknowledged."

Damona nodded. "I will."

She did not add that she had intended to accompany Lady Rionach from the first. And not necessarily for healing. Within her there pulsed a fear of what might happen when Muirchertac's wife arrived home. Sekhmet had been silent since Damona had ridden away from the *Tuisech's* hall. Yet the lion-headed goddess was not gone. As if in proof of this, a red haze billowed up beyond the queen's shoulder, glimmering and vague, yet unmistakable to one with Druid-sight.

But Rionach, if she was not aware of such things, could still see the sudden change in Damona's expression. "What is it?" The queen glanced sharply behind her. "What else is troubling you, *Banfhili?*"

Damona shook her head. "It is nothing, lady. But go you and bid your servants ready you to leave. We should depart from this house at once."

And so, as unexpectedly as the queen and her retinue had appeared at Bishop Cairnech's hall, it prepared to leave. When word was brought to the bishop of his guest's planned departure he came hastening to Rionach, appalled at her decision.

The queen was in the great room, supervising a group of servants as they filled panniers to be loaded upon mules. She looked up smiling as he approached and softly ordered the servants to leave.

"My lord," she started to greet him, but Bishop Cairnech waved a hand sharply, cutting her off.

"Lady, I do not understand! What has come on you that all of a sudden you are telling me you will depart? Lady, surely you must know this is not wise."

"Not wise, perhaps," Rionach replied. "But necessary. I have responsibilities, Holiness, and I must tend to them. My place is no longer here, under the shelter of your kind guidance, but back in the hall of my husband."

"Lady, your husband is dead! And it was the power of the old ways that killed him. The pagans have already attacked our faithful when they went to the hall to demand justice for his murder. To return now is not safe—"

The rest of his words trailed off. Damona had stepped out from the corner where she had been standing. She was no longer dressed in the bloodstained garb of tragedy; the queen had gently insisted that she bathe and had ordered a fresh tunic brought to her. It had been difficult for Damona to remove that torn, ragged clothing, as difficult as it had been to leave it on. It was a reminder, its bloodstains the last physical holds she had of her children. Yet, even in her fresh tunic, the heaviness of death and loss still clung to her. She was not free of them, and especially she was not free of Sekhmet.

Bishop Cairnech, though not a Druid, was still an astute man who walked in the hand of his god. He saw this at once. "You," he gasped, and sketched the sign of the cross in the air. "How dare you enter this house. Evil one, I command you to leave!"

"My lord," Rionach said. "I asked her to enter. I have overstepped the bounds of hospitality, and I beg you to accept my apologies for it. But she will soon be gone, as will I. We are leaving together."

The bishop looked at Rionach. The queen's face was set, her eyes distant and sad. He saw that the pagan woman was watching him. He met her gaze and found that he had to look away. This upset him even more. "Lady," he said urgently to the queen. "You are a Christian. You have renounced the evil of this woman and the ways she practices. Would you go back to them now?"

"I would not." Rionach drew herself up. "I have not. But there must be peace within the tuath. If there is not, there will soon be no tuath. Our neighbors will see our discord, and we will be overwhelmed by their warriors."

"But her!" The bishop gestured at Damona without looking at her. "She has called upon dark powers and committed murder. I can see the evil coiling about her. Would you ally yourself with this creature, this woman who put a spell upon your husband, and then slew him?"

Rionach clasped her hands together and gazed down at them. Then she raised her eyes and looked at Damona. "My husband," she said very deliberately, "deserved slaying. In his madness he caused many problems, and the greatest of those was his attack upon a sacred shrine."

"Sacred?" Bishop Cairnech turned on her with blazing eyes. "No Christian considers shrines to the old gods sacred."

"I do," Rionach said with quiet implacability. "If only because what was done to this particular shrine was wrong. Holiness, you know that as well as I. Or has the forgiveness our Lord preached now turned to killing children because a mad *Tuisech,* who was not himself a Christian, deemed them worthy of killing?"

Damona spoke for the first time. "Your words mark you as a queen, indeed, lady. And as a *Tuisech.*"

Her voice swung the bishop back to her. He opened his mouth to reply, but she went on before he could launch into a new protest. "I do not ask your forgiveness, priest of the Christians. I did not come here for that. Whether you curse or praise me makes no difference. Your ways are not mine, and never will they be. Indeed"—her voice became harder—"it is I who should curse you for what was done to my *fine* in the name of your religion. But you are right about one thing: evil is with us, and it must be stopped before it goes any further."

"The evil is with *you,* woman." The bishop sketched another cross in the air. "And you are the one who brought it here."

His glare of triumph slowly faded at the expression on Damona's face.

"Yes," she said. "I did. And now, I must send it away. For all our sakes."

The rain had not let up. All the way from Muirchertac's hall it had lashed Damona and the horse she had taken from the stables. It had continued while she was within the house of Bishop Cairnech and now, as Rionach led her people away from her host and the refuge he had given her, the downpour became an assault that slashed at humans and animals alike with thousands of watery drops as sharp as arrow points.

Rain was commonplace in Eire and people were used to it. But there was something different about this storm. In huts and cottages, raths and halls, the folk of the tuath huddled together, listening apprehensively to the fury pounding over their heads. They whispered of what they heard in the wind, convinced that Muirchertac was abroad, crying out for justice, and as mad as ever he had been. Christians crossed themselves and pagans shaped the sign to protect against evil, and though the symbols were different, those who made them were united in their fear of what lay ahead.

Unstable and dangerous the *Tuisech* had been in life, but who knew what menace he might present now that he had been murdered? No one knew, and to make matters worse, it now turned out that the mysterious woman who had beguiled Muirchertac to his death had been the *Banfhili* Damona in a magical guise. The folk of the tuath huddled around their hearth-fires and trepidation wafted about them as black and heavy as the woodsmoke from the fires.

Out in the deluge the queen and her retinue had no shelter other than their woolen mantles. They had pulled their hoods up over their heads, but the cloth was drenched, the gaily patterned colors dark and indistinct in the unrelenting rain.

And there was no more shelter from what was (storm than from the rain itself. Damona understoo too well. She was riding just behind Lady Rionach, and though the procession of servants strung out in an untidy line of twos and threes, Damona's gelding plodded along through the mud by himself, for not one person would ride next to Damona, the *Banfhili* who had come back from the dead. They were terrified of her, and the queen's determined acceptance made no difference.

Damona cared little about their fear. She was concerned with far greater matters. She knew, as others did not, that the spirit of Muirchertac was not what was shrieking through this dank and frantic day. The knowledge was small consolation. Sekhmet had still not spoken to her; the Goddess had allowed the queen's folk to depart as easily as She had allowed Damona to ride from Muirchertac's stables. But the storm portended Her anger, and that was only a hint of what was to come.

Drenched and shivering, the train made its way over the flooded track, moving steadily toward its destination. Darkness came early in the season of early winter, and on this day it was hastened even more. Evening was shrouding the weary travelers with dark wet arms when the bulk of the great hall loomed up distantly through the unceasing rain. Lanthorns had been lit and the lights flickered and danced crazily in the wind as the house folk carrying them streamed forth.

"It is the queen!" a man's voice shouted. "Praises to Danu, she has returned."

"No," a voice muttered loudly behind Damona. "It is our Lord who should be praised for bringing us safely here."

But as the rain lashed down over the heads of them all, a chill suddenly draped itself over Damona. It froze her bones and burned in her blood like heated metal. She knew that neither Danu nor the Christian god had brought them here. Another mind, another will was at work, and its purpose was malevolent.

An instant later, it began.

Something began to form itself, seeming to take its very substance from the wind and rain and darkness and flickering light. Damona at first thought it was Sekhmet, but on the occasions that she had seen the lion-headed goddess, Sekhmet had appeared as a blazing figure, burning with blood and flame. This was different. There was a darkness about what was coming. It whispered to Damona, and its breath smelled of dankness and death and power.

She was the only one who sensed the invading presence. There were no Druids at the hall; they had all left after the confrontation of the day before, and not one of them had returned. But the dark force was growing stronger and more distinct by the moment.

The animals were becoming aware of it now, and they were beginning to fidget nervously, tossing their heads and pulling at their bits. Other than taking up a firmer grip on the reins, the people on their backs paid little heed. After all, the beasts were surely as eager to reach warmth and food and shelter as their riders were. Indeed, they urged the animals forward, toward the approaching servants.

All at once the chill clamped over Damona like the jaws of a water monster. "Lady!" she cried to Rionach. "Turn back! Turn back!"

She screamed out the warning so that she thought her lungs would tear, but her voice was lost in a sudden wail of wind. She saw the queen's horse rear up. The mare's hooves flailed frantically against the dark sky, and Rionach clung desperately to the animal's mane. At last the horse came down, only to rear up again in even greater terror. Damona could do little to help, for all the other horses, including her own, were doing the same. All through the train people were toppling into the mud, screaming and cursing. The startled servants from the hall were rushing up to help, shouting and swinging their lanthorns wildly in the rain.

The wind added its voice to the tumult, and in its depths there was laughter. The sound jabbed through Damona like a sword blade, growing louder and louder until she clapped her hands to her ears. Feeling the reins loosen, her horse lunged forward, sending Damona tumbling onto the wet ground. She scarcely noticed the fall. The laughter was deafening, and attending it was magic, beating upon her in sheets as fierce as the rain. She crouched in the mud, frozen as irrevocably as she had ever beguiled Muirchertac.

"Look upon me!"

The voice was a deep tolling purr, like the growl of a great beast. It reverberated through the night, drowning out the sounds of wind and rain. Now Damona was not the only one who heard it. Struggling with panicked animals, climbing up off the muddy ground, holding up lanthorns to see better, people looked up in a confusion, which instantly turned to dread. Someone let out a ragged quavering scream. Others echoed the cry, while still others spun frantically about as if to run.

"Stay," the terrible voice commanded. "I have given none of you leave to go."

Under scores of staring eyes a dark shape shot up from the depths of that voice. It was enormous, framed against the wind-tossed sky. It resembled Sekhmet, and yet it was not the Goddess. This was a manifestation of Her: darker, colder, less solid, but no less powerful.

Lady Rionach's horse had dashed away, but the queen herself had regained her feet. In an astonishing show of courage she raised a hand and made the sign of the cross. "Away with you, evil spirit," she cried. "In the name of our Savior, I order you."

Her voice, though so brave, was puny in the vastness of the storm, little more than a child's shout in the midst of a roaring battle. The towering figure looked down at her, opened its great jaws, and laughed. The laughter was a sound that possessed form and substance. It hurled itself forth in a bolt of crimson and black and struck Lady Rionach squarely in the chest.

The sight of the queen tumbling backward released

Damona from her stupor. She clambered to her feet and darted to Rionach's side. To her immense relief life still beat within the woman, though Rionach was unconscious.

"She has no power," the mighty voice said. "And neither do you, Priestess. Sekhmet offered you strength. She gave you gifts and She brought you revenge. In thanks for Her generosity, you turned from Her. Did you think that She would forget?"

Damona found her voice. "Then deal with me," she shouted. "Punish me, if that is your will, but harm no one else."

The laughter roared again. "So even now you seek to make demands? Do not fear, foolish mortal. I have been sent by the Lion-Headed One Herself. There will be retribution indeed, and why should you think it would stop with you?" The figure raised her arms. "Long and long has my Mistress waited to reenter the world. She is hungry, my mortal children. Starving. Now She will not be denied. Misfortune accompanies me, children. Blood will soak your land. Women will lose the babes in their wombs and the crops you sow in your fields will wither and fade before you can harvest them. I have come here to see that these things are done, and not soon will I leave."

She thrust a giant dark hand at Damona. "Heed me, Priestess. It was you who brought me here. You will learn that well. And when I have done, you will come back to the service of my Mistress."

"No." Rionach had regained her wits and had heard the terrible predictions offered by the manifestation. "This must not be." She looked up at Damona. "You must stop it. You—"

The thundering voice cut her off. "She will stop nothing. It has already begun." The figure made a gesture. "Gaze upon the power of my Mistress."

The wind howled again with that wild laughing note, and Damona's flesh prickled at the coming of more magic. She saw another form take shape beside the first. There were gasps and wails as other people saw it, too.

This figure was smaller, and she wore the shape of a woman. But it was a twisted representation. Her face was a ghastly mingling of human and animal. The rounded ears of a lion protruded through her thick hair, and fangs gleamed in her open mouth. Her body was squat and her hands and feet were armed with gleaming claws. She was naked, and in either hand she clutched a snake that writhed up each arm. A hideous smile transfixed her twisted face. Within moments another had sprung up behind her, exactly the same in every detail. It was followed by another and yet another, until seven of the creatures stood in the darkness.

The incarnation waved a hand. "Go," she commanded with a snarling laugh. "Destroy, my fighters, destroy."

The creatures darted forth and people ran, screaming for their lives.

Damona felt as though she had been running for days. In truth, it had been long enough. The night was well advanced, and still she was fleeing through the deep woods, battered by the ceaseless lash of wind and rain.

She was staggering more than running now, her breath sobbing in her chest, her feet slipping on the slippery grass as she slogged along beneath the tossing trees. Yet she could not stop. Tearing through her mind were the sights she had witnessed before she fled: the creatures chasing down screaming people like wolves darting after deer. She had hauled Rionach to her feet and gotten her into the dubious safety of the hall. Then she had run for her own life, convinced that at any instant the apparitions would overtake her, and she would feel their fangs and claws tearing her apart.

But they had not, and Damona did not want to examine too closely the reasons for why they had not.

A familiar voice spoke out of the darkness. In spite of the storm's roaring, the light tone was curiously penetrating, reaching Damona's ears clearly. "It's about time you got here," it said.

Damona stumbled to a halt. A cave was before her. Light glimmered golden out of its depths. In the entrance a small form stood looking at her, its tail waving slowly in the air. Damona put a shaking hand to her eyes, staring incredulously.

"Well?" the Guardian demanded irritably. "Why are you standing out there putting down roots like a tree? Come inside where it's warm."

He spoke as though nothing had ever happened between them, as if the night on which she had refused to heed his pleas had never happened. But Damona could not adopt his aplomb. She looked at him through the curtain of rain, and her voice was as desolate as the night. "I renounced you," she said. "Both you and the Goddess of my mothers."

The cat regarded her with the serene gaze she remembered so well. "So you did," he said. "But that does not mean you must stand out there drowning. Come in."

"I *can't.*" The cry was torn from Damona. "How can you offer me shelter after the things I have done? I embraced evil and brought it willingly into my own land. Willingly! I am cursed. Turn from me, Guardian. It is what I deserve."

A gust of wind battered her, as if Sekhmet had heard her words and agreed, mocking this attempt at finding safety. The cat shook himself in annoyance as rain skittered through the cave opening. "It is not," he said, "for you to decide what you deserve. Now for Holy Hathor's sake, get out of that rain. I am not about to get my fur wet while you dither about beating your breast."

It was that matter-of-fact tone, more than anything else, that brought Damona forward. Stumbling a little as she stooped under the rocky overhang, she entered the cave and followed the sleek black figure to the fire glow. It was a small fire, but this was a small cave. Heat and light radiated out from the cheerful cluster of flames, illuminating the rough walls and low ceiling. Damona sank down gratefully. She did not question how a cat had come to light a fire. The Guardian was a creature of magic. That in itself was sufficient explanation.

Gracefully the cat settled himself before the fire, tucking his forepaws against his chest and curling a long tail about his flanks. "That's better," he said contentedly. "Sekhmet can blow Herself hoarse and we'll stay here. She will get tired eventually. Even goddesses get tired."

Damona's muscles were beginning to loosen in the unexpected warmth. Steam was rising from her mantle, and slowly she unpinned the brooch that held shut its folds. But the warmth she was feeling was outward, not inward. Deep inside she was still shivering. The memory of the demon was as relentless as the storm. Its eyes drilled into her, vivid and terrible, blinding her soul. She was in Sekhmet's possession still. She knew it, and intuitively she understood that the cat knew it as well.

"What"—she stopped, unable to continue.

The cat answered her unspoken question. "What attacked you was Sekhmet's Bau." His eyes were wide and unblinking. "It is a demon of sorts, only far more powerful, and far more dangerous. She is an incarnation of the Goddess Herself, sent to attack Her enemies." He regarded her with that huge stare. "Of which, child, you are now one. The others are called the Slaughterers. Usually only one at a time appears to human folk and the people of the Black Land used to call her *Beset*. She and her sisters belong to Sekhmet, and they, too, destroy whoever She tells them to."

Damona took this in silently. The trembling had almost stopped as the heat of the small fire slowly penetrated her chilled limbs. "They did not destroy me," she said.

"Not yet," the cat replied dryly. "And that was only because they were told not to. *She* is not ready."

"Then they, and this"—Damona faltered, not able to pronounce the foreign word the cat had used—"demon of

Hers must be destroyed. You heard what it said, that women will miscarry, crops will fail, and blood will drench the earth."

The cat lifted a front paw and examined the soft pads as if they would reveal secrets to him. "It is too late," he said in his light voice. "Much of that will happen. The Bau foretells; she does not threaten. There is little you can do to prevent these events from beginning, all you can do is try to stop them from continuing. And it will not be easy. Sekhmet's creatures cannot be destroyed, only sent away, and there is only one way to do that."

"How?" Damona was shivering again. She leaned forward, her haggard face limned by the fire glow. Her eyes were blazing as fiercely as the cat's. "If there is a way, then I will do it. For I brought them here. *How?*"

The cat lowered his paw, setting it neatly beside the other one. "The wands my Mistress once gave to your foremother Veleda will banish them from this world. But they are an ancient and dangerous tool in themselves, and obtaining them will be as difficult as the using of them."

"That does not matter." Damona tightened her hands, digging the nails into her palms. "Tell me where to find them."

"I cannot tell you," the cat said calmly. "I must take you there. We will leave when Sekhmet wearies of Her temper and allows this most uncatlike weather to cease."

Damona stared at him, and her hands slowly unclenched. "Why would you do this for me?" It was a painful thing to ask, but even more painful was to think of all that she had done since the idyllic days at the shrine. Yet she could not avoid the question, any more than she could avoid the brightness of the cat's huge orange eyes.

The Guardian continued to look at her with those serene eyes. "You no longer belong to Sekhmet," he said. "Not completely, and that is reason enough."

"But I am far from free of Her." Damona snarled out the words. She bent over, gripped by a pain so intense that it was more like anger. "And I do not belong to your Goddess, either. I do not even belong to myself. By all the gods, how can I ever belong anywhere again?"

"That," said the cat, "is what you must discover."

Gaul

10

NOW, WITH STARTLING SWIFTNESS the days of true darkness descended upon the tuath. The Bau's grim warnings came true with a vengeance. Women who had been nurturing new lives within their bodies lost those tiny lives in blood. Many of the would-be mothers died in the process, adding their blood to that of their infants. Husbands helplessly watched their wives and babies die, then found maggots and rats devouring the food supplies that were to have sustained the surviving members of their families through the long winter.

They have brought it upon themselves, Sekhmet growled as She watched from the Realms of Magic. *Just so did I set my creatures loose on those of My subjects who had displeased Me in the days when the Black Land was all-powerful in the world.*

These people are not Your subjects. Bast's deep musical voice was cold. *And never will they be. Not Your subjects or Mine. Many have given themselves over to the new god, and the rest will soon follow.*

The Lion-Goddess let out Her gurgling bloody laugh. *Then why is their new god not protecting them?* She demanded contemptuously. *Where is he while his faithful cry out in misery at what My power has wrought?*

Where is the woman You said would come to You and begin a line of Priestesses devoted to Your service? Bast

136

countered. She turned Her long green eyes upon the face of Her Sister and stared unwaveringly.

The barb struck home. Sekhmet's laughter twisted into a snarl. Her yellow eyes narrowed. *You are grasping at victory far too soon,* She snapped. *The woman has not come back to You yet. You have sent her Your cat and instructed him to tell her about the wands, but that means very little. A great deal can happen before they ever reach them.*

She swung around in a flare of crimson. *And I,* She added, *will* see *that it does.*

No more than a handful of days had passed since the night Sekhmet's creatures descended upon the tuath, and Damona had struggled through every moment of every one of those days.

The Bau had indeed spoken truly: not only of the misfortunes that would visit the land, but of Sekhmet's influence over Damona herself. The Goddess was sending pictures to her, and they would not leave her in peace. Images hovered about her, behind her eyes and beyond them. She saw herself as she had been, imbued once more with the power that had been stripped from her. Sometimes she was the Lady Niam, glowing in gold and red; other times she was Damona, but a changed Damona, aflame with the strength of hatred and dark magic.

The lion-headed goddess was playing with her, tormenting her the way a cat teases a captured bird. Damona felt it in her bones. And she could do nothing about it.

The clothing of power was a mantle she had felt about her for as long as she could remember. She had been born as the heiress to the shrine of her mother; the gifts of prophecy, of a *Banfhili,* had always been hers. Then Sekhmet's dark favors had come to her. Terrible those powers had been, but there had been a heady delight in them, as well, in their absolute lack of any quality other than the thirst for blood.

Now all those gifts, whether of a *Bhanfili* or avenging woman, were gone, torn from her so abruptly it was as if she stood shivering in a blizzard, her woolen tunic yanked from her, leaving her naked to face the storm.

The fearsomeness of the Bau and her demons had failed to sway Damona on that first night, so now Sekhmet was trying different tactics.

Come back to Me, She crooned. *Return to My service, and I will give you even greater power than before. The whole of this land will quiver before you.*

She spread temptations before Damona, gleaming with promise. She revealed her as a queen, clothed in power, mightier than the Ruiri of the province or even the High King of all Eire himself. In the guise Sekhmet laid upon her she was invulnerable. Neither the old religion nor the new one could touch her.

But neither could anything else: not love or joy or remorse.

Somehow, when the temptation of those images became too great, Damona managed to remember that simple knowledge before falling back into Sekhmet's spell. And it was up to her to remember it, for she was very much alone. The Guardian was with her, and yet he was not. This was her battle, and in the beginning at least, she would have to fight it by herself. She was aware of the cat's great orange eyes watching her as she stumbled through the midst of the visions and struggled with the urges to regain her lost power, but he said little to help her.

Plainly, he was testing her, waiting to see how she would handle the challenges from Sekhmet. And his Mistress, the Goddess Bast to Whom Damona had once devoted her days, was apparently waiting, too. Unlike Sekhmet, the Goddess had not spoken to Her erstwhile Priestess. Damona would have been surprised if She had. She had renounced Her; she could hardly expect forgiveness to come swiftly, even from a Goddess.

Soon, though, survival became more than a matter of magic and mortal souls. Damona's own people had begun hunting her. Perhaps Sekhmet was growing impatient at her stubbornness. Or perhaps the dark Goddess's intervention was not even necessary. The people were already terrified at the scourge that had attacked their tuath; they needed little motivation to seek out the one who had brought it here.

The Bau had taken over Muirchertac's hall. It was a *Tuisech*'s hall no longer. All semblance of its former status as a royal house was gone. An enormous fire burned in the hearth, a magical fire of bloodred flames that needed no wood to keep it burning. The flames were so great that the sounds of roaring and crackling could be heard from leagues away, yet they generated no heat.

A chilling cold radiated from the hall, freezing the blood of any person foolish enough to venture near. The Bau held court inside, squatting within the walls with a presence as vast and dark as the Goddess who had sent her. From there she sent out her demons to work her will, or she merely sat and watched the fruits of her Mistress's magic: the storms, the cold, the deaths, and the fear.

Some of the house folk had survived the attack of the seven demons. They had fled into the woods, seeking sanctuary at the halls of other chieftains and other raths. With them they took the terrible story of the night's events. They also took their accusations of the one who was clearly responsible for these awful misfortunes: the *Banfhili* who had turned herself into the murderous Lady Niam to avenge the destruction of her husband and children and the shrine to which she had dedicated herself.

The former servants of Muirchertac were not alone in their denunciations. There were Christians who had also escaped with their lives that night, and they were even more eager to implicate Damona than the pagans were. To them there were no mitigating factors as there were in the minds of those who followed the old religion. In their eyes, Muirchertac had not sinned in his attack upon the shrine, but Damona had sinned in the seeking of her revenge. She had used the dark powers of the old ways to create death and havoc, and the worst of it was the fate of Lady Rionach.

The queen was still inside the hall of her former husband. She had yearned to return to her home, and her followers had yearned to see her there. But not like this. With their own eyes the survivors had witnessed the *Banfhili* dragging Rionach into the hall. No one had seen her since. She was either a hostage inside those walls, or she was dead. Most were convinced that it was the latter.

Damona feared the same. She no longer had her gifts of divination to tell her otherwise, and that left only one way to know for certain. On the third day, when the storm—and Sekhmet—were finally blowing themselves out, she left the cave to return to the *Tuisech*'s hall. She had to. She herself had brought Lady Rionach inside the house thinking that there she would be safe. With her powers already taken from her, she could not have foreseen that the Bau would also take refuge there. Now it was her obligation to see that the queen was indeed restored to safety: true safety.

"This is beyond foolish," the Guardian warned as she stooped under the ledge of the cave opening. "There is nothing you can do to help that woman. Not now, not while you are as you are."

"I have to try. It was my doing that she is where she is."

Damona squinted up at the sky as she spoke. It was a glum tapestry of gray upon gray, the lighter patches forming a background for looming masses of troubled dark clouds. Rain was still falling, but it was splattering the wet earth in fits and starts, rather than in the driving downpour of the last several days. The wind had also died down, though every now and then Sekhmet remembered to send intermittent gusts that tossed about everything in their path before passing on.

However, while the storm had lessened, the power that had entered the tuath was far from gone. It breathed in the damp cold air. It smiled down from the gloomy sky. It chuckled in the restless wind. There was no way to see it, and no way not to feel it.

"The Bau will know that you are coming long before you

ever reach the hall." Damona started as the cat spoke from directly behind her. In spite of his disapproval he was following her, leaping distastefully through the wet grass, shaking droplets of water from each paw as he went.

"Then let her take me in the queen's place," Damona answered flatly. "And let the Lady Rionach go. If she still lives." She glanced at the cat. "But you know already, don't you, whether she is alive or not."

"I do," the cat said in the same tone. "However, that does not matter."

Damona's eyes narrowed. But she never had a chance to respond.

They had passed through a forest clearing and a thick stand of trees, and had come out onto a wide flat meadow. A rath stood in the distance. Its earthen walls were deserted, a forlorn barricade that had been able to protect its inhabitants from physical threats but not from those sent by magic. The farmstead was eerily silent. A tendril of gray smoke drifted up from the great house, merging with the larger gray of the sky. Yet the familiar sounds of a rath in winter were absent. There were no dogs barking, no cattle lowing or pigs grunting. Nothing broke the stillness of the dank air, only the ominous gusts of wind. The empty fields lay brown and sad in the damp light.

All at once a shout rang out. A man had come onto the meadow and was pointing at them. Damona jumped, whirling to stare at the distant figure.

The Guardian, however, showed no surprise. "I told you this would happen," he growled. "And now it has."

The man came closer. He was dressed for hunting, and he brandished a spear as he peered at Damona. Several other men hurried out of the woods. They gathered beside the first man, staring at Damona with the same intensity.

"It is she!" The first man's voice cracked wildly. "The *Banfhili* who brought this darkness down upon our heads. We must kill her. Her blood will cleanse the evil from our tuath."

The men with him took up his cry. Now others came pouring out over the earthen ramparts of the rath. They gripped spears and bows, and their faces were twisted with the agony of lost children and dead wives and the looming specter of starvation. They were terrified, and in the midst of their terror, they were filled with rage. It was a dangerous combination.

"You see?" the Guardian snarled throatily. "That is why what has become of the queen does not matter. These mortals want to kill you. It would seem that dealing with this situation first would be the wiser course of action, don't you think?"

Yet Damona hesitated. Death stared at her from the faces of these men who were her own people. Most of them had come to her in the old happy days, seeking wisdom. Now what they sought was her blood. The thought of giving it to them was suddenly sweet. Her own *fine* was waiting for her in the Otherworld. Oh, to see their faces! And surely in death, she would finally free herself from Sekhmet.

"No." The Guardian's deep growl jarred her. "Death will not free you from Sekhmet, nor will it reunite you with your kin."

An arrow slammed into the tree next to Damona's ear. She stared at it blankly, the feathers at the end of the shaft quivering before her wide eyes. In that moment, a pure animal desire for survival washed through her. These men wanted her blood, and now she possessed no powers, whether from Druidcraft or the darker gifts she had welcomed for her revenge on Muirchertac, to help her.

She ran.

A chorus of howls shredded her ears as she ducked back within the sheltering trees. More arrows whistled through the air, burying themselves in solid wood with rhythmic deadly thunks. But by some turn of magic, or perhaps by the protection of the Guardian and the Goddess Damona had turned from, not one of them touched her.

The men were determined, though. They pursued her with

a fanaticism born of their desperation. To their straining eyes the *Banfhili* was an elusive and maddening figure. She darted through the gloomy woods, just beyond their reach. They did not realize that she had lost her powers. To some she was Lady Niam, her snow-white hair flying behind her as she slipped through the trees. To others she was Damona, the well-known and once-respected Priestess of a sacred shrine. But to all, she was clothed in the darkness of her magic.

None of the pursuers saw the cat; they only saw the *Banfhili*. Their shouts of rage tore through the trees, growing higher and more frantic as she receded farther and farther away from them. She was going to escape, leaving them all in the grip of this evil. Their cries were practically sobs.

When the last of the agonized voices had faded into the wind, Damona's feet brought her stumbling to a halt. She was drenched in sweat, her white hair hanging in a tangled mass about her shoulders. The wind touched her mockingly, setting a shiver that went all through her.

"Well." The Guardian's voice came from overhead. He was stretched out along the branch of a hawthorn tree, looking down at her. "That was entertaining. Shall we seek out some more of your folk so we may repeat the experience?"

Panting, Damona stooped over, resting her hands on her knees. "They blame me for what is upon our land," she said, when her breathing had steadied. "And by She Whose Name I renounced, they are right."

"No," the Guardian said patiently. "They are not."

Damona scarcely heard him. "Mayhap I should give myself over to them. Why are you so sure that my death will not satisfy Sekhmet? Blood is blood, isn't it, whether it flows from my veins or someone else's. She craves blood. Mine may be enough for Her to call back the curses that She has set upon the land. And it is certain that my dying would satisfy the people."

"These people of yours do not understand." The

Guardian's voice was less patient. "And neither do you. The gods of this land are angry and so is the one god of the Christians. They are so busy fighting with each other that they are blind to everything else. They do not see how their anger feeds the situation."

"How can they not see it?" Damona stared at him in anger. "They are gods!"

The Guardian gave her the feline equivalent of a shrug. "And you are a Priestess. Even gods have their failings, particularly when they are struggling for the worship of mortals. You know that."

"I did once," Damona said bitterly. "But no longer. I am no Priestess. All that has been taken from me. Whatever I once knew of gods and their ways is gone."

The cat gazed at her through slit eyes. "Perhaps it is," he said enigmatically. "But I know, even if you do not, that Sekhmet has taken advantage of the discord. She took advantage of you in the same way. It is typical of Her. She has done it before."

A vision of the lion-headed goddess clawed its way into Damona's mind, and the memory of Her was as vivid and terrible as ever. "Then what can we do?" she asked, making no attempt to hide the hopelessness in her tone.

"We must leave."

"Leave?" Damona looked at him blankly.

"Of course." The tip of the Guardian's tail twitched. He gave it a stern glance, as though it had done so without his permission. "You can hardly stay here. What happened just now was not unique. You will soon discover that everyone in this land, regardless of what god or gods they worship, wants to kill you. I can protect you, but that will grow tiresome for both of us, especially for you, lacking any powers of your own. And eventually, even my protection may fail. I am a creature of magic, not a god. A lucky spear or arrow could be the end of you."

Damona lowered her eyes. "I told you before. Mayhap it should."

"Nonsense." The cat was truly irritated now. "What good would that do?"

Damona said nothing.

The Guardian sat and looked at her, clearly awaiting some response. When it did not come, he went on, his light sharp voice even sharper. "What has become of the anger I saw in you the night you came into that cave dripping like a waterfall? If I had told you that the weapon to banish Sekhmet and Her minions was out in the storm, you would have gone rushing back out to find it. And now you sit here, as huddled up in terror as a mouse waiting to be caught in my claws. Well, you are in Sekhmet's claws now, and if you are ever to get free of them, you will have to fight. If you do not, then, yes, you will die. But that will change nothing. The evil that has come to your land will continue unchanged."

He paused. His tail had been twitching ever more fiercely as he spoke and suddenly he spun around in exasperation and pinned the offending tip down with his paws. "If you want to send the Bau and her demons back," he said over his shoulder, "then you will have to get yourself back first."

The silence between them was long. At last Damona lifted her eyes. Slowly she came erect, stiffening each muscle separately, as if she were discovering her body for the first time. "Where would we go?" she asked in a low voice.

The cat's answer was immediate. "To the land that folk now call Gaul," he said.

Winter soon fell upon the five provinces of Eire in earnest. It promised to be a harsh one, harsher than any that could be recalled in even the memories of the oldest men and women in the land.

Sekhmet was a goddess of the desert; of the eastern sun and its heat that pounded the ancient kingdom of Egypt with the force of a hammer striking an anvil. But here in the green woods and hills of Eire, She called upon the forces of cold to work Her will. And they answered. Perhaps Cailleach, the Ancient One, was angry after all at Muirchertac's poor

observance of Samhain. Or perhaps She was angry at the
increasing influence of a new religion that had no room for
Her. Whatever the reason, She chose to strike the land of
Eire with Her own hammer. And they were terrible blows
indeed.

The fierce rain that had attended the Bau's entrance into
the world now changed to equally fierce snow. Flakes came
whirling through the air, falling in dense white blankets that
quickly hid the brown breast of the Mother. The snow was
driven by a howling wind that seemed more laughter than
wind, and as soon as one storm had ended, another began.
Cold wrapped itself around the air, freezing everything it
touched. It turned the ever-increasing layers of snow to an
impenetrable sheet of ice, and encased the trees in glazed
sculptures that glittered like newly forged sword blades.

Desperate men set out from their raths and halls in search
of game. But the stark woods were bare of their furred
denizens; there was nothing living to be found. Hunting during any winter was hard, but now it was impossible. Wherever the game animals had gone, the beasts that preyed upon
them had gone also. No howls of wolves or barking of foxes
broke the eerie stillness, not even the croaking of a raven.

Huddled inside their byres, the livestock—those precious
cattle, sheep, and pigs that were meant to breed and increase
the herds for the next year—froze to death. Their carcasses
provided a source of temporary meat for their starving owners, but with every bite the people took they shuddered.
They knew that they were eating their future.

The evil was not content to remain within the tuath. Soon
it spread to other neighboring territories, and the *Ruiri,* the
king of the entire province, was forced to take notice. Once
Muirchertac had aspired to be the *Ruiri,* but Muirchertac
was dead. Aodh, who was the *Ruiri,* listened in disbelief to
the stories brought to him by the chieftains of his train. The
tales swept in upon him, growing worse by the hour. His disbelief rapidly turned to horror and then to anger. Aodh was
not a Christian. He promptly called his Druids to him.

The Druids had not been idle during these days. They had been taken unawares by the Bau's entrance into the world, but they could not be blamed for that: Sekhmet had wished it so. The lion-headed goddess had acted swiftly, and in any case, the Druids vibrated to the powers of the Shining Ones of Eire, not those from a distant land.

Once they did recognize the threat, though, the Brothers of the Oak wasted no time. From the first moment they learned of what had happened, they began laboring with all their might, seeking some way of sending the invading horror away. They called upon the Shining Ones, and made countless sacrifices in the sacred groves. They engaged in the rituals of divination: chewing the raw flesh of a dog and then lying down in sacred postures to await the coming of knowledge, or else sleeping within the hide of a freshly slaughtered bull while they waited for guidance from the gods.

The High Druid and his attendants brought word of these efforts to Aodh. But the *Ruiri* was far from satisfied. Pacing the great room of his hall, wrapped in furs against the chill that clenched every corner of the room, he glared at the rapidly melting snow that clung to the mantles of the newly arrived Druids.

"Where are your powers?" he demanded of the High Druid. "You and your brethren are held within the hands of the gods. Why have they not helped you? Why have they not protected us from this evil?"

"My lord," the High Druid answered, "the Shining Ones were taken unawares. As were we, their students." His voice was quiet; he looked twice his age this day, the burden of years and worry weighing him down like a pack of stones. He held his wand of office as though it were as heavy as a mountain.

Aodh let out a ringing oath. "How can that be? They are gods!" Such behavior was uncharacteristic of him. Druids occupied an important place in the court of a non-Christian king; indeed they ranked above him in power and prestige.

No one was more aware of this than Aodh. Usually the *Ruiri* treated the holy men with the greatest respect. It was a measure of his own worry and the helplessness he felt in the face of what had descended upon his people that he spoke so harshly.

But the old man did not seem offended. "And it was a god that brought the darkness to our land," he said. "A goddess, actually. But she is a goddess who comes from beyond our shores. We must find new ways of dealing with her power."

The *Ruiri* glared at him. "Then perhaps we should turn to the Christians. Their god is also from another land. He may succeed where all of you have thus far failed."

The High Druid and his attendants looked at him, and their gazes were so cold that Aodh promptly dropped his own eyes and made an awkward gesture of apology.

"The impious ones have gone into the stone houses they call churches," the High Druid said when he was satisfied that the *Ruiri* had been sufficiently chastened. "They have been praying to their false god continuously. Have you seen the slightest evidence that their prayers have done them or us any good?"

It was true. While the Druids had been engaging in holy rituals, the Christians had been engaging in theirs. Less than fifty years ago, Patrick, the escaped slave who had returned to Eire to convert a nation, had brought with him fifty bells, fifty patens, fifty chalices, altar-stones, and books of the Gospels. He had left each of them in new places and his doing so had borne fruit. Adherents of the new religion abounded, and all of them were now crowding into the small stone churches that had begun to dot the land in order to pray to their new god.

Thinking of this, Aodh sighed. "No," he admitted. "It has done no more good than any of the holy rituals you have performed."

"Precisely." The High Druid's voice was still cold. "Cairnech, the man the impious ones call Bishop, has been on his knees until they bleed. And look you"—he gestured toward the icy day outside—"still the snows are falling. The woods have gone bare of game. Our women have lost their babes. The beasts lie dead in their byres and when our people manage to sleep, they dream only of starvation. And all of this, while that monstrosity from another world squats gloating in the hall that once belonged to Muirchertac."

This also was true. Bishop Cairnech, as well as all the other church officials, had been praying from the first. Ceaselessly they had been beseeching God, Jesus, and Mary, pleading with the Holy Trinity to send this darkness away. However, the new god and his divine son and mother did not seem to be listening; or perhaps he was as powerless in the face of this strange threat as were the ancient Shining Ones.

The *Ruiri* slammed a fist suddenly against his thigh. "None of it is working," he shouted. "And none of you can tell me why." He fixed the Druids with a stony glare. "But there is one thing I do not need to be told: who is responsible. The *Banfhili* from the shrine of the outland Goddess has brought these disasters upon us."

The High Druid sighed. "Have you forgotten, my lord, what was done to her by the ruler of her own tuath?"

"I have not," Adoh snapped. "But neither can I forget what is being done to all of us now. The woman must be found. I care not how it is done, or whether she lives in the doing of it. Only that she be found." He stepped close to the High Druid. "Do you understand me, Holy One?"

"Yes, my lord," the High Druid said quietly. "I understand you well."

He did not voice what he also understood: that the safest course for Damona would be to get out of Eire. Doing that safely would be no simple matter.

II

THE CONCEPT OF SIN WAS A NEW thing in the world. There were the sins of idleness, of impure thoughts and minor self-indulgence, and there were the greater sins: transgressions of sexuality or religious dogma that could result in a resounding public act of exclusion from the holy church and the Christian community.

Hand in hand with the notion of sin went that of penance. Only by coping with one's sins in a manner laid down in no uncertain terms by the clergy could the average man or woman hope to gain the palpable joys of the "city of God." Those who had committed grievous sins and then taken on the mantle of penitence—either by their own will, or that of the bishop—were little better than the non-believers who stubbornly refused to give up their gods and goddesses. Such penitents were excluded from participation in church ritual. In the very back of the church, they stood in specially designated areas, humbled, dressed beneath their station, beards unshaven and hair uncombed, waiting in full public view for a gesture of reconciliation from their bishop.

As she and the Guardian made their way east, Damona caught glimpse after glimpse of this peculiar sight. It was an irony indeed, she reflected, that bitter toward both old ways and new, she had herself become a penitent, and of the gravest kind. Yet it was true. She was as clothed in the darkness of her deeds as any sinner huddling in the back of his church. And just as that humbled Christian, she now found herself searching for a similar gesture of reconciliation, though hers would have to come from a source far different than any known by the upholders of the new faith.

Dressed in a voluminous laine and brat that she had stolen from a deserted farmstead in order to hide her face, she and the cat slipped through the land, heading for the coast. They kept to the woods, to the secret places and little-traveled ways, constantly aware of what would happen if Damona were discovered.

Past the sacred groves where once the *Banfhili* would have been welcome they darted. Ceremonies were going on in most of them; the ancient towering oaks and yews and hawthorn trees were jammed with worshippers, their frightened eyes fixed avidly on white-robed Druids whose arms were red with the blood of sacrificed beasts. Damona did not ask, but she was certain that the Guardian must be cloaking them in magic, for not once did the keenly attuned senses of the Druids detect their presence.

The churches were easier. Christians set themselves apart from the natural world; rather than embracing the trees and waters and winds and rhythms of life, they enclosed themselves in small rough buildings of wood, or more frequently, stone. They crowded inside the walls of their churches and huddled there. Their eyes did not turn to the sky or the voices within everything that lived. Instead, they kept their gazes fixed on the symbols of their faith, and on the faces of the priests who prayed for this evil to depart.

But the priests, unlike the Druids they had set themselves in competition against, possessed no powers of magic. The realms beyond did not speak to them, or perhaps the priests had no interest in listening. The ears of Christians were attuned only to that which came from God.

It was so easy to slip past them when they were gathered in the stone churches. It made Damona wonder about the power of this new religion that was so rapidly taking over her country. And not only her country, but also the great lands that encompassed far more than a small island surrounded by cold tossing seas.

Christianity had been declared the official religion of Rome, and therefore of much of the known world. In the year 312, the Emperor Constantine had been converted. His acceptance of the new faith had given it a public standing that had proved and was continuing to prove as decisive as it was irreversible. In the fervor of his conversion Constantine had encouraged the subjects within his realm to be baptized. Many had done so. Many others had not.

But the decrees of an emperor made little difference to those folk who made their homes in the most distant parts of the empire. The tribes there revered their old gods, and they had no intention of forsaking them. One hundred years later, that had not changed. If anything, the ancient tribal societies had grown stronger, as a once-mighty Rome weakened. Particularly in the west, in the unsettled areas that had comprised the Roman frontier, there were numerous Germanic tribes that lived as they always had. They saw no need to alter either custom or religion. They had not done so for Rome. They did not intend to do so for Christianity.

Eire, however, was the exception. Rome had built several small enclaves along the eastern coast, but the country itself had never been conquered by the notorious legions that had triumphed throughout the known world. Gaius Julius Caesar had coveted the fertile green island, as he had coveted first Gaul and then Albion. He had succeeded in obtaining both those lands for the empire, but Eire had eluded him. It had escaped the hunger of subsequent emperors and generals, as well. Rome had never succeeded in invading Eire; it had taken something less solid than soldiers and swords to accomplish that, something more ethereal but infinitely more powerful: religion.

"I do not understand," Damona said to the cat. "What is it about these Christians and their ways that draws so many to them?"

They had reached the eastern coast, and below them lay the harbor at Drumanagh. Here was the closest Rome had ever come to attaining a piece of Eire: a fort, which still sat

on the extensive promontory. Trade had always gone on
between Rome and Eire, and Roman hands had built the
structure with its defensive ramparts in the days of the
empire's greatness. Now the fort was inhabited by folk, most
of them merchants, whose blood was a mixture of Rome and
Albion and Eire.

Vertical cliffs bounded the promontory on three sides, and
beside the old fort lay the harbor itself. It was an ideal landing place, sheltered and wide. From the most ancient times it
had been a destination for traders traveling up the Sea of
Eire. Even before the days of the fort, it had served as a dis-
tribution center for Roman goods. From Damona's tuath it
was the closest spot to catch a ship bound for Gaul. With the
dangers now past, the difficult part lay in descending along
the cliffs that led to the wide protected beach where coracles
had been drawn far upland, out of the reach of the hungry
winter waves.

It was not the season for sea travel: Damona had warned
her companion of that fact frequently. But the cat seemed
untroubled by her concerns. His only complaint, he had told
her, was that water journeys of any kind were more distaste-
ful to him than any torture that mortals could devise.

"I still do not understand," Damona said, as they began
the laborious descent. "And you have not answered me."

If a cat could smile, the Guardian seemed to do so. "Of
course you do not," he said. "You cannot."

He was leaping gracefully from boulder to boulder, while
Damona picked her way cautiously along the narrow and far
more precarious path. Along these cliffs the wind whistled
even on the best of days in high summer. In this dark time,
the wind howled with unique savagery, biting through
woolen cloth and thick fur alike. Damona tightened the hood
of her brat about her head, gazing at the cat's sleek black
coat as the thick fur rippled in the ceaseless blowing.

"Never will you become one of these Christians," said the
Guardian. "You are no more likely to dunk yourself in their
holy water than I am."

"Water is also holy to those of the old ways," Damona reminded him. Her voice was sharp as the wind. "Long and long has it been so. Yet the Christian priests prattle on about their sacred water and claim it as their god's, when they took its very sacredness from the gods and goddesses of this land, and most likely, every other."

The cat flicked his tail as he balanced on a knife-thin edge of rock. "Precisely my point. Can you not see what is happening? No, I suppose you would not; not with everything else that has beset you. The Christians have learned something very valuable. It is a thing I have not seen in all the years of my life, and those years, human one, are many, indeed."

"All I can see," Damona said, tight-lipped and grim, "is that they hate those who do not follow their ways."

"Only some," the cat corrected her. "You cannot place Muirchertac among their number; as you have said yourself, he was no Christian. He was only mad, a state which is all too common among you humans. No, the priests of this new religion are crafty, disturbingly so." The cat went very still. His orange eyes narrowed and then grew wide, as if he were seeing far beyond this dark overcast day. "They have set their feet upon a path that will lead them far and far, and this path they take will cause an ending in the paths of we who are older than they."

Damona felt the hairs on the back of her neck prickle. This was a seeing, and she could do nothing but listen, as though she were no more gifted than any of the men and women who had come to the shrine during her other life. She ached for the return of her powers; without them she was as raw and sore as if she were rolling naked down this rough and rocky path.

"You are speaking wisdom," she said miserably. "But I cannot grasp it. I no longer have the gifts."

Instantly a familiar voice coiled through her mind.

You may have your gifts back anytime you wish, Sekhmet purred. *All you need do is ask . . .*

The promise rang in Damona's brain, echoing all the way down to her belly. Once again the ease of doing as the Goddess wished struck her. To have her gifts back, to be powerful even beyond what she had been, that would be greatness, indeed. Oh, how it hurt, to be so naked of the embrace of what was uniquely her own: the magic she had been born with. Bast had sent the Guardian back, but She had done nothing to prevent anything Sekhmet had done, not the taking of Damona's powers, or the appearance of the deadly creatures and events attacking the land.

And She will not. A scarlet haze accompanied Sekhmet's voice, whirling through the world behind Damona's eyes. *She has left you and your people to their own devices. Think you that I am evil? Let Me offer you this: come back to My service and I will restore the land to what it was.*

The redness grew thicker, as though it were alive, as though Sekhmet had charged it with the task of blocking out all other thoughts in Damona's mind. Was this a fate that was up to her alone? If she did as the Goddess offered, she could repair the damage she had caused. Perhaps it was the only way . . .

"What I speak of is not a matter of wisdom, but of sense." The cat's light voice penetrated the haze, calling Damona back to herself. He was sitting on a rock, watching her, his orange eyes studying her face as if he were fully aware of what had just occurred.

Drawing a deep breath, Damona returned the cat's gaze. She was about to ask if he indeed knew what Sekhmet had said to her, but something held her back. More than likely, the Guardian would say the Goddess was lying, as perhaps She was.

A gust of wind whipped up the folds of her brat, chilling her to the bone. She lowered her head, turning her eyes away from those of the cat, and began to walk.

The Guardian leaped onto the next boulder. "Think about what you said about the sacredness of water," he said, continuing with his discourse as if nothing happened. "Once it was holy to the old ones. Now it is holy to Christians. But that is just the beginning. The Christians have learned a very important lesson. Just as water does, they engulf, rather than destroy. It is a practice that has stood them in good stead, especially in Eire. The wisest of these Christians have come to realize that it is better to steal ancient customs and make them their own, rather than seeking to banish them from the hearts of those they wish to win. For that they will never do. Not in this land."

Damona glanced at him. "And elsewhere?"

"Elsewhere." The cat made a small sound that could have been a sigh. "Elsewhere the change has not been so gentle. But that, you will eventually see for yourself." He jumped to a massive outcropping of rock and peered down at the flat promontory that stretched out into the harbor. "At the moment, we have other matters to concern ourselves with."

"We do, indeed." Damona followed the cat's gaze. "Such as finding safe passage to Gaul with winter coming upon us and the hands of my countrymen turned against me."

"Someone will take us," the Guardian said grimly. "*She* will see to that."

"She?" Damona stared at him. "You mean Sekhmet? Why would She help me after all that She has done to hurt me?"

The cat narrowed his eyes in the familiar expression he assumed when Damona said something that irritated him. "She is not," he said with exaggerated patience, "helping you. No matter what She might say. At the moment, She wants you gone from Eire. And gone you shall be."

It happened precisely as the Guardian had said.

In the deserted harbor Damona found a lone merchant from Gaul, hurriedly supervising his crew of sailors—a motley combination of men from Albion, Rome, and Gaul—in the loading of his ship. Under normal circumstances the merchant would never have chanced the dangerous winter storms that could descend on a ship as suddenly as a gull diving on a hapless fish. He would have settled down in safe quarters in Drumanagh, waiting for spring and the arrival of favorable sailing weather.

But the strange and evil events that held Eire in their grip had spooked the Gaulish trader. His cargo was valuable, and in the wake of threatening famine, it had become even more so. The precious stones and fine gold jewelry he had amassed would not fill a man's belly or keep him warm. The same could not be said for the packs of furs and woolen hides, the haunches of salted pork, and the sacks of wheat and oats. Such goods would be impossible for starving folk to resist if conditions in the harbor town grew much worse.

The merchant was both a practical man and a superstitious one. In this case, practicality and superstition were working together. Dangerous the tumultuous seas off Eire might be, yet it was far more dangerous to remain in Eire itself.

The sailors were sweating in the cold air as they carried the heavy sacks and crates aboard the ship. The merchant shouted at them to move faster, his anxious voice cracking along with the leather sails that snapped overhead. The wind still blew, but not as fiercely. The rain had stopped, the tide would soon be going out, and the merchant was frantic to get his goods loaded so he could take advantage of this brief opportunity that had surely been granted him by the gods.

He had scant patience for the woman who strode up to him, her face nearly hidden by the enveloping hood of her brat. He scarcely favored her with a glance and threw up his hands in a gesture of negation when she inquired about passage.

"No," he shouted. "It's out of the question, utterly impossible."

One of the sailors dropped a sack, and the merchant raised his voice in a spate of cursing. "I have no time to make arrangements for passengers," he went on, watching keenly as the man recovered his load. "As soon as these last bales are on board we'll be gone."

"Good merchant." Damona stepped closer, raising her voice to be heard above the snapping sails and yelling sailors. "There is nothing to arrange. I am ready to leave as quickly as you say. I have no goods for your men to load."

"Hah, and nothing to pay for passage with either, I'll warrant." The trader cast a more thoughtful scrutiny upon his potential passenger, trying to ascertain what sort of face and form lay beneath the woolen folds of her mantle. "Lower that cloak and let me see you. If you're pleasing enough to the eye, I suppose we might be able to work out a bargain of sorts."

Damona did not move. "I am not without means to pay for my passage," she said in a tone as frigid as the gray waters of the harbor.

Her hand snaked out from the folds of her brat and she opened it to show the merchant its contents. On her palm gleamed three rings of gold. The Guardian had led her to a cache of gold some days ago and had insisted that she take those items small enough to be carried. The ones the gold had belonged to, he explained, no longer needed them.

"These should be more than enough." Damona watched the trader's face change as he saw the gold. "I will give you one of the rings now and the other two when I arrive safely on the shores of Gaul. I am an honorable woman. If you are an honorable man, you will accept these in token that I may travel with you unharmed."

The merchant eyed the glittering rings. They were of the finest gold workmanship; his practiced eye told him that at once. He reached out and took one of the proffered rings. "I am a man of honor indeed," he said grudgingly. "But I was not expecting to take on any passengers, especially a woman. No provisions have been made, so the accommodations will not be to your liking—"

"I will make do." Damona gestured to a lithe dark shape that had suddenly appeared beside her. "And so will my cat. He will more than earn his keep by catching the rats on board your ship."

"Ah." The merchant smiled down at the Guardian, momentarily distracted. "A fine beast. Cats are very valuable, you know. He would fetch a fine price in Trier or Namnetes. I would even consider taking him instead of one of your rings, Lady."

The cat's eyes opened wide, and he stared hard at the merchant. The man returned the animal's gaze for a moment and suddenly glanced away. "Cats are peculiar creatures," Damona said easily. "They alone decide who they wish to be with, and I fear, good merchant, that this one has attached himself to me. I have taken it as an omen. The god who sent him to me would surely be displeased if I were to part with him. Ill fortune would fall upon me, and possibly on you, as well."

"Yes, yes." The merchant's anxiety returned. He was not a Christian, and he had seen too much already. "No one with a grain of sense would part with an omen sent by the gods. There is more than enough ill fortune about these days without trying to draw more." He sighed and made an impatient gesture, his nervous eyes going once more to his ship. "Well, go on aboard then, you and the cat. I'll soon join you. The tide will not wait, and I intend to be on it."

Damona nodded. With the Guardian pacing alongside her she strode swiftly up the planks laid between the ship and the dock. It was a short distance and yet the difference between land and water was already strong. The deck creaked beneath her feet, its timbers muttering. The sails hissed and popped as if eager to be gone. Wrapped in her brat, Damona stood silently at the rail, ignoring the curious and speculative glances of the crewmen as they finished the last of the loading.

Eire lay before her: the beautiful island known by so many names. Eire, Fodla, Banba, all of them words that described the ancient Goddess of the Land, She Who had many names and had been sought by so many suitors. It was part of Damona, this country the Romans called Island of Wood because of the mighty forests that clothed it. But now it had become a land that was soaked with blood and death and magic and the lost echoes of those she had loved.

In leaving it she was going into exile, self-imposed perhaps, but a decision made because there was no other choice. And in any case, exile was still exile. To a man or woman of Eire, it was the most severe penalty that could be levied under Brehon law. The person so punished was stripped of the very core of life in Eire: the densely interwoven network of kinfolk, lords, retainers, and dependents. From the moment of a babe's birth he or she was swaddled in this community of *fine* and tuath, cocooned in a protective fabric of custom, attachments, and obligations. To be severed from it was to be alone, a defenseless individual in a hostile world.

But for Damona, that warm fabric was already gone. Her *fine,* unto the fifth generation, was destroyed. As the merchant shouted commands at his crew and the heavily laden vessel nosed her way out of the harbor, she stared at her country. The Guardian had told her she must undertake this journey to find her way back home.

She was not certain she wanted to come back.

Ever.

12

THE CHANNEL HAD LONG BEEN A highway for seafaring folk. The Germanic tribes along the northern coast had once used it to raid the rich pickings of Gaul. Now it was traveled by settlers looking for new homes in both Albion and Gaul, as well as by ships carrying a variety of goods. Commodities of trade, plunder, tribute, dowries, and gifts all flowed along this stretch of sea that united tribes and lands. Only in the winter season did the constant stream of traffic ever slow.

At this time of year the voyage to Gaul was difficult. The Western Sea allowed the lone ship to pass over her depths, but she was singularly ungracious about it. Storms lashed the coast of Eire and the waters that lay between it and Albion. The channel crossing to the vast lands inhabited by the Gauls and the fierce tribes beyond was even worse. Waves buffeted the eighteen rowers who sat at their benches struggling to keep the ship on her course. Winds lashed the already sodden decks, sending a constant spray of salt water over everyone on board.

When the battered vessel finally nosed her way into the port of Namnetes along the coast of Brittany, a province in western Gaul, the merchant, his crew, and his two passengers were both heartily grateful, and heartily glad to see the voyage end.

"If Bast wanted to help us depart from Eire," Damona asked the Guardian sourly, "why did She not simply use Her

161

powers to sweep us away to Gaul, instead of allowing us to go on this horrid journey?"

Left to themselves, they were standing by the railing. Both the merchant and the sailors were far too delighted at the sight of the harbor to take notice of the fact that Damona appeared to be conversing with her cat.

The Guardian's whiskers stood straight out at her question. He halted in the intent effort to set his bedraggled fur in order, and he bared his long fangs in a snarl of annoyance. "Because," he growled, "my Mistress has a peculiar sense of humor."

The moment the planks were run out to the dock, the Guardian leaped forward. He was the first one off the ship, even before the usual covey of scurrying rats. There were none to be seen, of course. The cat had occupied himself in hunting out virtually every one, a feat that had earned him the admiration of the merchant and all his crew.

After giving the merchant the two rings she had promised him, Damona followed her companion, more slowly, but no less eagerly. They walked through up from the docks. Lying at the mouth of the Loire River this busy port city had been named for the Namnetes, one of the five tribes of Brittany. They had settled along the river's north shore almost four hundred years ago and had been engaging in the business of commerce ever since. In summer, at the height of the trading season, the harbor would have been so filled with the activity of loading and unloading of goods it would have been difficult to negotiate one's way. But on this day, with the sky overcast and a cold wind blowing off the sea, the arrival of a trading vessel was more of a novelty than an ordinary occurrence.

Damona stepped gingerly; her legs were slow to adjust to the solid feel of dry land beneath her feet. She noted that the cat seemed to require no similar period of adjustment. He pranced along cheerfully, displaying all of his usual grace.

"Well, we are here," she finally said to him. "What happens now?"

The Guardian paused. "This is only the first stage of the

journey." His whiskers stiffened again. "And the next stage should be no more pleasant. We'll have to find a trader bound for the north and travel along with his train. With the cold weather upon us that will not be so easy." He muttered deep in his chest. "We'll likely have to go along the river, at least until it freezes. Another cursed water journey."

Damona let her gaze rove over the waterfront. The sights and sounds fascinated her. In spite of the reasons that had led to this journey and the darkness that hung over her, she could not repress a sense of excitement at walking though this port city. The Guardian had told her that Namnetes was little more than a harbor town, that there were other ports and other cities in Gaul that dwarfed it by comparison. But to Damona's eyes, this place, even in its quiet season, was still larger than any town she had ever seen in Eire.

Travel was a pursuit that few people—even the high-born—engaged in. With the steady crumbling of Rome's authority, roads had fallen into disuse and long-used trade routes were slowly and inevitably breaking down. The resulting dangers had made travel an activity that had become even more infrequent. During the whole of most folk's lives they never went more than a few leagues from the place where they had been born. In her training as a Druid Damona had journeyed farther than many. But that travel had only been within the borders of Eire, to the Druidic school in Munster. Never, even when she had been in possession of her powers, would she have guessed that destiny would one day lead her to the shores of Gaul.

Still looking about her, she absently said to the cat, "Bast saw to it that we got away from Eire easily enough. Why does She not do the same here?"

"By the sarcophapus of Hapsetshut," the cat replied in exasperation, "has She not done enough already? You still have gold, do you not? Use it."

Damona was about to say something sharp in response, when she thought of why she was here. Chastened, she said nothing more.

* * *

After many inquiries, Damona arranged passage for them. In the days of Rome's glory this would have been a simple matter, even with the winter season hard upon them. But much had changed. Drawn by the need for land and a desire to be part of the very empire they were weakening by their incursions, first the Visigoths had encroached steadily from the west, to be followed by the Vandals, and the Franks. Each tribe had grown stronger as a *federate* of Rome, and yet their presence had caused the Roman eagle to grow frailer and frailer.

These days the famous legions were filled primarily with tribesmen, men who were Romanized but who also bore loyalties to their tribes of their birth. Many belonged to the ancient tribes Julius Caesar had vanquished; many more were Visigoths from the southern part of Gaul, and Franks from the north. They were a strange hybrid, these new legionaries, an intermingling of Roman and barbarian, with characteristics of both.

It had not always been that way. Once the armies of Rome had held only Romans. After the conquests of Casear had ended, the main task of the Roman soldiers had been to build roads all through Gaul and then to maintain them, guarding the routes so that a steady stream of goods could pass along to destinations in and out of the province.

Now the situation was as different as the makeup of the legions. Trade had broken down, in Gaul as in every other part of the empire. But along the northern frontier supplies were still needed, indeed, with the incursions of the powerful and savage Franks from across the Rhine, they were needed more than ever. Corn was grown in the central part of the province, and long caravans of it were sent regularly to the north to feed the legionaries who manned the dangerous and all-important frontier. Even with soldiers to guard the pack trains from attack, it was a dangerous undertaking. But for traders who were willing to brave the difficult and often hazardous journey there were always great profits to be made.

Near the great storehouses at the edge of the docks Damona found such a man. His name was Carbo, and he was short and burly, somewhat advanced in years, and as squat as one of the sacks of grain he was taking to the frontier.

"This will not be an easy journey," he warned Damona. "Especially for a woman traveling alone. Are you certain you wish to—"

"I am certain," Damona said abruptly.

Unconvinced, the trader sighed. "It will cost. Ten *solidi* at least. I must have that sum if I am to buy you a riding mule and keep you provisioned and protected during the journey."

It was an exorbitant amount, and they both knew it. Damona opened her palm to show one of the remaining gold rings. "I have already shown you that I can pay. This ring is the weight of five *solidi*, which is more than a fair price for my upkeep as your passenger." She looked down, fixing the shorter trader with her amber gaze. "And if you are thinking to do me some harm, such as selling me as a slave along the way, I must warn you that I have protections beyond what you may provide."

The trader gestured his assent. "I trade in corn," he replied in a gruff voice. "Not in slaves. You will be safe in my train, at least as safe as the rest of us. If disaster strikes, well, you'll have to take your chances along with everyone else. Although"—he cast an appraising glance at Damona's hair, the glittering white offset by the streaks of red—"by the mark of magic you bear I'd wager those protections you speak of will bring my enterprise good fortune."

And so, at dawn of the next day Damona and the Guardian set off on the next stage of their long journey. As the cat had predicted so dourly they did indeed take the river route, packing themselves into several large rafts belonging to Carbo. They were flat utilitarian crafts utterly lacking in luxury, for their main purpose was not comfort but to ferry the all-precious cargo.

Under a pale sun, the oarsmen who would later act as mule drivers steered the rafts along the reaches of the calm, winding river. Taking care to stay out of their way, Damona stood and watched the panorama of the river valley pass by. Lining the shores at a discreet distance there were villas: beautiful, finely crafted homes that clearly had been built by wealthy Romans. The villas were surrounded by countless hectares of fields that stretched all the way down to the river. But oddly, the villas appeared mostly deserted, and the rich fields lay fallow, empty of either crops or farmers.

One of the oarsmen noticed Damona staring at the silent estates, and spoke to her. "The owners are gone," he said without preamble. "They left long ago. Most of them anyway."

Damona continued to gaze at the strange sad sight of these abandoned homes and fields. Under a winter sun that was still warmer than any that shone in Eire at this time of year, the fine stone walls and bright tile roofs glowed as if their inhabitants still lived within. Yet the beauty was illusory. Some of the buildings were already starting to decay, their perfectly fitted stones crumbling into heaps alongside the walls. "Where did they go?" she asked.

The oarsman shrugged. "Who can say? They have been fleeing the province for years, running from plague, the barbarians, the falling apart of the empire. It's said that many packed up and went to Rome, though little good that did them when the Visigoths showed up at the city's gates. Others may have gone to Constantinople, a marvelous place, I'm told. I'll wager, though, that most are probably dead."

Pain suddenly clenched Damona's heart, tearing as fiercely as if the jaws of Sekhmet had closed over her breast. Unwillingly she looked within her mind to the once-fertile fields and pastures of her destroyed rath and words sprang past her lips, aching in her throat. "Why does no one take over the lands, then, and farm them as the Mother intended? Such rich fields should be bearing life, to replace the death."

The anger in her voice caused the oarsman to glance up. He grunted in surprise. "Why should anyone do that? Do you know nothing of the barbarians? No, perhaps you don't, being from Eire. Well, it's simple. If we settle on these estates and start farming the land, we'll eventually be killed, or if fortune is with us, merely pushed off our homes by the next army of savages that comes through. The legions are too busy guarding the frontier to care what becomes of common freemen."

The man looked briefly at another deserted villa and spat over the side. "I was a farmer once. It may not be safer than farming to drive mules to the frontier, but it's easier, and more profitable." His brown eyes suddenly squinted as though at memories. He turned back to his rowing and said nothing more.

The procession of rafts continued to move stolidly upriver, and the weather under which they traveled remained surprisingly pleasant. In Brittany the seasons were gentle, with mild winters and sunny hot summers. But that, the trader told Damona repeatedly, was a comfort she would find short-lived.

"It won't take long," he said wisely, "and there will be ice on this beautiful river. And with it will come the cold—cold like you've never known. The farther north we go the thicker the ice will get. Your bones will shiver until you think they're about to crack in pieces."

Carbo did not exaggerate. He had undertaken this journey before.

Soon enough the days grew shorter, and the mornings frostier. The gentle sun was replaced by overcast skies and in the distance, broken sheets of gray ice began to glitter on the river's flat surface. The oarsmen wrapped themselves in mantles, cursing as they blew on their chilled hands to warm them to the oars. Damona took out the thick cloak the trader

had advised her to purchase. With a cat's usual acuity, the
Guardian sought out the warmest places to curl up in
between the bales and sacks and stayed there.

"The ice will not allow us to go much farther," the trader
told Damona, his breath steaming in the air. "We'll disem-
bark at a town a few leagues upriver. The mules I've
arranged for will be waiting there." He grinned sourly.
"Then the real trip will begin. At least, we'll have an escort,
thanks to the gods."

At a place where the river curved gently into the shore
they stopped at the town Carbo had spoken of. It had no
name, this small scattering of huts with a central market
square; indeed, it seemed more of a village, with small plots
of tilled land stretching beyond its borders. But there was a
small wooden church set in a prominent position next to the
square, and in addition to the fields there were large pastures, filled with grazing animals. They belonged to a freeman who bred mules. He was already on his way down to
the riverbank leading several strings of sturdy pack animals;
on arriving there, he immediately set about trying to renego-
tiate the price with the trader.

While the two merchants argued, the oarsmen busied
themselves unloading the cargo and piling it on the grassy
shore. Townspeople gathered around the busy assistants,
both to seek a market for their own goods and to hear the
news from Namnetes. Glad of the opportunity to be on land
again, Damona, too, left the raft. But unlike her companions,
she stood apart from the busy scene. The voices of the hag-
gling traders rose into the chilly air, blending with the shouts
of the oarsmen and the questions of the townspeople. Many
of these townspeople stared at Damona, their eyes lingering
nervously on her moon-pale hair with its startling crimson
arrows. None drew near her, and when her eyes met theirs,
they quickly looked away.

"They are put off by your appearance. You bear the sign
of a goddess and they fear to approach you."

Damona looked down. The Guardian was sitting beside

her; his orange eyes flickered over the villagers, enigmatic and glowing. A smile tugged at the corners of Damona's mouth. In the crowded quarters of these past days, there had been little opportunity for her and her companion to speak. It was an unexpected relief to hear the cat's light, dry voice.

"They are Christians," she pointed out to him. "You know they have no respect for goddesses, or gods, for that matter."

"Not all of them." The cat twitched an ear in the direction of the people. "Many hold to the old ways. They recognize the mark of magic when they see it. And as for those who don't: Christian or not, most still have sense enough to pay heed to omens."

"Ah." Damona suddenly found it hard to look at the people of this place. They were strangers to her, as much as she was to them, but there was no escaping the weight of her burdens. Here in this place, they marked her, as indelibly as the blood of the dead.

"The trader's men will not interfere with you either," the cat said. "They, too, are afraid."

"Of me?" Damona gave him a sad sharp glance.

The cat extended a back leg, put out his claws, and began to clean them with firm tugs of his teeth. "Actually," he said through his licking and chewing, "they are more afraid of me. They do not know why I am with you, and it worries them. None of these men know the name of my Mistress, but the knowledge of goddesses is an ancient memory in their blood that Christianity has not yet been able to wipe out. They see the power of the old ones in my eyes. They are drawn to it, yet their new god warns them that they dare not look too close."

He finished with his leg and stood up, shivering all his fur and then smoothing it down into place. "Look, there in the distance is a temple to Great Mother Isis Herself. She was very popular among the Romans not so long ago. It was they who brought Her to Gaul."

Damona followed his glance. The building was not large, but it was neatly constructed out of whitewashed stone and blocks of marble that must have been laboriously imported during other wealthier days; even from a distance one could tell that here sat a shrine to the old ways that was lovingly tended to. "There are still those who worship Her," she said.

A purr rumbled in the Guardian's chest. "Yes. It warms my fur to see a place where Mother Isis is still held sacred. There are so few of them left."

"Lady!"

Carbo's impatient voice broke into their conversation. "Will you stay in this town or continue on the journey you paid me for?"

He and the mule breeder had concluded their agreement at last, and their slapping of hands had sent the trader's men into a second flurry of activity. The cargo was on land and the townspeople had dispersed, leaving the erstwhile oarsmen to be transformed into their true occupation: that of mule drivers. Quickly and skillfully they were engrossed in saddling the newly purchased mules and packing them with the goods that would be carried north.

Carbo came toward her leading a saddled bay mule behind him. He proffered the reins to Damona. "You will ride, of course. Some of your gold paid for this beast."

Damona nodded, taking the reins. "I will also need to purchase a basket to carry my cat in."

The trader went silent. Frowning, he stared down at the Guardian for several moments. "Lady," he finally began, "I said nothing when you came to me seeking passage with that animal in tow. I said nothing when you brought him with you on the river. But now I must ask you: why it is so important to have this creature with you?" His eyes turned away from the cat's orange gaze with sudden unease. "Is he part of the protections you spoke of that you bear?"

"He is." Damona regarded him steadily. "Treat both of us well, and you will prosper in the journey that lies ahead."

The trader crossed himself. "Very well, then. Recently I became a Christian, and the priest who baptized me warns us constantly against heathen magic. But I am also a man of common sense. These days it is better to have the goodwill of both the old ways and the new, especially when one is heading into the frontier."

"Most sensible of you," Damona said. From his frequent references to the gods she would not have guessed that Carbo was of the new faith, but given his views she now understood why. She did not voice what else she was thinking: that it seemed obvious that a man could not have the goodwill of one god without incurring the ill will of the other.

There was no need to search for a basket; almost at once a woman called out to Damona. She turned, saw the power in the woman's eyes at once, and hesitated, wanting to turn away. It was too painful to answer this Priestess, to face one who stood in the light of her goddess, while she, Damona, stood in the darkness. But the Guardian had other ideas. He bounded toward the woman, his tail straight up, curving his body around her ankles as she stooped to stroke him.

The woman straightened up as Damona reluctantly followed, leading the mule after her. "The blessings of the Great Mother be upon you, lady," she said cheerfully. "And upon he who guards you." She was small and robust, olive-skinned and dark-eyed, a handful of seasons older than Damona. Her coloring and build marked her as a descendant of Romans, rather than the tall fair tribes of the Keltoi, though more probably she was a commingling of both. If she sensed Damona's unease in her presence—as she surely did—she gave no sign of it.

"You wish for something to carry him in," she went on, bending again to rub the cat under his chin, a gesture he responded to with closed eyes and a thunderous purr. "I have exactly what you need."

Damona did not question how the woman knew this. She was a Priestess; nothing more needed to be known than that. "My thanks, lady," she said politely. "I have gold to—"

The Priestess put up a hand. "No payment is necessary. This is a gift." She held out a round basket. It was large and beautifully crafted, with a cover and a leather thong so the entire affair could be attached to a saddle. "This one who guards you will be quite comfortable. I have lined the inside with a piece of soft wool."

The woman's eyes were dark and penetrating, filled with knowledge. Damona glanced into their depths and away. "Why?" Her voice was soft and low. "Surely you know what I am, what I have done."

"I know you have a long journey ahead," the Priestess said serenely. "And it is a journey of the soul as well as the body. This is but a small offering to make your way easier." She smiled. "Consider it a gift, from my Goddess to yours. Now take it." She placed the basket in Damona's hands. "The time for you to leave draws nigh."

Damona followed her gaze. The mule drivers were shouting at each other and the mules as they lined the burdened animals up for departure and attached lead ropes from one beast to the next. Carbo was pacing back and forth issuing last-minute orders as he watched these final preparations. Catching Damona's eye, he made brusque motions in her direction.

Damona looked down at the woman. "Thank you," she said simply. "May your Goddess be with you always."

The smile on the Priestess's olive face glowed. "She has always been with me, daughter. She always will be, from one life to the next."

A chill rippled over Damona. For the first time she truly looked at the woman. Darkness was hovering above her, shading the brightness of her power with black fingers. But there was no time to speak of what she saw: the trader had gone from gestures to shouts, yelling that if she did not make haste, he would leave her behind for certain. Still smiling, the woman bent down to stroke the Guardian once again. She rose and strode purposefully away.

13

THE PACK TRAIN GOT UNDER WAY. The road along which it started had once been broad and laid with flat, carefully matched stones. Now most of the stones were broken, and not only grass, but even young trees were springing up in the gaps, increasing the deterioration still more. But it was still a road, its outlines still defined, and its pathway would lead them north.

Damona's mule was a quiet, calm beast; as he plodded along, she looked over her shoulder at the line of men and animals coming behind her. The train was a long affair, unwieldy and noisy as the mules protested their loads and the leaving of their familiar pastures. It would take days for order to develop as the routine of travel asserted itself. The pack mules, loaded down with sacks of corn and supplies for the long trek, formed the bulk of the procession. Only the animals ridden by Carbo, his assistants, and Damona carried no loads, save for the large basket hanging from the saddle of Damona's mule.

There were no wagons, as there would have been when the empire was strong; with the crumbling of the roads no wheeled vehicle could hope to survive the pervasive mud and ruts and potholes of the journey, conditions that would grow worse the farther north they ventured. A squadron of Roman cavalry would round out the convoy. Carbo had told Damona the mounted escort would join them when they stopped at at the garrison he was leading them to now.

The people of the town and nearby farms gathered along

the ruined road to watch them pass. Pack trains were a relative novelty at this time of year, but Damona had the sense that there was more to their scrutiny; the eyes of these folk followed her, and from her they kept glancing to the sky, in the direction of moonrise.

She quickly saw the reason: the moon was indeed rising, and at a time of day it did not normally appear. In spite of the afternoon light it filled the eastern sky, glimmering with a light that was softer and yet more persistent than the weak winter sun. The light was pale, as moon white as Damona's hair, but there were streaks of red in that paleness, as distinctive as those which marked her own tresses. Standing by the road the people watched the moon and then her. Their faces were tight and closed; many made the sign of the cross.

The road led past the temple to Isis. Above the white stone and marble the moon hovered, washing the building with silver. A line of people was winding its way toward the sanctuary. Their arms were filled with offerings: baskets of autumn fruit, loaves of bread, and jugs of wine. In the doorway of the temple the woman who had given Damona the basket stood waiting for them. Her voice touched Damona's ears, faint but still sweet and rich, spiraling up in the melody of an ancient prayer.

Low in the sky, above the trees that fringed the river, the moon hung. She was in her full phase and she glowed with an eerie illumination in the sky that was still bright with daylight. The Priestess and the procession of worshippers turned toward the sight. Those in the convoy heard their voices grow louder as they raised them in a chorus of praise. A loud rumbling joined their prayers. In the basket that hung from the saddle of Damona's mule, the Guardian had begun to purr.

The men of the train had become aware of the moon's strangeness, and they were reacting in much the same way as the townsfolk, crossing themselves and staring with set, hard faces at the moon, the temple, and, more surreptitiously, Damona.

Carbo kicked his mule up alongside hers. "This is a bad omen, seeing the moon like this." The trader was muttering, as much to himself as to Damona, his nervous fingers rigorously sketching the sign of the cross along with his men. "It is an evil omen, indeed. Look how the moon rises just above the pagan temple."

"Where is the evil in it?" Damona could not keep from asking. "Could this not be a good omen? A sign of good fortune from the Goddess Whose temple this is?"

Carbo stared at her, his face pale. "You do not understand—"

A furious shout rang out. Directly opposite the orderly line of worshippers a dark-robed man was approaching. His strides were as furious as his voice. In his hand he held a wooden cross upright, brandishing it as fiercely as though it were a sword. He came closer to the temple and the words he was roaring grew audible.

"Blasphemy!" he bellowed. "Heathen evil! God will not allow such practices to continue!"

The folk along the road stirred and muttered. The priest's fury was palpable, its effect like dry tinder kindling to a fire.

"The Evil One has caused the moon of this pagan goddess to rise at this unholy time, so that Her unholy rituals may be performed. She and those who follow Her must be stopped. The true God has decreed that this evil be crushed forever and the heathen temple rededicated to Him."

A ripple went through the people, and one by one they began to take up his cries.

"Yes, there is evil!" a man yelled.

"Look upon them," shouted another. "They are superstitious fools who deny the truth."

"You bring your faithless heresies upon us all!" roared a third.

The procession of Isis worshippers continued their

advance toward the temple, and their chanting did not cease. Many cast blazing eyes on the Christians committing this sacrilege against the Goddess. Others stared straight ahead, refusing to acknowledge the heckling of their own neighbors and kinsmen.

The Priestess kept her place in the doorway of the temple, though her singing had stopped. "You," she said to the priest in her sweet, carrying voice, "are the one who blasphemes in this holy place. You, and these folk you draw along with you in your foolishness."

The priest jerked to a halt. Even with the distance that separated them, Damona could see that he was fairly quivering in rage. Abruptly he stooped down, then jerked upright. In his free hand he was clutching a jagged rock. He was too far away for the missile to reach its target, but in his anger that did not seem to matter: uttering a hoarse cry, he flung it at the priestess.

His action—a resorting to deeds, rather than more words—ignited a new reaction among the people on the road. They rushed toward the worshippers—these folk who were their own neighbors—picked up rocks, and began to throw them.

The mule drivers had been observing the developing conflagration intently and they were just as swift to be caught up in the anger and excitement. They, too, let loose with a chorus of epithets and began snatching up stones.

Damona brought her mule up hard against the trader's mount. There was little, if anything, that she could do about the actions of these townsfolk, but perhaps with Carbo she had some influence; she was after all a paying passenger. "Stop your men," she said loudly and angrily, as both animals shied. "They are committing sacrilege in a holy place!"

The trader returned her glare, his small eyes narrowing on hers. "The sacrilege is not in my drivers; it is in those faithless ones who persist in denying the One True God. I am aware, lady, that you belong to the numbers of those faithless, and perhaps I should pay heed to my men when they whisper that I should send you and that creature you carry with you on your way—"

"Not so long ago," Damona interrupted harshly, "you told me that a wise man takes care not to offend either the old or the new gods. Is this how you earn the goodwill of an ancient goddess, by allowing her temple to be desecrated?"

Carbo refused to answer her directly. "I am an honorable man. I have taken your gold, and I have no wish to return it. And since I do not wish to return it, I must live up to our bargain . . ."

The uproar grew louder, drowning out his voice. A full-scale melee was breaking out between the people of this town. The Goddess worshippers did not subscribe to the passive methods the Christians were known for in their earliest days; they returned anger with anger. They had set down their offerings and were seizing weapons of their own. Stones were flying back and forth, with many now hitting their targets. Pagans and Christians alike were bleeding, and several combatants on both sides were lying unconscious on the ground.

Damona's gaze flew to the Priestess of the temple. Stalwart and small, she had not left her place in the temple entrance. Her arms were raised, not in praise, but in fury. She was shouting, but Damona could not make out her words: perhaps they were to Isis, or mayhap she was cursing the priest who had initiated this sacrilege. The darkness around her small form had grown blacker. It hovered as low as the moon that hung above the tree line, and there was death in it.

"No," Damona whispered. "Not again. Oh, let her be."

In the clamor not even the trader could hear her. Yet Carbo had decided to act regardless of anything she might say. This incident, exciting as it was, was getting out of hand; it was delaying the journey, and anything that delayed the journey affected his profits. Worse, in their eagerness to fling rocks, some of his drivers were getting perilously close to letting their mules loose.

"Enough now, men," the trader yelled. "This does not concern us. Tend to your beasts. We must move on."

The drivers did not hear him, or else they pretended not to. Instead they continued to grab rocks and throw them with even more enthusiasm. A mule suddenly broke loose from its tether. Carbo cursed, kicked his own mule over, and caught up the freed animal's lead rope. "That is *enough*!"

Now the trader was truly angry. Laying about him with his riding whip he struck one driver after another. "Keep hold of those lead ropes," he raged. "I am paying you to drive mules, not throw stones over religion!"

The blows from his whip, more than his anger, had the desired effect. Reluctantly, the men broke off from their part in the melee and started again down the road, tugging the long pack train of mules after them. The townspeople did not appear to notice their departure; they were focused on the actions of the priest. For him, throwing rocks and shouting imprecations was no longer sufficient. From the folds of his robe he had produced flints and set light to a long dry branch. Brandishing the flaming torch he ran toward the temple.

"Abomination!" The screams of the priest shredded the air. Spittle flew from his mouth as he ran, the robe flying about him like black wings. The Christians among the townspeople followed after him, many stopping to light torches of their own.

The Goddess worshippers raced forward to protect their temple and their Priestess. The offerings they had brought lay tumbled on the ground in a welter of spilled fruit and bread, trampled flowers, and smashed jugs, the wine spreading out from the broken pottery pieces like spilled blood. The moon's light glimmered over her gifts, and over the Priestess who had fallen silent, though she still stood, unmoving, in the entrance of the temple.

"Run," Damona screamed, though she knew the Priestess could not hear her, at least not with her mortal ears. "Save yourself."

Holding his torch aloft, the priest reached the temple steps. But this was a building constructed out of stone. It would not burn. Perhaps the Priestess pointed out that very thing, for with an incoherent cry the priest suddenly rushed up the steps, raised the flaming branch high over his head, and struck.

It all happened very swiftly. The Priestess could have avoided the blow, could have slipped aside, for even with the speed of his religious fervor, the priest was clumsy. But she did not. She stood as if she had been waiting all along for this to happen. Her straight figure crumpled under the weight of the torch impacting against her skull, and she fell. Flames curled up in her unbound hair. Still shouting, the priest stooped and held the fiery end of the torch to her white robe.

But his attack upon her had not gone unchallenged. The worshippers of Isis plunged forward, gripped by a fury as white-hot as the robes of their priestess. Their rage overwhelmed the Christian townsfolk. In a matter of moments they had flowed up the temple steps, and beaten the priest, as well as any person who had dared follow him into the temple, unconscious. The remaining Christians slowly drew back, their righteous anger chilled by the sight of the unmoving bodies of the Christian priest and pagan Priestess.

Damona strained to see. Ahead of her the mule convoy was drawing steadily away; trotting at its head, Carbo refused to look back at her. Let her stay here, his stiff posture clearly said. He had given her the chance to do otherwise. Her mule tugged at the reins and sidled in the direction of the pack train, plainly wanting to follow after his companions. She held him back and continued to stare at the temple.

The Isis worshippers had flung the priest's limp body out of their sacred house. He lay on the ground surrounded by his followers. He was not dead, though obviously injured. Weakly his arms and legs were twitching and as Damona watched, the Christians gathered around him slowly began raising him to his feet.

But the Priestess was not moving, and by the attitudes of those who surrounded her Damona knew that she was dead. Now the significance of the Priestess's actions became clear. The small brave woman had given her life to preserve the temple of her goddess. The attack had stopped. The priest was too injured to continue, and the townspeople had lost the heart for battle as quickly as they had gained it.

The great round moon was still hanging low in the sky, but a cloud had drifted across it, obscuring its glimmering light. More clouds were gathering behind it, darkening the sky, turning it bleak as the events that had transpired here this day. What remained of the moon's light had dropped down to hover above the body of the Priestess. The blackness that had hovered about her while she was alive, the precursor of her death, was gone. Moon shimmer kissed her now, enclosing the still form, blessing the Priestess as though the hand of her goddess had touched her.

Damona gave the mule his head. He promptly broke into a jarring trot after the disappearing line of pack mules. For the first time she became aware of the silence in the basket.

The Guardian had stopped purring.

So that is the way of it. Sekhmet's voice burned. *They even dare to attack the sacred house of Isis Herself.*

That should not surprise You, Bast said. *Never have they made a secret of their hatred for the old ways. They cannot allow Us to remain in the mortal world. They are too afraid.*

The lion-headed goddess flung up Her arms in a shower of crimson. *On that much We agree, Sister. This new god must see Us destroyed, if he is to survive.* She eyed the other Goddess with blazing eyes. *We should join forces against him. It is foolish for Us not to. If We were to combine Our powers instead of using them to oppose—*

Bast cut Her off. *Our powers have ever been in opposition. And ever will they be; You know it as well as I.* She was silent a moment, Her enormous eyes looking far beyond the world of mortals. *And it is not the new god who wishes to see Us destroyed. It is his followers.*

Sekhmet snarled, long fangs gleaming. *It matters not to Me whether it is the god or his followers. The result is yet the same. How I despise these Christians. I will instruct My Bau to send doom after doom upon that island she now squats in, and when she is done punishing the faithless there I will bring her to this land . . .*

The Goddess paused and regarded Her Sister with narrowed glittering eyes. *Will You seek to stop Me?* She asked in a low purring growl.

The Cat-Goddess's green eyes stared into the cold distant reaches of Gaul. *She who is My instrument in the mortal world will stop You,* She said. *When the time comes.*

Sekhmet laughed. *You have forgotten Our wager, Sister. The woman will come back to My service. You will see.*

The garrison lay at some distance from the town and its tragic events. It was there that the cohort of mounted soldiers met them, galloping out to the pack train and trotting their horses up and down the ragged line of mules.

Damona studied the men curiously as the officer spoke with Carbo about the upcoming journey. They were the first legionaries she had ever seen, and they were not what she had expected. Tribal torques of silver or bronze glittered over their Roman uniforms. Their hair was long and unbound in the manner of tribesmen, indeed, in the manner of the men of Eire. It flowed to their shoulders in waves of auburn, yellow, or brown, bouncing with every movement of their horses.

"So those are Romans," she said to the cat.

She had removed the lid of the carrying basket, and the Guardian was sitting up peering at the riders with his enigmatic orange gaze. "They are very different from the men who invaded this land with Caesar. The Romans of that time were small men, and dark. They thought the people of Gaul were giants. Now there has been so much intermingling of blood it's hard to tell the difference between the two."

He fell silent, and Damona quickly saw why. Carbo and the officer had concluded their conversation, and the signal to move on had been given.

As the procession slowly settled into the routine of travel, Carbo led it toward its first destination: Trier, the city that had once been the Roman capital of Gaul. It was a detour from the route north, but a necessary one. There were a number of mules carrying empty pack-saddles; Carbo planned to load them with corn the transportation of which he had already arranged for.

Once Trier had been a vital metropolis, bustling with trade and the energy of being a center of Christianity in Gaul. In 313, a year after his conversion, Emperor Constantine had issued the Edict of Toleration for Christian worship. As a further adjunct of his Edict, Constantine and his family had officially encouraged and funded the building of churches. In Trier, that encouragement had borne fruit in a most spectacular way.

The imperial capital of Gaul had been the obvious choice for building a sanctuary that would comprise the center of the Gallic Church. Artisans and builders had set to work to build a cathedral, laboring with a holy zeal, matched only by the generous funding provided them by the Edict. The cathedral was meant to hold a large congregation, resembling the huge basilicas constructed by Constantine himself in Rome. But the designers in Trier had not stopped with one church. Eventually, a second, equally mighty, church had risen beside its sister.

However, much had changed since those glorious days. Quite suddenly the light had been snuffed out. The seat of government had shifted from Trier to Arles, taking with it all the influence, wealth, and patronage that went along with the status of being a capital. The barbarians had pierced the Rhine frontier in the winter of 401 and the Franks had attacked the unfortunate city four times in thirty-four years. Roman order had collapsed; so too had fallen the new apparatus of organized Christianity.

Many had died in the once-powerful capital. Many more had fled. Trier could no longer be considered a city; these days it was more of a town. But in the bleak and unsettled landscape of Gaul, there were few large towns, and those that existed functioned as all there was of government. Trier, despite its fall, still contained craftsmen selling their wares. It was still a center of trade for merchants such as Carbo, though it shone with only a shadow of its former glitter.

Into the remnants of this once-bustling city the trader caravan plodded. On their arrival at the corn warehouses, the drivers and soldiers fed and watered their animals, then scattered to indulge themselves in the last taverns they were likely to see for many leagues. While Carbo tended to his business, and the men to theirs, Damona, too, explored the erstwhile imperial capital. Attended by the Guardian, she walked about the city, wandering through the narrow streets. They soon came upon the centerpieces of Trier: the twin cathedrals.

The two enormous buildings stood side by side, occupying almost two blocks within the grid of crowded streets. Both were beautiful, of basilica shape with long naves and aisles and atriums at each end. Magnificent fresco portraits adorned the walls. Many were of women, for Helena, Constantine's mother, had donated part of the imperial palace as a site for the cathedral.

Each of the two churches had its separate function. A baptistery lay between them. The southern basilica was for newly converted Christians preparing for baptism. Once they passed through the baptistery they were then welcomed into the northern church, which was reserved for fully baptized believers. Regardless of whether one entered the northern or southern half of this double cathedral, though, one would find it crowded. The city might have shrunk to a fraction of its former size, but the Christian faithful had not. Many lived in Trier, to be near the great churches, and more and more converts were joining them every day.

Yet, unlike so many other places, including the town from

which the pack train had come, the burgeoning new religion seemed to be coexisting in an odd sort of peace with the older faith that had been woven through the fabric of life in Gaul for so long. Temples to the old gods still stood in the city, their graceful edifices of marble and stone brightening the dull winter sky. Yet even they had taken the place of far earlier deities. There were layers upon layers in this country, and over the centuries of Roman occupation, the Celtic Shining Ones and the Roman gods had slowly and steadily intertwined.

But it was an uneasy truce at best. Worshippers continued to make offerings and pray in the old temples, but there were fewer of them. There were other signs as well. As Damona and the Guardian walked past, they saw gaps in the proud temple faces, stark holes where blocks of stone or marble had been ripped out, stolen, in order to be put to use in some church.

When they paused before the cathedrals, Damona regarded them in frowning wonder. Never had she seen such structures. They were astounding; yet her eye did not find them beautiful. They were too big, too enclosed, like giant cages, she involuntarily thought.

As Damona stared at the churches, the cat studied the massive buildings with his enigmatic orange gaze. "It's a long way these Christians have come," he observed. "In this very city they were once thought of as cannibals and rapists of their own children. The Romans had them tortured and killed in that amphitheater we passed, while the local people cheered in approval. Most of them were not Christian, you see. Christianity was a religion of foreigners then, mostly Greeks and half-Greeks."

He broke off as several women walked past on their way inside. When they were safely out of earshot he glanced around. "There is probably a shrine somewhere about that venerates a slave woman called Blandina. She was sent into the arena with others of her faith to be torn apart by wild beasts, but the animals would not touch her."

Damona continued to stare at the double cathedral. The enormous shapes blotted out the sun and sky, separating both those outside and inside from the light and air of the world, and of the Shining Ones. She wondered if any of the people crowded within those walls or hurrying past to get inside ever felt that separation, and if they did, if it mattered to them at all. "Did the Romans free her?" she asked at last.

"They did not. Clemency in such matters has never been a Roman trait. They sent her into the arena again. This time, the animals killed her."

Damona looked from the massive buildings back to the cat. "You know a great deal about a religion that is not yours."

"I," the Guardian answered serenely, "know a great deal about everything. However, knowing about this subject is particularly important."

A large crowd of worshippers started coming out of the northernmost of the two churches. Men and women walked together, smiling distantly, their faces serious and transfigured. Damona watched them uneasily. "Tell me, Guardian," she said. "Why is it so important to know about them?"

The cat leaped off his perch. "Because," he said over his shoulder, "one day these Christians will rule the world."

14

CARBO CONCLUDED HIS BUSINESS quickly. So far he had been lucky; the gods had smiled on him: they had traveled down the river safely, obtained mules and the rest of the corn, and no major storms had struck as yet. But there was little time to waste. Trier was an attractive place, particularly with winter coming on. They would have to be on their way quickly, before some of his drivers decided to desert him permanently for the city's comforts. With that in mind, he soon had the long caravan of mules and its escort of soldiers plodding out of Trier as steadily as it had plodded in.

From that point on the days settled into a sameness that never seemed to vary. Dawn would find the camp already stirring, the breath of men and beasts steaming white in the frigid air. Throughout the day they would travel under overcast skies, jolting over crumbling roads, forging their own paths in places where the roads had vanished completely. Only when the last of the dull light had begun to fade would they halt to make yet another bleak cold camp. It seemed that they went to sleep in bone-chilling cold and darkness and awoke to the same. Storms provided the lone break in routine, and no one looked forward to the change. When the winds howled and snow twisted sideways, Carbo and the members of his train had no choice but to huddle in whatever shelter they could find and wait for the storm's fury to blow itself out.

Gradually, in spite of the delays caused by weather, they

inched their way north. The frontier drew steadily closer and the country more desolate and rugged and cold. Immense forests frowned down at the travelers, some of the trees stripped bare of leaves, their naked limbs as stiff as the limbs of the dead, others green with needles and layered with snow. Every stream they came upon now was frozen, forcing the men to chop ice and melt it every morning and evening for the needs of themselves and the animals.

In the dark and cold of a dawn like so many others, Damona suddenly started into wakefulness, jerking up in her furs.

The Guardian was sitting beside her; his tapping at her face with his paw had awakened her. "Get up," he said softly, "and come with me."

Damona looked about her. The encampment was still wrapped in sleep and darkness, its silence broken only by someone's snoring and the occasional stamp of a dozing animal. "It's not even first light yet," she whispered.

The cat flowed to his feet. "It will be by the time we get there," he said. "Now come, before the others wake."

Damona sighed, rising to her feet with considerably less grace than had her companion. The air was chill, speaking to her of winter and yet another day of bad weather. She snatched up one of the furs and bundled it about her shoulders as she set off after the cat's sleek form.

Woman and cat walked in silence, their breath steaming in the frosty predawn. Eventually, the camp was left far behind them, and still they continued on. With steadily increasing impatience Damona followed in the steps of her feline guide. He paced ahead of her, his tail held straight up, signaling her on like a banner, as the night darkness slowly grayed into dawn. She was about to speak, to ask how long he intended leading her on this interminable journey, when the cat came to a halt.

"Here we are," he said, and sat down, curling his tail about his paws in his familiar gesture.

Damona looked beyond him. Just ahead stood a small church. It had been crudely constructed out of blocks of stone, and its rough outlines were slowly beginning to clarify themselves in the morning mists. Next to the church was a larger edifice, or what remained of it. Whatever it had been, it was ruins now; the stones used to build the church had been taken from it.

"All I see is yet another stone house belonging to the Christians," she said irritably. "For this, you insisted that I leave my bed and go marching about in the cold and dark long before dawn?"

The cat extended a hind leg, licked at it fiercely, and flicked his tail. "Believe me, furless one, traipsing through wet icy grass is not something I would do, unless there were a reason. Stop complaining and look beyond the obvious."

Damona started to retort, then fell silent. "A place to the old gods is here," she said at length. "But why bring me out to show me this? Such places exist all through Gaul."

"Not like this one." The Guardian turned his gaze from the church and its accompanying ruins to Damona's face. "What lies here is a temple to my Mistress. The only temple to Her that was ever built in this part of the world."

"By my foremother?" Damona stared at the crumbling structure with new eyes. "The histories of our *fine* do not mention it."

"That is because it was not built in Veleda's time. Others who came to this land long after she had left it for Eire erected this House to the Lady Bast. The people who worshipped Her here were originally from Kemet, though by then, as almost everyone else in the world did, they thought of themselves as Roman. Still, they kept faith with my Mistress, and they were even joined by descendants of Veleda's tribe, who remembered the old stories."

The cat made an odd little sound in his throat. "It was a small temple," he added sadly. "Nothing at all like the great temple that once stood to Her in the holy city of Bubastis:

Her city. But this was a holy place nevertheless, dedicated to Her and Her alone."

"And now it lies in ruins." Damona drew in on herself, pulling the wolf skin closer. A great wave of sadness washed over her. She felt immersed in grief. Perhaps it came from the Guardian, or perhaps it came from far beyond him: from not only Bast, but all the old gods and goddesses whose sacred places lay abandoned, falling into ruin, their holy stones robbed to build new churches to a new god. She shivered, despite the warmth of the soft fur. "Why have you brought me here? What does this place want of me?"

"You know the answer to that." The cat's stare was unwavering. "Go into what is left of Bast's temple. I will wait for you here."

Damona's trepidation grew. "Why? If the Goddess wishes to punish me, must I enter these ancient ruins for Her to do so?"

The Guardian turned away without answering. "Go," was all he said.

Damona stood for a moment. Was this how it was to end, then? Had the Guardian brought her all this way, from Eire to Gaul, so Bast could mete out Her anger in the ruins of Her forgotten temple? In truth, there was justice in such a plan; it held a certain roundness that was fitting considering Damona's own deeds. And what if retribution was not the Goddess's intent? Damona no longer possessed the power to divine that either.

The cat was still not looking at her. Damona squared her shoulders and left him. She started off in the direction of the temple. Whatever the Goddess intended, did it truly matter?

As she walked toward the temple she saw that she was no longer alone. From out of the woods and along the crumbling Roman road, people were beginning to appear. Men walked together, young warriors adjusting their long strides to the slower steps of white-haired elders. Clusters of women followed along behind, many of them with children in tow. Damona drew a quick breath. For a single instant it seemed that all these folk were coming to the temple of Bast.

But of course they were not. Their destination was the small church built out of purloined stones. A man garbed in a coarse dark brown woolen tunic suddenly appeared in the doorway. A broad smile of welcome wreathed his beardless features. He stretched out his hands as the first of the people arrived, going forward to move among them with softly murmured words of greeting.

Anger stirred within Damona as the Christians assembled. It was not enough for them to plant their churches so that they sprang up all over the landscape like weeds in an untended cornfield. No, they could not be content with such victory, but must engage in the added indignity of using these ancient places of worship for their own ends. Was it fear that drove the Christian leaders so relentlessly that they could not abide any trace of the old gods to survive? Oh, it was a bitter thing to see this. Whether or not Bast's anger awaited her in the abandoned temple, this was still the Goddess's place, and these Christians had robbed Her of it.

Caught up in her growing anger Damona quickened her pace. The people gathered before the church turned to watch her approach. Some stared at her with curiosity, eyeing the white hair streaked with red that streamed about her shoulders. Others looked at her with hostility, wary of this stranger and her sudden appearance among them.

Damona paid no heed to their scrutiny, pausing in her steady strides only when the darkly garbed man stepped forward to block her way. He was young, younger than she, but he carried himself with an air of authority that verged on arrogance. A heavy cross suspended on a thick silver chain dangled to his waist; plainly, he was the priest of this Christian place.

"Have you come to pray with us?" The tone in which the young man asked this question robbed it of politeness.

Damona regarded him until the priest dropped his eyes. "I have come to show reverence," she said.

"Ah." The priest looked up, his expression lightening. "Then enter, sister. We are about to begin morning devotions."

"I will not." Damona's voice was even. "I have not come to show reverence to your god, but to mine."

The priest drew back. "You are a heathen." Behind him people muttered, their faces tightening with anger.

Damona did not move. "Perhaps," she said softly, "it is you who are the heathen."

"You dare"—the young priest's features turned bright red—"this is a holy place!"

"Indeed." Damona's eyes looked beyond him, fixing on the temple ruins. "And it was holy long before you desecrated it to build this house to your god with blocks of stolen stone."

A ripple went through the assembly. "You speak of stone?" a man shouted. "There are stones here in plenty, woman. Stay, and I will show you some."

A rock whistled past Damona's ear. Other people yelled and stooped to the ground to snatch up missiles of their own. It was as if she had stepped back in time to the day Carbo's train had left the town along the river. The faces of these people were the same, the mood just as contagious, a dark fever that spread as rapidly as a fire in dry grass.

Still, though she knew what was coming, she did not move. This, then, was the punishment awaiting her. There was no point in seeking to avoid it. From somewhere a thought whispered in her mind that the Priestess at the temple of Isis was surely not being punished when she sacrificed herself to protect the house of her goddess. She pushed the realization aside. The life paths of herself and that small dark Priestess were all too different—

"Hold," a woman's voice shouted.

Hands that had been raised with jagged stones froze in midair. People fell utterly silent. The priest stepped forward.

"My lady," he said, his eyes going past Damona. "I bid you welcome in the name of our Lord, and I most humbly apologize for the sacrilege that has met your eyes."

Slowly Damona turned her head. Horses were stamping and blowing behind her. A party of riders had arrived. A woman was in the lead. From the deference with which her companions flanked her it was clear that it was she who had spoken. She was noble; her clothing and her jewels proclaimed it. She was also heavily with child.

As the woman dismounted, two of the female attendants hastily scrambled from their own horses to assist her. She was clumsy with the burden of her great belly, but beautiful in her fecundity. The ripeness and promise of life strained at the folds of her richly embroidered gown, and Damona felt a churning pain in her own belly at the sight.

My children, she cried out in her soul. She turned abruptly away.

The royal newcomer's dark eyes followed her curiously. "What is amiss here?" The question was for the priest, though her eyes remained on Damona. Her voice was low and sweet, but it spoke of her expectation that she be obeyed.

"This woman seeks to profane our church," the priest said instantly. "She came out of nowhere spouting at me about heathen ways."

The newcomer looked at Damona. "Is this true?"

"Who can say?" Damona smiled a slight cold smile. "Blasphemy and truth are peculiar words. Their definition often depends on one's beliefs."

The woman studied her. "Be you a Druid?" she demanded suddenly.

Damona returned her gaze in some surprise. She hesitated, not sure what to say. "I was," she said at length. "But no more."

The priest leaped in. "Ah, then you have seen that to follow the old paths is wrong. You understand the strength of our Lord—"

The woman went on, cutting off the eager young priest as if he had not spoken. "I thought you were a Druid. For certain you speak like one. I am Clotilde, wife to Chlodweg. Know you who he is?"

Damona shook her head. "No, lady, I do not. Though it requires no Druid-sight to see that you are of noble blood."

"My husband is king of the Franks." Clotilde's tone was strangely neutral as she pronounced this. "He rules over a great kingdom, much of it taken through force of arms. The Franks are a people who much love their wars, and they are exceedingly good at fighting them, as well as at winning them."

"And you, lady," Damona asked. "Are you not a Frank?"

She was surprised again at the look Clotilde gave her: sharp, disdainful, burning with a deep and ill-concealed anger. "I am a Burgundian," she said. "The daughter of a king in my own right. I was given in marriage to Chlodweg by my father, and I honor my vows, as wife, and both as blood daughter and a faithful daughter of the Church of the true faith." She laid her hands protectively over her belly as she spoke.

The priest nodded in approval. "You honor your vows, indeed, my Queen. Unlike your husband and his nobles, who choose to follow heresy."

"It would seem," Damona said dryly, "that the gods you name as heresy have done very well by the king of the Franks."

The priest bristled, but Queen Clotilde raised an imperious hand. "Let us begin the mass, good brother. And you, stranger," she added to Damona, "you who were once a Druid but are no longer. Go to the place of your old gods. No one will interfere with you."

The priest stared. "Lady," he began indignantly, "you cannot do this; surely you see that. In allowing this woman to engage in heathenish practices you invite sin upon your own head, as well as hers."

The queen stared back at him, then let her gaze travel over

the crowd of worshippers. Many of them still held rocks in their lowered hands. "And is it any less of a sin to throw stones at a stranger who has come seeking no more than a moment with the old gods?"

The people looked away. Some glanced at the stones they held as if surprised to find them there and dropped the jagged weapons back to the ground. Others continued to grip their stones, watching the priest for his reaction.

"This is ill done of you, lady," the priest insisted, his young face filled with earnestness and anger. "We must turn our faces from the lure of false gods. In countenancing a pagan ritual you encourage the people to follow this woman, to slide from the light of our Savior back into the darkness. This is not the way of a Christian, lady—"

"And is it not our way to bring new converts into the fold of our Lord by gentle means?" the queen asked. "The Lord Jesus did not win followers by heaving stones at them; he succeeded by love and the offering of compassion." The queen's eyes were small and dark, yet they glowed with a serenity that made them beautiful. "God is all-powerful. I doubt it will distress Him if this woman shares a moment with her gods."

"Her gods do not exist!"

"Let her discover that for herself. Then she will come to the truth of her own will." Clothilde motioned at Damona. "Go. We will not harm you." She paused. "We will see each other again?"

It was phrased as a question, but meant as a statement. Damona regarded her. "I have told you, lady, I am no longer a Druid. I have no abilities to answer that."

The queen nodded. "We will," she said with assurance.

Damona inclined her head so deeply it was almost a bow. It was a gesture of respect, and one that was easily given; this woman was deserving of respect. But as she continued on toward the temple ruins she found herself reflecting on the grim thought that harm from Clotilde and her Christians was not what she should be concerned with.

The stones of the fallen temple reared up at the overcast sky, clutching at the clouds as though they were memories seeking to resurrect themselves. The power of the ancient place surged out to touch Damona before she reached the first boundary, a ring of broken marble blocks that had once formed a wall, or perhaps, a courtyard. She swayed, waiting for the voice of Bast, preparing herself for the terrible blow that only an angry goddess could deliver.

There was nothing; only the sighing of the wind through gaping stones and marble, and farther off in the distance, the voices of the Christians as they began entering the church. She wanted to be away from them, away from their voices, and from their sight. She crossed the ring of blocks and entered what must have been the sanctuary itself. Here the stones were taller, hiding her from view.

Abruptly she staggered to a halt. The cold and cloudy day dimmed before her eyes, and then re-formed itself with a burning clarity that stung her eyes. Suddenly the church and the ruins of the pagan temple that lay beyond were gone. In their place stood a building that was flame-bright, as white as the fiercest heart of a great fire. It blazed at her, glowing even brighter by the land that surrounded it.

Damona stared with blinded eyes at a land she had never seen, not even in dreams.

It was a land that was harsh and golden, utterly devoid of the lush thick forests and murmuring rivers that were Eire, that beautiful island that formed a part of her soul. A vast sky gleamed down like an unending sheet of bronze, all the rich blue leached out of it by a merciless sun. Cliffs of red stone rose into the colorless sky, glittering as dark and crimson as blood.

Heat engulfed Damona. It swallowed her up from head to toe. She almost fainted with the intensity of it. Sweat streamed into her eyes, stinging them, although everywhere else on her body, the terrible sun was drying every drop of moisture the instant it sprang up. She wanted to crouch and fling her arms up over her head, to hide from those rays that were pounding at her like the blows from a sword. But she was held in place by whatever power had brought her here. She could see and feel, but she could not move. Only her eyes had the power to travel, and it was her eyes that brought her sights.

Now Damona saw people. They were not the people of Eire, Gaul, or any other land she was familiar with. These were a small and dark-skinned folk. Their flesh was brown, deep and rich, its color set off even more by their clothing. In the heat of this land, men and women alike obviously wore very little. Thin white garments were draped around their hips and amulets swung about virtually every neck. Their hair was black as ebony: the men's was cut short, while the women wore theirs in long and gleaming plaits and curls. They were passing in and out of the flame white building, carrying offerings. The people neither laughed nor smiled as they walked. Their faces were set and stern, and the air of worry that clung to them was as palpable as the heat.

This was a temple, Damona realized, a temple such as the Romans and Greeks had built to their old gods before Christianity came sweeping over their lands. The moment the thought struck her she could suddenly see inside the structure. Her sun-blasted gaze followed the worshippers to their destination, to an inner courtyard, where a group of men waited to receive the supplicants.

These men were draped in spotless white robes, beardless, and with skulls shaven so smooth they gleamed like polished wood. A former priestess herself, Damona identified them at once. The hairless men were priests, charged with the overseeing of this place, as she had once been dedicated to taking care of the shrine to Bast. Was this flame-bright structure crowded with these dark people and their offerings a temple to the Cat-Goddess? Was she glimpsing a vision of how things had been in Kemet, the land of the Goddess's birth? Yet she had always been told that women in the land of Egypt had ever served Bast.

As grave and unsmiling as the worshippers, the shaven-headed priests accepted the gifts being brought to them. As soon as the offerings were taken the people stood back, gathering in the courtyard until its wide spaces were filled. Carved doorways inlaid in gold and silver beckoned into the darkness of the temple's inner recesses, but the people were apparently not allowed to enter through those doors. That privilege belonged only to the priests. In a silent procession they proceeded, their arms laden down with baskets of fruit and bread, jars of beer, and haunches of meat. Bleating goats and sheep almost certainly destined for sacrifice were tugged along on tethers.

Damona's burning eyes followed them. They were chanting, their voices rising in a tongue as unfamiliar as the temple itself. The melody was strangely beautiful, its cadence rhythmic and haunting. After the fury of the sun and the white and golden land, the darkness of the inner sanctuary was as blinding as death. Lamps gleamed inside, but they did little to relieve the shadows, enhancing rather than relieving them.

So you have come.

The voice hissed at Damona. It was wide and powerful, filling her ears. Then she saw the statue at the heart of the temple. Before her stood the lion-headed goddess Herself: an exact likeness carved out of pure gold. She towered to the very ceiling, every wrinkle in Her snarling mouth and each fold of Her clinging dress executed in perfect gleaming detail. Her fangs were as long as spears. In one enormous hand She grasped a fistful of arrows, each of which was as tall as a man. Her presence shattered the dimness of the inner sanctuary, drawing into itself every scrap of flickering lamplight until She burned as fiercely as the sun outside.

Yes, this is My temple, although it is only one of them. And this is My land, the land from which I sprang long before the history of your people ever began. I am strong here, Priestess. Stronger than you can imagine.

Damona still could not move. She discovered now that

neither could she speak. The only ability left to her was her sight, and the gleaming fangs of Sekhmet's bared golden jaws seared through her eyes and stabbed downward to her heart.

The immense voice rocked the sanctuary, falling into a purr as earthshaking as thunder, though surely thunder and the rain that came with it had never touched this arid burning land. *Feel My strength, Priestess. See My power. Know that you may share in all of it, if you come back to My service. Watch.*

The priests were laying the food offerings on the huge altar at the feet of the statue, arranging the baskets and jars with precise attention and care. Their chanting continued unceasingly. They were priests, dedicated to Sekhmet, and yet they appeared to have no awareness of Damona's presence inside the inner sanctuary of their Goddess.

They know. The Goddess seemed to laugh. *But it does not matter. They are my servants. They will question nothing. They would not dare.*

Acolytes—boys dressed in white, their tender young skulls newly shaved—were leading the sacrifices up to the altar. The oldest of the priests had picked up a knife, also of gold, even down to its glittering curved blade. The chanting intensified as he drew the knife across the throat of a white goat. Another priest stood by, catching the blood in a golden bowl so large he had to hold it with both hands.

To Damona, it was a familiar sight, even in this distant alien land. How many times had she watched similar scenes take place? The number was beyond counting. The only difference was the language and the surroundings, and the overwhelming sense of the lion-headed goddess.

Memories flamed through her, scorching her with a yearning as fierce as Sekhmet's gaze. But the memories were not what she missed; floating in this space between worlds, she acknowledged it. It was the power. She wanted to be standing among the priests watching the sacred blood flow into a shining bowl. She wanted to wield the sacrificial knife, to be warmed and embraced by the ceaseless flow of power. In that moment, she wanted it more than anything, more than goodness or mercy, or even the return of herself.

The chanting went on. Even in the words of this unknown tongue a deep note of supplication throbbed through the singers' melodic voices. The sacrifices piled up, the bodies of the animals resting in carefully arranged positions beside the baskets of offerings. Terror washed through the sanctuary, borne heavily on the scent of fresh blood. Those creatures whose turn had not yet come wailed at the sights and sounds and smells of death, and struggled frantically to escape from the acolytes who gripped their tethers.

Without warning the voice of Sekhmet roared through the sanctuary. Damona was not the only one to hear Her. Each word pounded at the priests. In a single movement they all flung their bodies down, prostrating themselves before the golden statue, raising their hands palms up in gestures of supplication and pleading. As the acolytes threw themselves down, several of the goats tugged free from the tethers and ran from the sanctuary in a flurry of bleating, their little hooves rattling on the golden floor. From outside the shrine hundreds of voices rose in a chorus of horrified cries. Plainly, it was a terrible omen that the sacrificial animals were escaping. It could only signify that the Goddess had not accepted them.

In confirmation of this, Sekhmet's words blasted Her priests. *The sacrifices are not enough,* She roared. *Is this how you worship your Goddess, with these paltry displays of devotion? I am not pleased. By the Seven Arrows of My Power you will now see the proof of My displeasure.*

No sooner had the words thundered through the chamber than the lights went out. Every lamp was suddenly and utterly extinguished as abruptly as if giant hands had clamped down over all their flames at once. The resulting darkness was complete. And yet, Damona could still see. She saw the fear on the faces of the priests. They knew, if she did not, what was coming, and the force of their despair drenched her as thoroughly as the darkness. As swiftly as it had come upon her, the desire to be part of this unknown ceremony and all its power left her. She was cold, shivering deep in her bones, in spite of this land's fiery heat.

"Lady," the eldest of the priests called in a deep quavering voice, "we have honored You as always. Spare us Your anger. Tell us what we may do to appease You—"

The roaring answer thundered over his weak mortal words. *In only one way may you appease Me. And you, priest, know what that is.*"

The giant statue seemed then to come to life. Rays of light burst up, tinted with crimson, shimmering all around the golden form. In that lurid glimmer the arrows Sekhmet clenched in one mighty hand appeared to be dripping with blood. To Damona it seemed that the hand holding the arrows was moving.

The priests apparently had the same thought, or else they knew for certain that the hand was indeed moving. The old man cried out again, and this time, his brethren joined him.

Another sound shattered through the temple, drowning out the voices of the priests. It shuddered along Damona's nerve endings, a screeching grinding noise, as if metal were moving in ways its makers had never intended.

Paying no heed to the desperate pleas of Her priests, the enormous arm of the statue slowly lifted. The shimmering fingers tensed themselves and then opened. Like a cluster of birds exploding from their cage, the arrows shot forth. Glittering as bright and bloody as the fingers that had released them, they sped through the doors of the great chamber and in the outer courtyard. Screams erupted, and though Damona could not see it, she knew that a wholesale panic was ensuing.

The eldest priest lifted his face, and Damona saw despair etched in the aged brown skin. Pity seared her: for him, as well as the terrorized people trying to flee whatever awful fate the Goddess had sent after them.

You need waste no pity on them. Sekhmet's voice was

thick and scornful. *Better to pity your own people, or even more wisely, yourself, if you do not heed My warning. I have shown you My beauty and My strength. Remember them. But remember even more, the sight of My anger . . .*

All at once there was silence. In the wake of that silence came a rushing cold. As intensely as the heat had suffused Damona's every sense, this drop in temperature now chilled her in every pore. Blackness shivered before her gaze, clouding and obscuring everything about her. Now she could see nothing. The darkened temple with the golden statue as its sole source of light was gone. So was the parched land in its searing cloak of heat, and the brown-skinned people running in hopeless panic. Damona herself wavered, caught up in a vast and distant darkness.

"Priestess," a voice said.

15

THE LIGHT VOICE CALLED DAMONA by her old title once again. Its tone was quiet and gentle.

Blindly she turned in the direction the voice had come from. Light seared her eyes again, but it was the seeing she felt, and not the heat. This was a different sort of illumination, soft and diffused, familiar to one who had grown up in the damp mistiness of Eire. Shapes sprang into focus around her. Slowly she became aware that she was lying on her side. Above her she saw the ruins of Bast's temple. The Guardian was perched comfortably on one of the large broken stones. His sleek fur was fluffed against the cold, and his front paws were tucked neatly against his chest.

The great orange eyes were scrutinizing her, and whatever he saw must have satisfied him, for a purr suddenly vibrated in his chest. "She misjudged you," he said, sounding sober and pleased at once. "It was foolish of Her."

Damona stared at him. "What do you mean?"

"She sought to draw you back to Her by showing you Her power, but She grew greedy. Sekhmet has never possessed a great deal of self-control in such matters."

Damona struggled shakily to her knees. "You said this was Bast's temple. Where was She then? Why would She allow Sekhmet to come into a place where She had power, or once did?"

If a cat could frown, the Guardian did so. His eyes narrowed, his whiskers drew downward, and his ears flattened. "My Mistress did not share that with me," he said. "But doubtless She had Her reasons. And so did Sekhmet. She wanted to show you yet another of Her faces."

"I," Damona informed him with weary anger, "have seen enough of Her faces. I have no need or desire to see more."

This was not quite the truth, and she sensed that the Guardian knew it. Shame burned through her, its touch as flame-bright as the heat of Kemet. The heartbeat of temptation she had felt during the ceremony was gone, but not the feelings that had aroused it. She had not gone back to Sekhmet, but oh, for that brief terrible instant, how she had wanted to!

She sensed rather than heard the voice of Bast. It rippled across her consciousness, as distant as the days when this temple had stood in all its beauty and She had been worshipped within its walls. There was strength in it, and ageless wisdom, yet the voice was so soft she could not make out words. Instead she heard the cat's light dry tones.

"Fortunately, She let Herself get carried away. She always does. Her excess kept you from Her. This time." The cat regarded her with his enigmatic gaze. "There is wood scattered about, and it has been cold as a slaughterers's heart waiting for you. I would appreciate a small fire while we talk."

Belatedly Damona realized that she, too, was trembling with cold. She pushed herself to her feet and began to gather up sticks and small branches, tugging them free from their bed of snow. It was a relief to move, to occupy her attention with a task so mundane, so familiar. "You said 'this time,' " she reminded the cat as she dumped an armful of wood near the stone where he had ensconced himself. "Am I, or is any other mortal, so worthy of another effort?"

The Guardian uncurled one of his front paws and gave it a few licks. "Sekhmet failed, but do not underestimate Her strength or Her determination. During the time of the Eternal Nile, many mortals with powers greater than yours, furless one, have bowed to Her will."

It was the first time he had called her "furless one" since

he had come back to her. Damona felt a small warmth kindle within her. She looked at him, wanting to say something, and in the end, saying nothing.

She set to work laying the fire. "Is what I saw"—she shuddered—"is that how it is in Her land?" She shuddered again, the memories of that burning land and the people's fear searing over her in one great wave.

The Guardian sighed. "No longer. But once, in the days of the Pharaohs, it was so. Sekhmet was a powerful goddess, worshipped and feared in equal measure. What She showed you was a scene from Her own memory, of a time crumbling into dust long before the birth of your foremother Veleda. The new religion now rules where Her temples once stood. The same, of course, is true for the temples of my own mistress."

"Why is She doing all of this?" Damona suddenly burst out. "Why is it so important for Her to have me? In truth, if She is so powerful, there must be a host of mortals, any one of whom would serve Her far better than I."

The cat was silent for so long she thought he was not going to answer her. At last, he spoke. "There are," he said softly, "no other mortals who are of your line. There are no others who continue to worship Bast in the ways of the Mothers. You are all that is left. And Sekhmet wants you for Herself. It would be a great triumph for Her to take you from Her Sister. She has always coveted the devotion of Veleda's daughters."

"Well, I cannot give that to her!" Damona's cry was ragged, torn from the very depths of her soul. She needed no reminders of the fact that those who would have come after her were gone.

"Ah, but you can." The cat's orange eyes were steady and bright. "You are young enough so that your days of child-bearing are not yet done. If you turn from Bast and embrace the ways of Sekhmet, you will start a new line of Priestesses, of women who are dedicated to Her ways: the ways of blood and darkness."

Damona looked away from the Guardian's steady gaze. "I have not turned from Bast," she muttered. "The Goddess has turned from me."

The fire flared into life as though to confirm her words. Small and bright, the flames licked eagerly at the dry cold wood; a tendril of heat flickered out into the cold, then another. The cat leaped off the stone. Fastidiously, he flicked his paws free of clinging snow as he settled himself against Damona and the warmth of her wolf skin.

"So long as you believe that," he said briskly, "Sekhmet still has a chance with you. And She knows it. But there is a way to stop Her, and now is the time to tell you of it."

The fire sent up curls of smoke, twisting along with their breath in the icy air. Damona fed a few small sticks to the flames. "I am listening."

"Magic," answered the cat briefly. "Very old and very powerful. If we find it, it will free you from Sekhmet."

Damona considered this. "There are all sorts of magic." She eyed the Guardian, and her next question was sharp. "Is this a magic of the physical realm or the realms of the mind?"

"Both. The strongest forms of magic always are." The cat twisted around, making himself more comfortable, moving closer to the fire. He stretched, yawned, and resettled himself. "This particular magic was given to Veleda, the foremother of your line, by my Mistress. They are wands, and contained in them lies the power of healing and transformation and rebirth and the finding of one's strength. A great tool, if they can be recovered."

"I know of them." The tone in which Damona reminded him was sad and bitter. "I may no longer have power, Guardian, but I have memory."

"Indeed." The Guardian's orange eyes stared into the flames. "They were lost in a great battle. Mud and snow and blood buried them far beyond the sight of mortals." The cat turned his brilliant eyes from the fire to Damona's face. Their orange depths burned at her, more piercing than the flames. "Veleda did not need the wands of Bast again. But, you, furless one, do. Therefore, we must go back to the place where she last had them."

"The sacred place which she and her people defended against the Romans."

"Yes, but it is a sacred place no longer. Once it was called the Nemeton of the Circles. Veleda's people worshipped their gods there. It survived the battle they fought against Caesar. Indeed, it survived the Romans' turning of this land into part of Gaul. What it could not survive was Christianity."

"Ah." Damona's exclamation was pointed and dark. "It seems that the Christians can allow not a single shrine or even a tree dedicated to the old ways to live or be remembered. In the present of Gaul lies the future of what will sweep over Eire, and it does not require a Druid or a *Banfhili* to see it. It is a grievous thing, Guardian, a grievous thing, indeed."

"We have more immediate problems," the cat said grimly. "The wands of Bast must be found, and that will be no easy task. The Nemeton of Circles will have been changed beyond my recognition. The spot where Veleda dropped them could be a barley field or someone's house or—"

"A church," Damona finished for him, her face set.

"Perhaps," the cat agreed, and flicked an ear as ash spiraled up from the fire. "We will not know until we arrive there."

"Well, I have no powers that will help find it," Damona told him. "But if it is the will of Bast that Her wands be recovered, will She not help us?"

The Guardian regarded her silently for a moment. "It is also the will of Sekhmet that they not be found."

He looked at the fire, then back at her. "Ever."

Sekhmet was incandescent with fury. The flames that burned at the source of Her power towered about Her, roaring in scarlet-tinted echo of Her anger. Here in the place where Her Sister had once been worshipped, She had planned the moment of Her triumph. The woman would have come back to Her. She *should* have come back to Her. Sekhmet had seen the desire in her. She had held the woman in the palm of Her great hand. And then, She had lost Her.

The One at Whom that rage was directed watched, unimpressed. *You owe Me,* She said calmly. *We made a bargain. You lost.*

I will honor it, the Goddess snarled, her long fingers curling like claws. *But the wager itself is still in place. I do not have her, but neither do You. Her heart is not Yours. She wavered once. She will waver again. When she does, I will have her, and Your wands will make no difference.*

Bast's long green eyes were cold. *Regardless, You will do as You bound Yourself to.*

I will. Sekhmet's reply was a thunderous growl. *But, in the future You will find Me more subtle.*

Squatting in Muirchertac's hall, the Bau suddenly shuddered. "No," she muttered, her hoarse voice deep and pleading. "Mistress, why? After all this lovely ruin—"

She choked, her squat form bending in upon itself. "Yes." It was a gasp of obedience and pain. "I will obey You, Mistress. As always."

Imprisoned in the icy flames of the hearth, Queen Rionach slowly looked up. Time had twisted in this place of dark spells; it was as deformed as the creature that held sway in what had once been her home. She could have been here years, or it could be days, even moments. Only one reality existed that she could hold fast to: the strength of prayer. That she had done, calling upon the Holy Trinity until her throat burned as if the flames themselves had crawled inside it, reciting the holy words to herself over and over and over. Now, after this dark eternity, it seemed that the Lord had heard her at last.

The demon had risen from its place. Whirling in shades of black and red, it moved toward her, towering to the rafters and beyond. Rionach lifted an arm to make the sign of the cross. The gesture required enormous strength; her arm felt mired in peat mud, her fingers encased in ice. Still, she persisted, and even managed to speak.

"In killing me, you grant me freedom to the City of Heaven," she whispered. "I am ready."

The demon snarled. "Are you indeed? Well, you will have to wait for that particular sort of freedom. I am granting you a more painful kind." Its immense arms made a wild motion. "Be gone!"

A wind sprang up, leaping from the creature's warped hands. It howled in the queen's ears, deafening her. The flames surged up, billowing over her face, enveloping her, burning and freezing at once. She wanted to scream, but found that she could not: all sound refused to issue from her lips, even the familiar cadence of her prayers.

Abruptly the wind died, and with it the flames. Rionach was standing in the hearth as she had been all during this dark spell, but now the hearth was bare of the unnatural fire that had imprisoned her. She looked down dazedly in the new silence, afraid to move, not quite aware of what had happened.

The demon's hollow voice beat at her. "The One I serve has decided to show you mercy, mortal woman. This does not please me, but there it is. My Mistress's word is law. I advise you to leave quickly, though. My Mistress has been known to change Her mind in such matters."

Rionach did not move. She struggled to grasp what her captor had just said. Her thoughts were sluggish, as thick as mud from the deepest of bogs. Could it be true? Could God have finally freed her?

"Have you no ears, woman?" The demon's voice rose to a shriek. "That whey-faced god of yours had naught to do with this. My Mistress has allowed you to be released. Now go!"

The queen's legs stumbled to life. She staggered out of the hearth. With each step strength came back to her, until she was running toward the wide doors that had suddenly swung open to allow her exit.

The demon's laughter billowed up, following her. "Yes, run," she shrieked. "Scurry out to your land like the little mouse you are. You will find, woman, that while you are free, your land is still not."

Fresh air struck Rionach's face, as fresh and sweet as spring-cooled honey mead in high summer. Gratefully she gulped great mouthfuls deep into her lungs, drinking it as though it was indeed mead. The air burned in her chest, icy with the grip of winter, but she ran on, desperate to leave the hall and its evil presence far behind. Snow lay deep and heavy on the frozen ground. The trees shivered in a frigid wind, their naked limbs reaching in supplication at a dark, overcast sky. The queen shivered, too, vaguely realizing that the brat she had donned when she left Bishop Cairnech's hall an eternity ago was not heavy enough for this type of weather.

Without warning her foot slammed against something half-buried in the snow. She tripped and fell hard, measuring her length on the icy unforgiving ground. Dazed, she lay still for a moment, then struggled to her feet. Her eyes fell upon the object she had stumbled over. She cried out and crossed herself.

The body of a man lay faceup in the snow. His eyes gazed up at her, sightless and distended in an expression that froze the queen's blood. He had been dead for some time; his limbs were distorted, fixed in the position they had taken when he fell. The place where his throat had been was a gaping hole. The blood that had poured from the wound had long ago congealed and frozen, spreading dark and hard against the snow.

Rionach crossed herself again, murmuring a prayer for the man's soul. Her voice trembled. Despite the expression of torment and terror that marred his features, she recognized him. He had been one of the servingmen who had accompanied her from the bishop's hall, when she left to return home on the dreadful night when her world had fallen apart yet again.

Staring down at the ground she saw other corpses strewn like carelessly tossed logs among the trees. The trembling spread from her voice to her body, and it had little to do with the cold. How many had died here? It was difficult to know for certain. She counted eleven bodies, interspersed with the stiff carcasses of horses and mules. Her terror would not allow her to count more. She knew that she must flee. There was too little distance between her and the demon. It might yet decide to leave the hall and imprison her again.

Queen Rionach forced her stiff legs into motion. Stumbling and staggering, she made her way deeper into the winter-gripped woods. The images of the murdered humans and animals accompanied her, forming and re-forming in her mind. A thought nagged at her: the bodies had been there for some time, but they were untouched by scavengers. Winter was a cruel season; food was scarce for the wild creatures. Wolves and foxes and ravens should have been at these poor people and their animals, devouring them until naught but their bones remained. Yet there was no sign that anything had been feeding on this tragedy. At least, no being that was composed of mortal flesh and blood.

Rionach ran on. She must find her people.

If any of them still lived.

The caravan continued to travel north. The land grew increasingly unsettled. Here the old customs remained in force, and nowhere was this more evident than in the vast stretches of forest that reached all the way to the Rhine and beyond. These territories that Julius Caesar had been so determined to conquer and that the ancient tribes of the Belgae had fought so tenaciously to hold had been absorbed into the province of Gaul, but never truly Romanized. They lay too far to the north, were too close to the frontier. Roads had been built, though there were far fewer of them than elsewhere in Gaul. Those that had been constructed had fallen into disrepair. The trees had reclaimed them: the oak and ash and yew that Caesar had once ordered burned as symbols of Druid power.

To the Romans, a people whose civilization had been founded on the olive, with wine and bread only slightly less dear, these impenetrable forests were an uncultivated waste. To the Celts and the Germans they represented something quite different. From the earliest days of the gods they had based their culture on meat, butter, and beer; these woodlands provided them all they needed. In the deep forest they grazed their pigs, searched for wild honey, made charcoal, and cut wood for use as stakes and beams. They pastured their oxen and cattle on the wetlands and their sheep on the heaths. They grew rye, barley, and oats for their bread and beer, though with the exception of beer, grain was secondary to meat.

And not only tame meat, but wild. Hunting was a pastime nearly as beloved as war. Increasingly, the vast woods and the beasts therein had become the property of nobles and kings. It was a pleasure and a duty for warriors to provide a regular supply of venison, boar, salmon, partridge, and rabbits. The flesh of the aurochs, a wild ox of enormous size, was a dish fit only for a king, and it, as well as all other game animals, were protected under Germanic law.

Into these forest wastes, the mule convoy entered, finding its way with difficulty along dim tracks carpeted with snow. New generations of trees stretched triumphant limbs over the crumbling stones of Roman might. Their roots spread out steadily, like great fingers, growing under the roads themselves, inexorably breaking apart the carefully designed thoroughfares meant to connect an empire.

The people of these distant reaches, too, had returned to the ancient gods and goddesses. Supposedly they had taken on the mantle of Arianism, the form of Christianity considered so heretical it had ignited controversy throughout the more civilized reaches of what had once been the empire. But in reality, whether or not Jesus Christ was divine or merely a mortal, albeit an extraordinary one, mattered little, if at all, to most of them. Ancient temples had been destroyed or claimed for the new state religion and rededicated as churches. Worship of the old gods was forbidden, but the practices and beliefs attached to them had always persisted, and here in the north those customs were stronger than ever.

The descendants of the warriors who had opposed Caesar and his legions had reclaimed the groves of their ancestors. Indeed, many had never given them up. When Chlodweg and his powerful Franks moved across the Rhine, little changed. The conversion of many barbarians to Arianism had nothing to do with faith and everything to do with expediency and carefully calculated strategy. As was the custom, if nobles took on the mantle of Chrisitanity, so, too, did the common folk. But it was a conversion in name only.

Damona smiled sadly as she came across shrines tucked away here and there in the deep woods. They were a familiar sight, reminding her piercingly of home, small personal holy places devoted to Shining Ones Whose presence stubbornly remained in the minds of common folk. Farmers, peasants, and the like gave only lip service to the official religion that had been declared throughout what was left of the empire. Such decrees played small role in their lives. Let the far-off emperors sit in their mighty cities that none of these people would ever see and issue their decrees. It meant little under the press and struggle of everyday living.

At one of the spots where they stopped to rest the mules Damona opened the basket so the Guardian could stretch his legs. Over the monotonous days of the journey Carbo and his men, as well as the cohort of soldiers, had developed a grudging respect for their female passenger. She did not complain about the cold and ice and ruinous roads, she did her share in setting up and breaking camp, and the long hours in the saddle did not faze her. On a journey such as this such qualities loomed far larger than differences over religion.

As the men made a fire and talked among themselves, Damona and the cat drew away toward the warmth provided by the body heat of the tethered mules to have their own conversation.

"This is an enormous land," Damona said to him, low-voiced. "Far greater than any place I have ever seen. Eire is like a pond beside the sea compared to it. How in the name of Tara can we ever find what we seek?"

Fastidiously, the cat stepped back from the swishing of the nearest mule's tail, glaring at the offending appendage. "I told you," he said blandly, "that it would not be easy. But then, the events that brought you here were not easy."

Despair shivered through Damona. She had slept badly last night, and every night since the visit to the temple ruins. Sekhmet had not left her in peace, taking the opportunity to torment her when she was most vulnerable, at night, when she was exhausted from traveling. During the hours of darkness, dreams plagued Damona, tempting and beguiling her, and leaving her to wake in the icy air, sweating with images of power and blood.

Lying awake in deep night, staring at bleak lifeless trees outlined against a black sky, she could feel her resolve weakening and her doubts growing. Why was she struggling through this land, hoping for a redemption she did not truly deserve? She had abandoned Bast and the Goddess had abandoned her in return.

"She has not." The Guardian's tone was firm as he interrupted into her thoughts.

"Has She not?" Damona looked at him. "You bring me to Her temple, and She does nothing, while Sekhmet comes to me instead. She sets me a task that is impossible to fulfill, for I have no powers to help me find these wands—"

"You are forgetting one thing," the Guardian broke in. "She has sent you me. And with me, you will find them."

16

CHLODWEG, SON OF CHILDERIC, was a powerful man in appearance as well as in speech and deed. The kingship had come to him upon his father's death, and in truth, it could have gone to no one else. Chlodweg was a young man, but a man possessed of power and ability. As a leader, he was as different from the doomed Muirchertac as a sacred grove was from a basilica in Constantinople. Madness did not fester in this king, at least, not the kind of madness that had set the *Tuisech*'s feet on a path to ruin. Chlodweg was a man in which everything was controlled and utterly subordinated to his will. And his will was to unify the Frankish kingdom under one rule: his own.

This task he had set for himself was well on the way to being completed.

On this night he lay wrapped in his furs, alone, as he had been since his wife had entered the latter stages of her pregnancy. He listened thoughtfully to the storm raging outside his royal hall. It was unusual weather for the winter season: instead of snow, a mix of heavy rain and blistering sleet, attended by fierce winds, thunder, and lightning, was pummeling Tournai, the city his father had taken for the capital of the Franks. Chlodweg lay with his eyes open. There were omens to be seen on such a night; he was determined not to miss them.

Omens were important to the Franks; they were interwoven throughout every facet of their life. Chlodweg's folk had always been a people linked to the forces of the natural world. They followed the seasons and their herds, hunting and fishing and cultivating crops within the vast wild lands beyond the Rhine. When they were not tending their animals or growing food, they were warring against other tribes, for war was a holy pursuit, the province of all men of free or noble blood. Theirs was a good life, a life that had been ordained by the gods, and always had the Franks been content to follow it.

But the world around them was changing. So was the world that lay beyond the Rhine, that great dividing line of water that had always marked the boundary between the Franks and their Celtic neighbors. Unlike many among those who attended him, Chlodweg was not a man who feared change. To him, change represented opportunity. In these unsettled times, there were opportunities to be had in plenty.

The Franks were a numerous people. A number of them, known as the Rhenish, lived along the left bank of the Rhine. Others, called the Salians, who had crossed into northern Gaul, had originally come from Salland, a small pocket of land on the lower Rhine. Regardless of their origins, the Franks shared an intense hatred of all things Roman. Memories still burned of events that had taken place only decades ago, when the people had fallen under the hard yoke of Roman rule, the authority of one of the last generals of Rome left in Gaul.

Those days of oppression were over, leaving only the hatred. And now, Rome's weakness, combined with the restlessness of the times, had set fire to that intense hostility, as well as to the Franks' own restlessness.

It was nothing new, this necessity to shuffle and resettle one's living space, even if it meant pushing another tribe out of its living space. Such movements had shaped the complexion of Celtic lands before the coming of Rome, and now they were reshaping the Rhineland and Gaul itself.

The Salians had advanced across the face of northern Gaul, eventually settling in the area around Tournai and

Cambrai. One of their kings, Childeric, had been determined to expand his people's territory even farther. His ambitions, in spite of an attack on the Roman-founded city of Paris, were never realized. He died sometime before 481 and was buried in his capital of Tournai, leaving it to his son to take hold of his unfulfilled plans.

And Chlodweg, whom history would one day know as Clovis, had taken on the task his father had set him with a vengeance.

His first step on assuming his father's position was to set about unifying the fragmented kingdoms of his people. Clovis was a brave man; he loved battle as much as any full-blooded Frankish warrior, but he was a wise and devious man as well. He was not above foregoing honorable combat and resorting to the ancient methods of deception and trickery and murder when circumstances appeared to warrant them.

He showed his deviousness by utilizing such methods to dispose of the petty kings whose lands bordered his own. He showed his wisdom by using diplomacy, rather than murder or trickery, to mollify the powerful and stubborn Bretons of Amorica by officially recognizing their independence. One day—sooner than he realized—he would demonstrate his battle prowess by stopping the armed migration of the non-Frankish tribe, the Alamanni, in a savagely contested engagement and driving them back to the upper Rhine.

King of the Franks.

The voice came in a flash of lightning. A growl of thunder followed so closely Chlodweg shook his head, thinking he must have imagined the calling out of his royal title.

King of the Franks.

This time the voice seemed to issue from the remnants of the fire in the center of the hut. The words curled up from the smoldering coals. Chlodweg felt a surge of heat, as though another presence had suddenly entered. He sat up, letting the bearskin he had wrapped around him fall from his naked burly chest.

"Who speaks to me on this night?" His deep voice was bold and unafraid. He was indeed king of the Franks; if he felt any trepidation at being addressed in such a mysterious manner on this omen-laden night, he must not show it. "Show yourself," he called out. "If you possess a form that can be seen by the eyes of man."

The wind shrieked, sending a wave of sleet rattling against the skin-covered enclosure. The voice spoke to him again, a hint of amusement twining through its fiery tone. *Are you certain you desire this, King of the Franks? Men have been known to go mad from the sight of Me.*

Chlodweg drew himself up. "I," he said with fierce dignity, "am not as other men. Show yourself. I am not afraid."

Very well, then.

Lightning seared through the wind-whipped hide coverings, and in the flashes of light a shape loomed up. Transfixed, the king stared. He had spoken truly when he said he was not afraid. But what was appearing in response to his demand was beyond any realm he had ever heard or dreamt of.

The head of a beast filled the flickering darkness. The image floated before Chlodweg's stunned gaze, framed in a reddish glow that streamed about it like a pool of blood. Fangs glittered in the vast open mouth, fangs longer than the length of several tall men. Flaming in that eerie light, two enormous yellow eyes blazed into the Frank's gaze. There were worlds upon worlds in those eyes. They pierced the soul of the Frankish king like arrows, and whatever secrets he had, even to himself, were bared.

Words battered at Chlodweg's ears in a rush of thunder. *Your rude mortal dwelling is too small to enclose the whole of Me,* the voice said. *Therefore, you may see only My face.*

Driven by instincts that hearkened back to childhood, Chlodweg made the sign against evil. The face that stared at him was unmistakably that of a lioness, but he could see shoulders wavering in and out of the lightning flares—human shoulders, and below them, incredibly, the breasts of a woman.

The king fought against the cowardly temptation to draw back into his furs. "Are you a demon?" he asked hoarsely. "A spirit of the wind and storm sent by my enemies?"

The creature laughed. The sound roared through the hut, drowning out the thunder. *Fool,* it said. *I am a Goddess. Your enemies did not send Me. No mortal bids Me do anything that is not of My will*

Chlodweg swallowed. "Then why have You come?"

To offer you My help, King of the Franks. You are planning great things, and you are needful of help.

Chlodweg held himself warily. Here was a goddess from some far-distant land suddenly appearing to him offering aid. What lay behind this visitation? Magic was abroad this night. But there was no way of knowing if it was favorable. Yet he should not allow this visitor to frighten him so. After all, he was descended from gods himself, from the mythical hero Merovech, as were all the sons of the Merovingian line; semidivinity was their birthright as rulers and kings of the Franks.

"By my oaths, Lady, I thank you with all respect." Chlodweg fought to keep his voice steady, to allow no trace of apprehension to seep through. He strained for all the careful formality of which he was capable. "But surely You understand, Lady, we have our own gods. I fear offending them."

So you would offend Me instead.

The hair at the back of Chlodweg's neck rose at the tone in that otherworldly voice. "No, Lady," he hastened to say. "But—"

You are a mortal. The fierce beautiful voice cut him off as cleanly as if those terrible fangs had sliced across his throat. *Think you that your paltry excuses can deceive Me? You have abandoned your gods, though you have no more loy-*

*alty to the new than to the old. Your god is power, King of the
Franks. That is why I am here.*

Some of the fear Chlodweg felt began to recede. The look
he gave his divine visitor suddenly held more interest than
terror. He spoke slowly. "In truth, Lady, I am a king, indeed,
and kings are ever ruled by the desire for power."

*Not all of them, mortal. And I have seen many. But you
possess more than the desire for power. You possess the ability to achieve it. Destiny lies upon you, King of the Franks.
Your fate is to go beyond the lands of the Rhine. One day you
could rule from one end of this country known as Gaul to
another.*

"You know of my plans, then?" Chlodweg hunched his
broad shoulders and sat forward.

A growl louder than the thunder rumbled from the visitor's throat. *I am a Goddess.* She said this as if that were
answer enough.

As indeed it was.

Chlodweg nodded eagerly. "I wish to take the kingdoms
of the Burgundians and the Visigoths. Will I succeed?"

Lightning slashed through the hut and the fangs in the
giant mouth gleamed in the lurid glow.

With My help, said the Goddess.

The Guardian's eyes jerked open. Wide and gleaming
they stared into the darkness. The night was whipped by the
storm, its fabric torn apart by wind and sleet and cold.
Beside him Damona moaned in her sleep, her rest as torn by
dreams as the night was by the storm. The soldiers and
traders of the caravan shivered and snored and grunted all
around them, too exhausted to be disturbed by the howling
wind.

With the sky lowering in ominous portent of the storm,
Carbo had hurried to get his men, mules, and cargo unloaded
and under shelter before the weather turned fouler than was
its wont. There were no towns, or even villages in these des-

olate wastes, so Carbo had pushed ruthlessly to get his convoy to the nearest garrison.

The Guardian narrowed his eyes to slits, calling upon his magic. He growled deep in his throat at what it showed him.

Yes, Sekhmet's deep voice purred. *My Sister has Her mortal, with you to help her. And now I have My mortal. But he will need no help other than My Own.*

The cat growled again.

By dawn the storm had moved on, leaving yet another cold gray day in its wake. The caravan traveled on through the morning, and by the midday break, they approached the first of the frontier garrisons.

Damona was surprised to see that the soldiers stationed along the stockade walls bore little difference from the men of Eire or Albion, or indeed the Roman cavalrymen accompanying them. They, too, sported long carefully dressed hair and flowing moustaches, and their Roman armor sat over brightly colored and patterned tunics. Trousers hugged their brawny legs; arm-rings and necklaces of gold and silver and amber flashed in the chill clear air. Only their demeanor marked them as more Roman. Rather than swaggering and standing boldly, as if they owned the very earth, they stood in stiff poses, peering nervously over the rough walls at the vast dark forests beyond.

"Why, those soldiers are tribesmen," she said to Carbo. "I would expect to see true Romans guarding the frontier. These men look to be no more Roman than I do."

The trader shrugged. "What does a true Roman look like? These days Rome will grant citizenship to anyone She can get to serve in the army, especially out here, along the frontier. Those troops you're gawking at are Salian Franks. The Emperor Julian recruited them to come across the Rhine and settle here." He shook his head at Damona's blank look. "The *Emperor* Julian. He ruled the empire one hundred years ago, at least, what's left of it. Great gods, woman, don't you people follow any world affairs on that island of yours?"

"The people of Eire," Damona said stiffly, "were never ruled by Rome, not one hundred years ago, or ever."

"Ha." Carbo flicked his driving whip at the rump of a lagging mule. "Perhaps not, but it doesn't matter. The Christians rule the emperors now, and that means they rule Rome. They'll rule Eire one day, too. You'll see."

Damona glanced at the Guardian. Sitting comfortably atop the swaying sacks of corn, he returned her gaze. She did not answer the trader.

"So when Julian convinced some of these Franks to cross the river," the trader went on, warming to his subject, "he settled them in Toxandria, and there they be to this day, happy as fleas in a bearskin, though everyone but the emperor knows that they still owe allegiance to Chlodweg, their king. Of course, what barbarian in his right mind wouldn't leap at the chance to leave those wilds over there for the riches of life in the empire, even if it is along the frontier? They maintain all these garrisons, running all the way from Tongres through Bavay to Odilienberg. And you have no idea what they get in exchange."

He flicked at another mule. "Horses for the cavalry from the empire's own stud farms; comfortable lodgings in the houses of the local people; regular wages; and daily rations of bread, meat, wine, and oil. And as if that's not enough"— he gestured expansively at the pack train—"there's us, the ones who supply the army with corn. Corn from Africa goes to the troops in southern Gaul and Rome itself. The rations I transport are grown in the plains of Aquitaine, the Paris Basin, and the Thames valley. Not a kernel of it is wasted, either. These barbarians have appetites like a herd of wild hogs."

The train of wagons made its slow way toward the garrison. It had been sighted long ago and was expected. The driver slapped his favorite mule on the shoulder and spat cheerfully. "We'll get a warm welcome. They're always pleased to see a ration train. We'll off-load this garrison's portion, have some wine and meat, and go on to the next garrison. I want to reach it before nightfall. You're free to spend the time as you like while I'm engaged in my business. Just make certain you're around when I start out again. I'll not wait if you aren't."

Damona nodded absently. Great circles shadowed her eyes, and her face was haggard. Her face seemed almost as pale as her hair. Her dreams had been terrible last night, the worst they had ever been. Sekhmet's presence had coiled through her sleep; the Goddess's eyes had blazed through the hours of darkness, coloring the nightmares with a lurid glow. Tangled images came and went. She saw again the burning land and its dark-skinned people. She saw a king and his warriors. She saw death, and felt its heaviness weigh her down.

The lion-headed goddess stalked her.

Today, more than ever, it seemed as if there would never be an escape.

17

THE LABOR HAD LASTED HOURS. The pains had gone on and on. Periodically they would ease for a blessed few moments, only to begin again, clawing at Queen Clotilde with relentless agony. Her screams ripped at the ears of every person in the hall. Those who could find an excuse to leave had done so long ago; those who could not stayed in misery and prayed to the gods to bring surcease, one way or another.

In the central room, a great hearth-fire of logs blazed as always to ward off the winter chill. Chlodweg sat in his royal chair, a goblet of mead in one hand, the knuckles of his other hand grinding into his thighs. His blunt strong-featured face with its wealth of beard was set and stern.

Typically men were not present at events such as this. They went hunting, drank mead with their kinsmen, engaged in any activity they could in fact, to absent themselves from the sounds of their wives as they gave birth. Chlodweg, however, was a king. The birth of royal children was an important matter, especially since he was waiting for a son. In any case, there was too much snow for hunting, and the nobles who had sat drinking with him had made excuses and fled long ago, unnerved by the sounds issuing from the queen's chamber.

Chlodweg drained his goblet. Birthing was not supposed to be like this. He had slept with many women and fathered children with a good number of them. True, he had not been present at those births, but he had seen the results: healthy babes and robust mothers.

He thought of his other son—his firstborn with Clotilde—and his scowl deepened. That child had been born healthy, and with a minimum of fuss. He was to have been the future king, the heir to all his father's plans. But Clotilde had taken care of that. She wished her son to be baptized in the Christian manner, her husband's objections notwithstanding. Ceaselessly she had nagged at Chlodweg, chiding him for his attachment to the old gods, promising that the act of baptism would make their son strong. But Chlodweg had remained firmly loyal to his gods. The queen, frustrated in her devoutness, had finally acted on her own. She had taken the newborn to her church and had him baptized.

The baby had promptly died.

Chlodweg's knuckles ground harder into his thigh as those bitter memories ate through him. The heathen act of Christian baptism had not only killed his son; it had been a clear demonstration of the Christian god's impotence. Over and over had he shouted this at Clotilde, making certain she would never forget what her actions had wrought. They had argued and grieved and blamed each other, but in the end they had come together as duty demanded of them both, to make another heir.

Chlodweg had gone to great efforts to appease the gods for his wife's sacrilege. Yet it seemed apparent that they were still angry with him, as well as with Clotilde. Her terrible labor was clear evidence of their displeasure. Chlodweg's own festering anger toward his wife had burned away with the long hours of listening to her screams. That was not the case with the gods, though. Chlodweg was beginning to fear that the gods would not be content with making this childbirth difficult. It seemed that they intended to punish him further by condemning this babe, and his mother also, to death.

"My lord."

A woman's tentative voice broke into the king's brooding

thoughts. He looked up. The oldest of the midwives attending Clotilde had slipped into the hall. She was a small woman, thin as an arrow, her eyes blue and piercing and set within nests of wrinkles. Her lined face, worn by exhaustion and strain, looked twice its age.

"The queen would speak with you," she said. In spite of her weariness, the woman's voice was steady and filled with authority. "Quickly, before the pains begin again."

Chlodweg frowned. "It is not meet for a man to be in his wife's bedchamber at such a time," he said, feeling both awkward and impatient; of all folk the midwife should know this. "Bad enough that I must sit here listening to her," he added.

The woman did not move. Her lined face was stubborn. "Nevertheless, your queen is asking for you, and I think you had better come." She gestured to him. "Now, my lord. There may be little time."

Chlodweg rose at once. The heavy goblet fell unheeded to the floor rushes. "What mean you, woman?"

The midwife cast him an irritated glance from her sharp blue eyes. The long hours of assisting at this fruitless labor had robbed her of both patience and respect. Her answer was short. "Have you no ears, lord?" she asked roughly. "Your wife struggles to bring forth your child, but the gods do not favor her. The babe will not come."

"What do the omens say?"

The woman sighed. "I am not a Priestess. My charge is bringing babies into the world, not reading signs. But it was said . . . "

She hesitated.

"What?" Chlodweg snapped at her, nervousness making his voice even harsher than was its wont. "Speak up, woman."

"A sparrow flew into this hall yesterday."

Chlodweg paled. This was an omen of the worst sort. Two birds flying into one's house portended great good luck. A single bird, though, meant death. "Are you certain of that?" he whispered.

"The bird came into the queen's very bedchamber," the midwife told him somberly. "And right after she saw it, her waters broke."

Chlodweg strode away. "I will see her," he said over his shoulder.

The midwife hurried after him.

It was a new thing and quite uncommon for either a husband or wife to have a separate bedchamber. Such rooms were not a part of the great halls resided in by kings and their retinues, where everyone slept in the central room, in places carefully defined by rank. In the case of Chlodweg and Clotilde the chamber had grown out of their religious differences and the death of their firstborn.

Chlodweg entered the chamber and halted just inside. The sights froze him in place. The smells struck at him like sword blows from an opponent in battle. Indeed, the chamber resembled a scene where battle was being waged, a battle for the life of Clotilde and the babe she carried within her.

The queen lay in the bed that had been made and remade for her, as her exertions stained and ruined furs and linen coverings. Half a dozen midwives clustered about her, some of them mopping her face and massaging her belly; others mixing potions of herbs and wine. They drew back as they saw the king standing in the doorway.

Clotilde's face turned toward him, and Chlodweg struggled to hide his shock. His wife was unrecognizable. Pain had ravaged her pleasing features, twisting them into a parody of her former self. Her glossy hair, which had ever been her pride, was lank and stiff on the pillows, stained dark with new sweat and old. Wide deep caverns had taken over her dark eyes. Chlodweg swallowed. Whatever vestiges of the grudge he bore her for the death of their firstborn dissolved in a wash of pity. She had been punished enough; more than enough.

"Husband." Clotilde's voice was breathy and quick, shorn of its usual firmness. Her swollen belly seemed grotesque to the king, thrusting in a huge mound up against the bedcovers. "I have a favor to beg of you."

Chlodweg came toward her. "Ask it of me, lady. If it lies within my power, I will grant it."

"There is a woman," Clotilde whispered. "I met her outside the church. She will be able to help. Bring her here to me. Please."

The king regarded her in uneasy silence. Conflicting emotions mingled and ran across his face. Although his anger toward Clotilde was gone, he could not forget that he had lost a son already because of her fanatical devotion to her religion. He dared not risk losing another. After all, what point was there to establishing a kingdom, if he had no legitimate sons to carry it on after him? He exchanged glances with the senior midwife, who had not moved from her position on the other side of the bed. The woman raised her shoulders in a helpless gesture.

"Wife," he said carefully. "What good will that do? You have about you already, the best and most skilled midwives in the land—"

Clotilde's back arched. Pain seared through her, leaching all humanity from her haggard features. She was no longer the queen; she was not even a woman trying to give birth. She was only the pain, reduced to its very essence, the fiery core of her agony shattering her into a thousand screaming shards.

The midwives drew in around her, murmuring comfort, laying compresses on Clotilde's sweat-drenched forehead, pulling back the bedcovers to rub soothing herbs over her straining huge belly. Her royal husband watched in horror. This was woman's business. These were not sights fit for a man to look upon, yet he found himself frozen in place, unable to turn away.

Chlodweg was a warrior. He had fought in battle after battle, had seen countless numbers of men wounded and dying, but never had he seen pain such as this. He could feel the color draining from his face, and yet he felt no shame. He had always known, of course, that there was no finer destiny than to be born a man. But in these endless moments, he thanked the gods over and over again for his fate. He had never felt so grateful to be a man.

The queen's screams tapered off into exhausted moaning. Awareness and rationality slowly returned to her wan features. She put out a hand, her eyes focusing on Chlodweg's face. He took the hand she offered, wincing inwardly at the frailty of those thin fingers.

"My lord." Clotilde's voice was scarcely audible; Chlodweg had to lean over the bed to hear. "You fear granting my request because of our first son. You think God will take this child, as He took that one . . . "

"Lady." Chlodweg found it difficult to speak. "It is a son I want. To see you bound in this suffering is not something I desired, even when I was at my angriest with you."

Her hand tightened on his, the sudden strength of it surprising him. "The woman I seek is not a Christian," she whispered. "She has not found her way to salvation, any more than you have, my husband. But God has told me that she can save me. She is the only one who can. She is a Druid, trained in the old ways. You will know her by her hair; it is white as new winter snow with blood upon it. Bring her to me, and both I and the babe will live."

The grip of her fingers loosened. Her hand fell away from his. The senior midwife left her place by the bed and came around to the king.

"You see how things are," she said to him without preamble. "There is little time. If you are going to do as she bids, you had better set about it."

Chlodweg glared at her. His angry gaze swept around the chamber to encompass the other midwives. "What do the signs say?" he demanded. "Is there reason to go searching for such a woman, or are these the ravings of a woman in childbed?"

The midwives flinched from his anger. But the old woman stood up to him, meeting his eyes square and unafraid. "We cannot answer you," she said. "And you know it well. We are not priests, of either the queen's new religion or the old ways our folk have always followed. Our business is healing and bringing life into the world. Whatever success we have at doing that depends on the judgement of the Great Mother. As for the signs: I have already told you about the sparrow. I can tell you no more."

Chlodweg stared at his wife. She lay motionless and exhausted, as if she were already dead; only the rise and fall of her grotesquely swollen belly showed that she still resided among the living. One of the midwives was holding a cup of raspberry leaf tea to her lips, urging her to drink.

"By my divine ancestor Merovech," the king muttered. "She has just cause to suffer from ravings."

"The pains are about to begin again," the midwife said bluntly. "She can take little more of them." She watched the king for a moment. "If I were king," she added in her quiet firm voice, "I would send out men to do as my queen bade me. And I would do it now."

Chlodweg looked at her. Abruptly he wheeled and strode from the chamber with its smells of women and pain. As he passed into the corridor the midwives looked at each other as they heard his voice.

"Kinsmen," he bellowed. "Attend me. At once!"

Lying in the tangled bedcovers, her eyes still closed, the queen sighed.

"May God speed them," she whispered.

His business with the garrison commander concluded, Carbo gave orders for the men to ready the mules for departure. Their camp this night would likely be another icy spot in the freezing wastes, but it could not be helped. Other garrisons waited for their supplies, and the next outpost lay a good many leagues away.

Damona watched the preparations with unease. "You said we were waiting for a sign," she murmured to the Guardian. "How much longer are we to go on waiting?"

The Guardian yawned, stretching wide his lips to reveal gleaming teeth. "Until it arrives," he said.

The mules had been gathered and loaded and the gates opened to allow their passage, when one of the sentries posted on the ramparts called out a warning. A rider came tearing through the woods, riding at breakneck speed. He cleared several fallen logs, raced over the cleared land fronting the garrison, and tore on to the open gates.

The commander was already racing forward, armed soldiers at his heels. Their steps slowed as they saw that the rider was alone. He was also a barbarian, and of noble blood. His clothes were fine and jewels glittered through the mud spatters and caked ice of his hard riding. He spurred through the gates and came to a halt. The commander raised a hand.

"Greetings, warrior of the Franks," he said cautiously. "What is your purpose in dashing in amongst us like this?"

The noble's horse was lathered and blowing. The man himself was panting, his hair disheveled, the rich mantle he wore coming loose at the shoulder. He slid off the saddle pad, one hand clutching at the reins.

"I seek a Druid," he said hoarsely. "One trained in the healing arts."

The commander regarded him. "We are Christians here, my lord. I do not think we can help you."

"Not all of us are Christians." The voice of the mule driver who had been so persistently hostile to Damona rang out. Carbo glared at him and gestured sharply for the man to be still, but the driver pretended not to see. "Some still cling to the ways of evil," he shouted, and cast a triumphant glance in Damona's direction.

The noble's bloodshot eyes fixed on the man in a glowering stare. "I have not," he snarled, "ridden my best stallion nearly to death in order to debate religion. I want no Christian—priest or otherwise. Chlodweg, my king, he of the strong arms and mighty sword, has sent me, to find a priestess of the ancient ways. A Druid—"

One of the drivers spun about to stare at Damona. Before his eyes could meet hers he wheeled back. "My lord," he cried out. "There." The man's voice was thick and gloating. He thrust a hand at Damona, standing beside her saddled mule. "There is the one you seek. It must be her. I have traveled with the woman, and I have seen that she has unholy powers, the powers of a pagan. Look you upon her hair, lord. Is that not the sign of one marked by magic?"

Damona stood very still. She was astonished to hear Carbo burst out in defense of her. "She is a decent woman," the trader protested.. "And she is under my protection. No harm must come to her, lord, I beg you. My honor is at stake. What travelers will ever pay to take passage with me again if she is taken away before the end of her journey—"

"Silence," the noble snapped impatiently. "No harm will come to her." He paused. "Unless my king declares otherwise." He swung around to stare at Damona. "Be you a Druid?" he demanded.

She shook her head, the words of negation springing to her lips. "I am not," she began.

Go with him.

Achingly familiar, the voice twined itself about Damona's soul. The command was fleeting and soft, so gentle it might have been the wind itself speaking to her. Could it be? Had Bast Herself truly spoken to her? No, it could not be. No doubt this was some cruel trick of Sekhmet's. Never had she thought to hear the Goddess's voice again.

She sought to finish her reply. "I am not—"

A loud meow cut her off. The Guardian had pushed the lid off his basket and leaped out. Rubbing against Damona's ankles, he let out another piercing cry.

The noble's exhausted eyes narrowed, studying Damona. "White hair marked with red," he muttered. "So did the queen describe it. Yes, you are indeed the one I seek."

"The queen?" Startled, Damona met his eyes. "Lady Clotilde, of the Franks?"

The noble's head jerked in a tired nod. "It is her time, but the babe will not be born. She has it in her mind that the Druid she met at her church can help her. She will have no other. That is why men have been sent out all over the country in this accursed cold to find you." The noble swung back to the garrison commander. "Bring out a horse, a fast one. That mule of hers will be far too slow. Hurry," he snapped, when the Roman hesitated. "The beast shall be returned to your garrison. My lord's word on it."

Affronted, the commander stiffened at the man's tone. Chlodweg, however, was far too powerful and well-known a king to risk offending. He motioned to one of the soldiers. "Do as he bids," he ordered curtly. "Fetch the chestnut mare."

"Lord," Damona said, as the soldier ran off to the stables. "I told your lady I was a Druid no longer. I know not that I can be of any aid to her."

Go with him.

The silent voice was louder. The Guardian meowed again. The driver who had pointed her out crossed himself.

The soldier came trotting back, tugging a fine-boned mare along behind him. "I know not that you can help her either," the noble said. "Our midwives have not been able to. But you are the one she wants, and my lord has honored her request. It is not for me to decide otherwise. My task has been to bring you. Thanks be to the gods, that I have done."

Queen Rionach wandered through a land of nightmares.

This was not the Eire she remembered: the Eire from which the demon had snatched her. Darkness and death and cold were the mantles this country wore, so much so, that at times Rionach wondered if she had escaped the Bau at all, if instead, she was only fleeing through the realms of dreams.

Her fear that none of her tuath might still live had intensified. As hard as winter was for both humans and beasts, what had come over her home was like nothing she had ever seen. There was no letup to the snow that had lain thick and icy outside the hall that she and Muirchertac had once shared. It extended everywhere, making walking difficult, and at times impossible. Rionach sought out the rath that lay closest to the hall; there she would find shelter and aid. Shivering and praying, the images of the dead faces in the snow still burning in her mind, she struggled through the woods, breaking though the hard crust with every step.

She was exhausted when she reached the earthen walls of the rath, only to find the farmstead utterly deserted. Walking through the enclosure she called out again and again. Only the wind answered her, whistling through chinks in the wattle-and-daub walls. Rionach knew there would be no other answer. Death sat in this place, its presence stark and unmistakable. There were no bodies, but that made little difference. Life had fled this once-prosperous rath, and not even the ubiquitous rats remained.

The queen soon gave up trying to find anyone. She would have to push on through the hostile forest, alone. It was a daunting prospect, but an alternative that was easier to face than staying in this eerie place so bereft of life. She set about searching for food and warm clothing. Of the first, she found not a scrap; of the second she managed to find a brat and a pair of soft leather boots that laced up over her calves and were far too big, but were better than the thin thoroughly ruined shoes she had been wearing.

Thus garbed she started out again. The trees closed in around her. The paths that led through them were obscured. Rionach found her way by instinct, gradually coming to realize that she was heading in the direction of Bishop Cairnech's hall.

"It is a long journey on foot," she said aloud. "God will have to help me if I am to reach him."

Her voice came out small and weak. It was promptly swallowed up and then mocked by the cold vastness around her. Somewhere she thought she heard the laughter of the demon. She shut her ears to it and began to pray, fighting to make her voice strong, so that her prayers would reach beyond the demon's power. Periodically she would stop praying and call out as loudly as she could. Then she would fall silent, waiting for someone to respond. Each time she waited in vain. Not even the howl of a wolf or the croak of a raven broke the stillness.

Perhaps, Rionach told herself, it was best that there were no wolves about. The creatures did not prey on living humans, but if their keen noses were to sniff out a body lying motionless in the snow . . .

And the will that it took to keep on moving, rather than lying down in the snow, was growing more difficult. The queen was becoming colder and colder. She was limping badly. The too-large boots she had found were soaked through and slipping back and forth, blistering her feet with every step she took. The brat no longer seemed to keep her warm. Still, she forced herself on. Her thoughts were growing foggy. She was not aware that her prayers were falling away into the silence about her. Her voice had become too hoarse to continue anyway. Her steps were slowing along with her voice. She was stumbling more often, falling to her knees, though she stolidly pushed herself up to continue each time.

The passage of hours had become lost to her; it seemed that she had been struggling through this bleak lifeless landscape for an eternity. Here and there she came upon other raths and smaller farmsteads. Her hope lessening, she investigated each one, and found it as utterly abandoned as the first rath had been. This land had once encompassed a vital tuath, one that even in the hush of winter would have stirred with occasional life as deer wandered in search of food, followed by lone hunters from those raths, or small groups of folk wending their way between one rath and another. All that was gone, as though the evil of the demon had swept every sign of life away.

Queen Rionach was no longer praying as she staggered

along. She was sobbing. She would not reach the bishop's hall; she had accepted that by now. But that was not the reason for her tears. She was weeping for her people and her land.

Eventually she fell, and this time, the effort of getting back onto her blistered, frozen feet was too difficult to face. She lay in the hard-packed snow, a fallen branch pressing against her cheek, and waited to die.

It would not be so unpleasant, she thought. She had always heard that death by freezing was much like going to sleep, and indeed, that seemed to be so. Despite the scratchy pressure of the branch against her face she was comfortable and warm, as she had not been in days upon days. Soon, even the discomfort of the branch ceased to bother her. Wherever the people of her tuath had gone, she would soon be joining them.

Footsteps crunched on the crusty snow. Rionach lay still, taking little notice of them. Once the sound of them would have sent her scrambling up, but now they seemed far away, of little significance anymore. The City of Heaven awaited her; surely the Christians among her folk already awaited her there.

A snort blew through the frosty air, directly over her head. The footsteps grew uneven, and someone let out a distinctly human gasp. Slowly Rionach opened her eyes. She was not pleased to have to turn her head, but it was the only way to tell whoever it was to go away and leave her in peace.

A bone-thin horse was standing above her. His round dark eyes stared sadly down at her. The long whiskers on its chin quivered with his heavy breathing. An equally bone-thin man was holding the horse's lead rope. He was bundled in mangy moth-eaten furs and his face peeked out from them, pinched and wan and hollow-cheeked. He, too, was staring down at her, his eyes wide.

"By the Cauldron of the Mother," he croaked in a voice made hoarse by disuse. "How did you get here?"

Rionach sighed, realizing she would have to speak. "I am Rionach," she began. "Queen—"

"Lady Rionach!" The man's shocked voice cut her off. "It cannot be!" He backed off, tugging the horse with him. "It's told that you are dead."

His response irritated Rionach. "Told by whom?" She pushed herself up onto an elbow. "There is life in me yet, though a little longer and there would not have been." She fought to focus her gaze on the man's face. "Be you of the tuath?"

He nodded, still fearful, still uncertain of her. "I am."

"Then come nearer," she snapped. "I am your queen. Can you not see that I am in severe need of aid?" Awareness was coming back to her. She was not to die after all. She had been rescued. The One True God had sent this hollow-cheeked man and his poor thin horse to save her.

The man jumped to obey before he thought about it. Taking Rionach by the elbow, he sought to help her up. Finding that a single hand was not enough, he dropped the horse's lead rope, got both hands under the queen's arms, and levered her onto her feet. Swaying back and forth, the queen leaned upon him heavily, too exhausted to care about the impropriety. She sent a worried glance at the horse. The bony gelding was loaded with an assortment of ragged bundles, though it looked as if room could be made for a rider on his back.

"Will your beast be able to carry me?" she asked. "I would not ask it, with the poor creature being so weak and all, but I vow I cannot walk another step."

The man gave the horse an affectionate slap. "He will carry you, lady, if the distance be not far. He is tough, is my Brownie. Pretty to look at he's not, but he is alive. And that is more than can be said for many of his fellows."

He rummaged about among the bundles, shifting them to make a place where Rionach could sit. Finished, he gave her his hand and helped her to mount, no easy task since starvation had weakened him until he possessed less strength than the queen herself. The horse flattened his ears in protest at the additional weight. Rionach stroked his neck and tried to sit as lightly as possible. Clucking encouragement, the man tugged at the lead rope. After a moment, the horse sighed and started forward at a slow walk.

Rionach balanced herself amidst the bundles, holding on to the gelding's scanty mane. "What has become of the other horses?" she asked uneasily, well aware that her question encompassed far more than just the fate of horses.

The man knew it, too. He answered with a detachment brought on by hardship. "Dead. Starved to death for lack of fodder, along with most beasts, whether tame or wild." His light brown eyes became distant. "I was a farmer. I had no rath, just my house and some small fields, but I had cattle and pigs, and a new wife. Now the cattle and pigs are dead, my fields lie buried beneath more snow and ice than any elder has ever seen, and my new wife is newly departed from this life. I have come to believe that she is fortunate."

Rionach crossed herself, her face shadowed with sympathy.

The man saw the gesture and frowned. "I am not a Christian, lady," he told her quickly. "And neither was my wife."

"That is of no matter." Rionach could not bring herself to point out that as pagans, neither he nor his wife would find places prepared for them in the City of Heaven. This sad, good-hearted man had saved her; surely God would be merciful after such a deed.

The man's original uneasiness was beginning to return. "And you, lady," he said, striving to coat nervousness with courtesy. "How is that you have been spared? Word went out all through the tuath that you were dead. It was said that the evil shape called up by the *Banfhili* seized hold of you and bore you into the hall." He shuddered and rounded the fingers of his free hand into the sign against malevolent spirits, casting glances at her from the corners of his eyes.

Rionach shuddered, too, both with memories and with cold. "I was borne away by a demon indeed. But do not blame the Priestess for it. This evil was not of her doing. In truth, she tried to save me."

"Think you not, lady?" The onetime farmer looked up at her in disbelief. "Then you are the only one who believes so. Look you, I follow the old ways, not your Christian God. But the *Banfhili* was angry when the *Tuisech* destroyed the shrine of her Goddess. She sought to punish the wrongdoers, and the magic got away from her. That is what the Druids said."

"Where is the *Banfhili* now?" The queen could not have said why she was so convinced of the *Banfhili*'s innocence. The woman was a heathen, and even other heathens were naming her guilty. But Rionach remembered Damona's eyes the day the Priestess had come to her at the bishop's hall. The *Banfhili* had not brought this evil to Eire, at least, not knowingly. "Is she among the dead?"

"If she is not," the man growled, "she should be. Every man who was able to hunted her, but she was never found." He shook his head. "So many have died since then. It seems impossible that you were not among them."

"I have suffered," Rionach said briefly. "But God has a purpose for me, and so I am here."

"So is the demon." The man flung his arm out at the stark silent woods. "Look upon what that cursed Priestess has wrought. There should be life stirring in this forest, as there always is when the time of Shoots-Showing nears. What do you see? And it is this way throughout the entire land of Eire, not just our tuath."

"And what of our tuath?" Rionach steeled herself to hear the answer. "What has become of our folk?" She could not repress the shiver that went through her. Even in the worst of Muirchertac's madness the people had been numerous and strong, with babies being born constantly to increase their strength. It was inconceivable that all those souls could be gone. Feeling the tension in her body the horse tossed his head, though he was too weary to do more. "Are there none left but you?" she asked in a low voice.

"There are others," the man said. "A few here and there.

Some wander about as I do, finding bits of food or clothing in the raths and huts and halls of the dead. We are scavengers, but there is nothing dishonorable in it. How can there be? The dead no longer have any use for such things, and we trade what we find to keep the life in our own bodies."

Fondly, he patted the gelding's thin neck. "The gods favored me when I found this horse. I have not met anyone else so lucky. I discovered him outside the hall of a noble. His master had long since gone to the Otherworld."

"Are there any nobles left alive?"

"Perhaps. If there are, they are doing as everyone else is. Those who have not died of sickness or cold or hunger are hiding like rabbits in a burrow. They hoard whatever scraps of food are left and pray—old gods or new, it does not matter—and hope they will live to see this curse end."

Rionach forced strength into her voice. "It will end."

The man looked up at her. Bitterness and despair were etched on his haggard features. "How?"

"With my husband dead I rule over this tuath, or what is left of it. I must restore things to their natural balance. It is my duty."

"Lady," the man said tiredly, "may the gods be with you in your endeavor. But in the meantime, where would you have me take you?"

The trees had thinned. They had come to an opening in the bleak woods. A well-trodden path had once led between the hall of one of Muirchertac's kinsmen and several prosperous raths. Now the path was covered with snow and blocked with trees that had toppled over from their burden of ice.

Rionach glanced about, trying to get her bearings. "Do you know where the hall of Bishop Cairnech lies?"

"The Christian Druid? I have been there to trade, though not recently."

The queen did not correct the man's characterization of the bishop. She gazed at him with hope rising in her eyes. "Does he still live?"

"He did when I was there last." The man paused. "Whether he has remained alive is something only his god and yours can say."

Rionach nodded. "Take me there," she said briskly. "As fast as you and this good horse can walk."

18

HIS MUD-STAINED MANTLE FLYING behind him, the noble led the way to Chlodweg's hall. Other nobles were already there, having given up and returned to inform the king of the fruitlessness of their efforts. The man who brought Damona galloping up to the hall on her exhausted mare wore a triumphant expression on his tired face. He had succeeded; rewards would be waiting for him in plenty.

If the powers of the Druid woman could ensure that the queen and her unborn babe lived.

Servants ran out to take the horses and assist Damona in dismounting. Waving away their help, she leaped to the ground and started unfastening the basket from the mare's saddle. The noble put out a hand. "Leave the cat in its basket," he said impatiently. "One of the slaves will bring it to you."

"I will see to this myself." Damona continued untying the basket. "The cat must come with me."

As the noble shifted his feet, chafing at the delay, she finished untying the basket, took it in her arms, and turned to the man. "I am ready," she told him, addressing the chieftain with a self-possession she did not feel.

The noble hurried her into the hall. Damona's vision filled with a swirl of color and movement. The hall was luxuriously appointed, and it was packed with servants and Frankish nobles, the latter standing in small groups muttering to each other, while the former rushed about offering them meat pastries and wine. Cluster after cluster of men turned to look as Damona's presence was noted. They stared at her, their murmured conversations intensifying. She stared back, her eyes passing over the bearded faces of these strangers. She was fully aware of the sight she presented. The Guardian shifted in his basket, and she tightened her grip on the handle, taking comfort from the feel of his solid weight.

A tall figure came swinging through the crowd. The servants and nobles instantly parted to allow him passage. Plainly, he was the king; his garb and bearing proclaimed it as loudly as if he had shouted it.

The hall fell silent as Chlodweg halted in front of Damona. The king wasted no time with courtesies, made no offerings of greetings and refreshment. "I am Chlodweg," he said brusquely. "So you are the one." He looked her up and down, his hard gaze lingering briefly on the basket she held, then dismissing it. "We have been waiting for you. My wife believes you can help her. May the gods will that it be so."

Damona looked back at him in silence. A pattern was weaving itself about this ruler of the Franks. She who had been shorn of her powers should not have been able to see it, and yet she could. Darkness suddenly veiled the king's tall form, but it was a darkness lit with movement. She saw faces, heard voices, felt the pain of others. Sounds of a battle crashed overhead. From somewhere the cry of a baby sounded. A fiery breath struck her, causing her to stagger.

You are seeing again, Sekhmet's voice said, *because I have willed you to see. This pattern is of My weaving.*

"Lady." The king's strong hand caught and steadied her. "Are you unwell?" His blue eyes were intent and worried, his concern obvious. If this priestess was ill, how could she possibly be of any help?

Damona straightened. She knew her face was stiff with shock, and her eyes were distant, not attentively fixed on the king as they should be, but she could not help it. Momentarily she was struck dumb, struggling to make sense of what had just happened. Sekhmet had returned. The visions the Goddess had shown her had meaning, but their secrets were still known only to Her. Sekhmet was toying with her, playing as a cat plays with a captured bird that yet lives.

The king's hand shook her. "I asked you if you are unwell," he repeated angrily.

Damona knew that she dared not speak of what she had seen to Chlodweg. "Be at ease," she made herself say. "I am quite well." She forced briskness into her tone. "Take me to the queen's bedchamber, my lord. That is why I was brought here, was it not?"

The king nodded at her, relief and hope shadowing his gaunt features. "Come with me then."

He scarcely needed to lead the way to his wife's chamber. The aura of labor beckoned to Damona almost as soon as they left the crowded hall. So many times had she been called upon to attend at these occasions, times that could be clothed in the brightest of joy or the deepest of sorrow. But this occasion was already heavy with sorrow, for Sekhmet overshadowed it. Even before the king stopped, she knew where the queen lay. As if the lion-headed goddess were giving her a warning, a scream rang out, echoing against the stout walls, causing the wood to vibrate with agony.

Chlodweg winced and sought to hide that he had. "Help her," he said gruffly. "I will wait for you in the hall. This is not proper business for a man." Unwilling for this woman to see how the queen's suffering affected him, he turned on his heel, hurrying to leave before another scream shredded through him.

Damona entered the bedchamber. The scene that met her eyes was so familiar it made her want to weep. The woman lay in the bed, her swollen belly proclaiming the life waiting to be born. The air was stale, but redolent with the odors of herbs and tinctures and salves. Dittany leaf, mixed with pennyroyal, vervain, and hyssop, was simmering in wine to ease the pains of labor. The tea's aroma mingled with the strong scent of lavender, for here, as in Eire, the herb was burned to bring peace and tranquillity to the mother in her travail.

Midwives were huddled around the bed. Their attention

had been focused on their patient, but at Damona's arrival, each face turned toward her with one motion, as though the half dozen women had suddenly combined into one.

The oldest of the midwives stepped away from the bed and came toward her. She gave Damona a careful scrutiny, her eyes lingering on the startling hair. Damona waited for her to say something fearful, to make a sign against evil. Instead the midwife moved back and motioned her to the bed.

"The pains have continued," she said in a low voice. "One just finished. They tear at her like the sharpest of knives, but without bearing fruit. The babe refuses to come, and the life in the mother grows faint. I think she has only held on to this world out of the hope that you would be found."

Damona struggled to speak, to think. The fact that she had been found would accomplish nothing, she wanted to say. She was no longer a healer. That power had been taken from her. But with a pain as sharp as when that power had originally been stripped from her, she was discovering that this was not entirely true. The power of healing might have been taken, but the knowledge that lay behind it had not. It was still within her, all of it: the herbs, the sense of touch, the lore handed down to her by her mother and all the mothers before her. Sekhmet had not been able to wipe it from her memory. It had sprung back into life and was swirling through her mind.

"Is the babe in the proper position?" she heard herself ask.

The question tore at her even as the words left her lips. Memories bore down on her as heavy as death. The scores of births she had assisted at came alive once again. The birthing of her own children clawed through her, the sense of it so vivid and painful that for a fleeting moment she became the woman in the bed, contraction after contraction clutching at her own belly.

The intensity of what she was feeling must have shown in her face. The midwife eyed her strangely. "It is," she answered after a moment. "And that is the worst of it. There is no reason why this should not have been a normal birth. The queen is healthy, and she has borne before. Her child is positioned correctly. It should have come. It seems"—she hesitated, studying Damona's face as if judging how much more to say—"that something does not want this birthing to happen. I should have realized it before. The signs—"

"What signs?" Damona looked at her sharply. She had a terrible sense that the woman was going to speak of visions of a lion-headed goddess. An inward sigh of relief rippled through her when the midwife described instead the bird flying into Clotilde's chamber.

"You are an outlander," the midwife said. "But you are trained in the mysteries, are you not? You know what the signs mean, unless they are different in the land from which you hail."

Damona was silent. Clotilde was beginning to stir again, the other midwives hovering about her. "Your queen should not have sent for me," she said to the old woman. "I told her when we met that I am no longer a Druid."

The midwife gave her a keen glance from her blue eyes. "Yet she wanted you. Perhaps that, too, is a sign. In truth, it matters not to me whether you are or are not what she thinks. But if you can do aught for her, Priestess, then do it, for we have done all we can."

"Druid." The queen's voice wafted from the bed, a mere thread of sound. "You have come."

Swiftly Damona went toward her. "I have," she said, and wondered at the soothing tone her voice automatically assumed, as if she had indeed become a healer once more. She forced the sense of wonder aside, and in a different voice, said, "Though I fear there be no purpose in it. I told you before, lady. I no longer have the ability to help you, or anyone else."

"You do," Clotilde breathed. "And only you. You have come to protect me. From her . . . "

A chill rippled through Damona. "Her?" she whispered.

"You should not speak, lady," one of the midwives broke in. "You must save your strength—"

The queen ignored her. "She has tormented me, Druid woman. She threatens to take my son. With her beast head and her awful fangs, she laughs at me. She makes a mockery of my prayers."

She gasped and twisted in the bed. Another of the women lifted her head and held a cup of the herb wine mixture to her lips. The eldest midwife nodded with a look of grim satisfaction. "You see," she murmured to Damona. "The signs were right. A demon is preventing this birth."

Damona stared down at the queen, frozen.

Painfully Clotilde gulped down a sip of the tea. "Save me," she whispered. "You must. The new cannot defeat the old; it has not the knowledge. She belongs to the old, and so do you. Only you can protect this child. My life is of no importance." She gripped the cross about her neck. "I am in the hands of the Lord. The City of Heaven awaits me in all its light. But if I die, so does the babe. I must not die."

"Hush." Damona found her voice at last. "You must hold on to all of your strength, lady. There is work to be done, if you want this child. Wasting breath in speech will only weaken you."

The queen's sweat-matted head moved in a weak nod of assent. Her cracked lips moved, but she said nothing more.

"If it be true that you can protect her," the senior midwife hissed urgently, "then use your powers. Lay your spells. Drive the demon out before it kills both her and the babe."

Sekhmet's voice burned in Damona's ears. *Even in her ignorance the fool has guessed the truth. Deliver the baby. I will allow it.*

Why should I, when You have been preventing this birth?

Damona did not speak the words aloud. Yet the eldest midwife and some of the others sensed that something was passing between her and an unseen presence. They stared at her. The old midwife still refused to insult her by making the sign to protect against evil, but the younger ones were not so fearless. Damona paid no heed to any of them. She was listening too intently for a reply.

The Goddess laughed in a deep rumbling growl of sound. *Deliver this baby,* She said. *And then give it to Me.*

"I will not." This time Damona spoke aloud, crying out her refusal before she realized it. The women gasped; even the senior midwife drew back at the expression on the stranger's face.

You will. Sekhmet's purr was inflexible. *For you will never be free of Me if you do not. Do as I wish, and I will give you what you seek."*

There was a sudden commotion at the other end of the chamber. The basket that Damona had set down by the door was jerking violently. One of the midwives pointed to it and cried out. The lid of the basket toppled aside. Two more midwives let out cries of fear as a lithe black shape leaped out. The Guardian flowed toward Damona, swirling like a streak of black smoke. His orange eyes were huge and blazing.

Do not listen to Her. The cat's light voice swept into Damona's mind. *She seeks to draw you back to Her—*

Silence, creature of My Sister. Sekhmet's tone was both mocking and threatening. *You know this is her choice. She must make it without interference. Priestess,* She asked, *do you want to be rid of Me?*

Damona's answer was torn from her, though this time she did not speak aloud. Thanks to you I am no longer a Priestess and I am driven from my home besides. More than anything do I wish to be rid of You. You know it well.

Then you must have the wands.

Damona started. Yet she should not be surprised. As ancient as the wands themselves were, Sekhmet would surely know of them.

I will give them to you, the Goddess said. *Think of it. The task of finding them, of going through the endless seeking in this land of unnatural cold and snow for them will be over before it must begin. With the wands in your hands I will leave you, never to return.*

Damona stood silent. Something was stirring in her, and it burned with the dark fire of the Goddess Herself. She was ashamed to look at it, to recognize the feeling for what it was. But in the presence of a goddess there was no escape. A part of her wanted this bargain.

Take what She offers, that treacherous fragment of Damona's mind was whispering. All this can be over if you do.

It can indeed. The assurance purred deep into her thoughts. *And not only for You, for your land, as well. I will call back my Bau. I will lift the darkness and cold and sickness. The game will return to the forests. Your people will no longer starve. Is that not a good bargain?*

But the price, Damona whispered in her mind.

There is always a price. The midwives were growing increasingly nervous, but Sekhmet was ignoring them, as well as the Guardian. Her answer was impatient. *You are a slow learner indeed, if you have not learned that by now. I demand a life for a life. So did you, once, else you would not have sought My help. Muirchertac slew your husband, and you slew him. I am still owed payment for the lives of your children. I had planned to take your life as compensation, but I have decided to compromise.*

The Guardian hissed, his teeth gleaming ivory.

Sekhmet snarled at him, but addressed Her words to Damona. *Your life for this child's. It is a small price to pay. Do not tell Me that either the baby or its mother means anything to you. Listen to the wisdom in you that whispers to accept My bargain.*

Damona looked at Clotilde. The queen lay motionless in the midst of her bedcovers. Her eyes were shut as though she were dead. In reality she was in a rest almost as deep as death, taking advantage of the blessed relief from pain.

Perhaps, Damona thought, Sekhmet had granted her surcease from the pains while She bargained for the heart and will of another. She saw that the midwives were staring at her, as well as at the Guardian. None would meet her eyes save the eldest. From the moment Damona had first spoken to this unseen presence, all of them had fallen silent. But it was a silence hovering with dread.

"Look upon her," one of them finally muttered, breaking the silence at last. "See her face." Her eyes flicked nervously to the others. "Something is in this chamber, and she is conversing with it."

She spoke as if Damona could not hear. It was understandable. For while Damona could indeed hear, she felt as though she were encased in ice, her senses aware, but unable to respond. Strange: Sekhmet was a goddess of fire, yet the power She sent out to enclose Damona reeked of cold and dark. She stood by the bed, as motionless as the queen herself. Her blood felt chilled and slow, but her thoughts were racing. Shame ate at her vitals. She did not want the Guardian to know, much less did she want to acknowledge to herself how much she yearned for the bargain Sekhmet offered.

One life, the Goddess had said. One life in exchange for freedom and safety, and not only for herself but for Eire as well. Sekhmet would call back the Bau; things would return to normal, for her people at least, if not for her . . .

Will they? The Guardian's voice was as piercing as Sekhmet's. *Think well on that.*

The Goddess's presence swirled stronger. *Why should she? You speak only with the voice of a small feline. You are but My Sister's creature. And where is She, My Sister? She sends you to do Her bidding for her. I come Myself.*

You come because You are afraid, the cat shot back. *You called upon Your own creature, the Bau, to do Your bidding, and despite the grief she has caused in Eire, You still have not gained what You seek. You are here out of desperation, offering yet another bargain.*

Sekhmet roared. The sound was deafening, though none but the Guardian and Damona could hear it.

Damona clapped her hands to her ears.

"We should fetch the king, Ticta," one of the midwives said to the eldest. Her demeanor was firm and experienced, despite her obvious exhaustion and disheveled hair. She was younger than the senior midwife, though only by a few seasons. "There is evil magic here—"

"And what will the king do about it?" Ticta shot back. "We know there is evil here." She jerked her head at Damona. "That is why *she* has come, is it not?"

"But what of the cat?" One of the women laid a cool cloth on the queen's forehead and stepped back, eyeing the Guardian. "It is not a normal beast. I feel it."

The cat ignored her. He was standing beside Damona. He had not taken his eyes from her.

"Mayhap she brought the cat to aid her in driving out the demon." The senior midwife cleared her throat as though to make Damona aware of her once again. "Druid," she said cautiously. "Can you hear me?"

Answer the mortal. Sekhmet's deep voice pierced through her. *I will not interfere.*

The chill that had frozen Damona loosened. Slowly she turned her face to the old woman called Ticta. "I hear you," she said. "I have been hearing you all along." She nodded at the other women who had spoken. "You are correct in what you say. Evil attends this birth, great evil, indeed."

Several of the midwives exclaimed. Ticta held up a hand to silence them. "What is the meaning of this cat you have brought with you? Is the beast good or evil?"

Damona answered more severely than she realized. "There is nothing you need fear in this creature. Magic is in him, but the magic is not dark. He is a companion of mine, and I am honored to have it so. Cats are sacred to a very ancient and very powerful goddess, a goddess whom I once served."

And has this Goddess helped you? Sekhmet sent the question snarling into Damona's mind. *You speak of Her with such devotion, but where is She? When will you admit that She has deserted you?*

"You see?" The old midwife was unaware of the fierce voice. She cast a satisfied glance at her own companions. "The creature is here to help." The women glanced from her to Damona to the cat. The expression on the faces of most of them was dubious.

She has not deserted you, furless one. The Guardian's light voice was soft. *Do not think that She has.*

Damona flung her gaze down at the cat like a blow. "Then where is She? Why does She not speak to me Herself?"

Why, indeed? mocked the lion-headed goddess.

Without realizing it Damona had spoken aloud again. The effect upon the midwives was immediate. They drew back, and this time, the eldest drew back with them. "By the groves of the gods, what do you keep speaking to?" she demanded. "Is it the evil that has come here to attack our queen?" She thrust a hand out at the Guardian. "You said the cat was not—"

Damona spun on her. "The cat is not the threat, I have told you that!"

"Then what is?" Ticta's tolerance had been strained beyond the breaking point. "Whatever you must do, Druid, do it. Look at her!" She pointed furiously at Clotilde. "She will not remain among the living much longer, if you do not act. Cease talking to what the rest of us cannot see and save her."

Damona's own anger died. Suddenly she was unable to meet either the midwife's eyes or those of the Guardian. "I—I do not know if I can," she whispered. "I no longer have the skill—"

"Try." The old midwife stared searchingly at her. "You must try. For you are all she has."

Damona felt the touch of unseen hands. Power enfolded her, but she could not tell which goddess it came from. She moved to the bed and laid her own mortal hands upon the queen's belly. Pain surged out at her, flashing from the pregnant woman's flesh to hers. It was a tearing pain, reeking of fear and hope and life, sensations that were terrible in their familiarity. She focused on the life, spreading her fingers wide over the great mound of flesh and baby.

Yes, Sekhmet purred inside her head. *Do as you must.*

In a movement so swift it caught even Damona off guard, the cat leaped onto the bed. His eyes burned into hers. *My Mistress is waiting for you,* he said. *But you must find the way back to Her yourself. I wish,* he added softly, *that I could help you more.*

Clotilde stirred suddenly into life. Her eyes opened. A faint smile creased her mouth as she saw Damona above her. "Now the baby will come," she murmured. Her face changed, her eyes squinting shut.

"Another contraction is beginning," one of the midwives said unnecessarily. She looked from the cat, to Damona, to Ticta. "What shall we do?"

"Wait," said the senior midwife. Her eyes watched Damona. "Will your magic enable her contraction to bear fruit?"

Damona glanced up. The automatic response sprang to her lips and died there. It was no longer true. Magic had returned to her, though she shrank from the reason it had. The source and the purpose of this power suddenly flowing through her were things she did not want to speculate on too closely. They had Sekhmet's face stamped upon them too closely.

You know, the Guardian told her. *But the source is not important. The question is what will you do with it?*

Clotilde gasped and moaned, throwing her head back as the contraction's grip upon her strengthened.

"Well, Druid?" Ticta pressed. "Can you bring the baby?"

"Soon," Damona said. The act of birth carried its own intrinsic magic, and she was becoming caught up in it. Old habits and training took over. Compassion was necessary in a midwife, but so was objectivity. Damona took on the man-

tle of the latter as she bent to the woman in labor, both for
her own protection and that of Clotilde.

The contractions came harder. The queen bit at her
already torn lips, too worn out to scream. In the brief lulls,
one of the women spread balm upon her lips, while another
held a tied cloth for her to bite on.

Damona urged and encouraged her with soft words. She
massaged the great belly, moved down to stand at the
queen's feet. The baby was coming at last. Damona caught
the merest glimpse of its head crowning between the queen's
straining thighs. "Help me," she snapped urgently. "We must
get her into the birth position."

Together the women joined in lifting Clotilde from the
bed and helping her into the squatting stance that would
make it easier for the baby to slide out into the world. It was
a difficult task. Exhausted from the long hours of grinding
fruitless labor, the queen was near death. Hanging limply,
she was a heavy burden, weighing like a sack of grain in
their arms.

"We may yet lose them both," the senior midwife said.
"Her strength is all but gone. If she cannot push out the
babe . . . "

Damona reached out and touched Clotilde's face. "Lady,"
she said, speaking with quiet sharpness.

The queen did not respond. Her eyes were closed; her hair
hung in tangled matted strands about her shoulders. She
looked twice as old as the senior midwife. Death hovered
about her.

"Clotilde." Damona made her voice sharper.

The woman's eyelids fluttered. The midwives murmured
words of comfort and encouragement, straining to hold her
upright.

"You asked me to save you, to bring this baby into the
world. Do you still want that?"

"Yes." Clotilde's answer was the merest thread of sound.
Her eyes struggled to open. "The baby must live."

"And so must you." Damona placed both hands on either

side of Clotilde's face. The queen's cheeks were damp and burning beneath her palms. She felt the beginnings of the magic stirring through her; it pulled in her belly, almost like the pain of childbirth itself. "Your child cannot be born if you die. And once born, he will not live without his mother."

The woman's glazed eyes sought to focus on her. "Does your magic tell you so?"

"I need only the magic all women share to know it," Damona said. "The magic of giving life to a child, of being a mother." There was a break in her voice as she spoke, but no one noticed.

"My first son died." Clotilde's last word ended in a gasp. The gasp spiraled into a moan, and then a hoarse shadowy scream.

Working as one, the midwives tightened their hold. Their voices surrounded the woman in her struggle. The voice of the senior midwife rose above the others. "Push, dear heart," she shouted, exhorting and coaxing at once. "Push and push and it will be done."

Damona's hands flew to Clotilde's belly. The power in her leaped up, finding its full strength in rhythm with the contraction. It hurled through her, darkening her vision, sending her reeling into the pains that had attended the birth of her own children. How like Sekhmet: to give her the sheerest of power and the sheerest of pain, all in one massive blow. There was screaming in her ears, and she was not certain if it came from her throat or the queen's. The terrible flaming pulling sensation increased, her hands shook upon Clotilde's belly.

Suddenly she felt an easing. The midwives cried out, and Damona knew the baby was born.

It came sliding out through the birth canal, the limp bedraggled form dropping into the eldest midwife's eagerly waiting hands. Its tiny body was as bloody as the cord that attached it to its mother. The midwives hurried to sever that thick and knotted bond.

"A boy," Ticta announced triumphantly, as the task was done and other women supported the queen. "Lady, you have borne your husband a boy."

Clotilde moved her head, too weak to do any more.

Damona kept her hands on the queen's stomach. "Where is the tea for the afterbirth?" she asked without turning her head.

"Here." The eldest midwife was already there with another goblet, this one containing wine simmered with basil and thyme. "Dear one," the old woman said gently, holding the goblet to the queen's lips, "I know this is hard, but you must push again. The afterbirth must come."

Distracted, her exhausted attention on the child she had finally birthed, Clotilde sipped at the mixture. "He does not cry," she croaked.

Damona looked at the women gathered around the tiny squashed figure. "He will."

With swift skill those midwives not supporting the mother were cleaning and swaddling her newborn, wiping mucus from his nose and mouth so that he could take his first breaths. Red-faced, wrinkled, and incredibly ugly, he gulped in air, and promptly voiced his displeasure at the sensation with an angry shriek. The midwives smiled. Their fear of Damona was gone, washed clean at least for the time being, in the warmth and happiness of a birth in which mother and child both lived. Their quiet joy permeated the air with a scent sweeter than freshly picked sacred mistletoe.

New herbs added their scents to the chamber. The baby was being anointed with an infusion of holly, sprinkled on his tiny kicking body to ensure protection. Hawthorn was being placed in the cradle that would hold him to shield the tiny occupant from evil spells. On this night more than the usual amount was being laid about; the midwives might have forgotten their fear of Damona, but they had not forgotten the malevolence that had sought to prevent this birth.

A smile spread across Clotilde's wan features as the smells of the protective herbs wafted to her. Hawthorn and holly were never used when a babe was born dead or disfigured by dark forces, but only when the child came into the world healthy. "My son lives." Her voice was a whisper of relief and joy. "And he is whole."

He lives, the voice of Sekhmet agreed. *Now, give him to Me.*

19

OUTSIDE THE LYING-IN CHAMBER, Chlodweg's hall resounded with noise. The clamor of happiness and relief at the birth of an heir after these long hours of waiting were loud enough to disturb the rest of the tired queen. That was not a consideration to the men in the hall, though. Surrounded by his chieftains, the king was guzzling goblet after goblet of mead. His broad face was flushed with firelight and drink and joy.

The midwife who had brought him the news had promptly gone back to the queen's lying-in chamber, leaving the men to their celebrating. Women's business, she observed dryly to herself, as she left, was laboring to bring forth life. Men's business was to take the credit.

Her departure went unnoticed. The men roared and laughed and spilled their mead. The tension had been nearly unbearable, with most of them convinced that there would be only one end. Instead, the chieftain they followed had an heir. The dynasty, and their place within it, was assured.

"This birth is an omen," one of the nobles said to Chlodweg. His name was Mannius, and he was ancient by Frankish standards; he had fought by Childeric's side when the old king led the people into Belgica Segunda. He raised his creaky voice to make certain he would be heard above the uproar. "Now that your son is born, the time has come to continue with your plans. Remember the charge your father laid upon you as he lay on his deathbed."

The king emptied his goblet and held it out to be refilled.

"I know it well, Uncle," he said curtly. "I have had other signs besides this birth."

Chlodweg's eyes glinted. The words of his mysterious visitor rang again in his ears. Goddess, or demon, or whatever creature she was, she had been right. In truth, he was not satisfied with the lands he had taken from Syagrius. He had spent years battling the troublesome inhabitants of western Gaul, the Visigoths, in particular. Now that they were subdued, his aspirations were driving him to eastern Gaul and the lands of the barbarians there.

"Lord," a new voice broke in, "what are these signs you speak of? What have the gods told you?" It was a priest who had spoken, and no Christian priest, but a man of the old religion. He and his brethren had been in attendance from the first, offering sacrifices and prayers for the child of their king. They were glowing with satisfaction at their success.

Chlodweg studied the priest. Intuitively he knew he must not say anything of the strange Goddess. Let the priest think the people's own gods had spoken to him. Perhaps, through that terrifying vision, they had.

"First the Ripurians must swear allegiance to me," he said loudly, so that others would hear.

A roar of agreement went up in the crowded hall. Chlodweg had struck with unerring accuracy at a sore spot that rankled within every Salian Frank.

The Ripurians were a branch of the Franks, but they had not followed the Salians into Toxandria and then south into Belgica Segunda. Instead, they had chosen to cross the Middle Rhine from the east and take advantage of the ruin of Roman trade and culture. Towns had suffered, buildings had been destroyed, walls fallen into disrepair, and populations greatly reduced in this former enclave of Rome. Yet life continued to go on.

The Ripurians established themselves among the villas and cities on the great river's western bank. Just as their kinfolk the Salians, they were barbarians. They had little fondness for moving into the half-deserted villas that had once been great estates belonging to wealthy Roman citizens, or inhabiting the ruined towns that had once bustled with natives and Romans both. Still, settling down in these half-abandoned places was far better than the harsh struggle that attended life in the bleak forest clearings of central Germania.

Chlodweg watched the reaction of the chieftains to his pronouncement with satisfaction. If he was to achieve his ambitions, it was essential that the two branches of his people be united into a single tree, with himself at the crown.

"The Alamanni are on the move," one of the men said. His words were slurred with drink, but his thoughts were obviously clear. "They will move even faster, once word reaches them of your son. That you have an heir will embolden them. They know they must act before you grow too much stronger."

A rumble of assent went up, and Chlodweg nodded. "I am already strong," he said, terse and confident. "And once the Ripurians have surrendered themselves to my protection, I will be even stronger. The Alamanni are fierce in battle, and they have declared themselves the enemies of our kinsmen. A foolish move on their part, for once we have all joined together, neither they nor any other force will be able to defeat us. When the Alamanni lands are mine, Theodoric himself will take notice of me."

Men roared again, clanking their goblets. It was well-known that the Alamanni were terrible fighters, perhaps the fiercest of all the west Germanic tribes. But there was not a man in the hall whose blood did not race at his king's boasts. Chlodweg was a man to be reckoned with, a man who would lead his warriors far; everyone knew this. The gods smiled upon him.

When the shouting had subsided, the priest spoke again. "You belong to us, my lord," he pointed out. "And to the old gods. As for the emperor in Byzantium, he does not acknowledge you, and he will not. To him, you are a pagan."

Chlodweg grunted. "One day," he growled, "he will acknowledge me. As I said: I have had signs."

In Clotilde's chamber, the voice that only Damona and the Guardian could hear was more terrible than a sword cut. Utterly engrossed in the act of bringing life, Damona had forgotten Sekhmet. All her being had been taken up in the beauty and wonder of the birth. Oh, the joy of it: of seeing this baby arrive whole and beautiful.

But now it was done. Now the baby squalled and kicked in his first moments in the world, and the weight of the bargain she had been offered descended again, tormenting her with its horror and its temptation.

The birth cord and the placenta had been carefully wrapped in linens to be buried later in a secret place while the ceremonies that would protect both mother and child from harm were performed. The bed had been stripped and laid with clean linen. Clotilde, too, had been washed, clothed in a fresh bed gown, and helped back into bed. She lay on her back, breathing faintly. The fur coverlet had been drawn back, and Ticta was massaging her belly in order to shrink the blood vessels that had been so strained by the endless labor.

The old woman hummed softly as she worked. Her smile was a broader version of the one on the queen's exhausted face. "She will live," the midwife said happily to Damona. "There will not be any great bleeding. We will start brewing the herbs to bring on her milk, and cook oats to give her strength. Thanks be to you, Druid." Her smile reached to include the Guardian. "And to your cat. He has brought good luck, after all."

The Guardian sat motionless, his orange eyes fixed on Damona.

She stood in silence, her gaze fixed on the baby. She could not answer, could not speak, to either the midwife or the cat. Her voice was knotted inside her throat, as thick as the birth cord had been, engorged with the blood of children: the blood of her own, and the blood of all those children left behind in Eire, at the mercy of evil. One of the women brought the swaddled baby to the queen and laid the bundle in her arms. Weakly she clutched it, nestling her son to her breasts. The baby nuzzled at her warmth, instinctively seeking the thin yellowish substance that would sustain him until Clotilde's milk began to flow.

Damona stared and stared at the sight. Smoldering within her a new emotion was being born as surely as this babe had been born. Here was this woman, lying safe in bed, secure with her faith, her husband, and her new son. She possessed all that Damona had once had—all that she had lost. The unfairness of it was suddenly overwhelming. That she should have helped this Christian keep not only her life, but her child, after all that Christianity had taken from her. What had she been thinking?

Keenly she felt the weight of the cat's gaze. She could not bring herself to meet his eyes. She looked at Clotilde hugging her son, and her arms ached for her own little ones. It felt as if her very breasts were weeping, the swollen nipples seeping not with the substance of life, but with the bitter salt tears of grief. A sour taste filled her mouth. Jealousy welled up in her. The hatred that she had thought dead along with Muirchertac was all at once alive again. The intensity of it shook her. Had Sekhmet used Her powers to kindle these feelings in her again?

I have not, the lion-headed goddess said. *Whatever you are feeling is true. I have placed nothing within you that was not already there. Knowing this, it should make it easier for you to choose.*

The Guardian drew closer. His fur brushed against her ankles. *She is right,* he said in his light dry voice. *You must choose. But choose wisely.*

Damona wavered, staring at the baby and its mother. Clotilde finally became aware of her and returned her gaze. She smiled at Damona, her haggard features radiant. "All praise to the One True God." She was whispering, still terribly weak, but glowing with happiness. "He saw my travail and answered my prayers."

Damona teetered on the edge of a precipice. "I thought," she said coldly, "that the old ways answered your prayers."

The queen did not notice her tone. "Of course. But it was the Lord Jesus Christ who sent you to me. It was He Who used your old powers as a tool against evil." She touched the cross about her neck with reverent fingers. "May His holy name be praised."

Do you see? Sekhmet's voice was insidious, piercing to the core of Damona's pain. *How quickly she loses her gratitude to the one truly responsible. These Christians are all alike. And you would protect her and her babe? It seems that the blood of your own children who were murdered by Christians has grown unimportant to you, Priestess.*

Damona flinched. She searched within herself for a retort, and could not find one. It was true; she could not deny Sekhmet's words, any more than she could deny the reality of her murdered *fine.* A red mist obscured her vision, and in its glow she saw the bodies of her children. Crumpled and bloody, they lay superimposed over the tiny form of Clotilde's son. A Christian child, born to a Christian mother, whom she herself had helped, while her own lay dead at the hands of Christians. And now the woman could only prattle on about her god, a god who was surely more cruel and bloodthirsty than Sekhmet Herself.

The cat's brushing grew more insistent. *Take heed,* he warned. *Is what you are seeing from you or from Her?*

Sekhmet hissed. *What difference does it make? Truth is truth, whatever the source.*

Damona still could not look at the Guardian. *You will give me the wands, and the people in Eire will be freed of your demon?* she asked in her mind.

I have said that I will.

Then free my people, Damona said, steadfastly ignoring the Guardian. *And I will do as You ask.*

A thick purring laugh shook the chamber. *The bargain is struck,* the Goddess said. *Let it be done.*

A wave of heat surged up in the chamber. At the same moment the candles all went out as if a single great hand had snuffed them. The midwives, engrossed in their various tasks, were taken unawares. Startled, they looked around, their glances going to the hearth-fire to see why it had flared up so suddenly.

It had not. Beside the bed of the queen the source of the heat began to take shape. From out of nowhere a tall flame leaped up. Instantly it was followed by another flame, and yet another. Within moments the bed was surrounded by fire. The flames coiled and writhed like snakes, blazing red, and yet eerily silent. Surrounded by them Clotilde cried out, clutching both the baby and the cross to her breasts.

The midwives stared at the sight in terror, their eyes huge and round. "Do something," the eldest shouted to Damona.

Damona did not move.

Now the fire in the hearth was drawn in. Unlike the flames about the bed, these flames had voices. They crackled and hissed, snapping up into the air, moving as if they had been given a life of their own. In the midst of the crackling a figure was forming.

The figure grew brighter and brighter. Heat billowed forth, clothing the room in flame and smoke the color of freshly spilled blood. The midwives screamed and cowered. Only Ticta had the courage and presence of mind to fling her old body forward in a desperate attempt to protect the queen and her child.

The flames struck her down.

None of the women dared look at the figure that formed the heart of this unearthly fire; even had they wanted to it would have been impossible, for it burned too brightly. They did not see the figure stretch an arm out to Damona. They did not see the bloodred smoke and flames obscure her.

As swiftly as they had appeared, the flames and smoke

began to dissipate. In moments the chamber was as it had been. Once again the fire burned in the hearth as it was supposed to. The only light came from the flickering candles.

But there was one difference. The queen's sudden shriek announced it.

Damona and the baby were gone.

The women awoke from their terror. Ticta lay on the floor beside the bed, so still it looked as though life had left her. Several of her companions ran to her. Others began frantically searching for the baby. Without speaking of it to each other, they knew it would be a fruitless search. Clotilde struggled to a sitting position in her bed. Her eyes were wild, her mouth rounded into a circle of horror and disbelief. She stared wildly about her.

"My child." The queen uttered the words in a hoarse whisper. "My child." This time she spoke louder. "My child!" At last, she was screaming, and once started it seemed as though she would be unable to stop.

The young midwife who had gone out before to announce the happy news to Chlodweg left again. But now she was running, her face frozen in terror. She stumbled into the crowded hall, trying to make her way between the men. At first, no one noticed her; carelessly they blocked her path, laughing and shouting, spilling mead on her from overfilled goblets. In her struggle to reach the king the woman became angry. Shoving furiously at two burly chieftains, she let out a piercing yell.

The chieftains gaped at her in annoyed surprise, and she screamed again. Her nerves were shredded raw by the vision in the chamber; she had neither patience nor respect to spare for these men who stood in her way. "Move aside and let me pass, you great oafs! " she yelled. "Are all of you so drunk you cannot see that something terrible has happened! I must speak to the king!"

There was a commotion at the other end of the hall. Chlodweg suddenly appeared. The king took one look at her and snapped, "What has happened?"

Having achieved her goal, the young midwife found that she was unable to tell him. "My lord," she got out, and fell silent.

"Speak!" Chlodweg roared at her. "What has happened?"

The woman gestured in the direction of the lying-in chamber. "Come," was all she could say. "Come at once."

Before the last word had left her mouth the king had drawn his sword and was dashing out of the hall. His closest chieftains followed on his heels. All of them burst into the chamber in a clatter of weapons and mead fumes. They stared uncomprehendingly at the scene before them.

Tables were overturned, tinctures and herbs and water lay spilled on the floor rushes. The senior midwife lay on the rushes, while her companions tended to her. The old woman's face was covered with reddish black soot that at first looked like blood, her tunic was shredded, hanging from her lean body in rags. In the bed the queen was raging and writhing amidst the fur coverlets. Beside her bed a cradle stood empty.

"She has taken my child, she has taken my child!" Clotilde shrieked the same words over and over, as if her lips were incapable of uttering anything else. Those women not tending to the midwife were trying helplessly to restrain her.

Chlodweg's face went as gray as the sky. "Who," he breathed. "Who has taken my son?"

"The Druid woman took him." The old midwife's voice was a gasping echo of what it had been; she sounded as though her throat had been seared. With the aid of the others she managed to sit up. Dazedly she wiped soot from her face and stared at it. She coughed violently, then shook her head. "I do not understand it. She delivered the baby. She saved both his life and his mother's. And then, she took him."

"Of course she did." The young midwife who had fetched the king had recovered her voice as well, and with it, her fury. She was still trembling with what she had witnessed. "She wanted the baby all along. She is evil, just as I said she was! I warned you, yet you would not listen to me. You thought I was being foolish. Well, now you see—"

"I see," the old one retorted hoarsely, "that if we had not accepted her help, the baby and the mother would have died. What choice did we have? Tell me that!"

"Cease your squabbling." Chlodweg's voice was terrifying in its calmness. "Else I have you all torn limb from limb and then burned for your part in this."

The men who had followed him into the chamber growled their agreement. Her eyes rounding in terror at this new threat, the young woman's mouth clapped shut. But her elder was not so easily cowed.

"You may flay and burn us or cut us all up into little pieces if that suits you," Ticta said sharply, still wheezing and coughing, but strong in spite of it. "But no such deeds will bring back your son. We had no part in what happened here. And you are too wise a chieftain not to know that."

Chlodweg looked at her with blazing eyes. "How did the foreign woman take him?"

The midwife rubbed her throat. Clotilde answered for her. The queen's voice was almost as seared as the old woman's. "With heathen powers," she cried. "In the name of our Lord, Jesus Christ, I trusted her . . ."

"Your Lord." Chlodweg snarled the words as though they were a curse. "You killed my first son with your religion, and now, after the gods saw fit to give you a second, you must sacrifice him to this foul Christianity. Curse your one god, woman! Curse him! And you, who have given up my son to an unknown fate!" He raised his great fists as though he were about to strike her.

"No." Clotilde was sobbing in great convulsive heaves. "I did not. I sought to protect our baby."

The midwives glanced at each other. Instinctively they drew together to protect their patient. They were all women, and these men, Chlodweg included, were intruders. Not a one of them could bear to watch their queen in such pain, not after the suffering she had endured in order to bring her baby into the world, and particularly not after the way they had seen that baby disappear.

Again, it fell to Ticta to speak up. "You accuse your wife falsely, my lord," she said firmly. "She did indeed seek to protect the child. This was not her doing, any more than it was ours." She hesitated. "In truth, I do not think it was even the doing of the Druid woman. She wanted to help the queen. I truly believe that she did."

Chlodweg spun on her. "This is how you speak of help? Old woman, your wits have been addled by whatever it was that struck you down."

The midwife stared at him. "There was an evil here," she said. "And it was strong, terribly strong. In the end, it proved to be stronger than the powers the Druid woman possessed."

The king glared at her a moment longer. Abruptly he turned away. "Then how," he asked despairingly, more to himself than to anyone in the chamber, "am I to find my son?"

"Lord," the old woman said, seeking to make her burned voice gentle. "I do not know."

A silence dropped over the chamber.

Chlodweg's gaze went back to his wife. He looked at her, huddled and weeping, and turned his back. Grief and rage and despair scored his rough features, half-obscured by his heavy beard. He strode to the hearth. Back and forth he paced. Several times he did so, then jerked to a stop.

His face was set, washed clean of the emotions that had ravaged it. The air of authority that he wore as naturally as a mantle was his again. "Summon every man-at-arms who can walk or sit a horse," he commanded. "We will mount a search. Magic or no, we will not stop until that woman is found." His stern eyes swept over the cluster of men. "Bring the priests to me, every one of them. They, too, must add their powers to our search."

As the men hurried out to do his bidding, Chlodweg went back to the bed. Clotilde turned a desolate face up to his. It seemed as though her sobs would tear her body apart. The midwives glowered accusingly at their king.

"I told you, husband," she groaned. "The evil was present before she came. I called upon her to help me. I believed that she would."

Chlodweg heaved a deep ragged sigh. "In truth, perhaps you did."

"Oh, husband." Clotilde struggled to contain her weeping. "The One True God will bring our babe back to us. You will see."

Chlodweg looked at her, engaged in his own struggle not to rail at her as he had done before. He put a large hand over Clotilde's. "If he does," he said quietly, "if my son is returned to me, whole and unharmed, then I will make you a vow. I will do as you have so long urged me to do. I will become a Christian." He removed his hand and straightened up, adding bitterly, "It is a vow easily made, for there will be little chance of my being called upon to keep it."

He left the chamber. The moment he was alone the voice hailed him.

King of the Franks.

20

THE BEAUTIFUL, BURNING TONE froze Chlodweg in his tracks. An image of an enormous beast face gleaming as if flames lit it from within filled his mind. He looked around, startled and fearful. He saw nothing. "Is it you?" he demanded. "The Goddess Who visited me in the night?"

The voice slashed at him. *Who else would it be?*

Chlodweg gasped in relief. Yes, this was fitting, he told himself. Magic dealt with by other magic. An unknown force had taken his son; now, an unknown force would return him. "You have come to help me find my son." It was a statement, rather than a question, and he exhaled gustily as he spoke.

Perhaps, or perhaps not. The decision is up to you.

Chlodweg had the eerie sense that his visitor was smiling, though he had no way of knowing; unlike the other time, She had not revealed Herself to him.

The king's relief faded. "Goddess," he said desperately. "Know you what took my son?"

Oh, yes, the burning voice replied. *I know.*

Chlodweg's fists clenched into big heavy knots. "Have you the power to see that he is returned to me?"

The smile was there again. *I do.*

The king exhaled again. "Do so, Lady, and whatever decisions you wish me to make, I will make them." He caught himself, realizing too late the significance of what he had said. What if this outlander Goddess demanded something untenable, such as renouncing his kingship? His power for his son; it was an awful choice, one he was not certain he could make.

Be at ease. The fiery voice held laughter within the flames. *Without your kingship you are of no use to Me. Actually, what I ask of you is a thing you should take joy in. You must fight a battle.*

"A battle?" Ordinarily Chlodweg would have been eager at the prospect. But this was not the proper time; indeed, there could be no worse time. "My son is in the grasp of an evil power," he tried to explain. "I cannot put my mind to fighting until I have him back."

The Goddess's voice was inflexible. *If you fight this battle, your son will be returned to you. Fight it in My name, and I will give you weapons to ensure that you are the victor. For you, this is no mere engagement. You are occupied with thoughts of your future. Well, this will determine it. Did I not tell you that Gaul would be yours?*

Chlodweg was engrossed now. For a moment, his overwhelming fury and fear over the disappearance of his son was forgotten. "What is this battle you would have me fight?"

One that you have been waiting for. Your enemies are restless. They have left their lands and are moving toward yours. That should be reason enough for any king to fight. At a place you call Tolbiac you will meet them. Assemble your warriors; gather an army and go there.

Chlodweg considered. He knew the enemies the Goddess was referring to were the Alamanni. They were a tribe as numerous as they were dangerous. Their very name meant "Men from everywhere," a reference to the many offshoots of the Swabian West Germans from which they were descended. Unless the Ripurian branch joined the tree, there might be no defeating them, even with the aid of this foreign Goddess.

The Alamanni were fierce fighters; they were well armed, and, in an unusual departure from the Germanic tribes, they were horsemen, fighting off the backs of their mounts with longswords, as did the non-Germanic Huns. That alone made them a foe to be wary of. The Franks were accustomed to move and fight on foot. Everything in their arsenal of warfare was geared toward battling a man on the ground. Their weapons-makers were skilled, but the arms they made—the *scramasax,* the short sword, and the *francisca,* the throwing hatchet that was the characteristic war implement of the Franks—were meant for hand-to-hand combat.

"And what weapons would You give me to defeat them?" Chlodweg waited intently for the reply.

That you will see, said the Goddess.

The king frowned. "But Goddess—"

The harsh voice interrupted him. *Where do you think your son is at this moment, O King?*

Chlodweg drew in his breath. "With the Alamanni?" He uttered the question in a low, dangerous tone. "Of course!" He slammed a heavy fist against his thigh. "They cast an evil spell over my house, and then bewitched my wife so that she believed the woman was here to help her. By the gods, they will pay!" He wheeled about, his wild gaze seeking out his mysterious visitor. "You demand a battle, Goddess. Well, by my head, you shall have it. Tolbiac will run red with Alamanni blood before I am through."

Satisfaction purred in the Goddess's voice. *I am pleased. Set about doing it then. You will have your weapons when the time comes.*

The burning voice faded in Chlodweg's mind, disappearing as unexpectedly as it had appeared. Immediately another voice took its place, but this one was mortal and recognizable.

"My lord." Mannius, the old chieftain who had served Chlodweg's father, was standing at his shoulder. "The freemen are gathering as you have commanded. There are already enough to start the search, as long as no storms descend upon us. And the priests have come as well. They await you in the hall."

Chlodweg stood silent.

"My lord?" The old warrior put a questioning hand on his king's arm.

"I heard you." Chlodweg stood an instant longer, his ears straining for the sound of that powerful flaming voice. No words came to him; the Goddess apparently considered their conversation finished. Chlodweg would have to make up his mind alone. He tugged at his beard. "The men are armed?"

Mannius gave him a curious look. "As always. And though it will do them little good if magic is involved, they bear enough weapons so that one would think they are going to war."

"Good." Chlodweg gave his orders briskly. "Continue to see that every warrior is assembled, and pass the word that each man is to go on arming himself for war. I myself will go to the hall to address those already here. And pack trains with provisions will need to be formed to supply us as we march."

"Pack trains?" The chieftain was regarding him blankly. "Who are we to fight against in the dead of winter? Your son is gone. Difficult enough will it be to hunt for him in this cold and snow without engaging in battle at the same time."

Chlodweg whirled on him. "Do you question me, old man?"

The noble's faded gaze met the eyes of his king. "Yes," he said bluntly. "For as you yourself point out, I am old. Death holds little fear for me. It did not when I was young, and it holds even less, now that my bones are stiff and my blood cool. Why are you so set on seeking out a battle, when your heir was stolen away by evil magic? Will shedding the blood of mortal men get him back?"

A grim smile lit Chlodweg's face. "It will, friend of my father," he said in a tone so strange that Mannius stared at him. "Go you and carry out my wishes. There is work to be done."

The army of Salian Franks assembled swiftly. Chlodweg's realm was a warrior world; even in the nonfighting season the possibility of battle always hovered near the surface. The nobles pounded through the woods and fields shouting out their king's order, and clusters of men followed in their wake.

Lordship was the basis of Frankish society. The chieftains around Chlodweg were his *gefolge,* his war band. As was customary they and their families lived in his stronghold, exchanging their fighting ability for the king's protection and generosity. Chlodweg was a powerful man; as a result, his *gefolge* was large, to match that power. But large as it was, his stronghold could not contain the numbers of men that came clomping through the snowy woods.

These men who assembled at their lord's call were peasants, though freeborn ones. Their homes were small farms, worked by children, parents, and the occasional slave, and they comprised the backbone of the Frankish king's power. These tall muscular farmers turned warriors were the infantry, the foot soldiers who faced the grim and bloody business of warfare as it was fought on the frontier. Thus far, they had been highly successful.

Breath steaming in the frigid air, laden with throwing hatchets and shortswords, and bundled in furs so that only their eyes showed, the free men-at-arms gathered and waited. Rather than reentering the stronghold, most of the chieftains elected to remain with them. The chieftains were mounted, but the freemen were all on foot. Summoned from the warmth of their families and hearth-fires, they shifted their numb feet in the fading light of late afternoon, muttering to each other of the command that had brought them here, and of the wild rumors that attended that command.

Here and there groups had kindled small fires to ward off the chill. They huddled close to the warmth, fingering their weapons. The horses of the chieftains stamped restlessly. The men around them stamped along with them, as the waiting lengthened. All at once a ripple went through the assembly. The talking fell off. The men brightened, watching attentively. Chlodweg himself was coming out to address them.

The king, too, was garbed for cold-weather travel and for war. The hilt of his *scramasax* was solid gold and set with precious gems. His *francisca* was similarly ornamented. Necklaces of gold and silver adorned the fur mantle that covered him. His eyes blazed out at the Franks, snapping at them like the flames of the hearth fire inside his hall.

"Kinsmen." Chlodweg's voice carried the sound of blood in its roar. "My queen gave birth to a son this day. My heart was filled with joy, but that joy has now turned to rage. The Alamanni have taken my son. Such a deed is beyond honor. They must be punished."

A rumble went through the massed warriors. The nobles exchanged astonished glances, especially those who had charged after Chlodweg into the queen's lying-in chamber. They had seen evidence of magic there; that the Alamanni had anything to do with that magic was something none of them had heard. The aged noble, whose old bones had earned him the right to stay in the warm hall until the king left, looked thoughtfully at Chlodweg.

"Lord," a chieftain shouted. "It is said that a sorceress took the child."

Chlodweg jerked his head in savage assent. "In truth, she did. But word has come to me that she is in league with the Alamanni. They thought to distract me from their incursions into lands that do not belong to them. They will find that they are wrong."

The rumbling among the men grew louder. The Franks were a people accustomed to obedience, but those of high blood had the right to question their lord's decisions, and there were always those who insisted on using that right. One of them did so now. "The Alamanni possess a great force," this man pointed out. "As strong in battle as we are, the odds and the weather might go against us, lord. We will need the Ripurians standing with us to be assured of victory."

Chlodweg stared at the chieftain calmly. "They will be with us. Have no fear of it being otherwise." His voice grew louder. "All any of you, my brave men-at-arms, need do is make your bellies strong and your arms mighty."

A number of the warriors cheered. However, not all of them were yet satisfied. "How do we know the Ripurians will fight with us, lord?" another noble called out. "Have they given you their oaths?"

It was not in Chlodweg's nature to lie or dissemble. His honesty was one of the qualities that drew men to him, and kept them loyal. "They have not," he said. "But they will." His fierce direct gaze swept out over the men. "There is not a man here who does not know the strength of my word. I give it to you now. The Ripurians are our kinsmen. They will fight alongside us, and they will share in our victory." His voice had been steadily rising, until it became a hoarse scream, a battle yell in the cold darkening air. "My word upon it!"

Cheering erupted again, and finally it was unanimous. Chlodweg watched the display with dark satisfaction. His bloodshot eyes burned red in his gaunt face.

"Let us march," he said.

Damona stood within a circle of leaping flames and wondered if she was dead. The fire held her within a border of light, not harming her, but not allowing her the freedom to move either. She knew she was not in Eire. Had Sekhmet betrayed her, taking her life as well as the life of the baby she had offered to the Goddess?

The newborn babe waved his tiny fists, nuzzling his mouth into her breasts as he searched for milk. Damona hardened her heart against that soft, seeking mouth. This child was condemned; she had seen to that herself. It was too late for regrets.

The flames about her were the same as the ones that had appeared in Clotilde's chamber: crimson and smoky, shining dark and bright as blood. Their origin was magic, and so they burned neither Damona nor the babe she held. Focusing her gaze Damona found that she could see past them.

There was a land beyond the wall of fire glow. It revealed itself to her in shimmering lines, dancing through the boundary of the flames. She saw vast stretches of forest clothing mountains that disappeared into an endless sky. She saw flat grassy meadows bisected by rivers and great placid lakes. Far in the distance she thought she glimpsed the edges of a desert, perhaps the burning land ruled over by Sekhmet. It was difficult to tell, for even as she looked the colors in this place began running together, earth blending into sky until all of it became one enormous tapestry of wavering, the brightness of which forced her to close her eyes.

"Well, here you are at last."

The voice shook Damona to her bones. She stared through the red haze of smoke and flames, the baby clutched forgotten to her chest. The man smiled back at her. "Muirchertac," she whispered.

"Indeed." His smile widened. He stood outside the flames, tall and muscular, looking as he had in life, before she had driven him over the brink of madness. His auburn hair stood up, stiffened with lime in the fashion he had always been fond of. A jeweled fibula glittered at the shoulder of his brat; even the gold torque he had worn about his neck was there.

Damona regarded him with something like resignation. "So I am dead."

The former *Tuisech* shook his head. "Not precisely, though you did quite an efficient job at sending me to my own death."

The tone in which he spoke these words caught at her. She peered through the dancing glow, staring into Muirchertac's face. The madness that had tainted him all through his days in the mortal world was gone. His green eyes were bright and calm, gleaming with secrets and joy. Peace rested upon his features; he smiled at her with genuine humor.

"You see correctly, *Banfili*. The madness of my mortal life has left me. I should thank you. It was a favor you did me by sending me here." The *Tuisech* waved a hand. "Why have you not stepped through the flames, *Banfhili?* You, of all souls, should know they will not harm you."

The baby kicked, reminding Damona of his presence.

Muirchertac smiled at it. "It is time for you to begin your travels," he said mildly. "Both of you."

Still staring at him Damona stepped through the boundary of fire. The flames rippled over her as she passed through them, rustling against her skin with an odd, tickling sensation. She found herself within an enormous grove. The fire blazed within the exact center, burning soundlessly upon a patch of grass the color of a summer sky. Trees that had never put down roots in Eire or Gaul enclosed the grove. Their branches grew in great spirals, crowned by leaves as circular as the grove itself. They were not green, these leaves, they were no single color at all. Scores of different shades twinkled within their depths, darting and shimmering like hordes of spirit flies.

Damona stepped away from Muirchertac. It was too difficult to be near this man whom she herself had killed. The sight of him aroused so many memories and feelings within her she could not make sense out of any of them. She hated him still, and she hated herself for what had been wrought in her land as a result of that hate. The hatred tingled over her flesh, burning her more fiercely than any flames ever could.

The *Tuisech* continued to smile, obviously aware of this. He moved away, giving her plenty of room. "Go," he said. "Be on your way." He gestured, and Damona saw a path laid with bright stones winding out of the grove.

She took a step toward the path, and paused, looking at him over her shoulder. "Where?"

"Why, anywhere. In this realm all paths will lead to the place you seek, the place where you are supposed to be."

Damona's gaze started to go down to the child. She pulled her eyes away. "To Sekhmet?" she asked quietly.

"That," Muirchertac said, "is up to you."

"It is a choice I have already made, as you would surely

know." She did not try to keep the bitterness from her tone. "Is this Her country?"

Muirchertac shrugged. "It is the country of a great many. The real question is: will it be yours?"

He let out a hearty laugh. As the sound of it rang into the brightly colored air, he walked into the flames. They shot up with sudden brilliance. When the flaring ceased, he was gone.

Damona had blinked at the flames' glare. She did not see the madness that had flared up in Muirchertac's green eyes at the same moment the flames swallowed him.

The fire was dying down, as though its task were finished. As swiftly as it had blazed up, it dwindled to a pile of glowing embers. Damona watched the last few tendrils of smoke twine up into the multihued light. Sinuous and black the smoke left a stain against the luminous sky. When she could no longer see any trace of the blackness, she turned away and began to walk.

The baby had grown silent and motionless. Damona's heart constricted. Hastily she glanced down, wondering if Sekhmet had taken Her price after all. But the baby still lived. His blank little face peered out of the swaddling cloths. His eyes, blue and dazed-looking, as the eyes of all newborns were, gazed placidly back at her.

Damona pulled her gaze away. How many children had she helped bring into the world who had those same eyes? For an instant she saw her own babies reflected in those blue depths. They, too, had looked up at her as this child was doing, nestling against her as she held them in her arms.

Bring the child to Me.

Sekhmet's voice burned through the clear colors. Damona halted. "Where are You?" she demanded. "Why am I not in Eire? I honored my part of the bargain!"

And I will honor Mine. Keep walking, and you will come to Me.

Damona made her heart small and hard again. She dared not look at the small bundle in her arms. She hurried on.

The grove of giant trees with their circular limbs and twinkling leaves was soon left behind. But beyond it stood another grove, and yet another. Damona's strides slowed as she realized that she would have to pass through each one of them. She was a Druid, or had been, once. She knew the meaning of these groves. This was a place of magic, and the source of that magic was contained in these groves.

She drew a breath and followed the path steadily toward the next one.

She is coming. Sekhmet swirled up from a desert of gold and blood, bursting through the glimmering pink stones of Bast's temple and into the sacred sanctuary itself. *She has paid the price, and she is Mine.*

Bast glowed in colors deep with thought. *Not yet,* She said. *She must still pass through the groves.*

Damona walked past the barrier of trees and into the grove. A blast of heat struck her. Sunlight dense as an armful of woolen blankets flowed down over her. A wide flat plain stretched out before her, growing wider and wider even as she looked. It was covered in grass, strands upon strands of it, thick and tall and pale as new-minted gold. As in the first grove, earth and sky blended together, the sky as glittering and yellow as the grass.

The plain was not empty. Animals wandered about in herds, heads down as they grazed. All of them were beasts such as Damona had never seen.

Small tawny-colored creatures that faintly resembled deer leaped above the tall grass, slim legs carrying them in bounds high above the ground. Horses striped in startling patterns of black and white moved among them, tails flicking. Here and there, lone trees rose above the plain. Enormous animals spotted in hues of cream and brown stood next to these trees, so tall their heads rose above the topmost branches. They bore impossibly long necks that swayed in the air like the blades of grass.

Damona had no idea how long she stood at the edge of the plain gaping at these creatures before she resumed walking.

The pale gold grass enclosed her at once, its strands waving above her head, tossed by a quick hot wind. The path was still before her, though barely visible amongst the thick growth. She pushed her way along it, holding the silent baby against her. Pressing down a handful of grass blades, she peered ahead. Far, far in the distance she glimpsed the edges of the grove. The border of trees shimmered through wavering lines of heat. She must pass through this plain with its otherworldly beasts in order to reach it.

Behind her there was a sudden rustling in the grass. Damona hesitated. Should she keep walking or go around? She no longer had her true powers to tell her, only those vestiges Sekhmet had seen fit to tease her with.

The rustling grew louder. From alongside of Damona a huge cat appeared. It was as lithe and graceful as Mau, but on a far larger scale. In other ways as well, this animal was no Mau. Wisdom glowed on the broad whiskered face, but no compassion. Its fur and eyes were as pale and golden as the grass and sky. it seemed to be hunting her. Muscles bunched and coiled under its smooth golden hide as it moved toward her. The dark tassel at the end of its long tail beat slowly its flanks.

Though she had never seen one alive, Damona knew what this animal was. She had seen depictions of it in paintings and on pottery. Yet she needed no lifeless images to tell her what she knew in her soul.

This was a lioness.

Sekhmet Herself was stalking her through the tall whispering grass.

21

THE CREATURE'S GOLDEN EYES held Damona. It spoke to her, its tone burning and familiar. The voice beat along her veins.

This is the realm of My power. I rule here. I, and no other. Thus it was in the beginning, and thus it shall be in the end. Here is the source of My strength. It can be yours, as well. Look upon what I can give you.

The lioness sat down, curling her tail about her paws in a gesture eerily reminiscent of Mau. She turned her great head, and Damona followed the merciless pale gaze.

Before her the flat plain with its strange animals dissolved into a scene from the Black Land. Thousands of men and women clothed in white were preparing and drinking from golden jars. Red liquid stained the ground, and the people's brown faces and white garments. At first Damona thought they were drinking blood, but as the liquid bubbled and foamed she realized it was beer: jars and jars of bright red beer. The people's voices spiraled up into the hot clear air.

> *Hail to Thee, Lady of Plague*
> *Sekhmet the Great, O Person of Gold*
> *We make petition so that You may hear*
> *We make supplication that Your heart be turned to us*
> *The Two Banks are under Your power*
> *We, the sun folk, are Your flock*

The lioness stood up, moved closer, and sat down again. Damona caught the odor of her: wild and musky and redolent with untamable strength. *They are celebrating the festival in My honor,* the beast said. *Once a year, for ages beyond counting, they would pour out the red beer in My honor. Their prayers would fill the air as they pleaded for Me to spare them from the plagues that always ravaged the land in the hot days, when the Mother Nile was low.*

The lioness lifted a huge paw and examined the deadly curved claws. *Sometimes,* She added casually, *I would grant their prayers, if it pleased Me.*

The chanting continued. People drank from the jars, gulp after gulp, until the beer ran down their chins. Many of them were intoxicated. They stumbled, holding the jugs with unsteady hands when their turn came, spilling more than they drank. But theirs was a troubling drunkenness. Damona came from a people who loved their mead; all her life she had attended celebrations where the drink flowed as freely as the laughter. And that was precisely what was so troubling. These brown-skinned folk were drunk, obviously so, but there was no joy in it. No laughter rang out, no songs, other than the sober chant of petition. The faces Damona saw were somber, marked with fear, rather than joy.

Joy. The lioness snorted. *It is a simple emotion, worthy only of a Goddess such as Bast. I never sought that in My worshippers. Respect was what I desired, and there is no respect without fear.*

"And what of love?" Looking at these grim-faced people dutifully downing jar after jar of bloodred beer, Damona was revolted, as well as saddened. "A goddess should be loved by her people. Did not the folk of the Black Land ever love You?"

If they did, came the hissed reply, *it never mattered. Creation and destruction are embodied in Me. That is why the physicians of the land always supplicated Me, especially in the plague times. They knew that I could heal or I could kill. There is no place for love in either.*

Damona said nothing, and the lioness bared her teeth. *You loved My Sister, did you not?* She asked slyly. *How were you rewarded?*

The great cat did not wait for an answer. She stood up, tail lashing at her pale flanks, and leveled her golden gaze at the supplicants.

The scene dissolved before Damona's eyes. She drew a shaky breath. Eire shimmered before her now, the green and misty island of home. But it was a terribly changed Eire, green and misty no longer. The lush meadows where cattle had once grazed were barren fields of ice. The trees drooped beneath a burden of snow, their naked limbs coated with ice. The hills had lost their majesty, even mighty Tara, the seat of kings. They seemed to have shrunk in upon themselves, shivering in an intense and unfamiliar cold. The rivers and streams were frozen solid. The beautiful River Sinann, named for the ancient Goddess, was a broad sheet of winding ice.

Damona let out a low cry. All rivers and streams were sacred to some goddess, but the River Sinann belonged to the Mother Herself. To see it lifeless, held in the grip of this nameless force, tore at her, sharp as the broken shards of ice glittering over her land. "What have You done?" she whispered.

Why, I have given you your revenge. The lioness widened her eyes, affecting surprise at the question. *It is what you wanted.*

"No! I never wanted that. I never asked for it!"

Revenge is a door that once opened is difficult to close. One never knows what is going to come through it.

Here and there Damona began to catch glimpses of people. They were struggling across the bleak landscape, and she gasped again as she saw them. The folk of Eire were skeletons, ragged and sick and starving. Some of them walked, but others had stopped moving. They lay on the uncaring fields of white, motionless bundles of rags.

Heat is more My element than cold, the lioness said in a great purr. *But you endowed Me with the ability to call upon the use of winter.*

"I?" Fresh horror stabbed at Damona. She had known Eire was in the grip of the evil creature Sekhmet had sent on that stormy night. But this was beyond comprehension. This Goddess she had called upon had ravaged her land. And she was responsible. "I gave You nothing," she said brokenly, trying to convince herself more than the lioness. "Nothing."

Ah, but you did. The coldness in your heart strengthened My power. That coldness is still there. But you are afraid. You still do not understand that the coldness, the lack of mercy, is the source of your strength, as it is Mine. Or would you rather be like her?

A new scene revealed itself. Damona recognized it at once. There before her was the hall of Bishop Cairnech. She saw past the walls into the interior. It was stark and cold inside; only a meager fire burned in the hearth, but the people gathered around it were alive. They were praying in the manner of Christians. The bishop himself was leading them, and beside him, there was someone else.

"Rionach," she whispered. "The queen."

Queen? The lioness growled in annoyance. *She is the queen of nothing. That title will now be yours. Look at what you will rule over.*

The dark cold hall disappeared. Sunlight took its place, sudden and dazzling in the bleak sky. The grayness receded, fleeing from the long fingers of burning light. A deep soft blue took over the sky, broken by small puffs of cloud. Damona could almost feel the warmth returning to the land. The looming weight of ice and snow melted with a speed that could only occur by magic. Startling shades of green popped up all throughout the fields and forests, as grass sprouted and the trees regained their leaves. Everywhere, the music of birdsong and rushing water poured into the air.

Unaware that she was doing so, Damona clasped the baby closer. People were coming into view. They were strong and healthy, as folk had been before the evil. Children ran and played, dogs barking at their heels. Women chatted as they drew water, and men sowed their fields. Herds of cattle, fat and sleek, grazed in meadows that had grown lush again. The woods teemed with nesting birds and graceful deer and bears lumbering in search of grubs and berries. Life breathed throughout the length and breadth of Eire, as present as it had been absent. It was joyous to see.

And all of it can be your doing. The lioness's burning voice broke in upon the beauty. *You will be a queen, hailed as the one who rescued Eire from My evil magic. The people will worship you, and you will worship Me. Not only will you have had your revenge, but you will have new power to make you forget your loss.* The lioness growled deep in her throat. *Or you can be your land's undoing. Its fate is in your hands.*

"You said You would lift the spell," Damona said.

And I will. If the price is paid. If it is not—

The warm and fertile day was wiped clean, as if by a giant hand. The cold returned, sweeping across the land with numbing ferocity. In the blink of an eye the snow and ice clothed Eire again, leaving no patch of land touched by the sun. The vision returned to the bishop's hall. Rionach stood where she had been, beside the struggling fire, her hands clasped together as though she were praying.

Numbness spread over Damona as intensely as the cold. She stared at Rionach, praying that she could somehow communicate with her.

The lioness snarled softly. *Who do you pray to, Priestess? My Sister, or to Me?*

"To Whoever will free my land." Damona shuddered as she spoke. The words ripped their way out of her throat, each one tearing at her like a wound. Yet she meant every one. Her heart had expanded at the vision of Eire in the sunlight. Now it grew small and hard again. In only one way could she restore her heart to the way it had been.

The lioness saw her thoughts, and she was implacable. *Then you know what you must do.*

All this time the baby had been still, but now Damona suddenly felt it stir against her. She winced as though the soft little form had stabbed her. She dared not look down at the bundle in her arms. She fixed her eyes on those of the lioness. The great cat sat motionless, watching both her and the babe. She parted her mouth, revealing her long fangs, and licked her whiskers with a hungry pink tongue. The enormous golden eyes drew Damona in. She stepped forward.

Wait.

The voice rippled through the hot dry wind like music.

Let her see the rest first.

It was Bast. The Goddess's presence flowed over Damona, brilliant and confusing. Yet there was no sign of Her, only that voice, throbbing in the air.

The lioness sprang up. Her pale fur bristled, making her seem even larger than she was. The great yellow eyes blazed. *This is My world,* she snarled. *You have no place here. Get out.*

Not until You have told her the whole of it. The deep voice was a quiet counterpart to the lioness's hiss.

The huge cat bared her fangs. *She has made her choice. You cannot interfere, Sister.*

"She has never interfered!" Damona was shocked to realize that it was she herself who had spoken. But once begun, she could not stop. "Where have You been?" she was raging, and she did not care. "You abandoned me. You left me to the mercy of evil. I suffered, and You cared nothing for it. Why should I not embrace this world? What else is left for me?" She fell silent, panting as if she had been running throughout the length of Gaul. She took another step toward the lioness.

There is knowledge.

The simple answer stopped Damona as nothing else could. The baby kicked and cooed and held his arms up to the sky.

The Goddess's voice was deep with compassion. *You have been sorely tested, Daughter. But there are reasons.*

You think I have abandoned you. You have chosen your way out of anger and pain. But visit all the stops along this path before you make your final choice. There are other groves to be seen. Follow the path, and you will see.

The lioness let out a roar. The sound of her rage was thunderous, deafening Damona with its fury. *The path leads nowhere,* she snarled. *It begins and ends here. This is the place of power. Leave it at your peril, Priestess. Your peril, and that of your island.*

The path continues, Bast said. *Look.*

Before Damona's eyes the path she had followed past the grove and into this plain of tall grass and visions opened up. Light touched it, making it appear even broader than it was, a road, rather than a path. Glowing with all the colors of sunset, it beckoned to her, winding in a great curving circle out of the plain. She stared at that glimmering road with a sudden yearning.

With a great spring, the lioness leaped in front of her. The enormous golden body blocked Damona's view of the path. The creature's tail whipped furiously against her sides.

You made a bargain. The lioness roared out the words so that Damona could scarcely understand them. *Will you betray Me once more, as you did after I gave you the man who slew your kin? Think you that I will forgive you a second time? Give Me the baby. Its suffering will soon be over, but anger Me, and the suffering of Eire will continue on and on, and all because of your weakness.*

And what of your suffering? Bast's voice was gentle and sad. *Will giving Sekhmet the life of this baby heal your heart? Once you thought that blood would heal blood. Were you healed when you watched Muirchertac fall into the vat of wine?*

"Ah." The cry was wrung from Damona. The Goddess had seen into her soul. She had glimpsed the grief and the doubt, and above all, the guilt.

My Sister spoke truly. Bast's voice was as soft as the roaring of the lioness was loud. *This is not My place. I have no power here, other than to show you the path. It is up to you to follow it.*

Damona stood for a moment. At last, she looked down at the baby in her arms. "If I take him from here." She spoke slowly, the words halting. "If I return him to his mother, what will become of Eire?"

You know what will become of it. The lioness glared at her with blazing eyes. *I have told you.*

"Lady," Damona said in despair, "what will happen?"

Ah, My Daughter. The Goddess's voice touched Damona's ears as softly as the hint of a breeze. *That you must discover for yourself.*

Silence fell across the wide plain. The lioness sat down on her haunches. Bast said nothing more. The baby grew quiet again. In the distance, the strange and wondrous animals stopped browsing and lifted their heads, staring directly at this human intruder who had entered into their world.

At Damona's feet, the path still shone through the tall grass. She stared at it. The lioness fixed her with the weight of her golden eyes. She broke the silence, growling deep in her throat, as if in warning.

Damona did not look at her. She lifted a foot, set it down on the shining surface of the path, and lifted her other foot. She began to walk, expecting at any moment to hear that deafening roar, followed by the shock of the lioness's spring. It did not come, at least physically. But in her mind Damona felt the impact of Sekhmet's rage, heavier than if a score of lionesses had leaped upon her.

She followed the gleaming trail. It curved through the waving grass, then veered off to the left: sunwise, as the Druids would have said. She walked along over the flat smooth stones, letting her feet carry her and the babe. The grass began to thin; the trees that marked the boundary of the grove suddenly loomed up, their branches curving into circles of magic. Now was the point where she could change her mind, turn back, and seek the Lion-Goddess's favor once again.

She went through the trees and out of the grove.

Once more she found herself in the unreal beauty of the Otherworld.

More groves along the path, Bast had said. She went on to the next grove. The same circular trees enclosed it; the same path wound in amongst them. She walked on, and then stumbled to a halt. An anguished cry ripped out of her.

The rath of her family, whole and unburned, stood before her.

At night, when the first camp had been made, Chlodweg issued a new order. He set the men-at-arms to cutting the straightest tree limbs they could find and carving sharpened stakes out of them. They obeyed him with curiosity and muttered questions. It was a strategy neither they nor the chieftains were accustomed to; spears were used for hunting, not warfare. But Chlodweg was adamant.

"We will need something effective to use against horsemen," he said. "Spears can bring down a racing stag. Why not a horse?"

The next night and the next he had them do the same. During the short winter days he marched his army hard, heading for the territory of the Ripurians. He knew that such a great force would not go unnoticed. On the third day of marching his certainty was borne out. One of his mounted chieftains who had been riding ahead of the train to scout for danger came galloping through the trees. He pulled up beside the king, satisfaction gleaming on his bearded face.

"The Ripurians have sent you an envoy, my lord," he announced. "They await you three leagues hence."

Chlodweg nodded, unsurprised. "Now we will be strong, indeed." His eyes burned through the trees, glaring in the direction the scout had pointed out. "Soon, " he said to himself, "my son will be back with his father. And my power will be greater than ever."

He glanced up, half-listening for the fiery voice of the foreign Goddess. He heard nothing, yet he was not concerned. She had said that She would give him the weapons to defeat his enemies.

He believed Her.

Holding the baby in one arm, Damona pressed a hand to her mouth. Tears that she had long thought dried up forever welled up in her eyes. Sobs bubbled up and choked her. She stared and stared.

The earthen walls stood again, strong and whole. There was commotion from the buildings within; the familiar comfortable sounds of dogs barking, people calling to each other, and pigs grunting. Smoke curled up from the house, carrying the odor of cooking meat. Damona heard dogs barking. Beyond the walls a great herd of cattle grazed contentedly in a wide green meadow.

Damona's gaze was drawn to the placid beasts. She knew these cattle by sight and by name. There was the red cow with the twisted horn, and next to her the black heifer that always persisted in wandering off to the woods. How often she had walked out to the herd to find her husband, either to bring him a meal of meat and bread and cheese, or simply for the pleasure of looking upon him. Would he walk out from these cattle now? She did not know how she could bear it if he did. She did not know how she could bear it if he did not.

"It's my turn. Let me hold him!"

"No, I have a little longer. You said so."

Children's voices.

The voices of her own children.

Damona groaned. She closed her eyes and opened them. Two little girls had come out of the rath. One of them was cuddling a brown-and-white puppy. The other was trotting alongside, frowning as she tried to pet the small creature.

Dark-haired and with blue eyes, they were identical. Deirdre and Eichne; her twins. The little girl without the puppy looked up and saw her.

"Mother!" Her delighted cry rang out.

The other child followed her gaze. A huge smile broke over her face. She dropped the puppy and ran toward Damona. Her sister was close on her heels.

"Mother, Mother!"

The twins swooped in upon Damona, the puppy barking excitedly around them. Damona dropped to her knees, tears choking her. She reached to embrace her daughters, then realized that she still held the baby.

The girls had already noticed him. "Ooh," they cooed in unison, and crowded in close. "Mother, where did you get him?" "Has he come to live with us?" "Is he a new brother?"

Damona struggled to find her voice. "No, my darlings," she finally got out. "He has a home and family of his own."

"Can I hold him?" Deirdre asked.

Eichne nudged her. "Me first. You were holding the puppy!"

Trembling in every limb, Damona held out the baby. "Eichne first," she said shakily. "For a few moments only, then you, Dierdre. Be careful now, watch his head." The cautions were automatic, the instinctive responses of a mother. But so too was her next response. She clasped both little girls in an embrace that made them squeak in protest.

"Mother." Deirdre put her small arms around Damona's neck. "Where have you been? We've been waiting and waiting."

Eichne was cuddling the baby as tenderly as she had held the puppy. "Yes, Mother," she added, her attention momentarily distracted. "We missed you so much. Libran cried for you—"

"Libran." Damona closed her eyes briefly. "Is your brother here?"

The twins gave her looks of identical surprise. "Well, of course, he is, Mother," Eichene said. "He's with Cliodna, his nurse. Where else would he be?" She glanced impatiently from her sister to Damona. "Can I hold the baby now? You said a few moments only."

Tears pouring down her cheeks, Damona helped Eichne shift the baby over to the other twin's arms. At once Eichne clasped her neck as her sister had. "Don't cry, Mother," she said with a child's kindness. "Libran is happy again. Father told him you would be coming."

Damona swallowed so hard her throat hurt. Cuchain, Cuchain: her heart cried the name over and over again. "Where—where is Father now?" she whispered.

The twins were absorbed with the baby again. "Where he always is at this time of day," Deirdre said absently. "With the cattle. You know that, Mother."

Damona rose to her feet. "Come," she said as steadily as she could. "Let us go find him."

She led her daughters towards the grazing cattle. As they neared the herd a tall achingly familiar figure stepped out. Damona froze. She put a hand to her mouth again, pressing the knuckles into her lips. She dared not move.

"Mother," Eichne said, tugging at her. "Come on. Don't you want to see Father?" She darted forward. "Father, Father, look. Mother's come at last!"

Cuchain broke into a run, his long legs bringing him swiftly toward them. He held out his arms. With a sob, Damona flung herself into his embrace. He smelled uniquely of himself, as only he could: of cattle and sweat and life. She pressed her face against his shoulder as though she could shut out everything that had happened to her since his death.

"My love." Cuchain's voice was trembling. "My love." He lifted her face to his, and kissed her. His lips trembled as much as his voice.

"Look at the baby, Father." Deirdre was growing impatient with her parents' tenderness. "Mother brought him."

Cuchain raised his head. "Girls, give him back to your mother and then go off to play. Mother and I must talk."

The twins pouted, protests formulating on their lips. Gently, feeling protests of her own, Damona pulled free of her husband. She took the baby from Deirdre's arms and nodded. "Go on, girls. Do as Father bids."

The twins trotted off, glancing back over their shoulders as they went. Cuchain looked down at the baby. He touched the child's face with a callused finger. "You do not belong here, little one," he said gently. His blue eyes met Damona's. "And neither do you, love."

Damona felt as if her body would fly apart with yearning, breaking into a thousand pieces before she could speak. "No, Cuchain, no. I want to stay here with you and the children. Oh, husband, here is my place."

"Dearest." There was pain in Cuchain's face, and knowledge. "You cannot. For one thing, you have not died."

"I have." Bitterness blended with the yearning in Damona's soul. "Ah, Cuchain, I have died over and over since that night. Death walks with me wherever I go. I taste it with every breath. It reeks in my nose like old blood. I long to be of it, to be with you and the children once again."

"And for another," Cuchain went on gently, "there is the babe. This is not his place."

"But it is mine!"

Cuchain looked at her. His eyes were sad. "That is not worthy of you, my wife."

Damona laughed harshly. "There is much that I am not worthy of. I have changed, husband, more than you can ever know."

"Do you think that we who are in the Otherworld can no longer see what happens in the land of the living, where our dear ones still bide?" Cuchain reached out and touched her hair. "Do you think I do not see the differences?"

Damona put her hand over his. "The differences lie in more than the color of my hair." She caught herself, her eyes going to her hair. It shimmered black before her startled gaze; the white was completely gone.

"Yes," Cuchain said. "Here you are as you were. In all ways, my love, my Priestess of the Shrine."

Damona jerked as though he had struck her. Her arms tightened on the baby so that even his preternatural stillness was disturbed and he whimpered. Unconsciously she comforted him. "I have lost the right to call myself a Priestess. If you saw what happened in the world after you were killed, then you know what I have become." She could not meet his gaze. "Perhaps you are right. I do not belong here. I can never be as I was."

Cuchain kissed her. "That is not why you cannot stay. You have tasks to attend to in the realms of the living. Tasks that only you can perform."

"Because they are my fault."

"Ah, my love." Cuchain's breath was warm upon her cheek, as real and vital as the feel of him had been in her arms. "It is not a question of fault. But Eire is suffering. Would you let that suffering continue?"

They stood in silence. Then Damona spoke: "You said everything is as it was. Does that mean the shrine—?"

"Go to it. It will lead you home."

"Home." The word was like a stone in her breast. "I thought I had come home. It was foolish of me, so foolish. I do not deserve this place."

Cuchain kissed her forehead. "Do what must be done and you will. Go to the shrine. Take care of what must be taken care of." He put an arm around Damona's shoulders. "Come, I will walk with you."

Through a fog of tears Damona saw the shining path that had brought her into the grove. Now it led her down ways so familiar she could have walked them in her sleep. There was the sacred spring, beautiful and pure, as it had been in the days before Muirchertac and his men profaned it with blood and death. The trees that screened it stood tall and beautiful again, no longer charred and burned by torches. The path wound on to the shrine. The boulders that had been rolled against the entrance were gone. The opening glowed as if it were alive.

Cuchain stopped. "Here is where I must leave you." Love

and regret ached in his voice. "But then, you know that. You always entered the shrine alone."

"Cuchain, husband." Damona wanted to hold him. She turned toward him, but the baby was in her arms.

"Yes," Cuchain said. "He is between us. He will remain so, unless you take him back. That, too, is one of your tasks."

Damona turned back to the shrine. It was an effort that wrenched every thread of her soul. She started toward the entrance. The glowing light reached out to her. In the distance, yet so close she wanted to run and find them, she heard her twins shrieking and laughing as they played. She looked back at Cuchain. He was listening to the girls, too. He smiled at her, and she saw longing in his blue eyes, the same eyes he had given to her daughters.

"Farewell," she whispered. She turned around.

A sheet of flame shot up in front of the shrine entrance.

22

THE BABY, AS IF SENSING THE DAN-ger to himself, broke his silence and let out a wail. Cuchain shouted an oath. Damona said nothing.

Muirchertac was standing within the flames. He stared at Damona, and in his eyes she saw the madness she had thought gone. In both hands he held a longsword, raised in readiness for a blow. "Do you wish to see your man die again?" he shouted. "And your children with him? If not, then go back to Sekhmet. If you are fortunate, perhaps She will forgive you."

Hatred flared up in Damona. It washed over her as intensely as the love she had felt for her vanished family. "You have no right to be in this place," she spat. "You profane it with your presence."

The *Tuisech* laughed. "And who are you to speak of rights? I have more right to be here than you. *I* am dead, which you well know, having killed me."

"Leave." Damona was trembling with the force of her hate. The shock of seeing him as he had been, aroused all the rage, all the desire for revenge that had sent her down this dark road she had taken in the first place. "You can never harm my *fine* again. They are safe from you for all time."

Muirchertac's eyes narrowed. "Shall we see if that is so?" He leaped from the flames, brandishing the sword at Cuchain. "Come to me, foeman," he yelled. "Let us see if I can take off your head again."

Damona hurled herself between them. The baby wailed louder, but she paid no heed. She felt power surging up inside her. The feel of it momentarily staggered her. Here was the power she had once possessed, before Sekhmet had stripped it from her. Strength roiled through her, magic in all its sublime force illuminated her soul with a thousand colors. She gloried in it, in this feeling she had despaired of ever experiencing again. She freed one arm from the baby and leveled it at Muirchertac.

"Beloved," Cuchain said.

Something in his voice made her pause. She looked at him.

"Do not do this." Cuchain's eyes were steady upon her face.

"Everything is as it was," she cried at him. "That means my powers have come back!"

"No." Cuchain ignored Muirchertac, his attention fixed solely on Damona. "What you are feeling is not the return of your gifts. Do not let yourself be drawn into what She would have you feel. Think not of power, but of your gifts. Your true gifts."

Muirchertac swept his sword in a great circle at Cuchain. "Kill me," he screamed at Damona. "Before I kill him." He swung again. The heavy blade sang, cutting through the air with a keen whistle.

Damona shook with the desire to slay, to send power arching from her hand to this madman that would send him away once and for all. Muirchertac had begun all of it: the death, the grief, and the revenge. Was it not fitting that it should all end with him, again? "Husband," she cried despairingly. "How can I not slay him? I failed all of you once. Do not ask me to fail you again."

Muirchertac danced toward Cuchain. "And after him, your children. Heed me, woman, use your powers, or the children in Eire will die." The baby squalled, as if to emphasize his words.

"Beloved," Cuchain said. "Will you do as you did before? What will you set in motion, if you do?"

Muirchertac leaped at him again, and once more Damona

interposed herself between them. The sword blade slashed down, stopping a hairbreadth from her skull. "It is not you who are to die," he snarled.

Cuchain's breath was warm on her neck. "Go into the shrine, Damona," he whispered.

"Oh, husband," she cried. "If I do, how many more will die?"

"Go, my love. Follow the path that has been offered to you." He stepped back. "I will be waiting for you to return."

Damona hesitated, slowly turning to Muirchertac as he circled them with his sword raised. She heard the beating of her heart, and that of the babe's. She felt life swirling through the power that had been given back to her, and death.

"If I go, will he kill you and the children once again?"

Cuchain did not answer. She drank in his presence, aching with love and with loss. She turned, exposing him to Muirchertac, and entered the cave. Instantly the baby fell silent. Behind her she heard a furious scream. It came from Muichertac. She glanced back over her shoulder. The flames that had brought him to this place had sprung up again. Engulfing him with a cracking fury as great as the madman's own rage, they bore him away.

The cave drew her back. Ahead of her lay the passageway. She stepped into it, past the light. Darkness enfolded her; the passage wound before as it had in her memory, as if all these black and bloody days had never happened. Every fold and curve between the stone walls was familiar, as though she had just walked here yesterday. Holding the baby against her, she set off.

The passage was utterly black. There was no lanthorn to guide her, as there had been when she was a priestess, yet she still found her way. She stooped as she walked, for the corridor was as narrow as it was dark. The teachings came back to her: that it had been shaped that way for a purpose: so that all who passed through it would lose their pride before they came to the inner shrine. Ah, she thought, pride was something she had lost long and long ago.

The glow that had vanished when she entered the corridor returned. She was nearing the inner chamber. Once it would have been bright with torchlight, from the torches that she herself had placed in the wall niches. Now the glow came from some other source. Damona's breath tightened in her chest; her steps faltered. What would she find in there? Her old life, or a terrible punishment? She stepped inside.

At once she saw the source of the glowing light. The long golden couch stood where it had always been. It gleamed with its own brilliance, drawing in the light and throwing it out again, so that the chamber blazed.

The Guardian was sitting upon the embroidered cushions. He looked at Damona, blinked his great orange eyes, and let out a resounding purr.

The battle between the Franks and the Alamanni began as all battles did, with noise. There were countless trumpeters and horn-blowers on both sides, and at the command from their leaders they let loose with all the power their lungs possessed. At the same time both armies started shouting their war cries. Outbursts of song and chanting mingled with shrieks and howls and the clashing of weapons against shields. The result was a confused conflagration of sound that echoed and reechoed until the countryside itself seemed to be joining in the battle.

The horses of the Alamanni pranced and curvetted at the clamor, eager to surge forward. Their riders held them in, waiting for the order to charge. From his place on the rise, Chlodweg watched intently. Now he would see if his strategy against these mounted men would bear fruit.

"Signal the spearmen to ready themselves," he shouted.

The squadrons of freemen drew back their arms. They were burly, powerful men, chosen for their aim and accuracy in casting a spear.

The Alamanni had been steadily whipping themselves into a frenzy. Now, as if one man and one horse were animating their movements, they broke into their charge.

A sound like thunder rolled up, drowning out the trumpets and horns and shouting. The horses came sweeping across the plain. Crusty snow and balls of ice flew up from their hooves. They tossed their heads as they hurled themselves forward, splattering gobbets of foam from their ornate bridle bits onto the men astride them. The men howled out their war songs. Scorning the use of saddles, they rode by balance, clinging with knees and calves with the same effortless skill with which they handled their longswords. As they neared the massed Franks, they leaned forward over their mounts' necks, bloodlust twisting their faces into hideous masks. The howling intensified.

Chlodweg's arm slashed downward.

A hail of spears arched up into the air, then tore downward, rending into the ranks of horsemen like lethal rain. Horses screamed and reared. Men fell to the snowy ground, tearing futilely at the shafts embedded in their flesh. More horses fell atop them, crushing those who still lived. The Franks let out roars of triumph and charged forward.

"No!" Chlodweg yelled. It was too soon. The next rank of spearmen had not yet time to ready itself. "No!" he roared in fury. "Who gave the order to charge! By the tomb of my father, I will slay the dog with my own hands!"

The old chieftain was watching with narrowed eyes. "No one gave the order, lord. I think the excitement of seeing your strategy's success carried them away."

Hacking and chopping with their axes and shortswords, the Franks swept into the melee of rearing and fallen horses. Chlodweg raged at the sight. There were a great many Alamanni, too many; one volley of spears would not be enough to swing the tide of battle irrevocably in his favor. Indeed, more enemy horsemen were already charging into the fray. The engagement was joined in earnest, and Chlodweg's strategy fallen by the wayside. If the spearmen threw their weapons now, they would strike down their own comrades as well as their foes.

Beside him his handpicked circle of nobles fidgeted and drew their swords. The light of battle was blazing in their eyes, especially the eyes of the aged chieftain. "Always have I prayed to the gods to keep me from dying in bed," the old man cried. "I think that on this day they will grant me my wish."

"Wait." Chlodweg held up a hand. His mind was churning furiously, debating and discarding new strategies. Below him swirled the familiar chaos of combat. He could see the rear ranks of the spearmen scrambling in confusion, seeking to pull out throwing hatchets and shortswords in place of the spears. He snarled an oath. And yet, he told himself, there might still be time. "Mount your horses," he snapped out, swinging onto the back of his stallion. "Each of you ride as fast as he can. The spearmen must not discard their weapons. Tell them to use the spears to stab into the bellies and legs of the horses."

Suiting action to words, he led the way, driving the stallion into his fastest gallop. His bellow preceded him as he thundered down the slope. "Men!" His voice lashed at the Franks as furiously as he lashed at the flanks of his mount. "Use your weapons to disable the horses. Stab at their bellies and legs!"

The small cadre of nobles tore after him. On reaching the main body they split apart, each man echoing the king's orders. The more enterprising of the warriors did not need to be told. They were already deep into the engagement vigorously disabling as many horses as their spears could reach.

Chlodweg leaped from his own mount to join the fray. Fighting on horseback was not in his nature, even if he had possessed the appropriate weapons to do so. The sight of their king wading into battle, tall and broad-shouldered, his *scramasax* in one hand and his *francisca* in the other, sent a wild chorus of shouts and howls blasting through his men. They vied with each other to follow him into the thick of the fighting. Soon they lost sight of him, and the battle took on the characteristic of all warfare, whether fought on horseback or on foot: each man found himself striving against the strength and skill of another for his life.

Within that melee of hoofs and arms and thrusting blades it was impossible for the Franks to keep track of their leader. Still, even though they could not see him, the horses of the Alamanni fell before Chlodweg's tactics. The animals went down in droves. Rearing up in panic to escape the sharpened wooden spearpoints they exposed their bellies to the very peril they were trying to avoid. Those riders who kept their mounts from rearing struggled to protect the horses' fragile legs from being sliced to pieces by swords and hatchets, while at the same time they sought to protect themselves.

More and more Alamanni warriors soon found themselves on the same footing as their foes, slashing and tearing at the Franks with the longswords that were not meant for the close-in combat at which the Franks excelled. The fighting turned ferocious.

But the Alamanni warriors were not the only ones being cut down, and they were numerous. They poured onto the field like waves upon the beach, and all of them were mounted. There were not spears enough to contain them. The odors of war laid themselves over the battlefield, reeking with the unique miasma of death. Sweat from man and beast, the coppery tang of blood, and the heavy stench of spilled entrails burdened the nostrils of those who still lived. So far, the tide of the battle had not yet swung in either direction, but slowly, as more horsemen came racing in amongst the combatants, it began to seem that the Alamanni would be favored this day.

Chlodweg was a mighty figure in the heart of the fighting. Rage, the determination to regain his son, and, above all, confidence in the outlander Goddess, drove him to heroic feats of arms. He appeared oblivious to the forces arrayed against him, and he was virtually tireless. Legs planted like oak trees, he swung his brawny arms in rhythmic patterns, creating around himself a swath of destruction. Blood poured down his arms in rivulets, staining his face and body. Wounded and dying horses screamed in agony, men groaned in their death throes, or lay twisted and motionless, and Chlodweg himself remained unscathed.

The Alamanni began to avoid him. Clearly some powerful force protected him. But their avoidance did not extend to his men. This was too important an engagement; too much lay at stake for the loser. Sensing an advantage, the Alamanni chieftains shouted encouragement to their men, relentlessly pressing forward.

Chlodweg, too, sensed this turning of the tide. He flung himself to the aid of his warriors, as though he were a one-man army. Chopping his crimson-stained *francisca* into the throat of an unhorsed Alamanni, he leaped back to avoid the fountain of blood spraying forth, swinging about in the same motion to stab his shortsword into the belly of a rearing horse. He tore the blade deep along the animal's underside; the beast collapsed with an unearthly shriek, and before the rider could prepare himself, Chlodweg used the same blade to cut his throat.

"Goddess," he bellowed as he yanked out the blade, "I am fighting as You asked. Where are the weapons You promised me?"

There was no answer. Chlodweg fought on, listening for that burning voice to ring inside his head. "Come to me, Goddess!" he trumpeted again.

Both his own men who were within earshot, as well as the enemy warriors heard the king's summons. It heartened the Franks to hear him calling a divine force to his aid. It worried the Alamanni, confirming their thought that he was magically protected.

"We must slay their king," they cried to each other, "before the Goddess he is calling to replies to him."

Sekhmet exulted as She watched the battle from the Otherworld. Many men sprawled on the ground, either dead or wounded. Their blood was engorging Her with steady force, increasing Her strength. Surely She would soon be strong enough to overcome Her Sister and take the wands from their secret place. Bast would not be able to prevent Her.

Will I not?

The voice was sudden and unexpected, even for another Goddess. Sekhmet wheeled, and Her own reply was a snarl. *Why are You here? Should You not be with the mortal seeking to recall her from My influence, or have you finally seen that You are defeated?*

Bast's long green eyes seemed enormous in the glowing light. *You will not have the wands.*

They will be Mine soon. The woman has already come back to Me. She is My Priestess now.

Is she?

Sekhmet's yellow eyes blazed through the multihued light of the Otherworld. *The one I sent to bring her back to Me will not fail. You may have persuaded her to leave My grove, but she will never enter Your shrine, not after the magic I have worked. I called upon the places in her where she is weak and My powers are their strongest. Your faith in her has been misplaced, Sister. You should not have waited. You should not have left the decision to her. I was too wise to do that.*

Your impatience, Bast said, *is greater than either Your wisdom or Your power. It always was. And You have misjudged the weaknesses in My Priestess. Look for Yourself.*

The cat-headed goddess spread out Her hands. Between them a scene appeared. Sekhmet stared at what Her Sister had called up. Her enormous eyes narrowed to glittering slits. She saw Damona carrying the baby: the price of her soul, that was to have brought the mortal back to Her. The mortal's man walked close beside her, his arm about Damona's shoulders, as they took the path that led to the shrine.

The Goddess hissed in irritation. *You show Me that of*

which I am already aware. Why else would I have sent the one I did to intercept her?

Wait, said Bast.

Muirchertac appeared, waving his sword. Damona wavered, caught between the sweep of her own returned gifts and the desire to protect her loved ones. The colors of her torment swirled about her. Sekhmet purred Her satisfaction.

The purr abruptly became a growl. Muirchertac had thrown up his arms. His face was distorted with rage and madness and frustration. Flames had already engulfed him, the flames Sekhmet Herself had set to swallow him up if he failed.

The scene changed again. Damona stood within the inner chamber of the shrine. The baby was in her arms. The Guardian sat upon the golden couch.

Does it look, Bast said in a quiet and cold voice, *as if You have gained a new Priestess?*

Sekhmet's roar shook the Otherworld. *I am not done!* She screamed. *Her land is still in My grip. We will see how long her goodness lasts.*

Damona stared at the Guardian for a long time. She wanted to speak, but the words would not place themselves in her mouth. The cat seemed content with the silence. He sat as he always sat, as she had seen him sit uncounted times, occasionally licking a paw, his orange eyes blinking slowly as he watched her.

At last, Damona made herself speak. "My gifts have come back." She cuddled the baby, listening to her voice ring against the stone.

"Sooner or later they were meant to." The cat's voice was as it always was, light and precise. "Though in what form, and whether for good or ill, even I could not have seen."

Damona gazed about her, at this holy place she had never again thought to see. "When I saw the children, and Cuchain, I thought it could be as it was. I thought I could stay here, in peace and happiness." She looked down at the baby. "But that can never be. I have not earned it." Her eyes went to Mau. "Nor have I earned the return of my gifts, but they are back. Tell me why that is so, Guardian. Did Bast give them to me, or did Sekhmet?"

"That depends," said the Guardian, "on what you do with them." He regarded the baby in Damona's arms. "I've never been overly fond of humans that young. They are noisy and smelly creatures, and most of them have a disconcerting habit of grabbing at my whiskers or my tail. Thank the Sacred Souls, that this one has a quieting spell upon him."

"I must take him home," Damona said. "And I must return to Eire."

"Yes, you must." The cat flicked an ear, and turned to groom the end of his tail. "But have you not forgotten something?" he asked when he had licked to his satisfaction. "You do not have the wands yet."

Damona moved nearer to the golden couch. The light emanating from it was so intense she had to blink. "And will I have them?"

The light took on a familiar brilliance. The voice of the Goddess suddenly filled the chamber, echoing and reechoing with musical power. The words were loud and soft at the same time. *In a battle they were lost, and in a battle, they will be found. Mau will show you.*

The light faded, though it still remained bright enough to illuminate the chamber. Mau leaped fluidly off the couch and glided toward the corridor.

Damona followed him, though apprehension slowed her steps. "What battle was She speaking of?" she demanded. "Guardian, what other deaths are to weigh upon me?"

The cat paused in the opening that led out to the narrow passageway. He sat down and stared at her, and his orange eyes were very wide. "These deaths are not on you, but on Sekhmet. And," he added after a moment, "on the new god of the Christians. Now, are you ready to go back?"

The question created a bubble of grief in Damona's

breast. "Ah," she said softly. "The answer to that is simple.
Never would I leave, if it were my choice. But it is not. I
have debts to pay. And this one"—she glanced down at the
baby—"needs his mother."

Cats normally do not nod, even magic cats. But Mau
moved his head in a gesture as explicit as that of any human.
"Yes, furless one," he said. "And it is time for you to go
home, as well."

23

IN THE WORLD OF MEN THE CON-flict continued to rage back and forth. The shadows of the short winter afternoon were lengthening, and Chlodweg's concerns were growing along with them. The hordes of Alamanni horsemen continued to pour over the field, fighting with a ferocity that was turning the tide more and more in their favor.

Chlodweg had been calling upon the outland Goddess until his voice threatened to leave him entirely. Still, there had been no reply, even worse: no sign of the weapons she had promised him. He could not know that Sekhmet had deserted him. To Her, he had been a tool, one that was no longer of any use. Her interest in him had waned as quickly as it had kindled.

The interest of his foes had not waned, however. The Alamanni were determined to slay the Frankish king. The more he shouted for the Goddess, the greater were their efforts to slay him. Only Chlodweg's enormous valor kept them from accomplishing their task. He fought like a man possessed. His arms were red to the elbows with the blood of those he had killed; the blades of his weapons dripped with it. More blood had clotted in his beard and spattered his chest and face, some from minor wounds he had suffered, though most of it came from Alamanni dead.

Yet the battle itself was not going well. Chlodweg knew it. He had fought too many engagements not to know it. Inevitably there came a point in every battle when the gods made clear the man they favored as the victor. Chlodweg had grown accustomed to being that man. Today, for the first time, he was beginning to fear that the fates had arrayed themselves against him. Had all of this been some evil twist of magic? Had the outland Goddess lured him here with promises of greatness, only to abandon him?

He should not have trusted her, Chlodweg roared to himself. This is what came of listening to foreign gods. In his excitement and confidence at the predictions the Goddess had made, he had neglected the proper sacrifices and prayers to his own gods. Now, even if he begged them, they would be well within their rights to ignore him. Savagely, he sliced at the legs of an Alamanni horse, hamstringing the animal. As the beast came crashing down with an unearthly shriek, one of the nobles fighting beside the king killed the rider.

"Lord," the noble cried, "you must beg help from the gods. They are not favoring us."

It was Mannius, the old friend and comrade of Chlodweg's father, who had spoken. Amazingly, the old man was not only still alive, but fighting as fiercely as any of his younger cohorts who had deployed themselves to protect the king. An Alamanni warrior who had been unhorsed charged at Chlodweg. Mannius interposed himself between them, whirled his *francisca,* and sent it thunking into the skull of the warrior.

"I have offended them," Chlodweg shouted back. "They will not heed me this day."

The old man narrowly avoided a slashing attack from another warrior. Chlodweg cut the attacker down, and the noble jumped toward his king and leaned close. "Then call upon another," he yelled near Chlodweg's ear.

Chlodweg stared at him through the chaos and clamor. "You mean the god of the Christians?"

"He is the god of your wife, and she has always pleaded with you to turn to him. Call upon him, my lord. What is there to lose?"

"This battle!" roared Chlodweg.

"If the gods are angry with you, then the battle is already lost—"

Mannius's words ended in a gurgle. A sword blade was suddenly protruding grotesquely from his chest. The other nobles converged upon the Alamanni warriors that had surged in to attack. But the *sacramax* and *francisca* had dropped from the old man's nerveless fingers. He started to fall, and clutched at Chlodweg's arm to hold himself up.

"Call upon the Christian god," he rasped. "It is our only chance." His eyes rolled up in his head and he was gone.

Chlodweg held the limp body for an instant, then left it to join the other dead. "I will bury you as a hero," he promised.

There was no time to promise anymore. The fighting was sweeping in to encircle him. All over the field of battle Chlodweg could see that his men were becoming isolated, cut off into pockets of desperately fighting men. He must act, and act quickly.

"Very well, God of the Christians." He sent up his voice, making it loud as he could, despite his hoarseness. "I call upon You for Your help. I pray You: Give Me victory this day. Do this, and I vow that I will become a Christian to the end of my days."

At first it seemed that his plea had not been heard. The battle continued as it had. Chlodweg found himself caught between despair and fury as he fought within the circle of nobles valiantly trying to protect him. But then, he saw the change. It rippled across the field, subtle as a breeze, and yet, to the king's straining eyes, unmistakable. The tide was turning back in his favor.

Suddenly the pockets of trapped Franks were breaking free. An eye untrained in warfare would not have been able to discern the difference in the swirling commotion. Chlodweg, though, was ecstatic. The Christian God had heard him. New strength poured into his voice. "Hear me, Franks!" he bellowed, all traces of hoarseness gone. "Follow me to victory. A powerful god is with us!"

An answering wave of shouts roared over the field. The

fighting took on a new intensity, and even to an inexperienced eye the direction of the pending victory was clear.

From a knoll overlooking the field of engagement, Damona and the Guardian watched the fighting.

"Chlodweg will win the battle," the Guardian said dryly. "He has asked the Christian god to help him."

Damona noticed the disapproval in his tone. "And does the Christian god have the power to give him so great of a victory?"

The Guardian flattened his ears. "Perhaps he does, and perhaps he doesn't. It does not matter, because he has had nothing to do with it. My Mistress is responsible for the victory the king of the Franks will see this day." His ears flattened still more. "And Chlodweg will never know it."

Damona watched the combat with difficulty. To see these men covering each other with blood and death brought back vivid memories. Knowing that her loved ones were safe and happy now did little to ease the pain of how their lives in this world had ended. "Why would the Goddess do this?" she muttered. "What purpose does it serve?"

"Why, your purpose, of course. We must get you the wands if you are to free Eire."

In a battle they were lost, and in a battle they will be found. Recalling the Goddess's words, Damona sighed. "I would not have wished for it to be this way. Death begets death, Guardian. I have learned that to my sorrow. The cost of this battle may not matter to Sekhmet. Once it did not matter to me. But it matters now."

"Because you are yourself again. Remember this, though: sometimes, death begets life. It doesn't happen as often, and it is not pleasant when it does, but it's true nonetheless."

The cat stared down at the savagely fighting men. His eyes were glittering slits, enigmatic and cold. "I have seen many battles, furless one, more than you could ever imagine. This one at least has a purpose. You will have your wands, and Chlodweg will have his victory. The predictions

Sekhmet made will come true, despite the fact that She made them for Her benefit, and not his."

Damona stroked the baby's head. "He will also have his son."

"No," corrected the Guardian. "Clotilde will have *her* son. The rights of a mother are sacred to my Mistress and to all Goddesses. Clotilde has embraced a religion that over time will erode those sacred rights, but we who belong to the old ways must still honor those claims."

Damona remained silent, continuing to stroke the soft fuzz of the baby's skull. The Guardian studied her. "Your claims are honored, as well, furless one," he added gently. "Why else do you think that you were shown your children? You will be with them again."

She looked up, smiling sadly. "How will we return him to her?"

"You will do it, when you have the wands. It is fitting. With Sekhmet's help you took him, and with Bast's help you will give him back. Look"—the cat flicked an ear at the bat-tlefield—"the Alamanni are starting to flee."

And so it was. The once-fierce horsemen were losing their lust for battle. They had not been able to kill the Frankish king, and the victory they had thought was assured now seemed to be slipping further and further away with every newly fallen horse and man. It was obvious that a god or gods was influencing this battle; when the Shining Ones involved themselves so, there was little for mortal men to do save quit the field and wait for a day when the gods favored *them*.

"We must go," said the Guardian. "There is little time." He trotted off, and quickly broke into a lope. He threw words back over his shoulder. "Between defeat and victory there will a space when the wands call out to you. But you have to be quick. If you do not take them at the precise moment they speak to you, Sekhmet will intervene. And if the wands come into Her power . . ."

He did not finish. He did not need to. He led the way

along the top of the knoll, then angled down the heavily wooded slope. Damona struggled to keep up. The quieting spell still lay over the baby, yet it was awkward pushing through the brush carrying him and trying to shield his delicate face from the sharp branches. But she did not ask the Guardian to slow his pace. Panting, she followed the sleek black form, its long tail leading her on like a beacon.

The Guardian came to a stop, halting so abruptly Damona almost stumbled over him. So intent had she been on keeping up with him, she had not noticed that the trees and thick brush had opened up, bringing them into a small clearing. Over the sound of her labored breathing, Damona heard the sound of water.

A natural spring gurgled here. It was enclosed by a well house that looked as if it had been built long ago. With only the wide overhang of a rock outcropping to shield it, the holy well stood alone in the clearing. The small domed shape was of finely carved blocks of stone, covering the mouth of the passage that led to the well itself.

It was a lonely place. Massive boulders lay scattered about, squatting on the flat ground, their uneven shapes glinting with fresh snow. A lone oak tree grew next to the rock outcrop, its long gnarled roots stretching deep into the hard stony earth. Magic breathed here, imbuing every rock and branch with its presence.

The Guardian spoke, startling Damona with his voice. "Once only the Belgae, your foremother's people, knew of this place. Then the Romans conquered them, and in time, they discovered it, too. Fortunately, even they recognized the holiness that resides here. They were the ones who built the well house."

Damona stood in the clearing looking about. All water was sacred to her, and running water, most of all. In Eire there were many such places. She had worshipped at them, dropping small offerings into the waters. "Who is the Goddess of this place?" she asked. The baby nestled against her.

"She was known as Burmana." The cat paused. "Or by

Her other name: Damona." The Guardian made a sound that was plainly the feline equivalent of a laugh at the expression on Damona's face. "Yes, your foremother Veleda herself once worshipped here. That is why the mortal who found the wands so long ago brought them here, not that it matters. All that is important is that you receive them. Go closer to the well, furless one. Look at the waters."

Damona did as he bade her. What she saw confirmed what she had sensed the instant she entered the clearing. This well was a place of healing; whoever had put the wands here had been instructed in the mysteries enough to know it. The wands had come from a goddess, and though they had not been returned to She Who had given them to Veleda, they had still been given to a holy goddess as a true offering.

Damona gazed down at the rippling waters. In Eire the place would have been called a Red Well, meaning that deposits of iron colored its waters. But there was another, more mystical reason behind the crimson waters. Here flowed the blood of the Goddess, imbued with deep and incontrovertible powers of healing. At night the sun sank beneath the waters, emerging from them again at sunrise. During the dark hours, the waters absorbed the illuminating and healing power of the sun. To sleep near those waters was to invoke the nurturing powers of the underground sun.

But Damona saw something else in the blood-colored waters. Her voice was hushed. "Sekhmet has power here."

"She could," the cat said. "It is up to you, whether or not She does."

On the battlefield below, the Alamanni king made the sign for retreat. His nobles took up the signal, and it spread like wildfire through the ranks. In the midst of slashing at the Franks, men suddenly began tugging their horses' heads around. The beasts started galloping away, leaving the enemy shouting after them in derision.

The flight was as rapid as the advance had been. From all

over the bloody place of engagement, the Alamanni began to
flee. The hooves of their horses splashed through ever-
widening pools of blood; they trampled and crushed the
bodies of dead and wounded that had already been trampled
and crushed in earlier charges. The Franks pursued them.
They roared and roared their delight, the sound pulsating
through the failing day.

In the clearing the Guardian lifted his head. His wet black
nostrils wrinkled as he tasted the air. "It has begun. Put the
baby down. Hurry."

Hastily Damona laid the small bundle on the grass.

"Keep looking in the well," the light voice said. "Be alert,
furless one. You must be ready."

Damona stared at the red surface. It glowed like the blood
of those newly slain on the battlefield, like the blood of her
husband and children when they had been murdered. "What
must I do?" She asked the question without lifting her eyes
from the well. "Tell me. How must I be ready?"

The cat stepped back. "From this point on, I cannot help
you. That is why your gifts are back. Listen to them, and you
will know."

From the depths of the well a silver light glimmered, as
though the moon had entered this well. The illumination
spread upward, moving with the speed that only attended
true magic. Damona saw a door open. It revealed a sacred
grove of massive oak trees. Inside the circle of holy trees
another battle was being fought, one that had taken place far
back in the mists of time. Romans and barbarians were striving against each other, and Damona felt a sinking sensation
in the pit of her stomach. A spasm of grief went through her,
old and strong, as though it were coming from someone
else. The Romans were winning.

In the midst of the fighting she saw a tall woman wielding
a sword. The woman's auburn hair swirled about her shoulders, disheveled in the fury of battle. She wore the garb of a

Druid. She wheeled, staring up through the silver light. Her eyes seemed to stare directly into Damona's, glimmering green as emeralds.

Damona caught her breath. "Veleda," she whispered.

At that moment a Roman officer sprang at the woman, his shortsword raised. Perhaps if she had not been looking into the light, Veleda could have avoided the blow. Damona would never know. She cried out as she watched the sword blade strike. Blood spurted from a mortal wound, and her ancestor staggered. Howling in rage, other barbarians swept over to kill the Roman. But for Veleda, it was too late. She started to fall, and as she did, she reached up toward Damona.

The wands glittered in her hands.

"Take them," Veleda cried.

At the same moment the door that had opened onto the ancient battle began to swing shut.

I will.

Sekhmet's voice shattered the peace of the clearing. Her power burned into the well, turning the water to blood and flame.

You have made your choice, She snarled. *Let the consequences be on your head.*

The well's surface grew brighter and bloodier. It roiled in response to the Goddess's anger, churning as though She were slashing at it with Her hot breath. Images flashed in and out of the waves. There was the beautiful rath in the Otherworld, where Damona had rediscovered her family. But it was beautiful no longer. Shadows swirled over the sunlit meadow. The odors of fear and anger billowed up from the well, striking at Damona like blows.

She saw Cuchain. He was running; Deirdre was gripped in one arm and Eichne in the other. Behind came Cliodna the nurse, carrying little Libran. The shadows swirled closer in pursuit. They coalesced, took on shape. They were the demons that had invaded Eire on the rainy night when Damona tried to return Rionach to Muirchertac's hall.

Yes, Sekhmet roared. *And now they will rip your family from the Otherworld. I will find other mortals to serve Me. With you, the bargaining is finished. This is your consequence.*

Cuchain jerked to a halt as if he knew that he could not outrun his pursuers. Lowering his daughters to the ground, he shoved them and the nurse behind him and whirled to face the invaders. It was hopeless, yet his mouth opened in a silent battle cry.

Damona stood frozen, her eyes fixed in horror.

"Hear me, daughter." Veleda's voice thundered over Sekhmet's. "Bast is with you. She has never left you. Use your gifts, and you will see Her."

"But, Cuchain." Agony writhed in Damona's cry. "My children."

"Illusion. It is naught but illusion. Once you had the power to distinguish between the two. Look for the Goddess, child. See beyond what is there. Pierce the deception. See the truth."

Sekhmet roared. The squat twisted shapes of her slaughterer closed in around Cuchain. The nurse and his children huddled in the meager shelter of his back. The fanged jaws of the creatures gaped open in anticipation.

Damona stared at the boiling red surface with all her might. Power moved through her, tingling in her belly. It was sluggish, slow with disuse, but it was there. She stared harder, feeling sweat break out on her forehead. All at once it happened. Her eyes became hands, pulling apart the curtains of falseness. At last, she saw.

The night of the attack on her mortal family and the mortal rath tore at her eyes. She groaned, not wanting to look, yet knowing that she must. Once more, she saw the flames, heard the bellows of cattle being slaughtered, watched the horsemen destroy her home.

Suddenly she saw herself, and with her, her *fine*. They were gathered around their fire in the woods. Cuchain had stood up, determined to race back and defend his home. She was pleading with him to stay. Oh, if only he had!

Image after image flashed before her, each one stabbing at her heart. She saw Cuchain running through the trees. She watched Cliodna and her children stand up after she had left them to follow Cuchain, and start back to the rath. And through the eyes of magic, she saw something else. A familiar form swirled above her family, touching them with long, burning fingers.

Sekhmet.

"You," she gasped. "You laid a spell upon them. You led them to their deaths!"

Mortal fool, the lion-headed goddess hissed. *Of course, I did. How else was I to turn you from My Sister and bring you to Me?*

Damona swayed, in body and in mind. Fury roiled through her, blinding her so that she could not think. She had no sense of how long she whirled in that state, before it was replaced by a terrible calm. She searched for Sekhmet, stared into those blazing yellow eyes. "I repudiate You," she said. "Never again will I listen to Your words."

The images from that night vanished.

A new picture lit the well. A chamber lit with pink and gold and silver dazzled Damona's gaze. In the center a goddess with the body of a woman and the head of a cat sat on a silver throne. Her long green eyes reached out to Damona, holding her in an embrace as real as any mortal's arms.

"Lady," Damona breathed. "Oh, Lady."

Without warning, Sekhmet's voice slashed the bloody water. *She is the illusion! Look at your husband and children as they are torn to bits, and know that they will suffer that death over and over, for all time!*

She seeks to distract you so that She can seize the wands. Bast's musical voice thrummed in Damona's soul. *Continue to see the truth, Daughter. The door is closing.*

And it was. Even as Damona watched, the light grew narrower, the images within the door dimmer. The scenes of

Veleda's battle and the demons surrounding Cuchain and the children jumbled together.

Veleda's eyes pierced through the fiery haze, gripping at Damona. The light in their green depths was fading. She had fallen to her knees, but she was still holding the wands straight up over her head. Around her the battle went on, as if no one else in that distant world was aware of what was happening.

"Use your gifts again, Daughter." The Druid's voice was still strong. Urgency rang in her cry. "Call the wands to you."

Damona strained with all her being.

"Call them!"

Strength poured out of Damona with a great rush. She gasped. Her hands opened and jerked out over the surface of the well with a will of their own. The wands left Veleda's hands. They came hurtling up through the water, in the instant that the door swung shut. At the last moment Damona felt a blast of heat; Sekhmet was trying to shoulder her aside, to seize the wands. She was a Goddess, but now, armed with the knowledge of what She had done to her, Damona's power was, for the space of a heartbeat, far greater.

The wands flew from Veleda to her distant, distant daughter. The weight of them filled Damona's hands. The strength of them sent her stumbling backward. The shining door slammed shut. The water instantly grew calm. Sekhmet's fiery presence vanished.

And the baby began to cry.

24

IN THE OTHERWORLD THE BABY HAD needed neither milk nor mother. Now he needed both. He advertised this at once. The unnatural quiet that had sat upon him all this time vanished. Screwing up his tiny face, he let out one piercing shriek after another. The angry rhythm of his cries filled the clearing.

The Guardian let out a low, annoyed hiss. "I knew this would happen once the spell was gone. By the Living Goddess, I would rather suffer another water journey than have to listen to this wailing. Hurry up, furless one, let us get the creature home before he drives me to distraction."

Slowly, Damona came back to herself. She looked at what she was holding. The wands were like living things in her hands. Their warmth flowed up her fingers, into her arms, and on through her entire body. They were crafted from a snowy white stone that reminded her of frozen moonlight. Signs of magic and animals were carved into their surface, crafted with infinite detail, some of them familiar, most of them not. The power in them throbbed, a more palpable force than any magic Damona had ever experienced. They humbled and exhilarated and frightened her, all at once.

Dazed, she looked from the cat to the baby. The latter's cries had grown louder. He was kicking his tiny feet as he wailed. Carefully, she gathered the wands in one hand, went toward the babe, and knelt to pick him up.

"Yes," she said absently. "We must return him to his mother. And we must arrange passage to Eire at once." A hard shudder clamped her as images of what was happening in her country filled her mind. The state of distraction left her. "Sekhmet's evil must be driven out," she added briskly. "I cannot bear the thought of any more delays."

"And I," said the cat, "cannot bear the thought of traveling over first a river and then an ocean. However, I need not worry about that again."

"Guardian," Damona began impatiently.

The cat twitched his tail. "Why do you think we have the wands? They are here to be used."

Damona glared at him. "I don't know how."

He glared back. "Yes, you do. Veleda herself gave them to you, and with my Mistress's blessing. The knowledge is within you."

Damona's anger left her. She looked down at the wands; they began to glow in a deep and silver shimmer. The light entranced her; she felt herself grow dizzy. She heard the cat speak to her. His voice sounded as if it were coming from a great distance.

"Lay the baby on the ground again, then stretch the wands out over him."

Slowly Damona did so. Instantly the infant's wailing grew louder, though to her, it sounded as far away as the Guardian's voice. She put out her arms, holding the bright wands over the tiny form. Their light took on a deeper intensity. All at once she knew what to do.

"Ah," she said in wonder, speaking to the cat as well as to herself. "I *do* know!"

She closed her eyes. The light from the wands shone silver in her mind. Within that deep glow she searched for Clotilde. The queen sobbed in Damona's mind; she felt the pain and loss of the new mother sweep over her, and inside that silver light Damona herself cried.

"Take this baby home," she said to the wands. "Return him safely to his mother."

The light grew brighter still. The baby's crying abruptly stopped.

* * *

Clotilde's weeping had not ceased. She lay in her bed, curled in agony, her empty arms reaching out at the air. The midwives stood about her, despondent, utterly at a loss as to how to help her.

"She will die of grief," whispered Ticta, the eldest one. "And we, unable to help her."

"Perhaps the king will find the child," another said hopefully.

The old woman gave her a scornful glance. "Chlodweg is a great king, indeed, but his greatness lies in the matters of men and not magic. Charging over the countryside with weapons drawn will not help him recover his son."

The other midwives nodded in grim agreement.

A shriek tore apart the gloomy silence. It came from Clotilde. The midwives rushed to comfort her.

"Lady," Ticta soothed. "Lady."

She drew back in astonishment.

Clotilde was still weeping, but now joy transfigured her worn face. Her arms were no longer empty. A loud angry voice was adding its cries to hers. "My baby," the queen sobbed. "My baby."

The baby butted against her, searching for her breast. Finding it, he began to nurse. His grunts of contentment filled the chamber.

The midwives stood staring. One by one, the eldest one first, they began to smile.

The battle was over. The Alamanni had fled back to the reaches of the upper Rhine, leaving their dead and wounded behind. Not again during Chlodweg's lifetime would they attempt to expand their territory.

The Franks were celebrating in the manner of all victors, by roaming over the field and killing those wounded who had not yet expired on their own. Others were gathering up the wounded of the Frankish army and arranging the bodies of the dead who were of noble blood to be taken home for proper burial.

Chlodweg stood by himself. Earlier his elated nobles had surrounded him, showering praise upon their king for this victory. Chlodweg had chased them all away, roaring at the startled nobles not to return until he bade them to. A black mood sat upon the king of the Franks. His own exultation had faded almost as swiftly as the enemy had galloped away in retreat. Yes, he had defeated the Alamanni, but the outland Goddess had not kept her promises, the most important of which had been the return of his son.

"King."

Chlodweg whirled. His eyes bulged; an expression of utter rage twisted his muddy, blood-spattered features. The foreign woman stood there. Her cat companion was at her feet. Both were bathed in a strange silvery shimmer that made the eerie whiteness of the woman's hair even more startling.

But in Chlodweg's present mood, strange lights—magical or otherwise—were of little concern. "You," he snarled, and whipped his bloody sword out of its scabbard. "Where is my son? " He advanced on the woman, leveling the sword. "I will slay both you and the evil that enabled you to take him—"

"Then you would hardly know where your son is, would you?"

There was a note of humor in the woman's voice, and, hearing it, Chlodweg lost all self-control. "You mock me?" he bellowed, and charged at her, swinging his sword in a mighty blow that would take off her head.

A jolt slammed against the king's sword arm. Tingling pain ran all the way up his shoulder; the sword dropped from his nerveless fingers. Neither the woman nor the cat had moved. The weapon had impacted against the silver light and rebounded as if it had struck a shield made of iron.

The woman looked at Chlodweg from within the light. "I was not mocking you," she said gravely. "If anything, I would seek your forgiveness."

"My forgiveness." Chlodweg rubbed his arm, studying on

how he could get to her. "Give me back my son. That is all I care about!"

"I have done so."

"You have"—Chlodweg stared at her, momentarily nonplussed. "Then where is he?" he shouted, catching himself. "I see no sign of him."

"Of course not. He is where he belongs. With his mother."

Chlodweg regarded her, his massive chest heaving, as though he had just finished the battle. "I," he said through clenched teeth, "do not believe you."

"Look upon him then."

The woman moved one of the wands. Chlodweg's mouth fell open. A block of color was opening inside the silver light that enclosed the woman and cat, and within that block he saw figures and movement. There was his wife's chamber, he saw the midwives gathered about the bed, and Clotilde herself propped against the pillows. The last time he had seen his queen she had been utterly torn by grief. Now a beatific smile bathed her features.

A baby nursed at her breast.

"By all the gods," the king breathed, forgetting that he had sworn himself to the Christian God. He lifted his stunned gaze to meet the woman's steady eyes. "Is this a true thing that you have shown me?"

"It is." The woman moved the wand; the scene vanished. "Go home, King of the Franks. Go home and see your son." Her eyes grew as deep and shimmering as the light that surrounded her. "A goddess has played with you and your kin. She has tossed you about as a cat plays with a mouse. But that is over. She will not trouble any of you again."

Chlodweg lurched forward. "You know of her!" He stopped, eyes narrowing. "Ah, but you would, for you are as foreign as she. Indeed, the two of you seemed to appear at much the same time. She must be your Goddess."

"She was, once." The woman's voice was as hard as her eyes. "You are not the only one She betrayed."

The feeling had come back to Chlodweg's arm and hand.

He slammed a fist into his palm. "So that is why She did not aid me. She lured me here with promises of greatness, and left me to die. But why? I did nothing to anger Her. On my father's head, I had never even heard of Her!" He glared at the woman through the shimmering barrier, spitting out more questions without waiting for an answer to the first. "And the predictions she made? Were they only lies, nothing more than a part of her toying with me?"

"You will be as great as you wish, King of the Franks." The cat stood up as the woman spoke. The light around them began to fade, and both of them along with it.

"Wait," Chlodweg cried. "How do you know? What has your magic shown you?"

He could no longer see the figures of the woman or the cat. Only her voice hung on the air. "Perhaps," she said, and the note of humor was back in her tone, "even greater."

Chlodweg was left staring at the empty grass, blood-stained and torn up from the fighting. "I will be greater," he growled after a moment. "In the name of the Christian God that gave me this victory, I will!"

He spun on his heel and went stomping toward the main part of the battlefield, where his men were still engaged in their tasks.

"Hurry!" he bellowed. "We must start for home!"

In the clearing by the well, Damona turned to the Guardian.

"And we, too," she said quietly, "must start for home."

Bishop Cairnech held his hands out to the fire. The hearth was large, but the fire laid in it was small and gave out little heat. The bishop moved closer. He regarded his hands grimly. Once they had been strong and muscular. Now they were the hands of an old man, blue-veined and weak, as pale as though he were about to die.

Closing his eyes he began to pray. His voice was raspy, as weak and thin as his hands. Beside the fire Queen Rionach stirred. Slowly she rose from the chair that had been provided for her, only to slump to her knees. Clasping her hands together, she added her exhausted voice to his.

The words of the familiar prayers twined through the dank hall. Other voices joined in, though the response was halfhearted and automatic. Rionach looked up, and the flicker of hope that burned stubbornly in her heart faded a little more. Fewer and fewer were the number of folk who added their voices to those of the bishop and herself. Every day it seemed that death took more of them. For all Rionach knew, their small number could comprise the last Christians left in Eire. Isolated as the bishop's hall was by the relentless snow and cold, it was impossible to know for certain.

Without warning the great outer doors slammed open. The crack of the wood slamming back jarred those inside. The droning prayers dissolved in a flurry of gasps from some. Others stared apathetically, too worn to react in any other way. Rionach was not among the latter group. She jumped to her feet, swaying with weakness, her eyes huge.

"You," she gasped. "You have come back."

Damona gave her a strange sad smile. "I have."

Belatedly, Bishop Cairnech opened his eyes. He glanced around, wondering why the prayers had stopped. His gaze fell on the figure in the entrance of his hall, and he uttered a cry of fury, shouldering Rionach aside as he stumbled forward.

"Cursed one!" He leveled a shaking finger at Damona. "Have you come to gloat over the evil you have wrought in this land?" He gave her no chance to answer, but shouted, "Kill the creature," at the men gathered around the weakly burning fire.

"No." Rionach's fierce tone overrode the bishop. "I forbid it. We have death enough, without adding to it by killing each other."

"Wisely said, daughter." Another gaunt, white-bearded figure entered behind Damona. Somehow the Chief Druid had survived through this terrible winter. He was painfully thin and looked older than ever. But he was alive, and that was more than could be said for many others.

Bishop Cairnech stared. It was hard for him to decide which was worse, the appearance of the pagan *Banfhili,* or this man who was the head of all the Druids, and therefore, even more powerful than she. "This house is dedicated to our Lord," he finally said. "The One True God. Those who follow the old ways of the heathen are not welcome here."

In spite of his weakened state, the Chief Druid's eyes were oddly clear and bright. He looked through the dim light, toward the bishop, and his face was sad. "You seek to argue in the midst of a burning wood. Wisdom is wisdom, regardless of the god one follows. After all the suffering that has been visited upon us, have you not learned that yet?"

There was a long silence.

Bishop Cairnech broke it with a deep sigh. "I have learned it," he said wearily. "And it seems, Chief Druid, that neither your prayers nor mine have made any difference." His gaze went to Damona. "Many searched for you, but you were not found. Why have you now returned? To witness the culmination of the curse you placed upon us?"

Damona's gaze did not waver. "More than Eire has been cursed. But with all of your help that can change."

"What can we do?" Rionach asked quietly.

Damona looked at her. "Pray," she said. "Each of you must call upon the power of your gods. And you, lady," she added to the queen. "You must come with me."

"She will not," the bishop exclaimed in horror. "Once before you lured her from the safety of my hall and into the grasp of evil. I will not allow you to do so again."

Rionach drew herself up. "Eminence," she said, still speaking with quiet dignity, "this is not your choice to make. I will go with you," she said to Damona. "But where? Travel is well-nigh impossible, as you must have seen."

"We must go back to where the evil first came into Eire." Damona paused. "To the hall of you and Muirchertac."

Bishop Cairnech gasped, but the queen cut him off before

he could start a new protest. "It is a long way," she said calmly. If she felt any terror or apprehension at the thought of returning to the place of her imprisonment, she did not show it. "We have neither food to sustain us, nor animals to carry us there."

Damona smiled again. "We do not need them. Come outside, lady, and you will see."

"Magic," the bishop growled, as Rionach strode away from the meager warmth of the fire. "Pagan magic is what began all of this." He crossed himself fiercely.

"And if we are fortunate," the Chief Druid said, "pagan magic is what will end it."

A trickle of warmth stirred in the wind. Here and there lines appeared in the ice and the rock-hard snow, attended by crackling sounds so faint mortal ears would not have been able to hear them. The Bau heard them.

Squatting in the darkened hall, it shifted restlessly. Its huge shape swirled, forming ominous patterns as it searched for the source of these suspicious breaks in its hold over the land. Growling, the seven slaughterers came stalking forward from different corners of the hall. They, too, sensed the change, and silently they asked the Bau for guidance.

The Bau could not give it. "Mistress," it cried. "What is upon us?"

The answer came swiftly. *One who would destroy you. Keep the land frozen and send My seven arrows out to guard you.*

The Bau obeyed. But even as the demons charged out to do its bidding, the tingles of warmth grew stronger.

Damona lowered the wands. Their silvery shimmer had not dimmed as it had when its power brought her and the Guardian back to Eire. From the moment her feet had touched the ground of home, frozen and sick as it was, Damona had felt herself growing stronger. It seemed as though the wands were growing stronger, too, taking their power from her. Even the burden of conveying Rionach, along with herself and the Guardian, had not sapped them.

Rionach was staring about her dazedly. "How—how did we arrive here?" She crossed herself as her eyes fell upon what Damona held. "Those rods you carry—they grew so bright. In truth, they blinded me. I felt so dizzy, as if a great bird had picked me up and was flying through the air with me. And now, here we are." She crossed herself again. "The Bishop spoke truly. This is magic, *Banfhili,* great magic."

"It would have to be," Damona said grimly, "to rid Eire of the evil I brought to it."

Rionach studied her, her eyes lingering on Damona's flowing hair as white as the snow around them, save for the blood-colored streaks. She stepped forward and laid a gentle hand upon the other's arm. "It matters not who brought it here. All that matters is that you see it gone."

Damona's bleak expression lightened. "I thank you for that, lady—"

Her voice trailed off; she looked at the cat. He was already staring at her, his eyes orange and round. Rionach could hear him purring.

"What is it?" Rionach asked, hearing the nervousness in her voice.

"Warmth." Damona answered her absently. "Can you not feel it?"

Rionach tried. She struggled to feel for a change. Oh, how blessed it would be to know what being warm felt like again. But there was nothing. The skies were dark and gray as ever; the snow and ice as thick as they had been all these long winter months. "I am sorry," she confided dejectedly. "But the cold burrows into my bones as terribly as ever."

Damona laid a hand over the queen's and squeezed. "Soon," she promised. "Soon, your bones will be thawing under a spring sun." Rionach saw that the *Banfhili*'s eyes were no longer hazel-colored, they shone silver, almost as bright as the strange rods she held. "Come," Damona said before she could comment about her eyes. "The hall is just ahead. We must go there."

The road that had once led to the courtyard was packed with ice and layers of snow, indiscernible to any person who had not traveled it many times before. Damona and Rionach found their way by feel and memory. The cat followed in their wake, lifting each paw with fastidious distaste. Suddenly he bounded ahead, stopping in front of the women with a deep rumbling growl.

Before them lay the courtyard or what was left of it. Seven figures stood there, darkly outlined against the snow. A scream rose in Rionach's throat, and she could not hold it back. These were the demons that had attacked her and her house folk on that black and evil night. She screamed again as they charged.

The slaughterers flew at the women, their twisted forms leaping with eerie grace, their long fangs gleaming under the dank sky.

Damona held out the wands. The silvery light that bathed them shot out. A tinkling music filled the air, the sounds like nothing either Damona or Rionach had heard from any instrument known on Eire. The music grew louder, and a deep lovely voice thrummed out over the rhythm of the notes.

By the songs of My sacred sistrum, I bid you gone. Yes, and My Sister, as well. The warmth is coming, and you cannot stop it. She who took the beauty of this land with her has returned, and with her has returned the beauty.

The demons leaped forward and back. They snarled and slavered. Then they wheeled and fled back into the dark hall.

Damona's face was transfigured. "The warmth," she said to Rionach. "Can you feel it now?"

And Rionach could. A look of disbelief spread over the queen's face. So long had it been that at first she was not sure. But even as her fingers flexed in the unfamiliar luxury of this new sensation, she saw the sky brighten. And she knew beyond doubt that the change was real.

"Stay you here," Damona said. "I must go inside, and I must go alone. The cat will stay with you."

Her words jerked Rionach back to herself. She snatched at Damona's arm. "*Banfhili,* do you know what bides in there?"

The look of elation was still on Damona's face. She smiled. "I know, indeed," she said. "And it is time for it to leave."

She ran toward the darkened hall, as though it was not dark and a thousand candles were lighting it, as though a great feast was being held inside, and she was the guest of honor. Rionach watched in admiration and in dread. The cat rubbed against her, as if he knew she needed the reassurance.

The moments dragged by, or perhaps they flew; in looking back, Rionach would never be able to know which. A howl suddenly shattered the waiting. It was followed by another howl and then another. Seven times, Rionach thought, though she had not realized that she was counting. Wind swirled out of the hall, black and formless. It swallowed up the brief tender warmth, struggled with it savagely. Rionach wept at the loss, fearing that now the cold would truly be permanent. She saw Damona appear in the doorway.

And the cold was gone. The searing wind went with it. In the ensuing silence the tinkling music was suddenly louder, and now it was joined by other sounds. Rioanch uttered a soft cry as she heard them. Everywhere ice was crackling and shredding, falling in chunks from the tree limbs it had encased. The regular ping-ping of dripping water accompanied it, growing steadily louder with every moment.

The snow was melting; even as Rionach looked, patches of brown earth began to appear beneath the heavy white layers that had enshrouded it for so long. A bird chirped. The single note was hesitant but unmistakable. Tears burned Rionach's eyes as she heard another bird. Her skin twitched as warmth spread over her limbs. The brats that the bishop had pressed upon her to wear were rapidly becoming uncomfortable.

The cat darted past her, heading for Damona. The *Banfhili* was still holding the odd rods she had brought with her. She put them in one hand as she bent to stroke the cat. Straightening, she looked at the sky and smiled. Rionach looked up, too. Her mouth dropped. The sun was breaking through the dank sky, pulling apart the heavy clouds as though its rays were great hands. Behind the grayness swept incredible swaths of blue.

Rionach walked toward the *Banfhili*. Damona's eyes still shone silver. Her white hair with the startling streaks of crimson gleamed even whiter in the new sunlight. Tentatively, the queen put out a hand and touched that snowy hair. "You have not changed," she said softly. "The magic is gone, yet you have not changed."

"Ah, lady." Damona's voice sang with mysteries. "I have changed, indeed. I carry this hair to remind me of one change, and the color of my eyes to remind me of another. Life will never be the same."

Rionach nodded gravely. "For any of us."

The rebuilding of the shrine and the nearby rath was almost finished. Many more folk had survived than had first been thought, and now they came bearing gifts of food and livestock and labor. Among them Damona saw people whom she recognized from the queen's hall as Christians. She accepted their gifts with the same gratitude in which they were offered and asked no questions.

On the day the shrine was to be dedicated again to the Goddess, Damona arose at dawn. Within the ring fort a house had been built for her. Queen Rionach herself had supervised the building, consulting with Damona and yet insisting that it be comfortable enough for the *Banfhili*'s needs. Damona had wondered how it would be to live and sleep in this place where she had known such happiness and such pain. But it had not been nearly so difficult as she imagined. The spirits of Cuchain, the twins, and little Libran walked the rath with her. They laughed and sang and visited her in dreams. They waited for her to join them. They were ever with her.

As the sun peeked over the green hills Damona went to the sacred spring to bathe. The spring gurgled its greeting to her. It had been cleansed and purified, and hawthorn trees replanted to screen it. The trees were only saplings, but with the hand of the Goddess upon them, they would grow rapidly. After she was done, Damona dressed, lit a small torch, and walked on to the shrine itself.

The shrine, too, looked as it had, before the dark time descended on them all. The rocks and debris that had been piled against the entrance by Muirchertac and his men were gone. People had rolled away the boulders, carted off the filth and defilement. Sacred holly bushes had sprung up around the shrine's entrance. Oak saplings waved in the warm breezes of a true spring.

For a long time Damona stood before the reborn shrine. Thoughts filled her mind, swirling about her as gently as the sunny breezes that toyed with the flame of her torch. She and this shrine had been reborn together. Now she must think of what this new life meant for them both. The power of pagan and Christian together had contributed to the driving away of Sekhmet's Bau. But would that tolerance, that willingness to accept the strengths of the other, be able to continue?

"It must," Damona said aloud. "I must see that it does." The breezes carried her words to the holy spring and into the shrine itself. Standing in silence, she watched them go. The path before her was clear. In honoring the old, as well as the new, would Eire grow strong.

She stirred herself at last, and entered the passageway. The corridor was as narrow and dark as ever; she had to stoop as she always had in the past, paying heed to the eternal reminder to shed all pride before coming to the inner chamber. And then, the womb of the Goddess was there before her, gleaming with the unearthly light of Bast Herself. The gleam intensified, smoke eddying from the small torch, as Damona used it to light the larger torches that stood in the wall niches. Light sprang off the walls, turning the stone as pink and shimmering as the courtyard of the Cat-Goddess's temple.

The Guardian was curled on the golden couch, resting contentedly on newly embroidered cushions. Damona looked at him and smiled. She felt the presence of Bast sweep over her in a silence filled with music.

"Lady," she said softly, "when we were in the courtyard of Muirchertac's hall and You said: she who has taken Eire's beauty has returned, was it You whom You were speaking of?"

The tinkling silence intensified.

No, My Daughter, the Goddess said. *It was you.*

The fiery red glow that illuminated Sekhmet had faded. Her overwhelming rage had given way to a sullen, smoldering anger. She paced across the vast sunlit plain, paying no heed to the herds of zebra and antelope that scattered through the tall grass in clouds of black and white stripes and gleaming fawn at Her approach. In the heat of Her initial fury the Goddess had taken on Her purely lioness form to chase after the beasts, roaring, Her teeth and tongue flecked with foam.

Now She had resumed the form most familiar to Her worshippers. Towering over the plain, She raised one enormous hand and spread Her fingers, opening a space in the arid sky that revealed the courtyard of Bast's temple to Her narrowed gaze. The cats gathered on the pink stones lifted their heads, the tapestry of gold, orange, green, yellow, and blue eyes gleaming as they stared unblinking at Sekhmet through the space She had opened.

The lion-headed goddess moved Her fingers again. The courtyard with its guardians faded, and the inner sanctuary sprang into view. Sekhmet snarled as Her Sister's face filled

Her vision. Bast's long green eyes stared into the yellow orbs of Sekhmet, their emerald gaze serene and bold.

What do You wish of Me now, Sister? The Cat-Goddess asked the question calmly. Her voice was as direct as Her eyes.

The ivory fangs gleamed. *I was expecting You to visit Me so that You might gloat over Your victory. Why have you not?*

Gloating is Your province, O Sekhmet, Bast answered. *Not Mine. Things are as they were, at least, as much as they ever can be in the world of mortals. With that I must be content.*

Well, I, Sekhmet snarled, *am not content. Nor will I ever be. There has always been history between Us, Sister. And now, there is more.*

If She expected Her Sister to respond in a similar vein, She was surprised. Bast looked at Her solemnly, the long green eyes luminous with the glimpsing of far-off events.

Yes, She said at last, and Her musical voice was barely a whisper. *But the history is not yet finished.*

Sekhmet said nothing more.

She knew it, too.

Author's Note

As Christianity slowly became the official religion of Europe, those who followed the old ways were forced underground, holding to their ancient beliefs in secret. This was particularly true for the great Goddesses and their Priestesses. Isis, Artemis, Hecate, Diana, Danu, and, of course, Bast and Sekhmet, were discredited. The concept of a Great Earth Mother who both gave and took life became heresy, and insofar as cats were a symbol of the Goddess, they, too, came to be despised.

Yet the old beliefs did not disappear entirely, much as the new religion of Christianity would have liked them to. Indeed, Churchmen discovered that folding the ancient beliefs and traditions into Christianity and imbuing them with the blessings of the Church was the most effective, and perhaps the only, way not only to draw converts into the fold, but keep them there. So the Ancient Harmonies endured. The Druids disappeared, but in France, Wales, Scotland, and of course, Ireland, a secret and subtle devotion to the Celtic gods and goddesses lasted until well into the eighteenth century.

As for the *Franci*, or Franks, as they were referred to in Roman sources, they changed the face of the Western World. Taking advantage of the troubles in the empire, they launched devastating raids into Gaul, even penetrating as far as Spain. Chlodweg, whom history would know as Clovis, succeeded his father in 481 A.D. and became a great warlord, who extended Frankish dominion in every direction. He was also the first Christian king of the Franks, and a convert to Catholicism, rather than the heretical form of Christianity called Arianism, which had theretofore been more popular amongst the barbarians.

Clovis's actions were not due to an Egyptian goddess, of course; nor is it likely that religious zeal was responsible. Clovis, in fact, had little reason to love the new religion. He strongly believed that his acceding to Clotilde's pleas to have his newborn son baptized had resulted in the child's death. But Clovis was a supremely practical and ambitious man. He knew that if he accepted the Catholic religion, he would be the only orthodox Germanic king in not just Gaul, but all of western Europe. As the Catholic champion he would find it easier to gain the allegiance of the Gallo-Romans as he proceeded with his conquests.

The exact date of Clovis's conversion is unknown. Accounts written by Gregory of Tours, the spokesman for the Frankish church in the sixth century, claim that in the midst of his battle against the Alamanni Clovis called upon Jesus Christ to grant him victory, promising conversion in return. The tide of battle did indeed turn as I have depicted, and the Franks carried the day.

But to conquer is one thing; to govern is another. The Merovingian dynasty that Clovis founded turned out to be far less effective as rulers than as warriors. The kingdom Clovis left to his successors included all of France and a large part of Germany—far too much territory for the limitations of the time. Almost no attempt was made to maintain the Roman administrative system. In the century following Clovis's death, the chief interest of succeeding rulers lay in killing each other, so that the history of the Merovingian family is one long account of carnage and treachery.

By the seventh century the dynasty was left with only a shadow of its former power and only a small portion of the enormous realm Clovis had made his own. Nearly all of the seventh-century Merovingian rulers were mentally deficient, or—in the eyes of the early Middle Ages, possessed an equally disastrous handicap—they were either women or children. Such "unthroneworthy" rulers always signified the death of royal power.

But in the eighth century, another Frankish king would arise whose reign would be a turning point for both Christianity and paganism. His name was Charlemagne.

Sarah Isidore
Seattle 1999

AVON EOS PRESENTS
MASTERS OF FANTASY AND ADVENTURE

ARAMAYA
by Jane Routley   79460-8/$6.99 US/$9.99 CAN

LORD DEMON
by Roger Zelazny and Jane Lindskold
                                               77023-7/$6.99 US/$9.99 CAN

CARTHAGE ASCENDANT
The Book of Ash, #2
by Mary Gentle   79912-X/$6.99 US/$9.99 CAN

THE HALLOWED ISLE
The Book of the Sword and The Book of the Spear
by Diana L. Paxson   81367-X/$6.50 US/$8.99 CAN

THE WILD HUNT: CHILD OF FIRE
by Jocelin Foxe   80550-2/$5.99 US/$7.99 CAN

LEGENDS WALKING
A Novel of the Athanor
by Jane Lindskold   78850-0/$6.99 US/$9.99 CAN

OCTOBERLAND
Book Three of the Dominions of Irth
by Adam Lee   80628-2/$6.50 US/$8.99 CAN

....

Available wherever books are sold or please call 1-800-331-3761
to order.   FAN 0300